HELEN KELLER
REALLY LIVED

Elisabeth Sheffield

A NOVEL

HELEN KELLER REALLY LIVED

FC2
TUSCALOOSA

The University of Alabama Press
Tuscaloosa, Alabama 35487-0380

Manufactured in the United States of America

FC2 is an imprint of The University of Alabama Press

Book Design: Illinois State University's English Department's Publications Unit; Codirectors: Steve Halle and Jane L. Carman; Assistant Director: Danielle Duvick; Production Assistant: Eric Austin Longfellow

Cover Design: Lou Robinson

Typefaces: Garamond, Courier, and Trade Gothic

∞

The paper on which this book is printed meets the minimum requirements of American National Standard for Information Sciences—Permanence of Paper for Printed Library Materials, ANSI Z39.48–1984

Library of Congress Cataloging-in-Publication Data
Sheffield, Elisabeth.
Helen Keller Really Lived : a novel / Elisabeth Sheffield.
pages cm
ISBN 978-1-57366-181-2 (pbk.) -- ISBN 978-1-57366-848-4 (ebook)
1. Divorced women--Fiction. 2. Self-realization--Fiction. 3. Ghost stories. I. Title.
PS3619.H4515H45 2014
813'.6--dc23

2014006719

Dedication

For T.C.D., S.D.D., G.V.B. and W.H.S.

The cradle rocks above an abyss, and common sense tells us that our existence is but a brief crack of light between two eternities of darkness

—Vladimir Nabokov, *Speak Memory*

She is fellow to Caesar, Alexander, Napoleon, Homer, Shakespeare, and the rest of the immortals. She will be as famous in a thousand years as she is today

—Mark Twain on Helen Keller,
in *Everyman's Eggheads Editions*

Writing is the rabbit hole down which the subject endlessly disappears

—Unknown

HELEN KELLER
REALLY LIVED

Give me back my body, give me back my body. Really, I'm not joking, *lyubov moya.* Give me back my body right now. Or else. If you don't give me back my body, I'm gonna come and take something of yours, something you'll miss, missy. Like that three legged monster of a rabbit that lurches around the lawn of the house you bought with my insurance money, performing a grotesque fusion of the bunny hop with a sidewinder snake dance. Give me back my body, give me back my body or the rabbit dies.

Alright, alright. I was just trying to get a rise out of you, like you could always get out of me, sometimes three times in one night. I know you can't give me back my body—at least not the body I had. Before it went to hell, so to speak. I'm not stupid. Let me remind you that I was thirteen years old when the *bratva* got me in—couldn't speak a fucking word of fucking English. One year on the streets and I had street cred American, one year on my knees and I was on my feet with a green card and "supportive" American foster rents (four years, all expenses paid, at Scarsdale High). And when the supportive rents proved unsupportive (after a little free trade incident), I hooked my way through SUNY, four years of medical school, an internship and a residency until finally I reached the promised but by no means guaranteed land of a successful private practice. You don't do that with a case of faecal encephalopathy, a.k.a. shit for brains. But you never respected me when I was alive—why would you respect me now? God I sound like Rodney Dangerfield another kiddo from the old Eastern Bloc, bet you didn't know that (he was born Jacob Cohen). You knew me for a stooge though the moment I walked into the exam room, the moment my eyes dropped like pants. The clipboard in my hand provided cover as I pretended to scan your chart, but you could probably already tell I had it bad, see right through me even as I was let's see over 200 by then... no 90 kilos... always liked the slimming effect of the metric system... far from being a ghost.

Yeah right through me even though you were the paper doll a real flimsy floozy your motives completely transparent the way you'd wrapped your sun-browned bod in the standard pink gown, like a piece of eye-candy or a goddamn sex bonbon. My *vatruska*, it was obvious what you were up to, rigged as a Viagra erection, and I'd had my fill of sweet, young, and not-so-young things (yeah even then I could see your expiration date). But somehow you knew that too. Knew that after a while they all look the same, from the PHAT downtown trophy wives to the morbidly obese suburban breeders, smell the same. Take your pick it's all just the stale estrogen reek of *pizda.*

So you knew not just to wear the shoes but also to leave them on. Yes my sweet tart, my *limonka*, those shiny black, granny tie ankle boots with the six-inch heels were what finally piqued my ruined appetite. But not because of the way they forced your long boy's feet to do what anthropologists call the courtship strut, though I wish I'd seen you wobble through the door in them. You were already posed up on the exam table however, looking yummy but by no means irresistible in your strategic pink wrapper. So like Spike Lee said, "money, it's gotta be the shoes." The way the platform soles curved and arched like two frightened pussies (pun intended) the way the black patent vamps spat back the fluorescent lights.

In Russian there's a very old curse, *poshol v pizdu*—literally "go back into the cunt." But it's worse than that—a wish for someone's death. I don't know why I chose a profession that had me up inside them all day. It wasn't a turn on, for god's sake. Maybe to convince myself I was out. I dunno, if I were interested in introspection I would've joined the Freud Squad. What's certain is that the whole time you were on the table I was thinking about the boots and I was still thinking about the boots when I suggested an upstate follow-up at Bosky House, my Kinderhook manor-in-the-woods. You looked at me like I was some kind of *baba yaga* leering from her fowl-legged forest hut, like I was going to snatch you up and gobble you whole, and I fell for that too, the little lost lamb act, though I was the one who was going to get eaten, who couldn't see how things were going. Couldn't see that those boots were taking me right back to where I was trying to get away from, straight into the old *pizdu.*

So keep the body, you bitch, you *blyad'* Selina Van Staal—I don't want it. And that crap about the cell phone tapping—*poshol ty na khuy.* You can use the one that was mine.

Not Okay: A True Crime Story,

by Selina Van Staal

Chapter One

"The Truth Sounds Like A Fiction That Can And Will Be Used Against You"

This story, which is not a story but more of a memoir recounting actual events, is being written against legal counsel. According to Caroline Rose-Hickman, Attorney at Law, trauma survivors often tell their "stories" in an agitated and disjointed manner that undermines their credibility and even makes them sound like liars. Also, it is not uncommon for survivors to speak of themselves as if they are someone else. They do this to disassociate.

Here is an example of disassociation: when Selina Van Staal was a little girl her mother would act like she did not exist. So Selina would go pull a heap of scarves out of the dress-up box, remove all her clothes and replace them with the scarves. Then she would do a striptease for the whole family. How ignominious. Selina pretended it was not her spinning around the room to the Donovan recording, flinging filmy pink and yellow scarves on the floor one by one, but a bare-naked slave girl who had no choice.

According to Caroline Rose-Hickman, the truth sounds like a fiction that can and will be used against you.

Written on an old, hacker-safe Smith Corona electric typewriter kept hidden in a secret hiding place, with the Mac inherited from Timor used for research purposes only, the truth may be worth money someday. Even though this will not be one of those neat, convincing little stories where every piece fits just so. At times, it may even feel as if things are going in circles, like a broken record or a bare-naked slave girl, spinning around and around the room. Well, please remember that trauma survivors often tell their stories in an agitated and disjointed manner that undermines their credibility and even makes them sound like liars.

Selina's mother acted like Selina did not exist, no matter what she did, like spinning naked around the room or reading all of Rosemary's Baby at the age of seven. When Selina asked her mother if she would still love her if she was part devil, her mother said, eyes glued to Valley of the Dolls, not now, I am reading. The book Rosemary's Baby naturally led to the movie Rosemary's Baby and a crush on the director. So if Selina later became susceptible to older, Slavic men, it was not her fault.

Selina's mother acted like she did not exist and her father was never there—driving up and down the eastern seaboard (sometimes all the way to Florida!)—even when he was. Not completely—he was missing an eye, and also a piece of his brain. That explains a lot.

Once people realize that they need to be patient, the pieces will begin to fit together. Maybe not perfectly, but that is fine. Just fine. For now, people need to be patient because they are not going to get everything at once. They need to wait, the way children must wait until Christmas to open their presents. Selina's greedy sister Cara could never wait, but instead would peel back the tape at the end of the box and then slide the box out of the wrapping paper to preview its contents. Then Cara's Christmas would be over and her SAD would begin. SAD can be blamed for both depression and manic behavior such as compulsive shopping, but not for killing your husband.

Anyways, Cara did that in the late summer.

Patience is a virtue. Consider "Selina Claus," a one-page essay written at eight-years-old about what Selina would do if she were Santa. Selina Claus would give everyone the one thing they truly wanted, after listening attentively to find out what was that one thing. But they would not get it if they acted like pigs, without self-restraint or strategy. They had to behave themselves, and not just before but after they received their gift. Otherwise, the gift would be rescinded. Its composition hampered by a lack of proficiency in script as well as an unhelpful mother who was too busy reading to help with homework, the essay received only two out of the three gold stars it deserved.

Once people realize that they need to be patient, the pieces will begin to fit together. Not perfectly, but this is not the kind of story where every piece connects just so. To be honest, mistakes were made. Mistakes were made because, at times, self-restraint and strategy were lacking. Life is not a lab, you see. Fritzi Akdikmen once said that. Meaning a place where controlled results can be achieved, not the dog breed.

More about Fritzi later.

Selina met the first woman, Lyndon, during a period of intractable depression. The date was April 22, 2010. Timor, Selina's ex-husband, had been dead, due to a fatal stroke on October 31, 2009, almost six months. According to Winona Irving, M.S.W. and author of Loss and Recovery, intractable depression often ensues from a loss of self-esteem. A loss of self-esteem is commonly the result of divorce and the attendant financial difficulties. Divorce in turn often follows earlier losses, the series of voluntary physical and emotional sacrifices that can occur over the course of a marriage. Not to mention thefts (such as robbing someone of the best of her reproductive years). So thank Timor, Selina's ex-husband, for the intractable depression that led to Lyndon and all the trouble. And nevermind, as also stated by Winona Irving, M.S.W., that the road to recovery starts with you. Nevermind that you can counter the loss of self-esteem at the root of intractable depression by taking up a cause. That a charitable activity such as collecting money for impoverished people or mistreated animals or even the environment can make you feel better about yourself, and so less susceptible to intractable depression. Andy and Wesley could have been a cause. But without a husband or a documented income it is very hard to adopt.

So thank Timor for Lyndon, encountered at a Nike outlet in Massachuesetts during a period of intractable depression, even though at the time Timor had been dead for half a year.

First spotted flitting from one rack of discounted running shoes to the next, Lyndon looked to be a fairy without the wings. The mythological figure Nike had wings, but she was no Tinker Bell. She was a goddess who flew around the battlefields rewarding the victors with glory and fame. Would Selina have won a better settlement if Timor had not died before the divorce proceedings were completed? Hard to say because even though Timor was an evil bastard, the judges in New York State are sexist pigs (although according to Caroline Rose-Hickman, they are even worse in Connecticut). But Selina was alive and Timor was dead, and that was a kind of victory in itself. If you ever feel like a loser, just remind yourself that you are still alive.

Why was Selina at the Nike outlet in Massachuesetts? Well, Timor had store credit there, according to a slip under a pile of unpaid bills. Timor had had store credit there. The drive over the state border from New York to Massachuesetts had guzzled a quarter tank of gas, but the run later in a new pair of running shoes would be worth it. The cool spring breeze would flap your braid like a banner and sweat would dampen your thick white t-shirt, and with Timor's Etymotics earbuds in your ears, you would listen to that old Love and Rockets song, "I'm alive, Oh Oh, so so alive…" Incidentally, April 22 was also someone's birthday, her forty-third. That is still young, if you think about it. Many people these days live to eighty or more. If you think about it from the perspective of eighty or more, forty three is still young. Still young and so so alive, unlike Timor, now almost six months dead.

Selina ignored the flitting woman, the only other customer in the store, as she tested the shoes for suppleness. You do this by bending them. If the shoes bend easily between your palms, you can be sure they will not chafe your feet.

Excuse me, I need some help.

[A note to the reader: Quotations marks will not be used for dialogue in this true account of real life events. According to Practical English and the Command of Words, formerly owned by Dolores Van Staal, quotation marks "indicate the words actually spoken by the person quoted." But it is almost impossible to remember the words actually spoken by the person, especially if time has passed: the human brain is not a recording device! When you are quoting someone from memory, probably you are substituting your words for theirs. Well, in Practical English and the Command of Words, it also says that "if someone is quoted in words other than his own, no quotation marks are needed." Nevermind if it is sometimes difficult to tell who is saying what to whom. Nevermind.]

Selina turned. Big blue eyes popped out of a fake tan (not that a real one is any better. Especially a real one you cannot get rid of, due to too many childhood summer weekends at Staten Island's South Beach with a mother who was always reading and never applying sunblock). The big blue eyes blinked at Selina:

Sorry, I thought you worked here.

Thin but with the soft boned look of a small child or a kitten, in a silver velour hoodie with a pink sequined JUICY scrolled across the chest and matching drawstring pants, the woman did not appear to be a runner. As stated above, she resembled a fairy without the wings. Or a doll in a tracksuit. Yet, her sequined velour ensemble looked expensive. Never throw away an opportunity Selina's dad with the one eye used to say. What looks to be trash just might be treasure.

I might be able to give you some help, Selina said.

At the cash register, the wingless fairy, whose name turned out to be Lyndon, explained that she was going through IVF treatments and afraid of putting on weight. Grateful to Selina for helping her find fat fighting footwear, she reciprocated with an offer of baked goods: there's a cute little place with the yummiest muffins three doors down from here, my treat.

Dolled up in pink chintz curtains, lace scalloped tablecloths set with regency stainless, and cherry veneered bookcases lined with Dover Thrift Editions, spines even as crustless sandwiches, it was supposed to be a real English tea room even though it was not in England, as Lyndon so astutely pointed out. But that's okay, she laughed. I'm not a real blond, either.

Talk about good fortune: Lyndon with her openly acknowledged processed hair had the makings of a real dupe. You see it is not true that a sucker is born every minute. Perfect patsies combining stupidity with candor are hard to find. Or as noted by Winona Irving M.S.W., no one in our modern tell-all society actually does so (that is why it is so hard to share your loss, Irving says. And nevermind that it is impossible to give someone else a portion of what you do not have.). Lyndon had only just met Selina and here she was, being open as a 24/7 convenience store.

A waitress in a frilly white apron came with tea lists. Lyndon wanted the green but changed to herbal after Selina dissuaded her from it. You see, you should not drink caffeinated drinks if you are trying to get pregnant. You really should not run either, because running diverts the blood flow away from the uterus to other body parts. That is fine if you do not have one because your husband pressured you into having it removed, but presumably Lyndon did. Selina smiled across the table.

Lyndon stared back blankly, as if suddenly she did not know who she was, let alone whether or not she had a uterus. Then she said, I'm sorry, my name used to be Lucy, but Lucy sounds like a little girl, so now I go by my middle name. But sometimes I forget, especially with old friends. You're not an old friend, but already I feel like I've known you forever.

How sweet. Selina resumed: If you are trying to get pregnant, the best thing is yoga, any kind but bikram, of course. Acupuncture and reiki are very good as well, as supported by those trial studies.

How do you know all this? Lucy Lyndon bit into a blueberry scone. An enormous diamond dinner ring that looked to be genuine sparkled on her finger.

Well, Selina had trained to become an R.N. (after her mother had inferred she was not smart enough to be a doctor!). In fact, by the end of her training she had become so disenchanted by the masculine, patriarchal nature of western medicine that she decided not to take the NCLEX-RN exam. Oh sure there are aspects of western medicine that are second-to-none, but the problem is an approach to healing that uses just the body or just the mind. So Selina started exploring other options, including holistic healing. You see, people are not just the one or the other. Mind and body are unified with energy fields both inside and around that are part of the total health care system.

Lyndon's hand lay on the table palm side up, but even still you could see the diamonds glittering in the crack between her ring and pinkie fingers. As Selina extended her arm so that her own hand hovered just inches above them, Lyndon twitched.

I can feel one, Selina, an energy field both inside and around! Lyndon piped.

Selina did not need to touch Lyndon for Lyndon to feel the power that Selina collected daily, like a solar panel. Selina did not need to touch Lyndon's soft, thin-looking skin because energy fields in the universe are all interconnected. So they can be affected from really far away. Only one thing was necessary, Selina explained: for Lyndon to be receptive to the energy that Selina collected to help people like Lyndon for a nominal fee. And Lyndon did need help—she had said so herself.

Wingless fairy Lyndon was helpless even though she had money, as anyone could see from the Juicy tracksuit and the diamond cluster ring. More money than taste but even so, she deserved cheap healing energy as much as anyone. Maybe even more than some.

Lyndon went on to tell Selina about how she lived in Hudson, New York but her doctor husband was always at HVFC, a clinic for IVF, how he had given her the renovated Victorian mansion, a Volvo SUV XC90, in addition to four treatment cycles so far, but withheld himself. When they first started dating he could not keep his hands off her; now it seemed they spent more time in the egg retrieval room than they did in bed.

A semen sample is not love, Lyndon explained.

Plus he expected Lyndon to put up with his own two horrible children from his first marriage to a psychopath, which even with a full-time nanny, was asking a lot.

How sad Lyndon was, wiping her boohoo blue eye with a small supple-appearing hand—not the one with the ring, which might have scraped it. She deserved some inexpensive healing energy—oh absolutely. Fortunately for her, she was receptive to healing energy. If someone is not receptive, there is nothing you can do to make her more receptive. Fortunately for her, Lyndon had an open mind, in addition to a doctor husband.

In the parking lot of the outlet mall, Selina's old Beemer—the only presentable transportation she could afford after she totaled the Land Rover because she was so upset about the divorce settlement—would not start. Who can blame Selina for accursing both Timor and that piece-of-Nazi-crap car?

Your ex was also a Nazi? asked Lyndon, who had pulled up behind the Beemer in her Volvo SUV XC90.

What an airhead. Selina did not say what an airhead. Goddess forbid, Selina would never puncture another woman's self-esteem. Sisterhood means pulling each other up to a higher level, not bringing each other down to a lower one. Also, Selina needed a lift. So she briefly explained about what Timor used to say regarding BMW's Third Reich affiliations and so on (which is why he would never let her have a Beemer, and maybe even part of the reason why she bought that piece-of-Nazi-crap car, to defy him). Selina even claimed she was not sure if it was BMW or GM. As if she too were a scatter-brained simpleton. Then again, because imperfect, even muddled recollection is not uncommon when you have survived trauma (not to mention in human beings in general!), Selina's apparent confusion on the subject of car manufacurers with Nazi pasts could also have been genuine. You just never know.

No wonder I never liked Beemers, laughed Lyndon as she stepped down out of her Volvo. She pulled a silver iPhone just like the one Selina used to have out of a little silver pouch that hung on a strap across her chest. We can use my Volvo Care Plan to tow it and then I'll give you a ride home.

Rain began to fall, a light but cold spring rain.

Selina would never call Lyndon an airhead because after watching the auto serviceman attempt to jumpstart the Beemer's battery and then haul that lifeless hulk away, the drive in Lyndon's Volvo SUV XC90 over to Selina's house outside of Kinderhook, New York was like being on cloud nine. Like scudding over the blacktop as the Swedish suspension absorbed every shock and the wipers slicked the wide windshield above the silver glow of the dash and the speakers piped in frothy pop voices through the satellite radio system, as the pine dark bulk of the Berkshires flowed into blurry green fields and apple orchards and Selina ate organic milk chocolates from a little bamboo box in the recess below the cup holders and Lyndon babbled her big diamond flashing with each turn of the leather wrapped steering wheel about unsuccessful fertility treatments and all the meaningless surgical diversions before that, the Lasik, the collagen-injections, the boob job that could never take the place of a cute little baby.

Of course not. Babies and boob jobs are not the same: anyone who thinks anything can substitute for a baby is an idiot. But to say so would be to bite the bling-bling hand that was feeding you. Selina bit another chocolate instead and relaxed into the Volvo's heated leather seat. On that cold wet spring day, it was better than a warm bath.

When a person has experienced hardship and abuse it is only natural for her to seek an easy way out of her troubles. An airlift from an airhead, you could say. Plus it was not as if Selina had nothing to offer Lyndon in return. Selina did: her healing powers. So when Lyndon dropped Selina off beside the blooming apple trees that screened the peeling paint, shrink-wrap patched window panes, and weed sprouting steps of Selina's rural fixer-upper from the peeping eyes of 9H travelers, saying she wanted to come back for a treatment the next day, it was even steven. For both Nike and Tinkerbell.

Due to the hardship of the preceding months, Selina had evolved in many ways at a more rapid rate than humans generally experience. Plus she was highly responsive to the forces of nature. You could see this even when she was a child—by the way, for example, she would react to mosquito bites. One time at a backyard barbecue, a bite so swelled the left side of Selina's face that she appeared to be two different persons—a round cheeked Buddha on one side and a six-year-old girl on the other. More enlightened than most as well as acutely responsive to natural forces, Selina found the six-day Internet course, which came with a green silk caftan, two-day shipping included, totally sufficient to become a Reiki Master.

The problem was that people expect a Reiki Master not just to dress but to live like one. You know, all zen hoity toity and feng shui fancy. Due to an inequitable divorce settlement, however, Selina resided outside of Kinderhook in a falling down farmhouse with a rising mortgage (adjustable interest rates are never a good idea!). People want the soothing nature cds and the smooth white plastered walls and the rice paper watercolors and the joss sticks and the tatami mats, but you cannot get good chi without spending some money. Try installing a B & W speaker system in mice-infested walls. Try laying tatami mats on floors that rise and dip like you have just drunk three glasses of reisling that you cannot afford to drink, due to an inequitable divorce settlement.

Lyndon called the next day. Acutely responsive to natural forces but not clairvoyant, Selina checked weather.com before calling back: the chance of rain was zero percent. They would meet outdoors in back of the house because the healing power of nature is strongest out in nature. Selina waited for Lyndon at a trestle table with a view of the meadow, sipping a glass of boxed reisling. According to the New York Times, the French drink boxed wine all the time but Lyndon was not French and so the box was hidden in the pantry. A half-full carafe and an extra glass for Lyndon sat on the table. The reisling was potable. When you cannot afford alcohol, maybe the cheap stuff tastes better than it is. Or maybe you just appreciate what you have. In the apple trees beyond a cardinal flitted, here a spot of red, there a spot of red. Who needed recorded whale song when they had a live orchestra of crickets and warblers? Who needed aromatherapy when the guileless sweet of flocks wafted off their field? Sure it was no Chinese brush painting, as a wringer washer glowed white in the midst of the pink and purple meadow flocks. But even the abandoned appliance, stout and soothing like one of those old-fashioned nurses in the starched white uniforms, somehow worked. It all worked, a natural if not completely organic set-up for a healing experience that still would be as natural as any.

As natural or more so than Lyndon herself, who now came round the side of the house. She pranced through the tall grass in white velour sweats and aqua high-tops, a big orange satin tote bag in her hand. Her scrunchied hair was splashing bottle blond and black sunglasses covered her eyes like blinders. She was too cute, too cute to be true—a Little Phony Pony freshly broken out of her plastic packaging. But just because someone looks like a phony doesn't mean she is a phony, or that her pain is not real. Setting the big orange satin tote bag that with its pattern of orange embossed dots in fact looked to be a genuine Kate Spade on the trestle table, she took off the sunglasses. Her eyes brimmed boo hoo blue.

John says no more Clomid, Selina! He says after six months it's all just miscarriages. I asked him why can't I just go off for a month and start again but then he said my infertility is an "occult phenomenon" and that we could get two little Chinese girls for less than we've spent so far on fertility drugs. Like I'd want two more kids that aren't mine. They call me Lucy, you know. Lucy, like I'm the babysitter.

Lyndon slapped her hand down on the table: I want my own freakin' baby! Both empty wine goblets wobbled on their stems and the Kate Spade bag yelped.

Oh my baby did I scare you? Lyndon cried as she unzipped the top of the bag that you could now see, going on the discrete inserts of orange mesh at each end and the tiny dog she scooped up from its interior, was a pet carrier. The dog's brown mottled body was completely hairless except for a silky blond crest on its head. The crest was tied with an aqua ribbon.

Meet Cindy-Lou Who, Lyndon said holding the dog up by its chest. Lacking spunk as well as fur it dangled limply, gazing at some point beyond Selina's shoulder. Its breath smelled of rotten fish mixed with vanilla cookies. Crumbs flecked its fragile snout. People who are smitten by their dogs always expect other people to be smitten too. If you do not say how adorable they will think there is something wrong with you.

How adorable, Selina said lifting a dangling paw, then dropping it.

Thanks. You can't imagine what it's like with those rotten children. They're always after her spraying her with water trying to graffiti her skin with magic marker. I have to keep her with me all the time and if she's not with me she's at the dog sitter which John says is a ridiculous expense but it's hard to take her shopping she gets bored in her bag. And it is just not safe at home!

Lyndon gave the dog a kiss on her top knot then zipped her back up in her bag: Okay baby you can take a nap. Mommy has an appointment with this nice lady. Then turning back to Selina, her eyes once again welling up, she said I just don't know how much longer I can take it.

Selina tipped the carafe over Lyndon's glass. Lyndon needed to cheer up, to be receptive to the healing energy of the chi.

Am I allowed to drink? Lyndon sniffed, wiping her nose with her sleeve.

Drinking before you get pregnant is fine as long as you do not drink too much. Pregnant women all over the world have been drinking since ancient times. Did Lyndon know where the term "honeymoon" came from? Well in many parts of Europe it was the tradition to supply the young couple with enough of a honeyed wine called mead for a month, to ensure happiness and fertility.

Sign me up now! Lyndon exclaimed. Then she tipped the wine to her pink lips and gulped as the warblers swelled the air with free good vibes. The wine on the other hand was not cheap, though you would not know it from the box hidden in the pantry.

Another please, thirsty Lyndon gasped, thrusting out her goblet for more. Having drained that too, she exhaled. All around the warblers warbled in the trees and barn swallows swooped over the meadow trying to get a last bite before darkness descended and their beady little eyes could no longer see.

Can we get started? I want a baby so bad. The rim of Lyndon's glass was smudged with pink grease. If people knew how hard lipstick is to get off glassware, they would not wear it.

Selina explained that the session would be outside, down by that old washing machine where they would be drawing not just on the power of Gaia but of the feminine domestic force from bygone days. So Lyndon should just go there and wait in the grass while Selina went inside and got a tatami mat.

Nodding, Lyndon staggered off toward the abandoned appliance.

Tatami mats were originally a luxury item for the Japanese nobility, according to a big glossy book Selina's mother used to keep on the coffee table, Japan, even though she had never been to Japan. If you were poor, you had to make do with loose straw on dirt floors. The tatami mat spread over the meadow grass was actually a beach mat from the dollar store but Lyndon did not seem to notice. No surprise, since alcohol dulls the senses and makes the world less "there." This is why trauma survivors frequently abuse alcohol and drugs, to anesthetize themselves, you see. Selina had poured herself another glass of riesling on the way down to the old washing machine. That was to make Lyndon, who was a bit much, a little less.

Sprawled on her back, processed plume splayed, laser-corrected eyes closed, collagen-injected lips parted, silicone implants slid wide and to the side beneath the slubby knit of a white silk t-shirt, Lyndon would try the patience of a saint. Selina's own suffering had made her more tolerant than most, but she was not a saint. That may come as a surprise (ha). Who said trauma victims do not have a sense of humor? So pack up your troubles in your old kit bag and smile smile smile, as Selina's dad with the missing eye and hole in the head used to say. Pack up your troubles and count your blessings, one of which was that you were not a scatter-brained simpleton like Lyndon. As Selina's hands hovered six inches over her face (except for a quick swoop in to wipe away the bubblegum pink lipstick with a cocktail napkin), then her chest, her abdomen and finally her pelvis, Lyndon began to whimper I feel it, I feel it.

It was as legitimate a healing experience as any. As legitimate as any and maybe more than some as the bird song suddenly died away, leaving only the trill of the crickets, which maybe were just cicadas. Selina felt something that could have been healing energy drain from her body. That would explain that weak and tired feeling—Lyndon siphoning off some of Selina's healing energy. Or it could be no lunch. The not cheap box of riesling had cost a fortifying tuna on rye at the Kinderhook deli. Either way, Selina had lost something and Lyndon had gained something. You could see just by looking at her. She was still lying on her back, the violet tint of the early evening sky deepening the blue of her eyes, a smile flitting on her naturally rose (as opposed to bubblegum) lips. Thanks to Selina. With Selina's help, Lyndon had been visited with chi and improved her coloring.

As Lyndon lolled on her straw mat, the old wringer washer loomed in the grass behind her. People do not realize how much work women do, how much they rely on the largely invisible labor of women. Even women do not realize how much work women do. Women are in fact the worst, as they pay other women no better than slave wages to take care of their children, clean their houses and pumice the dead skin off their feet. They treat other women like appliances—like they can just set the wash and dry cycle before they leave the house for the afternoon. You could tell from Lyndon's now deep violet but no less shallow eyes that she was off somewhere in the outlet mall of her mind, already shopping for baby clothes.

In the basin of the old wringer washer, propped against the back, there was a wood and corrugated steel washboard. On the wood handle below the rusted ribbing the words IDEAL FOR SILKS, HOSIERY, AND LINGERIE OR HANDKERCHIEFS were printed in block letters. In a modern washing machine those would go in the Delicate Cycle, the setting for items that require extra care such as the green silk caftan. Selina herself was fine, delicate—that is what her father with the missing eye and piece of brain used to say. You've got such beautiful hands, hands like your Grandma Van Staal. You shouldn't bite your nails, honey.

But Selina could take care of herself, unlike wingless fairy Lyndon who had probably never worked a day in her life. Selina would get by, because she was a survivor. On the other hand, being a survivor requires something to survive on and so far, Lyndon had said nothing about payment. For that matter, where was the little silver pouch, or its white patent leather equivalent, to go with today's white velour sweats? Hopefully in her car—goddess forbid she had left it at home.

Lyndon sat up, stretched her arms and arched her back. Can I ask you a favor?

Selina sighed. What would the next question be? Maybe, do you mind if I pay next time? Or the time after that, as Lyndon put Selina through the wringer again and again, as each Reiki session would lead to another and the hope of a payment that would be endlessly deferred. Selina was a survivor but she could not survive on nothing.

I know you are against men and the medical establishment and everything but you've got so much to offer. You really do. John says they're looking for a new Cycle Coordinator at the clinic. An RN with experience in holistic health care, but with your background they might even consider an LPN. Won't you please apply?

The payment was in Lyndon's Volvo after all, an unwise place to leave it. Even out in the country, theft is a real possibility. Selina's father with the one eye, who sold the farm for a liquor store, used to say country people are the worst. You should never leave your money in the car, or your front door unlocked, honey. Country people are the worst, but people are people everywhere with mouths to feed and mortgages to pay. Next time Selina would caution Lyndon, because Selina could not be responsible for lost or stolen valuables, human nature being what it is.

For now, however, it was all good—the money (five Benjamins) beneath the green silk caftan, rolled up and tucked into Selina's running bra, Lyndon and her orange pet carrier belted into the great black sport utility vehicle that had transported her away, around the narrow tree-lined bend of Highway 9 and out of sight. All good, as down in the meadow bats swapped places with the barn swallows and three-legged Florence did lopsided binkies.

And who was Florence? Well besides a famous nurse known for her dedication to nursing, as well as her critical attitude (for the times) toward the male medical establishment, she was a three-legged Belgian hare whom Selina had adopted from the Humane Society in defiance of Timor. Not just a pet like Lyndon's little dog-accessory or even a companion, she was an inspiration. You see, though maimed by an unfortunate accident she still found joy in life by bounding, leaping and twisting in the air, even if her contortions more often than not landed her on her back. For then she would spring right back up again, throwing herself into the spastic gymnastics that had driven Timor crazy. He could not stand the sight of a survivor. Florence was a survivor who would just spring back up again on her three remaining feet, oblivious to Timor's threats to skin and stew her like some long dead wild rabbit who had stolen a carrot from the garden of someone named Baba.

So there you have it. You see, Selina was a survivor, too. Selina was a survivor who now had something to survive on, temporarily, and maybe even a job. So Timor could just take that carrot and stuff it you know where.

On average, the limits of a ghost's rationality are very narrow—no good, therefore, to explain to these astral *bolváns* that their bodies are non-returnable. Like toddlers and cretins, they just won't accept basic physical principles, like entropy, heat death and "no more." On average, but there are exceptions, and believe it or not, I'm one of them. So not only do I know I can't get that sack of shit back, I don't want it. I don't want my body because I don't want nobody. No body, no desire—it's that simple, *króshka.*

"Hmmmph," you'll say as you read this on the Mac you "inherited" from me, "hmmmmph," like there's a pubic hair in your throat. And maybe there will be one there, but who the fuck cares? Then lacing your long tanned fingers beneath your chin, you'll ask the computer screen "then why is he haunting me?" Fair enough. If I don't want nobody, least of all you, why bother? Maybe you think I've got nothing better to do now that I'm a spook but float around inside your Mac, playing with your pixels. Let me tell you, I've got plenty to do, plenty. All that reading I never had time for when I was looking up *pizda* all day—I was nothing but a cunt mechanic. No more ortho gel, no more latex gloves, no more twats, no more hands. Finally I can live like I always wanted to, like a member of the *intelligentsiya*, wallowing in words all day. I'm even doing a little scholarly work.

Yeah *détka*, I can do whatever I want now that I don't need to eat, to sleep, to fuck, to exercise, to lose weight, put on deodorant, pluck my eyebrows (yes, I did—they were always so bushy), pick my teeth, hold in my farts (which I realize were getting worse and worse), comb a head of still thick but grizzled hair. I don't need to worry about losing my looks (believe it or not, back in the Brighton Beach days they called me the James Dean from Odessa), because I no longer have any looks to lose. Really, it's nothing but the life of the mind for me now baby—an endless biblio-debauch in the original Plato's Retreat.

File 2010/Transcription of Revenant Dictation
(Former Sex: Female; Deceased 15.11.2010)

i live in a hole but i used to live in a house. i used to live in a house with a man. my husband, i called him. also mark. mark, i'd say, you're going to have to start treating me better. mark my words. but he didn't listen. he'd just keep on reading his new york times, or playing chess with his computer, or looking out the window at the boys playing croquet on the lawn, or going to work in the city while we all had to live out in west hartford because he said it was healthy even with all the lyme. but sometimes in the evening when he'd be drinking macallens or heinekins, when although he never listened i'd tell him my ideas to make money, because then maybe he'd listen just a little, because at one time he used to tell me that he thought i had great taste and a smart head on me even with only an associates, sometimes then he'd say that's a good idea, and we'll see, cara.

one night after seven eleven or was it nine it's all the same in this hole anyways one night when mark my husband was sitting in the library at his computer playing chess drinking macallens and taking some of my pills that i didn't mind sharing because dr. frolichstein would always give me more, i said i have an idea for a flip. but cara darling you just finished this house and it looks beautiful now you need to rest he said, it's not good for you to be haggling with contractors all day. you make yourself mad and then you have a relapse. and he petted my head. he petted my head then patted my arm his fingers grazing the side of my breast which meant he was interested in something else but i kept on with my idea because i knew my mark, knew that what excited him most was money.

so i reached over and closed the chess program, pulling up the pictures of the farmhouse on the hill overlooking the lake. people want to get out of the city now, i said, my voice a hiveful of honey. they want to get out of the city, away from the bad things the toxins and fumes to where the air is sweet, i said, oozing thick and sticky. they want to get out of the city but at the same time they don't want to give up the city. they want the simple but not too simple life the hay without the seeds the renovation that turns linoleum into florentine terra cotta. so i'll fix up the house to flip it. and in the meantime we can live up there make a sweet deal on the sweet air up there where there's no lyme but plenty of deer and other animals as well foxes and pheasants and field mice. if we can't live in the city because i don't mind the toxins and fumes they're not what made me sick, i'd rather live upstate. upstate closer to nature instead of in west hartford where all the people are phony and fake and do nothing but go to the mall and shop.

but you like to shop too, said my husband mark. you shop all the time.

that's different. i only shop for bargains, i reminded him pulling his hands up beneath the frogs of my chinese pajamas, a recent steal from saks online a bargain in blue silk jacquard. you don't know how much money i've scrimped and saved shopping for bargains, when it's so much easier to pay full price. now all i want is to move upstate for a while away from lyme and closer to nature closer to nature where i can be myself maybe build a little studio in the back yard and start making art again and andy and wesley can play indians in the woods and swim like otters in the lake, because this is not just about me. and you can take the train upstate every weekend. yes you can take the train sit back and relax in the bar car and i'll pick you up at the station in albany because this is not about me and drive you straight home to our king sized feather bed and a tumbler of scotch. a vacation for everyone only in the end we'll have money in our pockets.

let's sleep on it honey, mark murmured. but i knew i had him his hands inching under the waist of my silk pajama bottoms fingers crawling buzzing inside my panties buzzing buzzing. i knew i had him so grabbing his wrists i murmured back let's not sleep on it after all the scrimping and saving i've done i want an answer now. okay cara, he finally said and because a bargain is a bargain the next morning we made an offer on the house on the hill.

i live in a hole did i already say that, yes i think i did. it's not so bad this hole i softened it up with some feathers and cotton balls what did i used to use them for, oh for removing makeup, mascara so mark couldn't say, you look like a raccoon. but i liked raccoons liked the way they look with their domino masks, like little bandits. So friendly and cute. even in connecticut they were nice i didn't mind at all when they got in the garbage mark was the one who made the peanut butter and wayfarin sandwiches and left them on top of the cans. we're in this together i told them, you should see the way he looked at me back when i was a temp working my way through art school and i walked for the first time into his den at goldman sachs drooling like that disgusting lab of his i was going to be an artist you know he said he'd help me and instead he got me preggers. now he'd like to get rid of me too only it would cost him more than peanut butter.

after we moved to the house on the hill, the raccoons were the first to approach me. i was sitting on the new florentine tile steps between the potted dwarf cypresses, sucking on something what was it, a half empty tube of anchovy paste i think. anyways i was famished, famished and there was nothing in the kitchen everything mark hadn't eaten over the weekend the boys had polished off and then they all expected me to drive into town and go shopping without money for groceries because i'd spent it at target on the way back from the train station in albany, spent it saving money on all the bargains. give us the paste they said stretching out their small black hands and i said ok, but then help me find some dough.

so friendly and cute, and clever too. how they'd managed to spring the bungee cords old marky mark had stretched over the tops of the trash cans littering the grass with print outs and credit card and bank account statements so that now i knew about the other checking line is beyond me. anyways now i'd take out a few hundred here a few hundred there and he never noticed it was chicken feed compared to what he was spending on himself every week down in the city. i knew because a little birdy had told me it was all there in the inside pocket of his briefcase the crumpled bar tabs and credit slips. a little birdy told me or maybe it was a mouse because by then the mice were helping as well.

the raccoons were the first to approach me but the mice were the first to come inside. i'd see them out of the corner of my eye something darting across the top of my vanity as i was picking his underwear off the floor or skittering behind the hamper in the bathroom or even rippling the pattern of the kilim carpet that hung on the wall behind the bed. they were the first and i didn't invite them, they just came. i admit i also didn't tell them to go. i didn't tell them to go even though they say mice should not be living in a house but in nature, in a cavity under a root or a pocket in a field. but in nature the boundaries are sometimes not clear between nature and not nature and it's the same in the house, especially when you are living closer to nature. so much closer to nature i couldn't tell at first if i was seeing anything at all.

like with the lyme i couldn't tell i had it at first. was there a rash like a bull's eye or a target or was i just thinking after of the store logo on the way to the train station in albany? it starts with a spirochete dr. frolichstein said which means the thing passed on by the tick as it takes its blood meal, a thing that looks like a tiny corkscrew. because that's what it does it screws you makes you lose the thread the string that you tie around your finger to remember. that's why i've got string here too in addition to the cotton balls and the feathers, string to remember what it is i have to say. if i can remember i can move on, that's what they tell me. if i can remember i can get out of this hole that i'm in.

but it's hard you know i get so mad when that lab sticks its face in my hole blasting in its hot trashy breath sliming the dirt with its drool. i get so mad even though i know it's not mark's lab.

i know it's not mark's because she's gone. that was easy getting rid of her so easy i could have thought of it myself but it was someone else's idea. i can't remember whose exactly. probably one of the mice came up with that plan. most likely a mouse because of the traps mark would set up in suzi q's dish at night after he'd put her in her crate, the traps baited with peanut butter or sometimes cheese. the mice were never caught but boy they sure were pissed. i even found myself defending mark saying well at least he doesn't use the wayfarin on you guys. he doesn't use the wayfarin and when he catches you he has the boys set you free in a field on the other side of the lake. but we all knew that was only because he didn't want their corpses in the walls, stinking up the house so no one would buy it.

anyways they wouldn't have any of it. stop defending him, they said. he's no prince charming. we know all about it, how he promised to help you go back to risdi but then got you preggers. how he kept the money from the last house you flipped saying that he was putting it into a college fund for the boys but really it just goes down the old watering hole. how can you stand it he doesn't listen to you he won't let you be yourself you're supposed to be his fifties fantasy the perfect mother housekeeper sex doll rosie the robot who picks up after everybody even the dog. and you hate that dog it gets hair on everything and leaves steaming turds big as the boys' adidases all over the lawn. there's some wayfarin in the woodshed that was supposed to be your studio, just mix it in with the food in the dish. that dumb lab won't be able to tell the difference.

they were right about mark he was no prince charming far from it and now even worse. he expected me to pick him up every weekend in albany but when he got to the house he'd drink all night and then the next day hair of the dog so that even without suzi q it was more work than ever i didn't have a moment to just sit down and be me, let alone do my art. like a maidservant or a slave i did everything for everyone but me all the cooking the cleaning the yard work not to mention hunting for bargains while all the while fixing up the house to flip it. i had to do everything for everyone worked my fingers to the bone from morning to night for everyone but me. no wonder i started to have a relapse i could barely get out of bed it's not my fault i had to start shopping online, just to make my own decisions and be myself.

by this time everyone could see how mark was treating me, everyone, both inside and out. one day after mark had gone back to the city and the boys weren't around maybe i'd sent them to tennis camp or my sister's I don't remember anyways one day they all approached me. what can we do to help they asked. so i gave them each a different job to the raccoons i said you can wash his dirty dishes, to the mice i said you can whisk away the dorito crumbs from between the sofa cushions in his study, to the ravens you can lift his soiled clothes up off the floor and drop them in the hamper, to the sparrows you can peck up the screw tops and beer tabs and shreds of pot and tobacco that litter the carpet around his desk, to the garter snakes you can siphon the dregs from his empty bottles, to the spiders and crickets you can dispose of the flies that buzz around the kitchen garbage can he never empties.

then such a hubbub it was, everyone scurrying creeping crawling flapping flitting, slithering this way and that chittering squeaking squawking screeching hissing and chirping such a mad merry animation of friends. so that after when they all came up on my bed and said we're done, my eyes filled with grateful tears. unfortunately later after i finally got up and took a look around well i'm sorry to say they hadn't done such a good job. i actually started screaming.

but then i stopped because of course i had only myself to blame since i was the human and they were just animals without human standards of order or hygiene. they were just animals so of course the raccoons threw the dishes down like clam shells smashing them on the tiles after they washed them, that's what raccoons do. of course the mice left trails of droppings as they cleaned up the crumbs, that's their nature. of course the ravens and sparrows spackled the floors the counters the fixtures and furniture, of course the snakes remained coiled inside the yellowing bottles, of course the spiders spanned the doorways with their webs, how else could they catch the flies. of course the house smelled like the stinkiest zoo ever because why should they be toilet trained, they were just animals. so i stopped screaming because they'd only done the best they could. it wouldn't do to hurt their feelings. i'm sorry i said as i stood there in the middle of the kitchen in my blue chinese silk pajamas that i'd purchased online, it's just that i've never been so amazed. look at all the work you guys have done, the house is completely transformed.

there's just one problem however, mark's not going to like it. you know how boring he is, how he doesn't like anything to be different or funny. he's not going to be happy i said as a fly vibrated the web between the jambs of the mudroom door. and that will only make things harder for me.

well that really set them off next thing i knew they were all talking at once dashing around my feet hopping jumping tugging snagging the silk of my chinese pajamas purchased online the winged ones flapping around my ears so that it was really hard to tell where the idea came from it was a jostling mob a midnight madness of how dare he who does he think he is how can you stand it he won't let you be yourself he wants you to be someone you're not his fifties fantasy things just can't go on like this. no i really can't say but once it had been uttered everyone agreed. and now the room was suddenly so quiet it was as if there was no one there at all.

the idea remained however like a larvae in a cocoon quickening quickening until finally friday arrived and it was time to pick my mark up at the train station. we'll take care of everything they said. you just make sure he's happy they said, bring the macallens and some of the pills from dr. frolichstein. well i was happy to make mark happy especially since i knew he was unhappy he'd been calling all week about the on-line shopping saying things had gotten out of hand. things were getting out of hand but i was happy to make mark happy so it wasn't my fault. it wasn't my fault i was just trying to help him to relax, oh so hard to explain to remember. so hard to remember after what i've been through screwed by a spirochete i'd like to see them try remembering, try walking a few steps in my shoes.

i don't have any shoes here but i think this piece of string might be a lace a once white now gray lace from a child's sneaker maybe from one of my sons' before they started asking for the adidases. who could believe they were ever that small i liked them better when they were little like soft animals nuzzling my legs as i stirred their irish oats planting soft kisses on my calves. no kisses here or calves if i had shoes i wouldn't be able to walk a few steps in them, not even one. not even one oh how am i ever going to get out of here without the body that did whatever they say it did. but they say that's no excuse. i've still got to try to remember if i want to get out.

and i do i really do. even though it might not be any better out there. and it's not so bad here i've got cotton balls and feathers to soften it up and also did i mention a scrap of soft fabric it could be silk maybe from the chinese pajamas purchased online though the animals took everything in the end. i thought it would be better without mark that i could live closer to my own nature finally be myself. but the animals took everything in the end.

i don't know where the boys went after they did it maybe to my sister's you could tell she really wanted kids. or my mothers' if she was still alive she always said mark was such a good catch. they caught him alright though it can't have been much of a challenge after the booze and the pills from frolichstein I'm sure he had no idea what was happening to him until the final moments passed out snoring in the middle of our king sized bed. i had no idea either i slept in the guestroom that night it was all their idea though it's true that i was at my wits end with no time to be myself no time to be me close to my own nature. so i just closed the door. and i didn't open it ever again even though some of my nicest things were in there, my chinese silk pajamas among them. no i told them you can have that room that part of my life is over done sealed shut i'm starting fresh as if i was never married never walked into mark's den at goldman sachs.

but they weren't content with just that room they wanted more. you're finally who you were meant to be we must share in your happiness now that you're living closer to nature free to express your self. they wanted more which meant everything both outside and in but starting of course with the kitchen pulling all the boxes and cans down from the cabinets, the cartons and bottles and bags from the refrigerator shelves razor teeth and claws slitting cardboard and shredding plastic whiskers twitching tongues flickering and tasting proboscises unfurling slurping and soiling a foundation of filth of irish oats and spittle whole wheat flour and feces organic lemonade and venom covering every surface with skeins of gritty glistening slime which they then spun into cords tarps veils hammocks from wall to floor to ceiling to wall cris crossing in every direction spilling out into the breakfast room the dining room mark's study the living room the family room the twisting tendrils pushing each day weaving ever closer to the front door. each night i'd move the twin mattress i'd taken from my sons' room because by then they were gone for good a little nearer to the threshold until finally one night i was out on the lawn. yes and now i remember how i was blanketed in a viscous crochet a train of slime a glittering stinking sprawl squirming like spirochetes under a microscope or police examination extending from my neck back into the dim of the house. now i remember how i ran and ran until i couldn't run anymore out into the fields where i stumbled and fell. now i remember how when i woke up i was in this hole. it's really not so bad.

Editor's Note: In regard to the lack of caps: these are an editorial attempt to respect and preserve after the subject's death a stylistic affectation in life, exhibited in her infrequent correspondence with her sister. According to Norman Cantor, author of *After We Die: The Life and Times of the Human Corpse*, much of life is a preparation for death. Through our actions, gestures, and daily choices while extant, we compose what Cantor refers to as a "memory picture." "Even if cadavers [or here, ghosts] cannot sense the actual violation of a lifetime's legacy, their image and identity are things they have worked to establish that can be harmed." Certainly, we would not want to misrepresent anyone, especially such an attractive apparition as the above, who though past her prime at her decease (and who in fact was already in perimenopause when she became "preggers" at age thirty seven) nevertheless is a classic example of the succubus type, as well as a GILF—if intercourse was practicable, and she wasn't a total lunatic.

Not Okay: A True Crime Story,

by Selina Van Staal

Chapter Two

"Kick Me"

According to Winona Irving, M.S.W., the act of telling a story can alter the abnormal processing of a traumatic memory. Transformation of the traumatic memory can in turn bring the relief of many major symptoms such as insomnia. That is why people need to listen and to not just lumber on by like Selina's family did when she would be suspended from the lintel of the open cellar door in her Jolly Jumper. Trying not to think about the chasm at her back, Selina bounced for hours every day in her pink canvas sling, flashing her gums and simpering. Selina's mother, her sister, her brother—everyone always lumbered on by even though technically they were too thin to lumber because Selina's mother kept everyone on a low fat, high fiber and taste free diet. Not for health, by the way, but for looks. So that when she looked up from her book, she would not have to see fat people. Anyways, everyone always lumbered on by except for Selina's father, who would be out trying to make a deal or get a (good) free meal (and plus, was used to sneaking around). They lumbered on by with books in their hands, because when they were not lumbering by they were reading, and sometimes both at once. Oh sure, they were not always lumbering by and reading. Some of the time they must have been doing something else, like eating Wasa crackers or sleeping or going to school, not just Selina's sister and brother but also her mother, who was a secretary in the English Department at the University. Some of the time they must have been doing something else like eating or sleeping or going to school or even to a movie (preferably one based on a book, like <u>Doctor Zhivago</u> or <u>Rosemary's Baby</u>). But it seemed like they were always lumbering by and reading, as if poor Selina did not exist. By the way, what was that Jolly Jumper doing suspended in the doorway down to the cellar, and not in some less precipitous location such as the living room? Well one of the English professors had told Dolores Van Staal that the words "cellar door" form the most beautiful combination of sounds in the English language.

They say the story telling act can alter the abnormal processing of the traumatic memory, so here is a story. It was the end of the school year and Selina, though only in the second grade, had walked home all alone. That is another example of gross neglect but not an actual traumatic memory, so nevermind for now. All alone inside the house, having let herself in with the key under the geranium pot, Selina had nothing to do. She had nothing to do until she thought of something—a surprise. The surprise was for Selina's older sister Cara and brother Julius, who when they arrived home a little while later were told it had been prepared by Selina's mother, to celebrate the beginning of summer vacation. Even though Dolores Van Staal never would have thought of it—like the English professors she worked for, she was kind of a moron. Just because you are always reading does not make you smart.

The actual surprise, Selina told Cara and Julius, was at the very end of a piece of twine that began in the front hall, secured to an antique, cast-iron boot tree. Believing the surprise had been prepared by their mother, even though their mother had been at school all day helping English professors figure out how to turn in their grades, and still was not back, Cara and Julius were eager to discover what it was. Maybe books, they guessed.

Just follow the string, and you will see, Selina said, slipping out the front door.

The twine ran through the front hallway beyond the stairs, around the living room where every night Selina circled the sofa and chairs trying to get her mother, sister and brother to look up from their books, into the dining room under the table where they would talk about what they had read, under the swinging wooden door into the breakfast room where those idiots would even read the cereal boxes, through the sunroom around the woven wicker basket first of Puck a caramel colored teacup poodle that Selina's mother had adopted from an English professor offered a job in Scotland and then of Horatio an Irish wolfhound also adopted from an English professor forced to move to a smaller apartment after the loss of a rent subsidy who as the twine caught momentarily on a protruding bit of wicker seeped fecal gas but otherwise did not stir so that it was a great relief to slip out the back door onto the patio shaded by an awning which made it a perfect place to sprawl in the summer on a lounge chair with a…

Surprise! yelled Selina as she caught her siblings full front with the blast of the garden hose.

Well, people do not like surprises. Especially people who read all the time. They want to be able to open the book when they feel like it, and close the book when they feel like it. If they do not like what they are reading, they can even throw the book across the room, as Selina's siblings did to Selina, only it was outside. Her sopping sister grabbed hold of one Selina's ankles and her sopping brother grabbed hold of the other. Then they swung her around and flung her over the grass and into a trellis of rambling roses. Believe it or not, the traumatic memory is yet to come.

The traumatic memory comes with Selina sprawled in that bed of thorns, head still smarting from the smack of skull against wood. Looking up, she saw her mother (finally home!) looking down—not at Selina, but at the splintered bits of trellis and scattered foliage all around her. You ruined the roses, she said.

That was it, all she had to say: you ruined the roses. Can you imagine? All that Dolores Van Staal cared about was books, pedigreed dogs, and now, come to think of it, roses. Mindless plants that did not need love or attention, mindless plants that just stand there looking beautiful and most of the time do not even have much of a smell. No matter what the poets say.

Selina met the second woman, Kyle, one week after she met Lyndon. The date was April 29, 2010, exactly six months after the arrival of a certified letter from Giersten and Thurston, Attorneys at Law, stating that the note in what appeared to be Timor Zinkovsky's handwriting ceding the deed of Bosky House to Selina Van Staal was legally non-binding.

It might come as a surprise that Selina first encountered the second woman, Kyle, at a bookstore. Especially to people who read all the time and do not like surprises. Because even though she read all of the novel Rosemary's Baby at age seven, Selina probably does not fit their preconceptions of a bookish person. You know, a bookworm, an eye-sore cardigan wearer with holes in her sleeves. A fright of library paste and dandruff flakes and sour breath from eating hard candies all day because she cannot put her book down long enough to make a meal. Well Selina read more than any of them—Dolores, Cara, Julius—just not all the time (guess which little Van Staal got the highest score on the Iowa Test for Reading Comprehension?). Plus she did not act like books were more real than people.

The bookstore was in Hudson, New York—a former working turned shopping class town. On the day in question, Selina had an appointment with a customer who lived in Hudson. But the appointment was not until the afternoon. Hudson has two bookstores, one that sells used books, the other new. People who like to read all the time often only go to used book stores because the books are cheaper and they can buy more of them, to read all the time. But Selina always went to both because you never know what you will find. The first time Selina saw Kyle, she was at the new book store in Hudson. People who are always reading might have missed her.

Kyle sounds like a boy name, which it is. Parents think they are being creative when they give their daughters boy names like Kyle or Barry or Devon or for that matter, Lyndon. In addition, they believe that this act of creative naming will make their daughters creative. Kyle had a stake in this belief system. You could tell from her blue plastic framed glasses, bare arms tattooed with Egyptian hieroglyphics, and white ankle socks worn with black military-style oxfords that she thought of herself as an interesting and artistic person. People who are always reading would probably agree with Kyle's perception of herself. Kyle was not, however, in a section where constant readers, if they even bothered to enter the store, would expect to find an interesting and artistic person, like by the Poetry shelves, or Art and Design. Standing in the Pregnancy and Motherhood section, one big knuckled hand on her hip, the other holding a book titled <u>Empty Arms: Coping After Miscarriage</u>, Kyle was exactly where people who read all the time would be surprised to find an interesting and artistic person. But Selina was not one of those people.

That is probably why Kyle trusted Selina from the get go. Even though Selina did not necessarily look like an interesting, artistic person herself, but more like the sporty feminine type. She resembled an attractive gym teacher, but more mystic with her gypsy coloring. That would fit with the book in Selina's own hand, The Edgar Cayce Handbook for Health Through Drugless Therapy. Normally, Kyle would not give a sporty type a second glance, even a more spiritual looking one. She would be on the way to meet her interesting, artistic friends in their apartments decked with dead stuffed minks, crocodile skulls and Christmas lights, or to paint all alone in a corner of an abandoned pocketbook factory. But in this case, Kyle, or Tattoo Girl, as Selina thought of her, not yet knowing her name, could probably feel something was different. Looking up and seeing Selina's totally open smile, Tattoo Girl returned it with a small, sad smile of her own.

Selina asked Tattoo Girl if she was okay.

No, Tattoo Girl replied. Empty Arms fell to the floor as she covered her face with her hands.

It is hard to know when to give someone a hug. Even though people are hurting inside, they may have mixed feelings about comfort through physical contact, viewing it as a violation of carefully constructed personal boundaries. It is hard to know when to give someone a hug but sometimes you just have to trust your gut, as Selina's dairyman turned wheeler dealer father used to say. Well the gut was right, although it heaved a little, in hugging her. If you eat a lot of onions, you should try chewing on salt-dipped celery or parsley. And if you smoke—well, no comment.

To sell the farm or some such is an expression but it is also something people do. The small working dairy farm in Chatham, New York that Selina's father sold had belonged to Selina's father's mother, who bought it on a whim after her second husband, the stepfather of Selina's father, died. Not only did it belong to Selina's father's mother, but Selina's father had helped her run it, after he discovered that college was not for him. Through honest labor and frugal management, he turned his mother's bucolic conceit into a real farm (with the stink of twenty Holstein cows to prove it). Plus his half-sisters had inherited plenty from their own father. That is why it seemed fair for his mother to transfer the deed over to him on her deathbed. But then his sisters got really mad and although they did not contest the sale or try to recover the proceeds (which Selina's father invested in a liquor store) they made sure that he did not get even one French polished stick of a houseful of genuine Hepplewhite, which according to Selina's father turned out to be worth more than the farm.

So you should not sell what is not yours to sell. But you also should not buy what is not yours to buy. Even though people think that if they have money, they can buy anything they want, and it is theirs. You would not know it to look at her (although an observant person might note her privileged, spoiled expression), but Tattoo Girl had a lot of money—bestowed upon her and her sculptor husband by her father, who was a partner at a corporate law firm, and also by her grandfather, who had left her a substantial stock portfolio. She confessed that she had used some of it to buy the eggs of another woman. Human eggs that is, not the kind you can buy at the grocery store, although there are problems with those, too, admitted Tattoo Girl, who fed her ferrets raw chicken but was herself a vegan.

The two women were now sitting on a bench in a little public park in Hudson bounded on one side by a railroad track. On the walk up the street from the new bookstore, past windows cluttered with antique birdcages, chamberpots and imported pastas, Tattoo Girl had introduced herself. So now it is back to Kyle, although in the midday light, the black hieroglyphics more or less popped off her white arms. Having pulled out some rolling papers and a little pouch of tobacco out of her sleeveless, tunic-like top, Kyle rolled two cigarettes. Want one? Silver flashed in her mouth when she spoke—a bead fixed to the end of her tongue.

Selina shook her head, while maintaining an open expression. Smoking is a choice. Not smoking is a choice too, although if you are sitting next to someone who is smoking, their choice prevails over yours. Selina coughed as Kyle exhaled.

I never smoked while I was pregnant. Not once, Kyle said. Now it doesn't matter. She took another long ragged drag on her cigarette, then resumed as the smoke drifted past Selina's face. We tried for about a year before we went to the doctor. When he told me I had premature ovarian failure, I was looking out his office window. Beyond the clinic grounds there was a field, and at the top of the field, bordering the main road, an abandoned estate house. We must have passed it driving up to the clinic but only now did I see it, my awareness zooming up behind like a camera: the crumbling mortar of the limestone walls, the broken plywood-covered panes of the Georgian-style windows. That was once a beautiful house and now it's only fit for the wrecking ball, I thought.

A train whistle cut her off as the ground trembled. For several minutes, rail cars rolled by, cutting off the flow of traffic through Hudson along with poor empty armed Kyle.

As the caboose passed out of sight, she ground the cinder of her cigarette beneath a black military-style oxford and resumed. When the doctor told me that I could still get pregnant using IVF, but I'd need to use another woman's eggs, I was not interested at all. Grossed out, in fact. But as the months went by and it was just me, Jimmy and the ferrets, I changed my mind.

An understanding expression is important when someone is sharing intimate details or secrets. Fortunately, Selina had one. She had gotten her understanding expression from her father, who after he had sold the farm, had had some success as a salesman. Dean Van Staal had, in turn, taken his understanding expression from a cow. Which did not make it any less sincere. Animals understand our pain better than anyone, because they are still in touch with their bodies. That is what empty armed Kyle needed, to get in better touch with her body.

Selina explained that people today are expected to live like they are on an economic front of competition, like the soldier who once wore the shoes on Kyle's feet. They have to be constantly on the alert to maintain homeland security. You know, to keep the house and the family and the credit rating. And everyone is forced to participate, even people who feel like they are against capitalism—because they are still buying something, whether it is Blahniks from Barneys or Red Cross oxfords from Goodwill.

Kyle nodded, even rocked slightly, as if she were listening to her favorite band. So far, so good. Selina continued with her spiel, admittedly borrowed from <u>The Edgar Cayce Handbook for Health Through Drugless Therapy</u>, though updated for a contemporary audience.

Participation takes a physical toll, whether you know it or not. Look at all the cases of insomnia, obesity and self-mutilation. Because what is the difference between body piercing and a lab rat chewing on its own tail?

Kyle winced but the silver bead remained tucked behind closed lips, probably because she could not have said it better herself. As one-eyed Dean used to say, people like to hear what they already know. Yes, people like to hear what they already know, like rats chewing their own tails.

If you had only a mind, and not a body, the world of economics would disappear. You would not need a house, or food to put in your body, or clothes to cover it, or a health care plan with which to fix it. Yet the body that creates these needs, the body that causes all the elements of struggle and pressure and work, is neglected, abused, until it is fit only for the wrecking box.

The silver bead flashed. Ball. But you're right—it's crazy. And what can you do? You're always already fucked.

A sporty type might say Kyle had taken the (wrecking) ball and run with it. Game over. Being more spiritual in nature, Selina knew that Kyle needed guidance, to keep her from going afield into an attitude of doom and gloom. Dean Van Staal would use what he called "sweet talk" to steer his customers in a positive direction. But sometimes people's minds cannot be altered by words alone.

In Selina's backpack were gluten-free hash brownies for the customer, a pothead glutton with Celiac disease who lived in a mansion on Union Street. Illegal substances should not be bought or sold but the reiki alone was not enough to pay the bills and who knew if the job at Lyndon's husband's clinic would materialize. Plus if the pothead glutton did not get the brownies from Selina he would get them from some less wholesome source. Some people, for instance, would use wheat flour, which is easier to bake with and also cheaper than almond flour. Selina's brownies were dense and creamy without wheat flour or any gluten-containing ingredient, or even butter and eggs. So vegans could eat them too.

But if Selina gave empty armed Kyle a brownie, there would be one less in the order of the Union Street customer. Who might care more about total THC than texture, and in the future look to some less wholesome source for his supply.

Anyways, Kyle might not even want one. Some people do not care for cannabis because it makes them paranoid. Paranoia could be a risk factor with Kyle, who had dark circles under her eyes and an edgy appearance overall. On the other hand, she was stuck in an attitude of doom and gloom, resistant to healthy influences and positive suggestions that could not only improve her mood but her chances to conceive. A brownie might lift her out of her slough, into a more upbeat state: empty armed Kyle could be given a brownie for her own good. No need for fanfare about the ingredients, because if you are afraid of becoming paranoid, you already are. Plus cannabis is not an animal product. As for that customer on Union Street—well he was such a stoner, he probably would not even notice.

Four out of five people will take a flyer if it is simply handed to them, even if they do not want it. Churches and organizations such as Green Peace rely on this reflex to distribute their materials. Fishing a brownie out of her backpack, Selina handed it to Kyle, stating only that it was homemade, without eggs, dairy products or wheat.

A starling hopped up to the bench, eyes shiny as aluminum foil.

Chocolate is supposed to make you feel like you are in love. Kyle did not look like someone who liked to be in love, but then she also did not look like someone who would be found in the Pregnancy and Motherhood section of the bookstore. For a moment, she stared blankly at the foil wrapped packet, as if it had dropped out of the sky and into her hand. Finally she peeled back the wrapping, pinched up a moist bit of brownie with her fingers and brought it to her lips. The starling flew off, leaving a white splash on the gravel.

Selina did not partake of her own baked goods. Forced by an unfair patriarchal system as well as the untimely death of Timor to live by her wits, she could not afford to be a stoner. Goddess forbid. Selina had to get high on life, which is not always easy. Sometimes it is hard to keep an unhappy expression off your face. Just imagine Kyle sitting with the crumbled remains of the brownie on the foil square in her lap, like she had forgotten it was even there. Imagine her sitting and staring off into space, flapping around in her own private pain. How would _you_ feel? Hopefully empty armed Kyle would return in a better and more embracing mood, once the brownie took effect.

When you are bored or annoyed by the people around you, it is natural to look away. But according to Dean Van Staal, this is the time to pay attention. A counterintuitive strategy that can sometimes be useful. The hieroglyphics on Kyle's arms were not uninteresting. Selina complimented them.

Thanks, Kyle replied. An old boyfriend did them. They're from _The Egyptian Book of the Dead_.

Selina wondered what they said.

I don't know. It was kind of a joke. You know.

When Selina was little, the kids used to tape signs to each other's backs saying things like "kick me." That meant you could not complain if you got a foot in your backside—you were only getting what you had requested. Well it was like Tattoo Girl had taped the sign to her own back. But Selina did not want to make her feel stupid or put her on her guard: tact was necessary.

What if the hieroglyphics spelled out a curse? Something to do with blighting the crops and killing off the cattle. Maybe that was why Kyle had a miscarriage.

Kyle stared: You've got to be kidding.

She was just so negative. Fortunately, at that moment organ music began to play in the pocket of her tunic, the opening dirge of some old horror movie or television show.

With an iPhone just like Lyndon's, or just like the one Selina used to own, to her ear, Kyle stood up and walked to the other side of the small park, away from the railroad track, leaving the brownie wrapper on the bench. Folding the foil in half, Selina emptied the crumbs into her palm.

Another starling dropped down on the bench, ready to eat.

For twenty minutes Kyle alternately talked and shook her head, pacing back and forth, rubbing her tattooed upper arm with her hand and staring at the ground. Then her gaze shifted from ground to sky and she began to loop and weave, as if tracing a figure eight or an infinity sign on the gravel path. Abruptly, she pocketed the phone.

Weaving back over to the bench, she picked up the now clean and crumb free square of foil. Jimmy says we should try again, she said, smiling at her own reflection. Try again, try again, try again, try again she sang, to the tune of the nursery rhyme, "Mary Had a Little Lamb." Try again, try again, she sang and then abruptly stopped, the foil falling from her hand to the ground. Brow furrowed, she looked down at her lap. Then she looked up. The bead on her tongue appeared, like a fleck of foil or a bird's shiny eye: Do you think I should have these tattoos removed first?

Carl Jung said it is wrong to cheat people of their fate and to help them go beyond their level. Edgar Cayce, however, would do a reading for anyone.

Yeah, it's the life of the mind for me now, baby. But that wasn't always the case, and I'll be the first to admit it. I thought I needed the big country house and library with the wingback chairs for fireside chatting and all that highbrow crap first when all I really needed was the books. The books and the time to read them and maybe a kitchen table for kitchen talk. Like we used to sit at when we first married, *króshka*, after the sucking and the fucking, when we would go down the backstairs to the breakfast room and just talk. Talk about everything from who were you before you were you to what did people use to wipe their asses before there was toilet paper. Talk and drink, me with my Bombay Sapphire and you with your reisling, your Rhineland witches' piss. It must've been one of those nights that I scribbled my when death does us part-ing gift to you of Bosky House on a piece of grocery memo pad paper, though I have zero recall of that signatory act. Fortunately there was no date, let alone notary's stamp on the yellow scrap you presented to my attorneys.

Bosky House, Bosky House. Like an Egyptian mummy or a made man I would've taken it with me to the grave, if I could. Even though now I realize it was all just props, even the books. *Agitprop.* Because where did I get the idea that I needed all that shit in the first place? In American AP English, Tolstoi (in translation!), Flaubert, even Woolf, since stream of consciousness requires large airy rooms; that boat won't float in an efficiency flat. And because the opiate of literature leads naturally to the pusher, from a certain, bespectacled professor of English—Dr. Irwin C. Bliss. Even though at first his goods seemed second rate—Bliss specialized in folklore (a cottage industry if there ever was one). Still, for a while I was hooked.

Bliss came my third year of tricking myself through college. Picture me, if you can picture anybody beside yourself (unlikely, as I recall your "family" photo albums filled mostly with photos of you), a skinny, black-haired *banya* boy in a shared green shag-carpeted basement studio in White Plains. Rouse yourself to imagine me, rising just before noon from a futon on the floor to root for clean jeans in a swamp of soiled laundry, fast food wrappers and old Haitian newspapers (reading material belonging to my roommate, who left at 5:00 am to wash dishes at the Hilton), then out the broken security door backpack full of books thumping on spine over to Mamaroneck Avenue to catch the bus up to SUNY Purchase and pre-med courses mixed with a liberal dose of liberal arts. Then back down again to White Plains in the evening to hop the Metro North into the city (because as the name suggests, Purchase wasn't free), filling the time between tricks with snatches of cell biology or immunology (ha!), or if I didn't have an exam looming, a big fat novel borrowed from the college library, although those intervals were never very long. The three-piece suiters, the tweedy trust funded doctoral candidates, the smooth-faced, polo-shirted social workers and high school teachers, the artfully unshaven artists in paint spattered chinos, the off-duty policemen and corrections officers in fishing hats and docksiders, even the flat-headed thugs in leather jackets, they all got hard at the sight of the pale, Eastern European looking kid with the long black bangs and knapsack full of books. That pack on my back worked for me like a boob job on a stripper, not to mention the one in front, bulging beneath the belt of my jeans.

Picture me, and then picture him, with his lightly rippled silver hair and pythagorean tuft of paisley printed silk in the breast pocket of his navy sport coat. He didn't have an English accent or even a mid Atlantic, but his voice sounded like the kind of American voice that has sailed to Europe and back again as he sat next to me on the stairs of St. Mary's the Virgin Church (the lost altar boy look worked for me as well) in Times Square.

"Ah, the origins of life and all that," he commented, tapping a photo illustration of a human blastula in the open copy of *Developmental Biology* spread across my knees. "I'm more interested in what happens after."

I pulled a curtain of bangs behind my ear, glancing at him sideways. The bells of Smokey Mary's were ringing, or maybe it was just my tympanum. The last john had given me fifty bucks and a smack in the side of the head, saying that was for passing myself off as a kid when anybody could see I was at least twenty-five. I hadn't passed myself off as anything (I never *said* I was an altar boy), or even had my twenty-first birthday. And in the meantime, the final deadline for fall tuition loomed. So while Mr. Pocket Square had a little potbelly, I couldn't afford to retire. Fuck no. Or yes, I mean.

"The after life." Reaching round to the back pocket of his gabardine wool pants, he produced a tin of Altoids. "Want one?"

"An after life? Sure, who doesn't mister?"

"A clever fella. I like that." He popped the tin with his finger and handed it to me. The pill shaped mint was still warm from his ass and tasted like somebody's *baba's* breath, in some other place and time. "More precisely, I study tales of the afterlife—ghost stories, spectral sightings, things that go bump in the night. I'm a literary scholar and folklorist with a sideline in spooks. Dr. I. C. Bliss, Doctor of Philosophy that is. You may call me Irwin."

Well, I was the kid from Odessa, and it didn't go any deeper than that—ask me no questions and I'll tell you no lies about the Bolshevist conversion of aristocratic roots into the proper party line, all within city limits. Every Russian was once a serf, drooling village idiocy by the fireside, passing on the stupidities of the *skazkas* like cleft palates and clubfeet. Even if Professor Bliss studied the American versions, it would be that same old illiterate crap—the dimwitted *durak* who stumbles upon a hidden pot of gold, the crone's hut strolling along on chicken legs, as if in search of a trailer park. On the other hand, he didn't seem like a head smacker. And then he offered to buy me dinner.

"Shall we take a cab uptown to La Côte Basque? Or perhaps Lutèce, which frankly, I prefer for its *maman-et-papa* charm. There's one now: let's go."

I. C. Bliss. Safe and snug in a yellow checker, even as the curiously strong taste of peppermint lingered in my mouth, he started to look pretty good, at that. At Lutèce's, over a puffy onion tart and a glass of Bourgogne d'Alasce, his horn rim glasses and white, well-aligned teeth gleaming as he talked, moving in an orderly progression from his folklore research to his collection of American antique furniture to Riverside, his two hundred-year-old Federal style house in Cooperstown, New York, a charming village erroneously known as the birthplace of baseball but otherwise a genuine historical landmark, where I might just come and stay with him sometime, he'd pick me up at the bus station in Oneonta or possibly even drive down to White Plains to get me—he only looked better and better (even the little belly, round as a *durak's* pot of gold). Under Lutéce's soft pink lighting, beneath the white linen tablecloth, I started to get hard.

I'm not a fag, a fairy boy or *pyersik*. Hell I'm not anything now (although even at the end I still had skin soft and smooth as a nectarine), but I wasn't then either. You gotta do what you gotta do. And sometimes what you gotta do is also what you want to and so what I'm saying is that it was no hardship, as evidenced by the above-mentioned hard-on, to make it with Irwin. In fact, he smelled better than you, my stinking Selinka with your witches brew of psoriasis shampoo and fish house breath (not to mention the lobster between your legs). Imagine, if you can, his hygienic bouquet: skin soaped daily (yes, daily), fatted with shea butter and then lightly scented with French aftershave, like a meadow of hay bordered by spruce trees. Made by monks at some remote Alpine monastery, he claimed, when they weren't busy crawling under each other's robes.

It was no hardship to be with him or to stay in that house, every weekend for the next four years as I attended medical school at Weil Cornell in Manhattan (where I slept, Bliss-fully subsidized, in the dorms) and then full-time as I did my internship at Bassett Hospital in Cooperstown. Once again, I had the three meals a day (along with midnight snacks after our moonlit romps in Irwin's four poster bed), the clean sheets every week and hot water on demand—digs I'd had with my foster parents, but without the buckets of family-style bullshit. Those who know nothing of the fucking (literally) tedium of life on the edge, of the monotonous scuffle with menace, and I'm not talking about you, Sleezalinka, you've teetered there (though you'd never admit it), but about those satellite dish-heads who feed on digitally processed, choreographed representations of urban danger complete with reconstituted grit—those sofa fat *duráks* might have expected me to grow bored with old Irwin, but I didn't.

Shit, I was fascinated. Fascinated by the color sorted stacks of laundered cotton shirts on the shelves of his closet, each folded and pinned into a flat, crisp packet; by the alternating black, brown and cordovan rows of burnished wingtips and brogues, every pair stretched taut and smooth by wooden shoe trees, on the floor below; by the alphabetized spines of leather-bound classics in history, philosophy and folklore books in his study, all first and second editions (no volumes of *Everyman's Eggheads* for him). I owned three faded black t-shirts, a ripped pair of once red canvas hightops (Irwin called them my pinko shoes), and my only books were the ones I couldn't get out of the library—the jumble of textbooks and lab manuals in the backpack I carried everywhere, for fear of losing them. I wanted to know how the classy bastard did it—how he got the goods, and how he held on to them. So I studied him.

Studied him like there was gonna be an exam, not just an exam but boards given by a long table of middle-aged American men sporting mid-Atlantic accents and silk pocket squares, studied him so hard that soon I needed the horn-rimmed glasses and a pocket square of my own to polish them, so hard that after a while I had to get the teeth too, bruxism having ruined my dentition. Studied him so intently and finally, so successfully, that his passions, his bon appetites became my own (as evidenced by a little pot belly, just like his). A decade later, you wouldn't have recognized me, or actually you would, because you never knew me before. In your eyes, I was never what I *was*, but only what through Irwin's example (along with the purchasing power of my medical degree from Cornell), I became—a somewhat dated but nevertheless desirable version of the wealthy sophisticate, a knight in a navy sport coat and Gucci loafers, more wasp than *narjádnyy*, though the hint of a Russian accent was definitely part of the appeal. A hint that I knew to keep just a hint—too much would turn that foreign charm into chutzpah, the discrete *dacha* reek of black bread and caviar into the pickled herring cloud of the ghetto. In fact, as you'll recall, I scarcely ever uttered an actual word of Russian or Ukranian (unless I heard American mouths mangle it first—"glass nose", anyone?). The *mat* came post mortem, laid down especially for you—deployed the same way an old car (or cunt) mechanic, tired of his wife's fancy ways, stops using one, tromping the grease of the garage onto her clean kitchen floor.

Glass nose, *glasnost*, let's talk about transparency. After all, that's what I am, limpid as the air upstate in springtime. Is that me you feel, my Selinka, as you sit reading my words on the Mac you lifted from my office, or is it the breeze sifting through the window screen? In the interest of transparency, because I no longer have anything to hide, I'll admit I always loved to see you shiver. It made me feel like such a man. And now that I'm not, I'll also confess that it wasn't all about sex—the booties—like I said before. It was about the way you wore them, like some fragile fucking princess in a pair of glass slippers, about the way you looked at me, down your fucking glass nose. You thought you were slumming that day you came to my office, and again when you arrived for the first time at Bosky House, that one-eyed *kozël* in tow—lowering yourselves with the intent of rising higher again, slum lording over all. Irwin was the one who got me to buy Bosky House, by the way. So in a sense, he led me to you. Or more accurately, he led you to me. Because without Bosky as bait, would you have ever tottered into my exam room in your big whore's shoes?

Irwin persuaded me to buy Bosky House a year or two before we split up for good (since bliss cannot last. My body had lost its *banya* boy appeal while his pocket square charm no longer aroused me). I'd finished up at Cornell, as well as completed my internship at Basset. Having proceeded to a residency in Rhinebeck, I was living on my own in town at the top of an old mansion, in a sunny attic playroom turned Bokhara carpeted cockpit by my elderly, hearing-impaired landlady's son, who'd run off to Istanbul a decade earlier and never returned. With its mix of Wasp austerity and pasha opulence it was a fine place to fuck, but man does not live by fucking alone (even as all the young female nurses self delivered themselves to my door, like double-X rated meals on wheels). Especially an ambitious one. He needs a kitchen for the caterers to set up dinner, a dining room for the caterers to serve it to his medical colleagues and potential patrons, and a sitting room far enough from the kitchen to make the sounds of clean-up inaudible. I needed a place where I could live like the distinguished physician I intended to become. Then, just as my residency at Rhinebeck was up, the head of Obstetrics and Gynecology at Albany Medical Center called, offering a full partnership in a well-regarded and lucrative practice, and suddenly I was what I'd envisioned. Shortly after this, Irwin received a tip from an old friend at the New York State Historical Association that Bosky House was for sale.

Bosky House, Bosky House, a.k.a. Ye Olde Money Pit, or Piss It All Away House. Everyone who'd ever owned the place from 1729 on had walked in the end except for the scurvy ridden Africans who'd carved the sixteen inch solid oak beams that held up the sweeping ceilings and even they had paid through the nose, drained by the bleeds that had eventually sent them off to the slave cemetery in Kinderhook. Sure, Bosky House had a history of foreclosures but that didn't keep anyone from buying it anymore that it kept a certain movie star from getting nine husbands even though from thirty on she looked like a fat whore. And unlike the actress, the eighteenth century Dutch house in the woods would just get sexier with age, Irwin said—a hot number with a top-ten listing in the New York State registry of historical buildings that would only grow hotter. Plus, Irwin drooled, Bosky House wasn't just a valuable piece of real estate, but a trove of revenant treasure, bursting with ghostly legends and lore dating back to before the revolutionary war. Which is why, of course, he wanted me to buy the place—so he could get in there himself, root around for his spectral truffles, without the cost of maintenance or repairs.

And that was fine with me. Back then, I had no interest in ghosts. Irwin could have them all, I joked, and any other occult crap he could find tucked away in the closets and numerous built-in cupboards and bookcases—Ouija boards, rabbit's feet, divining rods, magic eight balls and evil eyes, you name it (little did I know your pop lost his first prosthesis in the tank of one of the second floor toilets). All I wanted, as soon as I saw it, was the house. I wanted the two entrances capped with pitched roofs like witches's hats; the six gabled windows; the slate tile roof; the twenty-two inch thick walls of limestone masonry; the three original Dutch-merchant built front rooms each with a fireplace big enough to roast a cow and her calf; the addition of the twenties dairy entrepreneur (he'd made a fortune pasteurizing milk) with its French doors, gleaming tile baths and nickel plated fixtures, a ten-room departure in period design that was nevertheless in communication with the older part of the house via a shared intention to spare no expense in materials, not to mention an intercom system that had been one of the first of its kind, and through which, according to Irwin, legend had it that the dead teenage daughter of the twenties dairy king, who'd been tossed skull first from her father's roadster into a tree, would call to her mother.

And then there were the choicely timbered grounds (chestnuts, maples, hemlock, spruce; no trash trees in those woods, nosirree); the pond continually refreshed by an underground spring; the clearing of pasture to graze a token cow and couple of saddle horses; the small but well-appointed barn complete with three stalls and a hay loft to house them; the chauffer's quarters attached to the side of the three car garage and the 30 foot square playroom with another huge fireplace above, all wrapped in an outer wall of vertical siding of clean yellow pine from Georgia (from the state, not the country—that was how far the kid from Odessa had come). I wanted it all, and I got it, and even now, it almost makes me hard to think about it, or at least makes me wish I could get hard. How about you, *króshka*? Did my little inventory just now of the features of Bosky House make you cream in your jeans, even though you knew the place as well as I did? Or better? Do I even need to ask, knowing you loved Bosky House like your own body (how you used to admire yourself in the mirror over our bed, how we both did)? I could check your panties (we can go anywhere, you know), but I don't think I'll bother.

I got it all—not only the house, but also the history. Yeah, the history. While ghosts bored me (I won't say to death, since that's when things finally got interesting), I was fascinated by the past, specifically the past of the objects that I purchased. Knowing that past, I felt like it became mine—displacing the dull heaps of gray snow and soviet cinder block, the hulking rule of the *bratva*, the oppressive pile-up of social workers, American foster rents and johns (I could hardly tell the difference between them), with something lighter, cozier, more whimsical and at the same time more complex. A kind of crazy quilt, you could say—like the patchwork your *baba*, or "gran," made when your father's family lived at Bosky House, back in the forties and fifties. Made not because they couldn't afford blankets, or had to make use of every scrap, but because folk art was becoming fashionable.

So when you brought your father with you to Bosky House, I was thrilled. Sure, not at first. At first, opening the door, all I saw was the one-eyed *kozël* standing next to you, smirking in his khaki pants and pressed white oxford, hands folded together over his loins as if he was about to raise them in prayer or imprecation. Worthless as tits on a billy goat. Even after you said he was your father, I had no use for him. Nor, it seemed, should you. Back at my office, you'd struck me as more than capable of taking care of yourself. And you looked no less so now, as you strode past me in your big black sunglasses, snug blue chambray workshirt setting off your permatan, black Ralph Lauren jeans and shiny, flat-heeled man-sized riding boots (no courtship strut in those)—a match for both country and gentry. Then you said, pushing a wing of brown-black hair, shiny as the glasses, glossy as the boots, behind your ear: "He used to live here."

Still standing in the entrance, holding the door (Dean had sidled after you), I scratched my head. I'd been through the town records, all the past deeds and census records, talked to the Kinderhook old timers as well as Irwin's pal from the NYSHA, who was a local historian. There'd been no mention of a Van Staal family.

Taking my hand, you gently pulled me into my own house, stood me before your father, who was already looking over his shoulder into my living room: "He was here back in the late nineteen forties and fifties with his mother, stepfather, stepsister and two half-sisters. The Holsapples."

The Holsapples. They had been the "real thing," according to Irwin's historian buddy—unlike the transplanted New Yorkers and Long Islanders who'd later nearly ruined Bosky House with so-called upgrades and improvements like the tile and mirror spangled Euro-Disney kitchen that I'd just finished ripping out. The wholesome Holsapples who'd lived by the New

England creed "if it ain't broke, don't fix it," even as they'd polished the place to a high historical shine, maintaining not just the house but the habits of the past, including churning their own butter from the cream of their three Friesian cows (and what they couldn't use they sold at the Kinderhook Dairy, same prices as everyone else's, even though nothing melted in the mouth quite like Holsapple butter). But then the son had accidentally shot himself in the eye, and a streak of financial misfortune had ensued (concluding this saga, Irwin's pal had intoned "curse or coincidence?"). The Holsapples sold Bosky House a few years later, at a loss.

And now here he was before me, the hapless Holsapple boy, who was actually a Van Staal, titanium-patched cranium and all. Studying him, I could see that the left eye was false—not only was the gaze a little off, but the upper lid crooked slightly at the center, probably due to nerve damage.

With a wink of the good eye, he stepped forward and thrust out his hand. I extended my own and he squeezed hard, like he was trying to wring something out of it. "Dean Van Staal, retired dairyman. Nice to meet you, Doc."

As he let go, you grabbed my still aching hand with yours and gave it another squeeze, equal to or even surpassing his. A double-wringer from the dairyman's daughter. I should've pushed the both of you back out the door, but instead put my throbbing hand in my pocket and followed, while your father gave me a tour of my own home.

Woulda, coulda, shoulda as Dean himself would say. But I didn't, because I wanted something too—now my appetite was whetted, *króshka*, for more than just you. With each room, that winking wanker revealed a little more of his intimacy with Bosky house. He knew that the robin's egg blue glaze (reconstituted from chips of actual, eighteenth century Dutch Colonial paint) that I'd chosen for the living room paneling, to complement the Delft tile surrounding the fireplace, was not original: "When we lived here, it was a kind of cream color"(an assertion verified by previous strata of paint scraped away during the restoration). He knew that the built-in maple and glass cabinets in the dining room, the only addition of the last decades that I hadn't ripped out, hadn't been there in the nineteen fifties, though, he added (to my secret gratification), "that looks like quality work." He knew that there'd been an oak beamed ceiling, "built by slaves," in the kitchen and breakfast room (which those *bolvàns* in the seventies had ripped out) just like the ones in the living room and dining room. Finally, he knew details from previous blueprints that I'd dismissed as insignificant because they'd done no aesthetic damage—such as the fact that the pantry had been on the left side of the kitchen (it was now part of an office/study), and now it was on the right: "Your grandmother used to arrange all her canning on these shelves. One Christmas time I nipped myself a jar of mincemeat. Kept it under my bed and spooned up a little bit every night while she was puttin' my sisters to bed up in the front bedrooms. Man oh man, that was good stuff."

By the time we got to his own former bedroom, a small room that must've once been the maid's at the end of the right wing addition of the house, I was sold.

"Yep, this is where I shot myself," he said, hands once again folded together over his crotch as he looked up at the pressed-tin ceiling, sucking on the insides of his cheeks. I thought of the basement corner room I'd been assigned by my foster parents in their sprawling sixties ranch in Scarsdale, away from the rest of the family and their thick-carpeted pads upstairs, each with its own set of sliding glass doors. Had he ever compared his little room with its one smallish window to his step and half-sisters' rooms, each twice the size of his, with two big gables or even three, all looking down on the great green gravel-driveway bound circle of front lawn?

"I got the gun from a guy in town—I was helpin' him clean out a house. I brought it home to show my stepsister—an old Smith & Wesson, without a trigger guard. Didn't know it was loaded." He pursed his lips together, squinted with his extant eye at the Empire-style double bed (a cast-off from Irwin) in the corner by the window. "There used to be a hole in the wall behind where that headboard is now."

That was your cue: "I wonder if it is still there." When sliding the bed away from the wall disclosed nothing but an unblemished tract of blue-ticking striped wallpaper, you knelt, the smooth globes of your Ralph Lauren-packaged ass resting on the backs of your riding boots, and lightly ran your hands back and forth, up and down until you found a spot where the paper caved to the touch. While it seemed dubious that no one had bothered to plaster in the hole before papering, the existence of the hole itself, fully revealed as you pulled a car key from your front pocket and punched through, was undeniable.

"I was going to be a doctor like you. It was all set up—my dad, my real dad, said he'd pay my tuition at Colgate University. But I'm not complainin'. See Tim, I've had to work with my hands due to what happened to my brain, and there's no shame in that." He looked up at the ceiling again, eyes (or eye) rolling (rollin'?) back, cheeks sucking (suckin'?) in as he waited for my reply.

Like I said, I was sold—even though I worked with my hands as well (try performing a gynecological exam without them). If your father had been a car in a showroom, I would've paid on the spot with my manicured mits and driven him home. On the other hand, the showroom, so to speak, was part of the appeal. What I really wanted was to install him right there, beneath that pressed tin ceiling, surrounded by those four ticking-striped walls, bed pushed aside so that the hole would be permanently on view, all visible through a plexi-glass filled door frame with a plaque over the lintel: *Here the Holsapple Boy Put A Hole In His Head*, even though technically, Dean was a Van Staal. Put him on display like a work of taxidermy, with two glass eyes instead of just one.

Hell, I wanted it all—the entire father-daughter-fallen-on-hard-times diorama. Wanted it all so I could step in and take the stock role of benefactor in your stock tale of genteel impoverishment—swapping my patchy hooker-to-healer success story for some more flowing narrative of philanthropic largesse (because as long as the money keeps coming, no one bothers to ask where it's coming from). You'd raise me up and I'd raise you… I started by lifting both your bags from the hatchback of your faded red Volkswagon Rabbit and carrying them inside and up the stairs—his a cracked but still supple leather satchel with a brass nameplate embossed with the initials DBVS (giving further credibility to his story of a solid wasp upbringing, though I couldn't help but wonder if the "B" stood for "Bullshit") and yours a more dubious affair with its beige and brown monogram pattern crookedly stamped on cowhide. I put your bag in the front right corner suite and his in his old room down the hall in the right wing addition, pretending not to hear him behind me as he said he'd always wondered what it would be like to wake up and look out over the lawn instead of into the woods, "like a Lord of the Manor."

That night, I lay reading in my own left front corner suite, listening with one ear for the creak of the old maple floorboards (because in the flowing narrative of philanthropic largesse, it never goes one way: we both knew you owed me a fuck). When no creak came, I put down my book. While there was no one outside my door, someone was up and about—I could hear faint thumping noises coming from the other end of the hall. I got up, roped my dressing gown and went to investigate. Outside your door, I paused, lifted my hand… The thumping had a rhythmic sound to it, like a dance, and it was intertwined with panting and little sprigs of muffled screams. I knocked. The thumping, panting and muffled screams continued. Knocked again. And finally, thinking maybe it was some weird kind of come-on, because if you didn't want me to enter, you could've said so—I turned the knob. The door swung open, and there you were, bare, bigger than ever feet leaping around in circles under the overhead light, brown-black hair flying and long arms waving, clawing at the air around your head, which was filled with insects—a swirling skein of mosquitoes spangled with lunar moths. For a second, your face turned toward the door and your gaze caught mine—your eyes wide with what you claimed, a few minutes later, after I'd grabbed your arms and seated you on the bed, was terror. "I have a phobia," you whimpered. But I didn't really believe you then, and I sure don't believe you now, you spooky bitch. You *baba yaga.*

Not Okay: A True Crime Story,

by Selina Van Staal

Chapter Three

"Helen Keller Really Lived"

Even though Selina always scored the highest on both the verbal and math sections of the Iowa test, their mother decided that Selina's sister was "the verbal one" and her brother "the math and science one." Cara was "the verbal one" because she wore glasses and was always reading Laura Ingalls Wilder and Judy Blume books. Cara was also "artistic" (even though Selina was the better drawer) because she liked to make things, such as multistory dollhouses out of cardboard boxes, each room wallpapered with sample paper from Pete's Paint and Paper Palace. But then when she was fourteen years old, she got contact lenses and stopped reading. She did continue to make things like trompe l'oeil trellises on the walls and window treatments piecing silk brocade swatches from high end fabric stores—until B. burgorferi wrecked her brain.

Julius was "the math and science one" and "artistic" as well, because in the sixth grade he got a score in the eighty-fifth percentile on the math section and a haiku published in the middle school magazine. Selina's mother wanted him to become a medical doctor and a poet like Doctor Zhivago in the novel by Boris Pasternak that was also made into a movie. Well Julius became neither, though he did continue to write poetry after his discovery of cannabis in the eighth grade.

Of the three Van Staal children, Selina exhibited the most potential, as demonstrated by high scores on standardized tests, if less than tiptop grades. The less than tiptop grades were probably due to Attention Deficit Disorder. This tragic condition that afflicts many more people than commonly realized in Selina's case sometimes led to missed or incomplete assignments. So you could say it all ADDS up, or up it adds, if you want to avoid a dangling preposition.

Anyways, Selina could achieve high test scores without even studying. This is because you can often figure out the answer by looking for clues in the question. Selina aced many a test by just thinking about the questions.

The only problem with using thinking as a test-taking strategy is that sometimes you can think too much. For instance, one time Selina was the only child in the class who got the pop quiz question (designed solely to give extra points to all the idiots who had flunked the last social studies test) wrong. The quiz consisted of a single True/False statement: "Helen Keller Really Lived." Well, had she? Blind, deaf, almost totally dependent like some over-sized toddler on her babysitter Annie Sullivan? What kind of life was that? Selina checked false.

Selina would not make that kind of mistake on the NCLEX–RN test. Going on the free study guide and sample questions you could download from the Internet, it looked to be a piece of cake. The kind so soft and moist with processed fats and sugars you do not even need to chew, as the multiple choice questions practically answer themselves. For example:

A mother calls the clinic to report that her son has recently started medication to treat Attention Deficit Disorder/ADD. The mother fears her son is experiencing side effects of the medicine. Which of the following side effects are typically related to medications used for ADD? Note: more than one answer may be correct:

A. Agitation.
B. Insomnia
C. Sleepiness.
D. Poor Appetite.

Well the "Note" already gives half the answer away, that there is more than one answer. Then you just have to figure out which answer does not fit with the others. It is true that poor appetite and sleepiness sometimes go together, but anyone who has ever tried cocaine recognizes that A, B and D are a classic combination. You do not even need to know that ADD in children and sometimes adults is treated with stimulants, which seems counterintuitive though there is probably a logical explanation for it somewhere or other, if you want to waste time looking on the Internet. At the same time, even in science things do not always make sense.

Because things do not always make sense, even in science, Lyndon's husband, Doctor John Asani, was interviewing Selina for the position of Clinical Coordinator at the Hudson Valley Fertility Center. The date was April 30, 2010, nine months to the day after Selina walked out on Timor.

Selina Van Staal, Asani read from a scribbled post-it stuck to the back of what looked to be a glossy brochure from a pharmaceutical company. Taking off his reading glasses, he looked across his desk: Any relation to Selina Kyle, the alter ego of Catwoman? Just joking, although I believe it was the American comic Batman that first instilled in me a weakness for the femme fatale.

Since the question was not really a question, Selina simply smiled in response, like a femme fatale. The framed certificate on the wall behind the desk said that Doctor John Assani's accreditation came from Weill Cornell Medical College in Qatar.

Doctor Assani put his reading glasses back on his nose, gazing down again at the post-it (the word ELONVA popped out from the brochure beneath, whatever that meant): according to my wife, you have some expertise in a medically controversial but increasingly popular method of massage known as reiki. Well, occasionally an effective treatment lacks empirical support. All we know is that the placebo effect is very strong. If my wife believes that your quote unquote healing hands will help her to conceive, then perhaps they will. And if other women with similar convictions then come to this facility as well, who am I to turn away their business?

So Selina's expertise in reiki (that on-line course had been worth every penny), in addition to her training in nursing, was just what the doctor ordered, Doctor Asani concluded with a smile, folding his reading glasses and dropping them into the pocket of his sports jacket. All she had to do was pass the NCLEX-RN. And maybe not even that, as he tapped a big white incisor with his thumb, his gaze resting somewhere below Selina's face. It was as if you were back in college again, applying for a bartending position.

Did the Doctor want to have a sexual affair? Possibly. With long straight dark hair that was only partially gray beneath the coverage of semi-permanent hair coloring and breasts that barely required the assistance of a barely-there bra, Selina was holding her own.

However, as a woman ages it becomes increasingly difficult for her to hold onto her own, let alone others. To be honest, an affair is not likely to lead to marriage or some other profitable, long-term arrangement. Doctor Asani would eventually return to little Lyndon, or move on to someone even younger. Besides, Selina had had it with doctors!

Then again, the income generated by the reiki and the brownies was not enough. Maybe Asani really did want to hire Selina to do nothing because sometimes nothing is just as effective, if not more so, than something. The placebo effect is very strong. Plus you could always continue with the reiki and the brownies on the side. Asani did not seem like the type who would object to moonlighting anymore than highlighting (the blonder the better, according to Lyndon). Looking at Asani looking at her breasts, Selina wondered what clinic Kyle went to.

At the end of the interview, Asani asked if Selina would like to take a tour of the clinic. Assuming that no was not an answer, Selina replied yes.

First we will slip into something more comfortable, Asani said, winking as he exited the office. When someone leaves you alone in a room, it is natural to have a look around. No surprise to find a copy of Hustler beneath the recent issues of The Journal of Reproductive Medicine on top of the bookcase by the window. A glance at recently visited sites on his laptop would probably reveal more of the same, but if the door opened suddenly it would be hard to explain why you were on the other side of the desk.

Selina sat back down in the visitor's seat. On top of Asani's desk was a large photo of Lyndon with longer, darker, healthier appearing hair. It is fine to pick up a photo of a friend, to study it more closely. Behind the photo lay a sleevless CD that had been labeled "Cat Stevens World Masters" with a black marker and also a newish paperback—a copy of The World as Will and Idea, by Arthur Schopenhauer. Probably the CD was for relaxing between patients or background for studying lab results. But the philosophy book—now what did that have to do with getting women pregnant?

When Asani finally returned, with two sets of blue scrubs, elasticized blue gauze hats like shower caps, and white gauze masks, claiming trouble locating the key to the laundry room, Selina was tempted to ask about the book, but did not. Everyone knows Schopenhauer was a misogynist who called women the stunted, narrow-shouldered, broad-hipped and short-legged sex (by the way, guess who was taller and had longer legs, Timor or

Selina?). In Selina's mother's copies of the once popular Ms. Magazine, there was a section called NO COMMENT, displaying examples of sexist advertising and such. Well, no comment.

Selina also did not remark upon the object in Asani's hand—a stainless steel water bottle embossed with a pink playboy bunny silhouette as seen on the mud flaps of big rig trucks. She did not remark upon the water bottle even though she suspected, as Asani swigged, then rolled his shoulders and vibrated his lips, that the liquid it contained was not Dasani. The suspicion was confirmed when Asani insisted on putting on Selina's mask. The first time his fingers fumbled with the elastic and the mask floated to the ground. Not to mention the fumes that penetrated the gauze when it was at last secured. But if you want a job you need to show you can be trusted to be discreet.

Asani steered Selina down a fluorescent-lit hallway into a room with a gurney bed. He nodded toward the bed, smirking: for egg retrieval and embryo transfer only.

The wall on the other side of the room was glass, with a door in the center leading into the embryology lab beyond it. Asani took another long pull from his bottle of not-Dasani, then led Selina by the hand around the bed and over to the glass wall. Immediately on the other side of the glass was a row of six white appliances the size of dorm room refrigerators, sitting on a long stainless steel trolley.

Gesturing with his pink mud flap girl embossed bottle at the glass wall, Asani announced: where life begins. With the petri dish hic union of egg and sperm. Schopenhauer asked if children were brought into the world by an act of pure reason hic would the human race continue to exist. Hic. No worries. No need for courtship here. Or for fore hic play. Premature ejac hic ulation? Failure to perform? Irrel hic vant! It's the complete disassociation of sex hic from pro hic creation. No worries if the male partner can't even hic produce a semen sample hic. The electro hic ejaculator will do the job. Hic. I think I need to lie down.

Asani collapsed on the gurney bed, lids flickering, then closing. As he snored, Selina tried the door to the lab but it was locked. Probably the key was in his pocket, but an attempt to retrieve it could be mistaken for fore hic play. Too bad though, to miss the opportunity to scope out the situation and maybe fill in a few holes. If you look at something carefully enough you can often figure what it is. By pressing up close to the glass and squinting, for example, you could see that the white appliances on the trolley had small metal brand name tags inscribed with the words "Biogenics Embryo Incubators." So that must be where they grew them. And if you could just see an autoclave again, you would remember what they are for.

Truth be told (and nothing but the truth), Selina's nursing school education was piecemeal, with certain pieces lacking. She had missed the final weeks of the course on Human Reproduction, which had included a special unit on the Assisted kind. That gap was due to a post Wall promotion package to Budapest including round trip airfare and thirteen nights at the Gellert Hotel and Spa. A one-time only deal, according to the travel agent, a friend of a friend from the bar, who had booked her ticket. Floating in the thermal twilight of the underground baths like some fawn petaled flower or delicious self-fertilizing but not necessarily autonomous plasm because it could always cross-pollinate with some other delicious plasm by retreating to the bedroom above with the crystal chandelier dimmed to recapture the watery gloam below had been completely worth the lost course credits.

You only live once, no matter how you are conceived.

File 1994/Transcription of Revenant Dictation
(Former Sex: Male; Deceased: 22.07.1995)

Nihil est in intellectu quod non prius fuerit in sensu—There is nothing in the mind that was not in the senses. Yes, I've got it all up here, Tim. Or somewhere. Hard to say, my boy, hard to say. At any rate, wherever "I" am now, in whatever form (the ideal being something suitably gauzy but not too revealing. Ghosts are more convincing when they cannot be examined too closely), I used to do the old body bebop, just like you. So it seems rather insensitive (regardless of the fact that neither of us is any longer, strictly speaking, sensitive) to ask me for my "story," as if the tale could be separated from the tail, as if the phantom appendage was not once the real thing.

And it's not even a story you want, but some sort of eyewitness account or report, it seems, of my "passing." Timmy, I loved your very gizzards and now you're asking *me*, a preeminent if no longer extant literary folklorist, to participate in *your* anthropological study? As if I were some Baffin Island savage bearing witness to civilization and its discontents? Christ, dying was bad enough—now I find out that you've joined the Franz Boas camp. What will you do with all your eyewitness accounts, once you've finished collecting them? Perform an ethnographic analysis of revenant rites of passage? Create a comprehensive catalog of spirit world taboos? I'm hoping your request for an account rather than a story is simply subterfuge, a strategy to keep the tale "pure," the teller from lapsing into self-conscious Propp-ological posturing (for who knows the conventions of the ghost story better than Professor I.C. Bliss?). In fact, I'm counting on it. So you can have your "report," you sly boots, but since we both know that the ghostly narrative, like all folklore, is a variety of literature, let me first provide you with a schema for its formal analysis and appreciation.

Ghostly narratives, or ghostlore, can be examined for the following defining patterns and features: Appearance (of Ghosts), Purposes and Character (of Ghosts), When and Where the Ghosts Return, Activities (of Ghosts), and Folk Attitudes (toward Ghosts).

Appearance, more specifically, refers to form—that is the form in which the ghost appears. One common form is, unfortunately, the form of the deceased body itself, or living corpse, where the corpse sits up, speaks to the assembled mourners, drinks, drools, etc. The living corpse, in my opinion, is a cruder and less imaginative construct than the "spectral ghost" (which I will discuss next), and as reflected by the popularity of this construct in Irish culture, may be simply a product of the alcohol addled minds of the informants. As you know, the hallucinations of delirium tremens are commonly the product of actual visual or sensory experience—hence lamp cords become snakes, and the casketed bodies of the dead suddenly rise up and serenade the living. No inspiration there whatsoever, not to mention taste as the undertaker's paints and powders only highlight the mortification, the whole necrotic foul-up that begins well before death—the bloating or falling away of flesh, the atrophying of muscles, the roping of veins and purple seep of broken capillaries, the shutdown of hair follicles and the attrition of teeth. I know that my belly lapped a little lower and wider over my belt each year you were with me, and that after, when the weight suddenly began to disappear, it didn't so much recede as empty out, draping over my newly skeletal loins. I know that near the end, you could hardly stand to look at me, which is why I made sure that our final exchanges were over the telephone. And because there's nothing in the mind that was not once in the senses, I know that my last image of you waving from the door of your manor in the woods—the pallid Polanski jowls, the bearish arms and torso that bequeathed no parting bear hug—is not a mirage. You packed it on too, larding over those exquisitely fluted ribs with fat skimmed from the well-fixed hausfraus (my god, how could you stand them?) who fed your thriving practice. But I would've overlooked it, Timmy. I would've overlooked it all.

Ghosts may also appear in spectral form. Spectral ghosts account for approximately thirty-eight percent of the whole spirit pie. When we begin to analyze the less clearly envisioned revenants we become aware of a change in terminology. Whereas informants describe entities that appear in the "living corpse" form as "ghosts" or the "dead," we now find them using words that betray a less defined concept in the mind. "Apparition," "presence," "spook," "spectre," "shrouded spirit," "cottony wisp," "shimmering transparency," and "evil plastic baggy thingy" have all been reported. Classification is possible, however, because all these wraiths possess attributes of whiteness and/or luminescence like your skin when I first met you, stretched pale and taut across your cheekbones, glowing like pure arctic snow under the dim security lights of Smokey Mary's.

Additionally, informants portray ghosts that take no form at all. What then do they portray? Generally, it is a sensation—"a cold blast of air," "a chill down the spine," "hair standing on end," "a sickening sense of malignity," "a gut feeling of evil," "a bad vibe" or even a "good one" (this is where the ghost story takes a religious turn, becoming another, less haunting genre). I'm all for sensation, or at least I was. I didn't love you just for your looks, but for your soft yet strong lips, your rough guttersnipe's touch, your moist dark armpits smelling like warm rye bread.

On occasion, ghosts appear as human body parts. As such, they may possess the substantiality of the living corpse, or a piece of the living corpse (e.g., the severed hand, complete with cuff of crusted black blood). They may also take on a more diaphanous aspect. It is always one or the other in the stories of our informants, however, though a moonlight vision of your shaft tenting the white sheet of my bed—the dark core of an icy upheaval—haunts me still. Talk about shivers down the spine...

By the way, only when the revenant is very old or very young does the informant mention the age. About one ghost out of ten is the spirit of a child or youth—a curiously low percentage.

As ghosts sometimes appear as parts of human bodies, they also appear in bodies that are less than human. A human ghost may be portrayed in animal form, but sometimes the ghost is simply an animal ghost, nothing more. This latter, baser and less symbolically suggestive type of manifestation may reflect the reluctance of the informant to let go of a beloved pet, like the old ladies who take their dead poodles to the taxidermist. Let me assure you that if I ever considered you to be a kind of pet, it was purely in the poetical sense, my boy. Nor did I ever expect you to give up your propensity to prowl or attempt to limit your range—even if *she* did look (not to mention smell) like something the cat dragged in.

In roughly twenty percent of their portrayals, ghosts are accompanied, or more commonly, conveyed by objects. Spectral clipper ships, steam engines and wheelbarrows figure in the older accounts, jet planes, minivans and ten speeds in more recent ones (I must admit my research ceased about a decade before the advent of the twenty-first century). If ghosts are the restless souls of the dead, what of these man-made vehicles which no modern religion would ever empower with spirit? They may be a continuum from earlier times, when souls were not denied to inanimate objects, or simply another example of the illogic found so often in folklore. Not that any of it ever made much sense, when I think back on it. You, me... You, her... I just don't understand the trajectory. Which is not to say, my boy, that the means of transport was unclear: you took me for a ride, and then she took you.

As ghosts may vary in form, so they may also vary in purpose (for return) and in character. Both purpose and character are closely related to the circumstances of expiration, or how they came to die. For example, over a third of the ghosts in informants' tales die violent or sudden deaths. In cases where the ghost was the victim of a murder, it is easy to see how that life-terminating event would shape his or her purpose and character in the hereafter—leading to vengeful and vindictive tendencies, and so on. Hence it is also important to note how the ghost became a ghost, although not something to belabor, since a ghost story is not a case history, and most of us would prefer to let bygones be bygones. The act of haunting notwithstanding.

Indeed, in some instances it is impossible to fathom the reason why a ghost returns. Or indiscrete, given that almost all revenants were once private citizens, entitled to lives lived off-the-record. So while the mores of Cooperstown, New York are straight and narrow as its maple tree-lined streets, my relationship with you (as well as your predecessors) remained uncontested. Because Bliss and his Boy (protégée, nephew, secretary?) were nobody's business—what went on behind the brick, federalist façade of Riverside had no more to do with my official role as folklorist and village historian than your long black bangs did with your full scholarship to the Life Sciences Program at Cornell (though my longstanding friendship with one of the trustees didn't hurt).

On the other hand, scholarly investigation is sometimes incompatible with discretion and further, many ghosts make no bones about their reason for recursion—a primary one being to reclaim said bones. Or in ghostly parlance: "Give me back my body, give me back my body." Various other reasons a ghost may come back include 1. to complete unfinished business; 2. to warn and inform; 3. to punish or protest; 4. to guard and protect; 5. to reengage in lifetime activities; 6. to reenact death; 7. to reward the living. One reason they do NOT come back is simply to pester people, as you once accused me of doing after I died. As you now know yourself, haunting is not easy... Indeed, coming back from oblivion is immeasurably harder than getting up in the morning, and I never liked doing that either. Especially after you left.

Moving on, we find that revenants generally display one of the following three character types: Indifference (58%);

Malevolence (29%); or Benevolence (13%). As the percentages show, the great majority manifests a disposition of detachment. There is about these ghosts an austerity of all relation, a mantle of deep abstraction and dignity. They are neither sad nor glad about mortal affairs, but preoccupied with their own sufferings. So it is simply not true that I somehow caused the toilet in the master bath to overflow on your wedding night. Even if the mal-intent were there, the agency was not (I really don't know how you manage all that electro-magnetic stuff, but then you always were more technically adept than I). Further, that woman regularly disposed of her feminine hygiene aids by flushing them, which cannot have helped the plumbing.

Given that coming back from the dead is less easy than pie (fyi, her crusts were store bought, and those "fresh fruit" fillings came from cans; did you really believe she could cook?), it is unsurprising that three quarters of informants' tales indicate a single appearance of a ghost. The fact, however, that some twenty percent of ghosts are sited during the day is a less expected statistic. If our interest lay not in the tales but in the ghosts themselves, we might observe that the large number of reported daytime hauntings could be taken as compelling evidence for the existence of the latter, independent of human imaginings. If we are simply the wistful fabrications of mortal minds, then one would expect us to be tailored according to the biases of those minds; i.e., the predisposition to expect things to go bump in the night. On the other hand, like the proverbial tree falling in the forest, the existence of the specter is to some extent contingent upon a spectator. If someone refuses to see you, are you really there? I showed myself to her three times, in broad daylight, once outside as she was pulling that Land Rover into your garage (the trunk was full of packages that must've been contraband; why else did she store them in the rec room above rather than bringing them into the house?), once in the kitchen as she was pouring herself yet another fishbowl of riesling in the midst of preparing her famous tuna with teriyaki glaze (which came right out of a jar), and one time in the bath (while I'm no connoisseur of women's bodies, I couldn't see the appeal. Bubble breasts aside, she was built like a boy with broken springs). Three times, and on each occasion her eyes immediately glazed over. Not one word of acknowledgment, let alone the customary scream. She wanted to make me feel like nothing, I'm sure—a nobody herself, the spawn of downstate suburban sprawl or maybe even jersey (I know the putative father had a pedigree of sorts but what's to ensure she was even his daughter?).

As for ghosts, in America they most often reside in upstate New York and New England—roosting in the eaves of farmhouses, millhouses and abandoned tanneries, floating along the riverbanks and rural byways, nestling in the hollows. While spirits, like mice, may be found in both city and country, the denser spectral population of the latter locale is a reminder that their lineage may be traced back to earlier, more arcadian times. The fact that we are almost never found in the fast food blighted burgherdom of the in-between speaks for itself.

Ghostly activity is, sadly, relatively circumscribed. Probably the most common occupation is walking, indoors and out. Other frequent doings are most invariably of a domestic nature, including the pulling of bedclothes off the living, the opening and closing of doors, shutters and cabinets, the snuffing of candles and turning off and on of light switches, faucets and spigots—with the exception of riding in and on automobiles and other conveyances. Although the ghost in the last case ventures out into the world, most often it is as a passenger, not as a driver (the headless horseman notwithstanding). This unwillingness to take the wheel (or the reins) reflects, perhaps, a certain lack of initiative—but also of vulgar ambition. I could've fought for you, I suppose, instead of playing along with the charade of old patron and benefactor, allowing myself to be panted in the pear-assed trousers of the unmarried "family friend." Or split with you entirely and spared myself the humiliation of hearing "Uncle Win"—not just from your lips, but from hers, spoken with that deferential lisp that was just another slight. Even then, she would never look me in the eye.

About one revenant in ten speaks to the living. The element of discourse is found more frequently in European ghost stories, a proportion that may reflect the greater stores of urbanity and wit in the old world, even amongst peasant populations. From the first, even with your still unrefined English, you expressed yourself cleverly, demonstrating an ear for the rhythms of the language and an eye for the manifold shades of meaning. Unlike that woman, who sounded as if she'd spent her formative years locked up in a tool shed or basement storage room, or more likely, in the split-level shelter of some suburban cul de sac. That lisping prattle, riddled with banalities and non sequiturs—thank heaven (or hell) most of the time she kept her mouth shut. On the other hand, her silence was just as grating, when she'd sit there during my infrequent visits to Bosky House regarding me in a manner that simultaneously disregarded me, as if I was the bimbo, the helium-breasted whore releasing one empty word after another. Especially as that silence would be amplified by your own, both of you staring at some point beyond my shoulder with dark, unwavering eyes, that were, now that I think back on it, remarkably similar. As if you were brother and sister. As if I was the outsider, not she.

Finally, in the analysis of the ghostly tale it is useful to take into account folk attitudes toward spirits and the spirit world.

In most cases the attitudes in question are those of the mortal informant who provides said tale. Here, admittedly, we are looking at a story of another stripe, as the ghost himself is the source of the narration. So I imagine you might like an account of my own "folk attitudes"—an account of my family and neighborhood tradition concerning ghosts, as well as my personal experiences as a youth. Some gush I never told you, say, about my dead Bubbe from Warsaw and Papa who changed the family name from Blizinsky to Bliss and went on to make good with his fur business in White Plains but then my *meshuggah* little brother climbed out the dormer of our ersatz Cotswold Cottage one night after Mama had been reading *Peter Pan* because there are no bars on suburban windows and none of us ever got over it...Well tough bananas, Timmy. I opened my heart (not to mention my wallet) to you for years, and now the door is shut, the latch hooked, the spigot screwed off. Once and for all.

However, since I did promise to provide an account of my passing, here you go: one day I was sitting at my desk. The next, I was not.

Not Okay: A True Crime Story,

by Selina Van Staal

Chapter Four

"A Reason to Fight"

Selina's ex-husband was lucky he had a stroke and died. Timor might have ended up in prison because tapping phones (which includes cell phones) is a federal crime. Although not many people believe tapping cell phones is possible, which meant that it was difficult to build a case against him. Both death and popular belief, or popular disbelief, were on Timor's side. Timor had all the advantages on his side. First, an M.D. degree gets you instant trust and respect, no questions asked. In addition, he possessed the ability to manipulate people, as he manipulated Selina for many years. Here is an example: if you called him abusive after he had called you a female body part, he would say Oh, am I hurting you? How am I hurting you? I don't see any blood or bruises but if you seriously believe you've been injured, I'll take you to the ER right now. Later he would say I'm so sorry I will never act like that again. Then he would hand you an expensive flower from an expensive florist that looked just like what he had called you. They say that is how men like Selina's ex-husband trap their victims, not with physical barriers but with promises of reform. And like insects that cannot resist the glow of a porchlight or the scent of a particular plant, the women just keep coming back.

But then Selina stopped. Timor tapped Selina's cell phone because promises no longer worked and it was a way of holding on to her. Or maybe he wanted to try to prove she was having an affair (which she was not) so that he could cheat her in divorce court and not have to make reparation for fifteen years of verbal if not physical abuse. (Even though verbal abuse is definitely abuse, as Selina once demonstrated to Timor with a copy of Webster's Dictionary. It was there under number three or four, defined as language that condemns or vilifies.) Or maybe the tapping was both—a means of holding on to Selina and a means of cutting her off without a dime. Anyways, there are plenty of reasons to tap someone's cell phone even though the federal agent Selina consulted (a Staten Island cousin) said it was technically possible but unlikely that a layperson could obtain and install the software. Besides, why would Tim, who'd always seemed like a good guy, do that?

Well, it did not matter why Timor had tapped Selina's iPhone, only that he had. If the slippery doctor slash con man had not died first, eventually Selina would have found someone who believed her. Someone young and ambitious like that cute state trooper with the crew cut and biceps who did the paper work after the Land Rover was totaled (thank goddess Timor had paid for the insurance through until the end of the year). Someone at the beginning of his career and willing to take a risk for a woman in distress. And then Timor, out of fear of prison, or maybe just pure guilt, would finally come clean.

Although the problem with the state trooper was that he worked for the state not the feds, which would have made the cell phone tapping out of his jurisdiction. Plus you could tell that under his pants he had chicken legs—upon which Timor would have been sure to remark. But if Timor had lived, eventually Selina would have found someone who believed her, because if you believe in something really strongly you can convince other people to believe as well. For example, how do they get people to fight wars? Think about it.

And as the cousin admitted, it was technically possible. Is. They proved it on 13 Eyewitness News. You can buy the cell phone spy software, or spyware, on the Internet, from places like Thailand and Taiwan for $3000 or less, which is pocket change to a man like Timor. Okay they said on the show that it is not easy to install, but if a journalist can do it, then why not a doctor slash con man? Maybe Timor was not as smart as he thought he was, but that did not make him an idiot. Here are three ways you can tell if your cell phone is being tapped: 1. If your battery is warm even when your phone has not been in use. 2. If your phone lights up when it is not in use. 3. If you hear an unexpected beep or click when it is in use.

Timor completely denied tampering with Selina's phone! I wouldn't know how to begin to install a spyware program, he said.
But then why was the smooth metal casing sometimes warm as skin—even though Selina had not talked to anyone for hours? Why did the screen sometimes glow softly for no reason, the insides making a tiny click or gurgle, if there was really nothing there?

These days, people can do practically anything they want: the technology is available, it is accessible, and it is done all the time. Timor knew that. But when you are dead, no one can make you admit anything.

Selina was explaining all about Timor and the cell phone harassment to Portia, whom she had just met in the old slave cemetery in Kinderhook, New York, which is now a children's playground with bright plastic slides, a merry-go-round and a bouncing motorcycle and rocket ship, each on a steel spring base. The date was May 1, 2010—the nine-month anniversary of the day Selina Van Staal walked out on Timor Zinkovsky.

Usually Selina would never discuss her private affairs with someone she had known for only an hour. But sometimes you need to make an exception. Say someone has an embarrassing but serious illness and you have had that same illness or one like it. You should tell that person about your own medical history, so they will feel less alone. While it turned out that Portia did not suffer from such an illness or even, probably, from a cell phone bug (though you never know), she did feel alone. Anyone could see that. You could tell from the way she had been pitching about on the bouncing rocket ship, the hood of her navy boucle wrap coat pulled up over her head, partially shading her face—tell that she was cut off or adrift somehow. All alone that frigid spring evening (the weather had turned cold again) on the deserted playground, she appeared estranged and even desperate—like a woman who has had a bad fight with a significant other, dashed out of the house and driven recklessly away.

Well, it turned out she had, in the new-looking silver Audi A8 next to which Selina had parked her Beemer. Although of course the cowled woman did not say so right off—she was busy riding her rocket ship as Selina took a seat on the bouncing motorcycle. At first, Selina just swayed beside the navy boucle cowled stranger, enjoying the cool moist spring air. The cold perfume of crab apple blossoms. You should not start talking to someone who is upset until you know you have her attention, like when you can see she is looking at you out of the corner of her eye. Even still, Selina waited until the cowled woman stopped her pitching, until she had thrown her long legs wide of her mount and dug the kitten heels of her brown suede boots into the gravel, before she finally asked the woman if she knew that there were slaves buried there, beneath the playground equipment.

Yes, I heard that, the cowled woman sighed. She pulled back her hood displaying a head of thick ice-blond hair and lukewarm gray eyes, the skin lightly crinkled at the corners. She was in her late thirties, at least, but with full lips like a sixties Swedish film star. You could tell she thought of herself as the kindly but smart type, as well as still attractive to men. She went on: A classic case of cultural amnesia. At the same time, the irony is hard to miss. You wonder what those guys—because probably it was a bunch of guys—were thinking when they decided to put a playground here.

She sounded like an English professor, which meant that someone else had bought her the expensive car. It also meant that she sounded smarter than she was as she flexed her long legs, giving the rocket ship between them a little jiggle.

Selina agreed. And as the sixties Swedish film star lips smiled, Selina added that women would never be so insensitive.

The decowled stranger stretched her hand out over to Selina: Hi, I'm Portia, after the character in Merchant of Venice, of course. Daddy was an English professor. So was I, for that matter.

Ha. They both bounced a little on their rides as Selina returned Portia's firm grip with her own. Was?

The biological clock was ticking harder than the tenure clock, my job was on the west coast and my husband's is here. And he makes an obscene amount of money. So I quit—to have a baby and be a stay-at-home mom. Dans cette mascarade de la fémininité…

That was French—all Selina could catch. She had taken French for a year at Staten Island Academy, before her deadbeat dad with only the one eye stopped paying tuition. C'est vrai is often a good response when someone speaks at length en Français. So Selina said c'est vrai.

Portia's lukewarm gray eyes heated up with l'excitement. But just as her sixties Swedish film star lips began to form more French, her cell phone rang from inside her wrap jacket. The ringtone was actually a ring, like the sound of a telephone in an old black and white movie. Dial M for Murder. Dismounting she stood, holding what looked to be the newest model of iPhone. She squinted at the oblong silver wafer for a few moments, frowning, then slid a finger over the screen and shoved it back inside her wrap. Restraddling her spaceship she stared down at the back of her hands.

That was when Selina related how Timor had hijacked her iPhone, just to make Portia feel better.

You don't think it was just acting up? Portia responded. Computers can do weird things—not because they've been tampered with, but simply because of already present and completely unintentional bugs in the software. It could've also been a case of PEBKAC—you know, problem exists between keyboard and chair.

Sitting there on her ride regarding Selina with her nose slightly lifted, as if peering through a pair of reading glasses, Portia seemed to feel better. Or at least superior, which is often the same thing. Fine. How could she possibly know, with all her advantages and fancy cerebral ways, what Selina had been through not just in recent years but also before, bartending her way through CUNY and then SUNY? What professors lacked in material possessions they made up for in airs. That is what Selina's mother used to say. Plus their children get free tuition. Without a word, Selina dismounted her tiny motorcycle. Wet pink crab apple petals and lime green tassels of elm tree pollen littered the gravel like left over party decorations.

To her credit, Portia did not lack sensitivity. As Selina began to walk away, she got up from her ride as well: Hey, I'm sorry. It sounds like your husband had all the power in your relationship, or at least it seemed to you like he did. I can't imagine what that would be like.

Selina probed the silk-lined pocket of her man tailored herringbone jacket (a Luciano Barbera beauty scored from Timor's closet after he died). Would the wad of bills crumpled in the silk pay both for gas and a pizza-to-go on the way home? As Selina was leaving the Lab last night, Asani had stirred on his gurney: Come back on Monday and we'll get the paper work started. But there is a big difference between a job offer and a first paycheck. Usually two weeks. No, Portia could not imagine.

Portia caught up, cupped Selina's elbow: Once you started believing he was a master of the universe, I bet it seemed as if there was no limit to his powers.

Well, Timor <u>was</u> very arrogant.

So is Michael, Portia confided as she threaded her arm through Selina's. Have you eaten yet? There's this great little Greek diner on 9H, falafel's on me.

With her arm hooked through Selina's, they stood shoulder to shoulder at about five feet nine inches tall. It could be Portia thought they were on the level. Selina was just happy to go along for the ride (or to tail Portia's Audi to the diner) as Portia continued: For investment bankers, arrogance is a basic qualification for the job. But now I'm leaving Michael and his pinstriped ass even though I gave up a tenure track job at a research one university to come back east. Leaving even though I just went through three months of IVF treatments at HVFC to have a family with that self-inflated subprime creep. And I'm taking my embryos with me.

Timor was lucky he died when he did, and also that before he died, there were no children. Then there really would have been a reason to fight. A reason to fight tooth and nail. But if there had been children, things might have been different. Maybe there would be something to do besides fight or at least a reason not to, because you should not fight in front of the children. You should not fight in front of the children, especially when it is just fighting for fighting's sake, fighting because you are tired of everything else. Because then the children will think everything else is not worth it.

I see you've just decided to ignore my e-mails, *króshka*. Ouch. I mean if I had any nerve cells, this would be a fucking prick. The kind you make with a pin, that is—not the kind you accused me of being every time you didn't get your way. Then you'd give me the silent treatment. Not just the silent treatment but the "I can't see, hear or touch you, let alone speak to you" treatment—the whole sensory deprivation spa experience (talk about "abuse"). So what I'm saying to you now is that I'm used to it. You're not gonna crush me or make me go away by pretending I'm not here, even if the laws of physics would seem to preclude my appearance on your PC.

You must wonder, by the way—how does he do it? How does he not only type in his messages but manage to send them from what appears to be his own, private account? How does he do this not only without hands but also without any programming skills, whatsoever (which is why we both know that cell phone harassment biz was crap)? Do we receive an automatic Ph.D. in computer science when we die? The ability to intelligently manipulate not only code but electromagnetic currents? Of course not. On the other hand, you didn't need to know how the Rover worked to drive it like some outback safari pro (accident, my ass; you just wanted the auto insurance money. How convenient for you that it was still covered under my semi-annual payment policy). Without going into a lot of technical detail about the specifics of spiritual existence—not because I don't think you could handle it, but because I know you couldn't care less about my life—I'll briefly explain.

Computer data moves from one place to another riding on the crests and troughs of electromagnetic waves. Data travels on these waves either as an analog signal, that is, a continuous electronic current that smoothly varies in frequency, or, as the days of the dial-up modem are numbered, through a digital signal, a series of discrete pulses. Either way—data is energy. Ghosts, or as we prefer to be called, spirit entities, also exist as a form of energy—what remains of the remains, since energy cannot be created or destroyed. In fact, a ghost is a type of naturally, or supernaturally, occurring bit stream (we went digital way before DSL). As such, we have the ability not only to travel through fiber optic cables (my fave; love that pure silica glass covered with reflective cladding, like spinning inside a disco ball) or ride satellite transmissions to enter any computer, but also to interface with and manipulate the bandwidths and content of the waves entering any PC, altering the data into the form in which we wish it to be read. And we don't even have to think (good thing; death is not an IQ booster). We just get into the groove. Like you and that Land Rover. Like you and me before Viktor, happy together. Although that now seems more farfetched, *détka*, than anything I've said here.

Not Okay: A True Crime Story,

by Selina Van Staal

Chapter Five

"You See Connections and Patterns Where there are None"

When you choose an IVF program, it is important to consider success rates as reported to SART, the Society for Assisted Reproductive Technologies. Success rates are based upon the ratio of treatment cycles to birthrates. The most successful programs can promise a birthrate in excess of fifty percent per treatment cycle while others report less than half that. Some report no success rates at all. Meaning they report nothing, not because they have nothing to report, but because nothing looks better than next to nothing. You know, they do not want people to know they stink. The Hudson Valley Fertility Clinic was one of the ones that stunk (including the essential oil-dispersing aromastones in the reception area). And yet all these women had given it their business—Lyndon, Portia and, as revealed by the patient database, Kyle. As Dean Van Staal would say, quoting somebody, a sucker is born every minute. Just not at HVFC.

Hudson Valley Fertility Clinic was not a good place to go if you wanted to have a baby. But it was an okay place to work, if you did not mind a low end salary (according to www.healthcarecrossing.com, the median salary for a clinical coordinator was $54,752. Selina's contract provided only $42,281, and minimal health insurance benefits, even though she was now in the health profession!), and a lack of direction. Not just a lack of direction but of a clear job description. Doctor Asani had said nothing more about the use of quote unquote healing hands. In the last month he had said nothing more about anything. He had only been spotted twice, from afar: at the end of a hallway, disappearing around a corner; flitting across the parking lot early one evening, vanishing behind the tinted windshield of his Porsche Boxster, so you could not tell if he even saw you. It was as if the interview had never happened—or as if the interview had been conducted by a ghost. Someone had put a pile of patient files on Selina's desk containing records of things like FSH and estradiol levels, whatever those were, as well as grainy gray images from ultrasounds and some kind of hystero-thingys. But they might as well have been pictures of asteroids in outer space. The job title of clinical coordinator suggested that it was Selina's responsibility to set up and schedule the various diagnostic tests, measurements and what not, making sure that Patient B's appointment did not conflict with Patient A's, and generally keeping track of who had what when with whom. However, the nurses and technicians who actually administered the tests and took the measurements seemed to know who had what when with whom better than Selina. Plus they had their own ideas about what next. It did seem like they should tell Selina what next so that she could then tell the patients. But they did not. What do you do when someone just passes by you? Well, you can take long lunches, in your office, or in the warm, dry weather of mid June, outside. Before and after lunch, you can also spend a lot of time googling.

HVFC, believe it or not, occupied the former corporate headquarters of Hudson Valley Cement, or HVC. The former corporate headquarters of HVC occupied, in turn, the former grounds of an empty estate house that had belonged to the Van Hoesen family, whose initials, VH, were etched in the limestone of the lintel over the front entrance. The house still stood on the main road, just before where you turned into the long driveway to reach the fertility clinic that was once a cement company. Looking at the accretion of initials from VH to HVC to HVFC, you might be tempted to see a pattern there (especially if you knew that "Hudson" comes from Van Hoesen, the first settler in the area). Probably it was just a coincidence. Timor used to say that the ability to recognize patterns is a component of intelligence (which is one reason why Selina was able to do well on standardized tests without studying. It is also why she would never go to HVFC herself, where there was a clear pattern of failure.). But to see patterns everywhere, darling, even in random data, is silly and paranoid. The technical term is apophenia, from the Greek apo, or away from, and phenia, from phren, mind or cognitive faculties (the "r" having been lost in translation, like so much of what we see and experience). Basically, it means away from mind.

Basically, Timor would say things like that to diminish Selina's belief in her own powers of perception. Which is another clear example of abuse.

Just before noon on June 16, 2010 nine months after the ruling of the New York State Divorce Court judge that alimony was unwarranted, given the relative youth and health of the plaintiff, Lyndon arrived at HVFC, hysterical. One of Lyndon's stepsons had stabbed Lyndon's hairless with a quick-release hunting knife he had received from his psycho-bitch mother. Asani was, as usual, nowhere to be found so Selina invited Lyndon to share her tuna on rye, in the field behind the old Van Hoesen house.

Sedated by tuna salad, Lyndon finally ceased with the sobbing. Also, after such a violent death, the dog would have priority for reincarnation. Cindy Lou Who would return as someone who would become very close to Lyndon, like a new baby, Selina explained to Lyndon, as the two walked down a slope of mowed lawn back to the clinic. Although the chances for getting pregnant at HVFC were not great.

You see, while the connection between the three sets of initials, HVFC, HVC and VH was probably just a coincidence, the random repetition and accumulation of letters had created a kind of gestalt, which is a functional unit with properties that are more than the sum of its parts.

I don't understand, said Lyndon, clomping over the buttercups in four-inch high espadrilles topped by what looked to be a tailored tan gabardine suit—depending on what your idea is of a suit. Do hot pants can count as the bottom half or not?

Nevermind, Selina told her. Lyndon should just think of the three sets of initials as a kind of spell, like abracadabra or open sesame—VH, HVC, HVFC!—spoken unintentionally, but they still worked. In the same way that it does not matter whether you press the remote control button for your garage door on purpose or if something in your purse presses it by accident.

Okay, but is it a good spell or a bad one?

Good or bad was not the issue. The question was what the spell spelled for you, Selina explained.

What does it spell for me? Lyndon asked as she pulled a wad of tissue from a tan calfskin clutch with a little gold clasp. Sorry—pollen allergies. She blew her nose.

What did the gestalt mean for Lyndon? What did it mean for Lyndon that her husband ran a fertility clinic where the live birth rate was so low that they might as well have been selling cement? Where Selina now had a job with benefits and a regular, although comparatively low, salary, but who knew how much longer that ship would sail? Asani was sinking in the not-Dasani waters of his own impaired judgment because you do not hire people without the necessary credentials—even people with a record of acing standardized tests. People who, to own up, may not have passed the NCLEX-RN after all. Steph the receptionist, the one HVFC employee who would actually talk to Selina, said Asani had been a topnotch reproductive endocrinologist at Uptown Procreative Specialists in Manhattan before he started his own clinic. The implication being that he was no longer. But that is all Steph would say about it. People around here are just trying to do their jobs, Steph admonished as she went back to her knitting and looking at ornamental shrubs on-line.

Well Selina would be happy to do her job too, if someone would just tell her what her job was. In the meantime, if Lyndon was ever going to get pregnant, she needed spiritual as well as medical help because of the unintentional but nevertheless potent gestalt of the letters HVFC.

Basically, Selina told Lyndon, sliding her ID card through the reader to a side entrance of the clinic, this gestalt combines the past with the present, immobilizing new life forms. Under current conditions it is impossible for fertilization to occur—because you cannot make a baby in a cement mixer.

Can you fix it?

Well, it would be a lot of work, but it might be possible to break-up the gestalt with good chi.

What?

It was one of the embryologists. She was usually on the other side of the building, in the lab. So Selina had never seen her up close. Up close, her smooth young face did not match her thick gray hair. Sometimes women do not dye their hair because they are pregnant. Beneath the blue bulge of her chest, her scrubs hung loose. But could be it was too early to tell.

Inside the building, Lyndon clopped off to search some more for her husband. Without thinking, Selina continued on with the gray haired but young faced embryologist down to the staff kitchen and lounge in the basement.

I'd love to hear more about what you were to saying to Asani's wife, the embryologist said, holding the door to the lounge. In the vee of her neckline a bit of silver snatched the light. A crucifix?

Selina hesitated. Asani had hired her, in part, for her quote unquote healing hands. While it was unclear exactly what services she was supposed to provide with those hands, probably he would not like to find out that he was paying for them twice (even though Lyndon said her husband had told her she was free to do whatever with the money in her personal checking account). But could be the gray haired embryologist wanted to hear more for personal reasons. The bottom of the crucifix was hidden behind the button of her lab coat but you could see the top had a loop to it. That meant it was not a crucifix but an ankh—an emblem of fertility from ancient Egypt. According to www.crystalinks.com, physician, priest and magician were one in ancient Egypt. So healing was an art addressed on many levels. Selina decided to share her theory about the repetition and cumulative effect of the letters in VH, HVC and HVFC.

Never waste your smarts on someone who is looking for a laugh, Selina's dad Dean used to say. Someone who is hooting with derision almost as soon as you open your mouth, her shoulders shaking, her thick silvery hair shimmying over her cheekbones. You cannot take back your theory, but you do not have to continue to share it. Finally, the gray haired but young faced embryologist stopped laughing: Wow, that explains everything. She pushed her thick locks back behind her ears, then held out her hand: I don't think we've formally met. I'm Fritzi Akdikmen.

Her handshake was firm, though her hand was cool. A firm handshake, Selina's father used to say, shows you can trust someone. But gray hair, if your face is still young, and further, your eyebrows are thick and black, is just as much an affectation as peroxide blond. Everyone should look the way they truly are, even if they are not.

I'm going to have a glass of Gatorade before I go back to work—want one? Fritzi asked, pulling a plastic jug out of the staff refrigerator.

The original Gatorade contained the sweetener cyclamate, a substance banned by the FDA but people continue to drink it anyways. In fact, it has spawned many imitations—sport drinks with different names and packaging but similar formulations. All of which contain way too much sodium. That means salt. Fritzi's friendly smile, when Selina declined the greenish yellow liquid, looked to be sincere.

Whatever floats your boat, she laughed as Selina went on to pour a packet of strawberry-flavored Emergen-C into a glass of water from the cooler. But you knew she was skeptical. Could be she just wanted to get more information about the moonlighting so that she could report back to Asani. Selina had met this type before, the type who seems like she wants to be your friend, but really wants something else. Fritzi did not dye her hair but she was hiding her true colors.

Sinking back into a cream leather love seat that looked to be a cast off from the Asani's house, Fritzi patted the cushion beside her: Let's hang out for a bit. I'm not ready to go back to that lab.

The only natural light in the lounge slanted through two small windows set near the ceiling. The fluorescent tubes above were turned off. The air conditioning hummed. Fritzi was hiding her true colors but sometimes it is nice just to sit in a cool, dim place with someone. Like a fish floating in a rocky cove or a girl in a basement recreation room watching television with her sister and brother, cool but also cozy. Cool but also cozy as bodies would slump into each other and feet would touch. Sometimes they would match their feet together, calling it a "foot five." Foot five, stay alive, they would say to each other. And once in a while Dean Van Staal, on the rare occasions that he was home, would join them, for a movie from the nineteen fifties like that one about the man whose best friend is a six foot long invisible rabbit. Selina would sit in her father's lap.

Before he drove off to Florida for the last time, Dean said, Honey I'll be in touch and if you ever need me, just call. But I know you and Tim will be very happy together.

Of course that was neither here nor there, like Dean himself who joined the church of Scientology and subsequently disappeared in or around Tampa circa 1997. Plus grown women do not sit on their fathers' laps.

Fritzi's feet, wearing white dansko clogs, rested on the glass topped metal coffee table next to her half drunk glass of Gatorade. Her arm was stretched out along the back of the sofa, behind Selina's neck.

When I was a kid, I had a best friend. We used to play a game where one of us would tell a lie or make some preposterous statement and the other would try to trip her up. Catch her in a contradiction or an inconsistency. Sometimes one would start a game without telling the other. Once we were at my house after school, eating some left over chicken stew that my dad had made. When my friend asked me what the little seeds in it were, I said cumin, the ancient Turkish term for dried deer sperm. She threw up, on the kitchen floor and my new moccassins. After that we always made sure that we both knew when a game had begun.

Fritzi's arm dropped as she drew her hands to her stomach. They rested there, as if in reminiscence of her friend's gastric upheaval. But maybe there was another reason. When a woman is pregnant, that is where her hands tend to go. But you cannot just ask if you do not know someone very well.

You and I would have gotten along as kids, Fritzi said, turning to look at Selina. Her eyes were a dark brown, almost black, which like her youthful face, contrasted with her silver hair.

On the other side of the room, on top of a rolling metal cart, there was a fancy coffee maker. The kind that can be programmed to brew automatically—so you can wake up and smell the coffee. Obviously, Fritzi was insinuating something. People can insinuate all they want, however. That does not mean that you have to take the hint. You do not have to take the hint just as it is fine to refuse a cup of coffee if someone offers you one. Or for that matter, a glass of gatorade. Still, it never hurts to give a polite reply: Oh. What does your friend do now?

I don't know. We went to different high schools and lost touch. But her parents were both corporate lawyers.

Well, that sounded like another insinuation. When someone will not stop with the insinuations, you should just change the subject. So Selina asked Fritzi how she ended up on her own career path.

Hmmm. Good question, Fritzi said, reaching for her glass of Gatorade. This was verboten in my house growing up. My mother was a health food faddist and the only drinks allowed were soymilk, water and homemade lemonade, sweetened with a hint of honey—which was about as refreshing as sucking on a lemon. She took a big swallow: ahhh. So where was I? Right, how did I get on this career path? Well, as an adolescent I aspired to lasting fame, I craved factual certainty, and I thirsted for a meaningful connection to human life.

Fritzi took another gulp from her glass. Wiping her mouth with the back of her hand she asked, How about you?

The air conditioning had stopped humming. All you could hear was the buzz of a lawn mower somewhere out on the grounds. Outside it was bright so that you needed sunglasses and even a hat but in here it was dim and soothing to the eyes. Fritzi said she had thirsted for a meaningful connection to human life. Was that true? Probably not. In fact, what Fritzi had just said sounded, as Dean Van Staal used to say, like horseshit. Be that as it may, you should have at least one person you can talk to where you work. Then you will know the scuttlebutt. Or at least be less isolated on the job. As Dean also used to say, a man out standing in his field is probably a farmer.

So Selina told Fritzi a little but not too much about Timor (people just don't understand about cyber harassment). Mostly she told about getting into the reiki business (leaving out the brownie franchise) and meeting Lyndon and how that had led to being hired by Doctor Asani. The specifics of the interview, such as the tour, went unmentioned. Except for the water bottle. Asani needed a better logo—like one of those snake-entwined staffs with the wings at the top. The mudflap girl did not help his image.

You can just go ahead and say it—no need to beat around the bush, Fritzi laughed. The man has a drinking problem. He didn't always have a drinking problem. Before it was just a thinking problem. In the sense that he thought too highly of himself.

Fritzi had used the past tense: Asani apparently no longer suffered from megalomania. Why not? It is always good to know about the past of your employer: you never know when such information will be useful, like that screw that you almost throw away and then later find is exactly the right size to hold the bed together (especially since you cannot afford a new bed, after the unfair divorce settlement). But Fritzi had fallen silent, her fingers fiddling with the ankh. She patted her lips with the looped end. If you want someone to keep talking about something, you can offer your own thoughts about it. Well Selina knew all about physicians who thought too highly of themselves, having been married to one. About how many of them forget that their names are followed by the initials M.D., not G.O.D. Maybe it was even worse in the A.R.T. field—doctors thinking they truly were Creators.

Fritzi let the ankh fall. Sighed and turned her gaze up to the two small windows.

I wish we could just let some air in.

She wished she could let in some air. In a dropped literature elective the professor had said that was a euphemism for abortion in a famous story by Ernest Hemingway. If someone wants to have an abortion, then probably she is pregnant. But again, you cannot just ask!

I hate air conditioning, Fritzi continued. In the lab we have no choice but I don't see why we need it here. Sure we'd all be a little warmer but with the windows open, at least we'd be getting more oxygen. I'm sorry, what were you saying?

Selina repeated what she had said about doctors who have a God complex. If that was Asani's problem, when did he stop getting high on himself and start drinking instead?

Fritzi extended her arm back up over the top of the loveseat. That snake-entwined staff with the wings at the top is called the rod of Caduceus, and it's kind of a joke, she said. Although not an intentional one. Back in the late nineteenth century, an Army officer suggested it as symbol for the medical corps—he'd mixed the rod of Caduceus up with the rod of Asclepsius, the Greek god of healing, which only has a single snake and no wings. The rod of Caduceus belonged to Hermes, the patron of the road and commerce. So it'd be a good logo for traveling salesmen and truckers—better, actually, than the mudflap girl.

When someone will not stay on the subject, that means that they either do not want to stay on the subject, or that they cannot. Beneath

Fritzi's dark eyes there were violet shadows, like she did not get enough sleep. Maybe she could not stay on the subject because she was tired. And maybe she was tired because of her unwanted pregnancy. While you could not just ask about that, you could talk about your own sleep troubles. Selina's sleep troubles had begun when she was very young. Never a good napper, unlike her older sister and brother, Selina had kept her mother from reading in the afternoons. So her mother went back to work as a secretary in the English Department. As Selina grew, she also had difficulty getting to sleep at night and boring thoughts would spin around and around in her brain until finally she got out of bed and did something else like reading <u>Rosemary's Baby</u> in the closet or sneaking around the house while everyone else was drooling on their pillows. But then you are tired in the morning and it is hard to get up.

Yawning, Fritzi nodded her head.

So what do you do when you cannot sleep?

What do I do if I can't thleep? She laughed. Thear theep. If I can't sleep, I work.

[<u>An aside to the reader</u>: Since speech impediments have no effect whatsoever on writing, Selina Van Staal's slight lisp has previously gone unmentioned. It is only brought up here to help explain why Fritzi was saying "thleep" and "Thear theep" instead of "sleep" and "shear sheep." Obviously Fritzi was making fun of Selina's small disability in order to steer the conversation away from herself!]

Undiscouraged by Fritzi's mockery, Selina continued with her questioning: why not take a pill, like Ambien or Klonopin? That is what Selina's ex used to do and Selina occasionally as well, though with Selina there was a rebound effect. So that the next night was even worse than the one before it. Plus you did not want to become addicted.

Fritzi picked up the ankh again, brought the loop up to her right eye and squinted: Not everything can be corrected or should be corrected, the miracles of modern medicine notwithstanding.

Not everything can be corrected or should be corrected, Fritzi had just said. That meant living with your mistakes. Once when Selina was waiting for her mother on the couch in the English Department Lounge, she heard her mother tell one of the English professors that Selina was a mistake. An unplanned pregnancy is a mistake that can be fixed by a medical procedure, but not everyone believes in having that procedure.

It seemed that Fritzi wanted to have an abortion but at the same time thought abortion was wrong. That is an ethical issue. Though eastern approaches are preferable to western ones in dealing with physical and spiritual issues, in the case of ethical issues, the Socratic method is usually best. Through a series of questions formulated as tests of logic, Fritzi would be able to figure out what was the right thing to do. But just as you cannot play tennis by yourself, you cannot employ the Socratic method without a partner. Someone needs to be the questioner. As a woman who was always ready to help other women with their problems, Selina would be happy to play that role. But you also need to know what you are talking about—you cannot play tennis without a ball. Or have an abortion without a baby. Fritzi needed to concede to her condition, starting with an answer to the question how long have you been pregnant?

Fritzi turned, brows raised, dark eyes wide: Pregnant? Me? Then she laughed: you've got to be kidding.

When people do not want to concede to something, they will turn it into a joke. The truth was that Fritzi was in denial as well as evasive. She did not want to talk about Asani's alcoholism. That is so typical! As in dysfunctional families, employees in dysfunctional workplaces are often close-lipped about destructive behaviors and relationships. The unwanted pregnancy, however, was another matter. You cannot keep a baby to yourself—it will come out, eventually. Being a woman who was interested in helping other women, Selina could not relent. If you want someone to take your words seriously, you need to accompany them with a serious, even stern expression. Silence can be employed as well, or in this case, the pregnant pause.

You're not kidding are you?

Selina folded her arms.

I suppose it's still possible, if unlikely. But why do you think I'm pregnant?

A feeling, an intuition. Selina did not bring up the undyed hair or the unconscious allusion to that Hemingway story about abortion—probably Fritzi would just call the one a preference and the other a coincidence. You have too much imagination, Timor used to say. You see connections and find patterns where there are none.

Sure why not? Fritzi smiled, tucked a long silver strand behind her ear. My own intuition about intuition is that it's right at least some of the time. So let's assume you're correct, Selina. What would you advise, from the non-western, anti-empirical perspective? A little massage for the mom-to-be, a few reiki sessions at a hundred bucks a pre-natal pop?

Well, that sounded a little aggressive, like a challenge even. But a challenge is also an invitation to prove your point. The point being that the western approach is not always the most successful, a point Fritzi herself had already half acknowledged when she said how not everything can be corrected or should be corrected, miracles of modern medicine notwithstanding. The western approach cannot do it all. At the same time, the western approach will not admit that it cannot do it all, so you need to prove your point without proving it. That means you cannot be obvious or pedantic, even though technically reiki is not massage. Technically reiki is not massage, because there is no physical contact between the reiki master and the patient, only an invisible current as the reiki master draws the bad energy from the patient's body and replaces it with good energy from the Universe. So you do not see the feet that were in the Dansko clogs because the patient leaves them on—the short, stubby toes with their scraps of pink and white nail, rimed and clumped with talcum powder. You do not feel the fissures and cracks in the heels, the thick calloused pads of the balls, or the smooth cool scoop of arch between. You do not smell the funk of talcum mixed with sweat, the moist close spongy smell of the locker room or rotted logs full of secrets like the shiitake mushrooms in the woods around Bosky House that Timor said could not be shiitake because you have to cultivate them, inject the spores into the logs first—so don't eat them, Selinka, they're probably poison.

You do not touch the person and vice versa, but if you need to prove your point without proving it, try a stroke or two.

Would you like a free foot massage? Selina asked.

Fritzi's expression as she lay back with her bare, stinking feet in Selina's lap was hard to read. Was she enjoying the massage or not? The slight one-sided curve of her lips could have been a half smile, or an unformed sneer. Fritzi's feet were chalky with powder but otherwise solid feeling and easy to grip, but Fritzi herself—unlike Lyndon, Kyle and even Portia—was not. Was she pregnant? Was her mind open or closed to natural healing? Was she a potential ally or an enemy? What did Fritzi want? Dean Van Staal used to say that people are people: if you know what they want, generally you can get along with them. But not always.

Unlike Dolores who owned many books, Dean owned only one: Dale Carnegie's How To Win Friends and Influence People. It was a book that was not even a whole book, as it was famously missing what was to have been its conclusion. According to the publisher's note, the final chapter was missing because Carnegie was offered a free trip to Europe just as he was about to start it—so he sent the manuscript off unfinished. But maybe the book's final section was missing because Carnegie could not bring himself to write it, not wanting to end his upbeat book on a downbeat note. In any case, the concluding chapter was supposed to acknowledge that there are some people with whom it is impossible to be friends or even peaceable rivals. You should divorce such people, sue them in court, or cut them to pieces.

Remember the winter I quote unqote dragged you to the Caymans, how on our return a security hound smelled someone else's coke on our cash? Sweet doggerina, you were always good at sniffing out secrets—just not so great at pinpointing what they were. So yeah, I knew you knew, even as I was sure you had no clue. An awkward internal rhyme, but STET. One of the things I've noticed since the great divide, by the way, is how much more aware I've become of words—their sounds and rhythms, their textures, their bodies, so to speak. It's as if my own lack of substance makes me more sensitive to substance—I now find it everywhere, even in the most abstract and rarefied language. One of the benefits, I guess, of being less dense. But to return to my point, however pointless, I knew you were on to me, suspected me of some kind of betrayal. I could feel your eyes sliding over my person when I rose from our bed and padded off to the bathroom, your intelligence softly probing, seeking the information leak my lips would not provide.

Why couldn't I just come straight out with it and tell you? Early on, during one of those cozy nights of kitchen talk, you said you were not interested in having kids. I repeat, **not interested in having kids.** You wanted to write children's stories or take photographs or do both like the woman you once said was the author of your favorite book as a little girl, *The Lonely Doll* (a glossy portfolio of nursery perversions unavailable to me during my pure Soviet youth and hence, at the time, unfamiliar. Otherwise Mr. Bear might have given Edith a spanking right then and there.). "I need to make something that is me but also more than me" you claimed. Then you went on to cite old albert-e, no doubt as quoted in the fools gold stamped pleather edition of *Everyman's Eggheads* you inherited from Ma Van Staal: some Nobel blah blah about how the artist and the scientist, each makes this self-created cosmos in order to find peace and security that can't be found in "the narrow whirlpool of personal experience." I was skeptical about the peace and security (already I sensed you couldn't get no satisfaction), but I was all behind the Big Bang, baby—the more of Selina Van Staal, the better. Bababoom.

You said you were **not interested in having kids** and then suddenly one day there you were, talking about time running out or making hay or seizing the day or maybe even just that your biological clock was ticking though I remember you saying once during a kitchen session that you hated that tick tock talk. Anyway, I don't recall because I wasn't listening—it was months before I could even believe my ears. But it turned out you were serious (I still remember the night—the rubicon of your turned back). Well, never let it be said I didn't do the least I could do, as the drunken doc says in that old American military sitcom (which was on TV the night of our short lived cold war). So then we tried, or you tried and I just fucking enjoyed myself fucking. My fortieth birthday present to myself (vasa deferentia all tied in a bow) remaining a secret between me and my urologist.

File 1993: Transcription of Revenant Composition
(Former Sex: Female; Deceased: 31.12.1993)

It was a Friday afternoon at the big, sunny Manhattan law firm. "In just another half hour," Kate LaLane mused, the while her slender fingers flew over the keys of her typewriter, "in just twenty-nine more minutes, the five o'clock bell will ring and I can be off." Yet Kate was not typically a clock-watcher. She loved her job. Indeed, she had wanted it very much, although not "badly," since according to *Practical English and the Command of Words*, the use of "badly" for "very much" is not good English, and had been thrilled when Mr. Hamilton had hired her, three months previously.

Why just to be sitting at a desk rather than standing in an assembly line like most of the other girls who had taken the high school secretarial course seemed like Heaven. And her salary of nineteen dollars, paid in cash every Friday afternoon, seemed a princely stipend when you had never earned any money before. On the ferry back to Staten Island, back aching and fingers throbbing from typing all day, she would still feel fantastic, thinking about the crisp bills, three fives and four ones, in her imitation leather purse. To be sure, there was not much left by Saturday morning. You see, Kate had to give Ma all three of the fives now that Brother Joe had come back from the war all shot up and dishonorably discharged to boot, while Pa had not worked for years.

It took a lot of planning and an almost heartbreaking amount of self-denial to make the pittance that remained stretch from one Friday night to the next. When you are only seventeen, and "pretty as a picture" (at least that is what the dashing Mr. Garrett Rockswold III, with his Italian briar wood pipe and black eye patch, used to tell her), why new hats and dresses and shiny leather pumps with very impractical spiked heels (especially for a farmer's wife!) seemed very, very important and often...alas, very, very unattainable.

Still, as of today Kate had managed, penny by penny and nickel by nickel, to save up seven dollars to buy a red felt platter hat adorned with coque feathers and a flirty spray of black netting that had been in the window display at Bergdorf Goodman for three weeks and now was on a shelf inside at the back of the store (without, unfortunately, any reduction in price). As soon as Kate could get over to the big department store with her hard earned cash, the hat would be hers.

It seemed to Kate that if she just had that red platter hat it would be a sure cure for all her troubles. Her chief trouble was occasioned by the growing conviction that Gary (as he had told Kate to call him, in happier times), during his all too brief visits to the firm from his farm upstate, was becoming increasingly attentive to Alice Peplinski, who worked for Mr. Montague in the office next door. To be sure, Alice always looked like a million bucks but then she was a stenographer and she made twenty two dollars and she could keep all her money but the five dollars for room and board that she paid to the aunt she lived with. "If I could buy things as nice as hers, I know I could put it all over her," thought Kate as the quick tears sprang to her soft brown eyes. "If I could just buy that darling red platter hat with the coque feathers and the black netting I could put it all over her and have him on a platter," even though *Practical English and the Command of Words* states that cheap puns should be avoided (because clear, fluent and concise English in business means keener thinking, improved communications and greater prestige).

Nowadays when Gary drove down to Manhattan in his Austin 12 convertible (his mother's old Lincoln Zephyr Continental was more comfortable for the long drive on the Taconic Parkway but with gasoline rationing and all, simply not a practical choice), he hardly took the time to say hello on his way to Mr. Hamilton's inner sanctum. Oh, Kate knew he bore the weight of the world on his shoulders since the loss of his mother (that on top of an eye, in a shooting accident when he was only sixteen years old!). And now his half sisters, Park Avenue socialites who could not tell a sheep from a goat, were trying to get the farm. But Gary had built it up from scratch, turning his mother's impulsive purchase of a charming if dilapidated old Dutch barn and the twenty surrounding green but milkweed ridden acres into a real working dairy farm. So that when he walked by you could catch the faintest hint of cow in his tweeds. Of course if you were a farmer's wife, living on a farm, you would not even notice it. Of late, however, that seemed less and less likely, as the smell of cow now collected in the office next door, even though it was Mr. Hamilton who was handling his case, not Mr. Montague. The truth of the matter, Kate secretly admitted, was that it was not preoccupation with legal matters that kept Mr. Garrett Rockswold III from lingering at her desk on his way in to see Mr. Hamilton.

But on Monday morning, according to Mr. Hamilton's appointment book, which had been lying open when Kate brought coffee in for Mr. Hamilton and Betsy Dorset, his stenographer, Gary had a meeting first thing. If Kate were to fall in right beside him as he entered the building (there was a little alcove in the lobby where you could stand out of the way), and ride with him up the elevator in that snappy red platter hat—why Gary would surely be very much impressed. Red was his favorite color. Which was kind of a surprise. You would think it would be green. Anyways, he had told her so one evening when after a late afternoon appointment with Mr. Hamilton, he had asked her to join him for a drink at the Oyster Bar. He had told her that she ought to wear bright colors. "Baby," he said, "with those black curls and big brown eyes, you'd be a knockout in red." But of course, that was a long time ago, before Alice Peplinski had replaced old Mrs. Dusenberry as Mr. Montague's stenographer, and the susceptible Gary had succumbed to her Titian charms.

"Miss LaLane, the boss wants to see you in his office." That was Betsy, as she rushed by with her nice beaver fur collared coat bunched up in her arms and tears in her eyes. "Wonder what's up?" Kate asked herself. Betsy was acting like she'd just been canned. Did that mean Kate was about to get promoted? Her typing skills were topnotch and with a little practice she would be great at taking dictation, too. Well, the red platter hat had a matching red coat, double-breasted with military style buttons. For a moment, as she smoothed her hair and straightened her skirt before pushing open the door to Mr. Hamilton's office, Kate dared to dream.

"You wanted to see me, Sir?"

"Yes, Miss LaLane. As you are aware, the war has come to a successful conclusion and our troops will soon be returning home. Before Miss Dorset, a young man worked for me—the best stenographer I ever had. Male minds focus better on the task at hand, you see. Now I would like to hire that young man back, but I cannot hire him on a girl's salary. To afford him, I'll have to trim the fat elsewhere, and as you are the latest addition to our firm, I shall have to reduce your salary to twelve dollars. I'm sorry, but it can't be helped. That will be all, Miss LaLane."

A seven dollar cut! And Ma expecting to pay the rent tonight! That meant Kate would have to give Ma the seven dollars she had saved up to buy the red platter hat. It was more important to pay the rent than to buy a red platter hat. With eyes swimming in tears and a great big lump in her throat, Kate LaLane nevertheless walked out of the office, rode the elevator down to the lobby and stepped out the revolving doors over to the curb and into the street with her head held high. "Oh well, maybe I wouldn't look so hot in red anyhow," was her last thought as the bus hit her.

Editor's Note: While no revenant subject can be a completely reliable witness of his or her own death, there are significant inconsistencies between the subject's report or "story" and actual circumstances and events. First, the subject did not die, as her report would seem to indicate, in 1945, or at the end of WWII, but forty-eight years later, at the age of 65, from multiple sclerosis (after two previous episodes of non disabling spinal MS at 35 and 48 years of age). Second, although the subject has adopted a fictive format complete with pseudonyms to obscure identities (do we see writerly ambition here?), it is likely that Garrett Rockswold III is the man she later married at the relatively advanced age, for the era, of 27. Four years her senior, the subject's husband was, despite a moneyed background, what is politely called in English a ne'er do well or less politely, a fuck-up. In Russian, the term *kozël* would be apt, meaning "a loser" or "worthless human being, from the phrase *ot negó kak ot kozlá moloká*, literally meaning "from him is like milk from a billy goat." Although the subject's marriage with the *kozël* lasted thirty-eight years, her narrative above may express the belief that she would have been better off dead.

Here's a story, *détka*: Halloween 1978, and I was on the southbound platform of the Metro into Manhattan. Tipping my hat to the holiday as well as my new, pending nationality (a green card was a coming), I'd gotten myself up in cowboy getup—a pair of chaps from the secret costume box in the basement of the Scarsdale house (a souvenir of my former foster dad), over levis that I'd later shove into my backpack, along with a blue gingham check shirt with pearlized buttons and a dirty white felt Stetson, both from the Goodwill. I'd also picked up a white domino for fifty cents but the only affordable cowboy boots I could find must've once been a cowgirl's—powder blue with three-inch heels. A bit too *golubóy* for the kid from Odessa, so I'd stuck with my high tops (then still a virile red).

Backpack cushioning against the concrete wall, I sat memorizing the names and symbols for fifty common ionic compounds (I had a General Chemistry midterm the next morning). Only as the scent of cannabis sativa pulled my nose up out of my textbook, did I see them—a group of what I took for fellow SUNY Purchase students (one I'd seen coming out of the Visual Arts building), all in what I took for costume. Although what the hell they were supposed to be, as they stood passing around a joint, I had no clue. Two of the girls were dressed in French maid outfits: stiff white headpieces, abbreviated black dresses that barely covered their white ruffled asses, little black aprons—only the aprons were pinned with postcard reproductions of abstract paintings. Images of red balls floating over black squiggles like clumps of pubic hair that I would later learn, under Irwin's tutorship, were Adolph Gottliebs. The boy in the group (who was also the kid I'd seen emerging from Visual Arts) wore a black plastic bag with holes for his head and arms as a top, cut off jeans that showed off his pale but chiseled legs, and a coil of garden hose over his shoulder, one end of which he'd duct taped to the gas mask he wore over his green grease painted face. Neither his costume nor the two girls' made any sense but at least they were erotic in a weird, Dadaist way—you knew they were somehow about sex, even if you weren't sure how. But the third girl's was about nothing but looking ugly and stupid: a big puffy brown ski jacket that only made her already bulky mass even bulkier, with a pair of kid-sized white gauze wings attached to the back, along with a little cap topped with a tin foil wrapped wire coil—a half assed attempt at a halo. Evidently she'd wanted to be an angel but either couldn't afford or fit into the rest of the costume (one size-fits-all robe or no). I saw her looking over at me and gave her a pitying smile. But instead of looking away in embarrassment, she smirked: "Hee Haw."

Only later that night, after I described the fat chick's costume to a Times Square colleague, a cute, red-headed runaway from Rochester, New York who'd come out as "Raggedy Andy," did I discover that she had been dressed as a figure of speech rather than of fun. Or as one of my Halloween tricks put it, when I dropped my levis and turned, cheeks chap-framed: "Holy shit!"

But why am I telling you this crap, this *kaká*, about Timor when he was still tiny, with a rather remarkable tush (hence the john's expression of appreciation) but a less than perfect grasp of idiom? Because you would have gotten it, even if you didn't get it: felt the tension of the inside joke, coiled to spring in your face. In fact, that's one of the things I appreciated about you—your ability to read people and seize their meaning, taking what you needed for your own ends. You'd have gone up to that puff coated *tëlka*, complimented her on the clever costume—then asked her to help you out with train fare.

I was the streetwalker, but you on your suburban cul-de-sac somehow became street wise. A sharp-sighted upstart spawned in a nidus of blind ambition, in an aluminum-sided split-level at the dead end of a dead end street, on the North Shore of Staten Island. Sure, I never encountered any of your family in the flesh—except for Dean (who now, interestingly, proves the most elusive). All you gave me of your youth with mother, sister and brother were a few ill-assorted facts: that Ma Van Staal (née Licata) grew heritage roses and kept a variety of pedigreed dogs, up to five at a time, each assigned its own tartan plaid. That Sis had saved money for a nose job by working afternoons at a deli. But then she lost her job after the surgery because she could no longer tell when the lunchmeat had turned. That Bro won a prize for a haiku composed while he was high (a "high-ku," you laughed, pantomiming a toke). That nidus of blind ambition I've constructed myself, gathering material here, material there (I have my methods)—a pile-up of pretention, self-deception, addiction and denial as well as simple bad medical luck—a kitschy American mess colorful as a heap of broken Fiestaware.

A pile-up of fuck-ups, a bloody *bardák* you more or less disowned like an old case of the clap, though it would've been fun, if a bit scary, to meet the homicidal hotty incarnate (FYI, due to the effect of Lyme encephalopathy on the brain's modulation centers, inhibitory pathways and stimulatory pathways, murderous ideation, urges and behavior can occur. Hence the fate of poor Marky Mark.). You were clearly the best of the bunch, the Van Staal with the most "potential." And now—the *only* one with potential, in the sense of a capability for actualization. By the way, that is one of the most frustrating limitations of spirit life—the basic physical impotence. Oh sure we can write—anybody can slide with a Ouija stylus, or slipstream a bit stream—but we can't publish.

I guess what I'm saying is that you can still make something out of yourself, if you don't end up in jail. You can do better than that asshole Asani. Oh maybe not as well as you think. Despite your self-touted aptitude for standardized tests (how many times did I hear the Helen Keller story?), you have no more talent for the sciences than you did for the arts. You do not have an orderly mind *détka*, and instinct will only get you so far. But the pseudosciences, well the sky's the limit—up, up and away. You have my blessing there—although contrary to popular belief, spirit entities do not reside at some higher level or sphere. As Huysmans writes in *Là-bas*, "space is peopled by microbes. Is it more surprising that space should also be crammed with spirits?"

The pseudosciences are yours for the taking, *détka*. Just don't say you have a dual background in both "traditional" and "alternative" medicine. No, better stick with the alternative. You might still get hired by a legitimate, SART-certified operation, because business is business, and if that's what those bimbos with ambitions to be babymakers want, then give it to 'em. A little reiki never did nobody no harm.

And actually, though I know it's all a big con for you, alternative medicine is not as "out there" as you might think. From the perspective of out there, or over here on the other side (which is, by the way, not really an other side, just as it is not another level or sphere, but rather a kind of mode), things start to look less quantitative, and instead more qualitative, more impressionistic. Even artistic. So I'm behind you, baby. As much as I can be behind you. Or above you. Or beyond you. As much as I've always been behind you, above you, beyond you, even beneath you. Yes, beneath you—I'll admit it. You don't believe me, do you? Even when we were good, you were sure there was something supercilious in my smile, an arc of triumph in my eyebrow. Somehow, someway I was always putting you down, or putting you up, my trophy wife on the solid mahogany mantelpiece at Bosky House. Only you really weren't such a prize. I could've found someone younger, prettier, better connected, www.Askmen.com. You really weren't such a prize and yet there were moments, *króshka*, when I felt unworthy to kiss the bottoms of your big boy's feet...

Such as? (Not only am I behind you, I'm inside you—right inside your head. Just kidding.).

Such as when I brought Loser, I mean Viktor, home from JFK. I was sure you were going to walk out on me right then and there. That was the worse part of it, in fact—your face after I pulled that flapping hooting microcephalic mess out of the car. Not the dawning realization as the passengers on the plane from Copenhagen (by way of Berlin by way of Moscow by way of Odessa) all gathered their luggage from the carousel and dispersed, that the only remaining child, swinging like an orangutan on the arm of a black-rooted blond in cork platform sandals as pocked as her face, was him. Not my growing horror, as the blond, having spotted me with my cardboard sign screaming VIKTOR in Cyrillic (why not just "shoot me"?), scuttled off as fast as she could on her little cork-hooved legs, which was in fact pretty fast, because by the time I thought to run after her she was already gone, swallowed up by the jet stream of sweat suits and rolling suitcases. Leaving me with him, passport and ticket stubs in a clear plastic packet, dangling from a black wire looped round his meager neck. The drooling six-year-old "wunderkind" of a cousin, a little "Boris Spassky" according to the e-mail from my cousin's mother, *Tjótka* Vera, who in America would reach his potential to become a "Bobby Fischer"—all he needed was lots of fresh meat and good air. Or good meat and fresh air, I can't remember how Vera put it in her e-mail, the mother of my cousin who had looked after me following my own mother's decision to tag after a bunch of loggers returning to their Siberian logging camp. What I do remember thinking as I read the e-mail one late May morning was that he'd be a distraction for the summer, to take your mind off the Cooperstown Regional Juried Art Exhibition of

1994—the only show your photographs ever got in, and only because Irwin pulled strings. Unfortunately he couldn't keep them from flopping. Amateur, clumsily perverse portraits of friends and family, including your own husband (was the wide-angle lens really necessary?) , they were dismissed by the judges as "Diane Arbus without the sensitivity or technical quality." Lack of talent exposed, you'd since retreated to some dark-room in your mind. Worse, you'd taken to sleeping in Dean's old bed on the other side of the house.

With Viktor, who was young enough for you to baby for a few months, but old enough to send off to a boarding school with a special program for chess prodigies in the fall, I knew I could lure you back. Young enough for you to baby, without there actually having to be a baby. The bathwater only, all warm and soft and sudsy with hormonal bliss (always good for sex)—minus the seven pounds of screaming sebum and lanugo hair slimed need.

Not. While the vernix caseosa was long gone, nothing but need remained. The kind of need best met in an institutional setting (or better still, by a snuff job in the NICU. Ask your friend Fritzi). Need with the universal face of Fetal Alcohol Syndrome, the collapsed nasal bridge, the small piggy eyes and epicanthic folds, the flat midface and smooth philtrum, as if all the features had been pressed by a mold, like the seal on a bottle of Absolut. Although it sure as shit wasn't some smooth Scandinavian vodka that had done that to him—no, it was good old russky rotgut. Which is what I felt like drinking after I'd released him from the back seat where he'd gibbered the whole way home, as I now stood there holding his clammy little hand, or pincer (the fore and middle fingers, and also the ring and pinky fingers, were fused), watching you watching us from the marble bench beside the entry to Bosky House. Something that would make me feel as poison as your look.

Which suddenly dissolved. So suddenly and completely I wasn't sure I'd seen it, like the flicker of a ghost behind a windowpane (you spooked me more than I'll ever spook you). Replaced by an expression of concern as you stood up and then strode down to the Rover, squatting and wrapping your long tanned arm around him, pulling him to your chest as you whispered something in his ear that made his mindless mug momentarily spark with comprehension. Then drawing away, still squatting, you patted your own back: "get on?" Instantly he scrambled up over your denimed haunches (who wouldn't want to get on that hayride?), wrapping his legs around your waist, though when I'd buckled him into his seat belt back in the parking garage at JFK, he'd writhed and screamed and grabbed the white oxford cloth of my shirt with his little grey teeth. Viktor clinging to your back, you turned and speed boated away in a pair of calfskin Moroccan slippers, disappearing together into Bosky House. Leaving me holding the little plastic ID packet, which had twisted off his neck in his giddiness to giddy on up.

I found you in the kitchen. You'd bungeed him to a bar stool at the cooking island, where you stood throwing bits of fruit flesh and vegetal matter from the garden into a blender, cooing "rock a bye baby, in the tree tops…" as he lolled his fourth percentile sized cranium from side to side. What a picture. You were so flawlessly maternal you looked unnatural, like a too perfect boob job (real breasts are never that symmetrical, which by the way is how I knew from the first yours were real). And him—no surgery in the world could fix him. And where did I fit in, as you hit the pulse button and the motley slop in the glass roared into life and the kid started back on his stool, tipping so that if I hadn't stepped behind and caught him, he would've crashed to the floor?

Once again, he attempted to sink his teeth into my forearm and so having righted him (or wronged him; assisted suicide might've been the better course), I stepped back. The contents of the blender were now a uniform ultragreen, a shade of pure chlorophyll so intense it would make a golfer's heart sing. Never was, despite Irwin's attempts to interest me in the game, but that afternoon I wished I could've driven off and done nine holes (any kind would do). Instead I stood there like a *bolván* watching as you poured two glasses of your witch's brew, one for him and one for you. I remained as you drank them, drained them, Viktor holding out his glass for more as he shot a sidelong glance at me, his smooth upper lip smeared with green smoothie. I retreated upstairs.

Later, I heard your tread, weighted by him, pass our door. Heard the floorboards creak down the hallway into the next wing and around the corner. I could guess where you'd gone, but waited until well after midnight to check. And there you were, both of you in Dean's old room, in the Empire-style bed. Half-sitting, back-pillowed against the headboard that hid your father's Smith & Wesson mishap, but thankfully, asleep (how exhausted you must've been), you had him wrapped in your arms, lips gaping against your collarbone, pincers tangled in your tresses.

What were you up to? Why wouldn't you admit, *détka*, that he was just another defeat? The drooling, the tics and spasms that would've been disfiguring if he weren't already a morphogenetic wreck. How could you face that face—liking nice things, beautiful things the way you did? The way we both did? And not only was he ugly, he was mean. Incorrigibly, irredeemably, congenitally mean (too late I recalled how my cousin used to send all the neighborhood's unwanted kittens to "Siberia."). I saw the first evidence that morning after I brought him home, the purpling alveolar imprints on your forearm as you peeled bananas for another smoothie, while outside in the garden beyond the big kitchen window he tore up heads of boston lettuce, flinging handfuls of the leaves into the air. The next day you came down in a dark, long sleeve turtleneck and jeans, even though it was the beginning of August, hot and damp, and you wore the same the day after that, and so on, because even as the heat continued so did the pattern of abuse, which as I caught a glimpse of you one morning slipping into the master bath, had really grown chintzy, flowery motifs of red on top of magenta on top of lavender on top of terracotta on top of ochre, dappling your arms, your calves, your thighs, even your ass.

So I made inquiries, talked to colleagues—doctors know where to go. In fact, the defective spawn of physicians make-up a significant percentage of the institutional population. Not because we produce more of 'em, but because we just don't tolerate 'em. Without a healthy separation between home and work, normalcy and disease, professional distance collapses and the diagnostic faculty flounders. Soon I'd secured Viktor a bed at facility in rural Vermont (what fun he would have, grazing over the lush green grounds. With those little gray gnashers of his, he could make his own smoothies.).

Early one morning, I snuck into Dean's old room with a hypodermic full of flunitrazepam and an ether soaked sock in my levi pocket. For a few minutes I stood watching you, assessing. You were deep in the throes of NREM, wrapped from neck to ankle in a cocoon of sheet (for protection against nocturnal predations?), which hid all the bruises, excepting a fresh red circlet on your left instep. Viktor, by contrast lay splayed on his back, naked except for a disposable diaper printed with a robot boy and his robot pup. Did you know, by the way, that the word *robot* is Russian? It simply means "worker." It was obvious, however, that Viktor would never be gainfully employed though I felt a twinge of pity as I saw the fleshy sinkhole at the center of his pale little chest. Never would he be able to puff it out with pride—he'd been preemptively robbed of potential, in a prenatal, vodka fueled heist. But then his eyelids slid back a centimeter or so, revealing a narrow white strip of sclera—*Chërt!* I plunged the needle in as I stuffed the sock in his mouth, then gathering him up to my own admittedly not too proud chest, swiftly exited the room.

In well under an hour I was on 87 North. I imagined you slowly crawling out of your winding sheet, not yet fully conscious and maybe even experiencing a sense of well being as your stretching limbs met only the softness of 600-count cotton. What followed as you ran through the empty house, discovered that the Rover was missing from the garage? I know there was anger (against which, I'm sorry to say, even the strongest vodka proved an inadequate anesthetic), but was there also maybe a shot of relief? Really *lubov moya*, the situation was not sustainable. What would you have done with him as he grew bigger, stronger, as the little pincers balled up into fists powered by androgen soaked muscles (deformed chest or no, he'd be a big guy someday—my cousin had been no Olga Korbut.)? If I couldn't save you from yourself, at least I saved you from him. But then I looked in the rear view mirror. The seat belt strap held him upright, but his head slumped forward and to the left, a position that emphasized the tender flexibility of his thin neck. I thought of a wilting spear of asparagus, I thought of those lurid green smoothies, I thought of my *baba's* garden in the country. She'd been merciless to the rabbits but had always tolerated the thefts of the village *durák*, and would even occasionally give him a bowl of borscht. We are all God's children, she would say.

As I turned into the gravel drive at Halcyon Acres, he began to scream—even though he should've been out for another two hours. It took two orderlies wearing padded sleeves and heavy-duty utility gloves to pry him from the car and even then, as one man let go for a moment to gather up the restraining jacket on the seat of an awaiting wheel chair, Viktor managed to sink his teeth hard enough into the other's thigh to trigger his own release. He sprang, stumbled and fell, leapt up again and took off toward the road, empty but for a farmer chugging along on a tractor—screeching, flailing, clawing at the hay-scented air. "Holy shit!" exclaimed the uninjured orderly, as he stood there holding up the restraining jacket. The other only groaned.

File 1984/Three Revenant Compositions
(Former Sex: Male; Deceased: 13.05.1984)

(*i am so wasted 1*)

floating foam drifting
flecks upon a glassy sea
glossary of me

(*i am so wasted 2*)

her arms are wicked
her legs are long jim morrison
made up this song

(*i am so wasted 3*)

live fast die young man
my old lady said to me
then we'll fuck some more

Editor's Note: In February of 1994, in the company of a sibling of the revenant subject, the editor visited the subject's former home at 80 Kreisler Circle in Staten Island, for the purpose of arranging an estate sale (the proceeds of which went entirely to settling the debts of the subject's mother, who outlived him by ten years). Two items from the subject's room were set aside and excluded from sale: a Smith Corona electric typewriter, circa 1978, and a cellophane tape bound cardboard box stamped with the label "Jim Beam" and bearing in magic marker the words "COMPLETE OPUS OF JULIUS VAN STAAL, TO BE OPENED ONLY AFTER MY DEATH—COMPLETE INSTRUCTIONS INSIDE." And examination of the contents of the latter yielded hundreds of "high-kus" as bad or worse than the above (the promised "complete instructions," however, were missing). Fortunately, death has reduced the poet's production, considerably.

Not Okay: A True Crime Story,

by Selina Van Staal

Chapter Six

"The First Cut is the Deepest"

When a person is forced to live by her wits, she becomes very perceptive about other people. She becomes very perceptive about other people, even if it turns out there is nothing to perceive: a month went by and Fritzi's stomach stayed flat. But it could be that she had had a procedure to quote unquote let the air out. Either way, whether she had never been pregnant or had been pregnant and then deflated, you could tell the silver haired but smooth faced embryologist was hiding something. You could tell by how in the middle of a conversation, her smooth forehead would suddenly cinch. You could tell by how she would then pull a cigarette out of the pocket of her lab coat—kept there for so-called emergencies. But what was the emergency? You could tell by how she would suck hard on the now lit cigarette, drawing it down to the filter, then grinding it under her clog and shoving it through the metal flap of the trash can next to the back entrance of the clinic. Why not just stub the butt out in the sand filled receptacle on top of the can, above the flap?

Yes, the silver haired but smooth faced embryologist was hiding something. But now and then she would also reveal something. Regularly now, Fritzi and Selina met for lunch in the staff lounge or outside on the grounds of the clinic, as well as for an occasional so-called emergency cigarette at the back entrance. Selina never had one because not only is smoking bad for your lungs, it can age your skin. When Selina explained why she did not smoke, Fritzi had revealed that smoking, ironically, made her feel young again, back in her childhood home sneaking behind her stern Turkish father's back: It's like I'm inhaling teen spirit.

Another revelation was that Fritzi used cannabis. Just once in a while, she claimed. To unwind. In fact, she had just smoked the last of her stash. Did Selina have a connection? What a question! When you have no safety net or savings, quote unquote connections, or ties to illegal commerce, are unavoidable. Even if all you do is buy peaches out of season at a discount supermarket you are engaging in illegal commerce. Because how do you think they keep the produce prices down? Only the socio-economically well-connected, the fair trade-ups and trust funders, can afford not to have connections. So what kind of weed did Fritzi like and when did she want it by? As Fritzi's friend, Selina would charge only a whiff of commission.

That was how on a Sunday morning, the first of August, 2010, Selina ended up driving in the Beemer out to the house of the silver haired but smooth faced embryologist. The date sticks because the Land Rover was totaled exactly ten months earlier, on the first of November, 2009. The auto insurance company did send a check for the replacement value of the Land Rover, but the amount of the check was only thirty thousand dollars. Needless to say, by the summer of 2010, that money was all gone.

Being tired and groggy from a night of benadryl-webbed dreams, Selina was drinking a bottle of Mountain Dew purchased at a gas station. By the way, why not take Ambien or Klonopin like Timor used to take instead of over-the-counter sleep medication? They are okay, if not great, to take if you are not pregnant. Well when you are living on the edge, or close to it (a salary of $42,281.00 is nothing these days, especially if you have a lot of credit card debt), you cannot risk a tumble into the valley of the dolls. Plus, as mentioned in chapter five, there was that rebound effect.

On top of that, Fritzi Akdikmen's house, located in a maze of back roads, was hard to find. Very hard to find because the signs designating such and such a road, or such and such a way were obscured by trees and overgrown hedges, or pointed in ambiguous directions. You could not tell if you should stay on the road you were on or turn. Also, roads frequently turned into drives, lanes and circles such that, for instance, Chestnut Drive became Chestnut Circle even though there was nothing round about it. Unfortunately the accident with the Land Rover ruined Selina's GPS. Though it is true that global positioning systems sometimes fail in off the beaten track locations.

On a road that could be Fritzi's road, but also not Fritzi's road, because the weed tangled sign at the top of the hill called it a "lane," the Beemer broke down. Leaving that piece of Nazi garbage behind, Selina stumbled upon Fritzi's house purely by chance. Impossible to see from the road, or lane, because of the way the property sloped down behind a hedge of arbor vitae, the house sprang up as you turned down the driveway: a big box of cobalt blue aluminum and glass, perched in a meadow scattered with flowers like yellow spears. It was like being ambushed by bad architecture. To boot, there was no address on the black metal mailbox at the top of the driveway. So you had no idea whose ugly house had ambushed you.

The long, empty asphalt drive ended in an overgrown patch of lawn, pooled in the shadow of the house's cobalt blue façade. A white gravel path divided the lawn, leading to two black granite steps and a matte black painted door with a brass loop knocker. On each side of the door there were two tall clay pots of wilting ornamental grass. There was no house number. To the right of the steps, on a wooden post, was a For Sale sign. Selina drank some more head clearing Mountain Dew. The sugar content is obscenely high but sometimes a good complexion must be sacrificed for business. Even if you are not quite sure what that business is. What did Fritzi want, besides a little cannabis? And how would Selina ever find out what Fritzi wanted, if she could not find her house?

The glass of the large windows on either side of the door was tinted black. All you could see was your own reflection: a tall woman dressed in twenty year-old Ralph Lauren jeans and a white linen button-down, fraying at the cuffs. Dressing like old money is cheaper than dressing like new. Plus skeptical Fritzi would never buy the reiki caftan.

There was no car in the driveway and no car in the garage, because there was no garage, only an outbuilding up near the hedge that could just as well have been a tool shed.

Was anyone even home? Would they answer the door if they were? People who live in the country often do so because they want privacy. Even though the blazing blue boxhouse screamed for attention. Well all Selina wanted was an address, so that she could figure out where she was and then call a towing service that she could not afford. Was that too much to ask? Selina lifted the brass loop. When suddenly the door swung in and as the voice of a man spilled out, wailing the first cut is the deepest, the body of a woman filled the frame.

Surprise, surprise: the body was Fritzi's (as opposed to the voice, which belonged to Cat Stevens). It was dressed in cut off levis and a dingy t-shirt printed with the faded image of a red-eyed fruit fly and the message Drosophila love PLoS. How cryptic. The feet were bare, stained chlorophyll green, completing a careless but somehow techie look, a look that said science was not just a profession but a lifestyle.

Hello, Fritzi said. Did you have any trouble finding my house?

How could anyone not have trouble finding her little hideout? Although once you got there, it was the opposite of a hideout—a big buzzing blue sensory assault weapon. But Selina just shook her head. No trouble at all.

There was no point in telling Fritzi how hard it was to locate her house, that finding it had been a matter of dumb luck. You would just be setting yourself up for a fake apology: oh, I should have drawn you a map. Or for some quip about a lack of spiritual guidance. So why mention it here? Well in hindsight that is how it was with Fritzi herself: a matter of dumb luck, in the worst sense.

Inside the house it was dark. You could not see much beyond the dim forms of furniture. Mostly, there was a smell like dogs, their drool and dank fur, and the wailing of Cat Stevens which as Fritzi flitted somewhere off to the right into the shadows, ceased. A whiff of unsuspected sap (Cat Stevens, who it seemed was enjoying a comeback, going on that CD in Asani's office), and then Fritzi grasped Selina's arm and conducted her to a set of French doors paned with more black tinted glass. Two black grids that as you stepped out onto a patio gave way to bright sun and the astringency of new mown grass, a clean sharp square of landscaped green like the grounds of a corporation or hospital. In the center of the square there was a semi-circle of manicured privet. In the center of the privet sprawled a bronze abstract sculpture resembling a woman melting into an amoeba. It was a riddle wrapped in a mystery inside an enigma, as one-eyed Dean would say. Not only that, but the open ends of the circle faced the house. Any fool would understand that was bad chi—they were sucking the good energy out. But Fritzi, unfortunately, was no fool.

Fritzi motioned to a pair of canvas deck chairs with a small bare metal table between them. You can get out your stuff there, she said. That is all. She did not offer anything to drink, although a glass of iced tea or fresh cold water would have been nice. To be sure, Selina had brought a beverage with her. But even if someone is carrying their own beverage, it is still polite to offer them a drink or at least a clean glass when they come to your house. Then Fritzi stepped off the concrete onto the grass: I'm going to finish picking up these clippings.

Together with her failure to offer refreshment, that was a snub.

In business you cannot take a snub personally. When someone will not let you in the front door, Dean Van Staal always said, figure out how to get in the back. Even though Fritzi had invited Selina to her house and had opened the front door in a literal sense, she was not being friendly. Why not? Rolling a joint while watching Fritzi scoop grass clippings into a big black plastic trashcan was an opportunity to think. About the <u>for sale</u> sign, for one. Moving is ranked by mental health professionals as one of the top five life stressors. Yet Fritzi had mentioned nothing about it. And the Cat Stevens? Fritzi was a cynic and a debunker, the opposite of the soulful and sincere folksinger (for whom Timor once claimed he had been mistaken, in his youth). It was as if there were two

Fritzis—a Fritzi who was secretly moving, soulful and sincere, and a Fritzi who was not moving, soulless and insincere.

Yipping noises rose up from a dark clump of trees about the distance of a soccer field beyond the meadow that bordered the lawn. One of the two Fritzis got to her feet and, hooking her fingers in her mouth, whistled—loud and long. First silence, then double streaks of white shot out of the darkness, high speed apparitions bolting up from the yellow spear scattered meadow below, speeding over the freshly mowed grass around the privet and finally collapsing at Fritzi's feet into two hot heaving mounds of white fur, some kind of eskimo dogs that in the winter against the snow you would not be able to see at all. One had something in its mouth. Give, Fritzi said.

The dog dropped a little wooden robot, silver painted blocks strung together, slick with drool, into her hand. She held the toy for a moment, giving it a weird look, like she both wanted to keep it and throw it away. And then she tossed it into the trash. You're my good boy, she said, turning to the dog, my baby.

My baby, she said, squatting to scratch behind the animals' ears. My two babies, she said, sounding like Lyndon who would normally be the last person you would think of in relation to Fritzi. Lyndon and Fritzi were polar opposites. Yet Fritzi wrapped an arm around each dog, pulling each to her chest as if they really were her babies. Someone could make a crack about trans-species gestation and tit for tat or paps for the pups. But if you start making fun of people just because they have made fun of you, you will never grow as a person or increase your personal worth. You catch more flies with honey than with vinegar, honey, Dean Van Staal always said.

So Selina found something nice to say to Fritzi about her dogs: what nice thick fur. By the way, going on the way they were rooting in said thick fur, black lips curled back and teeth nibbling, they obviously had fleas. Besides always reading and smelling the roses, Dolores Van Staal was always bringing home pedigreed dogs. Outside of a book, a dog is man's best friend (particularly if it has papers). Inside of a dog, Dean would joke, it's too dark to read. That was a one-liner from Groucho Marx that always made Dolores groan. Still, it made a comment on a woman who had no time for her own family but all the time in the world for dumb animals that could not talk, let alone parse a sentence.

Anyways, something nice was the right thing to say, to the right person. Because it was the soulful and sincere Fritzi who answered, you could hear the itch of feeling in her voice: Thanks, they're all I have left.

When someone refers to all they have left, indirectly they are referring to what is gone. So what had been lost? If you could be sure that the right Fritzi would answer again, you could find out. But if the wrong one responded, all you would get in return would be some kind of smart remark or gibe. Better to go ahead and smoke—maybe intoxication would tease out Fritzi's mellow side.

In the meantime, the insincere and soulless Fritzi ruled. She mocked Selina's rolling skills: better not give up your day job. Then after a long hit that, by the way, drew as evenly as one of her teen spirit supplying cigarettes, she proceeded to tell a bad joke she had heard at the lab. Evidently she had noticed the almost empty green plastic bottle in Selina's hand because the joke was about Mountain Dew and a new soda named after Princess Diana. Ending with a tasteless punch line (dew or di?), the joke was a mean dig at a woman who had suffered at the hands of an older, more powerful husband.

Silent, Fritzi no longer made any effort to talk. It was as if she could not be bothered. Sitting out there on Fritzi's patio in the August sun not talking and smoking the high grade but still harsh to the throat weed supplied by Selina, it seemed like there should be something to drink other than the syrupy sweet, lukewarm and almost depleted soda also supplied by Selina. A glass of chilled white wine or even a beer sure would be nice.

Great idea. I'll go get us a couple. Fritzi got up, shielding her face with one hand. Like she was trying to hide her expression, for some reason. As the dogs stood too, she motioned with the other for them to stay. The double grid of the doors closed on her back.

Five minutes passed. Then ten. Somewhere beyond the distant clump of trees a buzz saw droned. The sun beat down and the bronze woman in the privet continued to melt into an amoeba as Selina began to sweat. The dogs had returned to rooting in their fur, probably seeking fleas, but you could not be sure without looking close, and even then, you might need a magnifying glass. Especially if you are farsighted. You cannot really be sure of anything unless you see it with your own eyes, and even then, visual evidence can be misleading. Probably that is why Princess Diana put up with Camilla for so long: being together in the tabloids did not mean they were together in real life. At the same time, there is such a thing as intuition. Sometimes you just know things about people, even if you cannot prove what you know. You can call it a business sense like Dean Van Staal had or something more new millennium sounding and marketable like chakra perception.

You knew Fritzi was hiding something, maybe even secreting something away, because otherwise why was she spending so much time inside? All that time inside, and outside in the sun Selina was sweating, especially her groin area. With the moisture trickling between your legs it can feel like you are menstruating. But if you no longer have a uterus that is no longer possible. Fritzi was not pregnant although presumably like most women she still had a uterus. Presumably Fritzi like most women still had a uterus and it was also safe to say she was hiding something. Why else was she spending so much time inside, if she was not slipping something into a drawer or a closet, or even a safe?

Selina stood up. Sweat soaked her inner thighs but the white linen shirt was long and not tucked in so you could not tell that the Ralph Lauren jeans were damp. When you are pointing out someone else's rude behavior, you do not want them noticing your crotch. Both dogs had given up rooting for fleas and were now sprawled out on the concrete, panting. Selina stepped over their hot heaving sides to the French doors.

It seemed even darker than before, after all that time out in the sun. Like walking into a cave only there was furniture, most immediately what felt like the back of a leather chair. When you walk into a dark, unfamiliar room, you should proceed with caution. You could stumble into, or onto, something. Eyes adjusting to the lack of light, Selina gripped the leather upholstered back and listened. Far off to the right there was the faint hum of an appliance, probably a refrigerator. A refrigerator, which meant Fritzi's house had one of those open floor plans designed to foster family life, a great room for great conversations, for the sharing of warm but never heated words. Like a glossy brochure from a new housing development but still it would be nice. With Timor it was always the bedroom or the kitchen. So much space, so many rooms that were never used.

The refrigerator hummed and forms materialized: another leather chair and a couch clustered around a low glass coffee table in front of a fireplace set in the left wall, a countertop island and cabinets to the far right. Over on the other side of the room were three shadowy recesses, the center one a hallway that no doubt led to the front door, the other two leading to additional rooms beyond additional pairs of French doors. Set with clear glass, they were like big windows, only inside. And then Selina heard it: a clicking noise, followed by a snap.

Click, snap. Click, snap. Click, snap.

The sound was coming though the set of French doors to the left, one of which was a few inches ajar. Slowly, Selina slipped through, holding the cool metal lever with one hand, reaching for the dark form of a table lamp with the other. Click. Light sprawled across the room. Over on the other side, in an armchair backed by bookcase shelves lined with what looked to be science text and reference books, a couple of framed photos propped against the spines, sat Fritzi. Fritzi with her hand wrapped around the handle of a knife, her cheeks gleaming wet. The curved blade winked. And then—snap. It was gone.

Gone, so that all you saw was the black grip in her hand. She raised her thin tear smeared face, looked across the room at Selina. At Selina, who was a guest in her house, who had come there in good faith, bearing premium marijuana. Who did she think she was? And <u>who</u> was she? Which of the two Fritzis was holding what looked to be a switchblade? The soulless and insincere Fritzi number one, or the soulful and sincere number two? Number one seemed like the obvious choice, the deadly debunker always searching for an opportunity to cut people down. But you could not disregard number two. The soulful and sincere types are sometimes the worst. For example, like when Cat Stevens said to kill that famous writer.

Who was sitting in the chair on the other side of the room?

Mack the Knife? Fritzi suggested. She smiled, then reaching around behind her, put the folded switchblade on the shelf of the bookcase.

You cannot just smile away a deadly weapon. Especially when you have tears on your face. Selina crossed the room. Next to Fritzi's chair stood a reading lamp. Selina turned it on, then stood over Fritzi with folded arms. In the literature, they call it "towering." Timor used to do it to Selina. It is wrong to intimidate people by standing over them and making them feel small. But so is flicking a switchblade at a guest who has come to your house in good faith. That is treachery, the opposite of good faith.

Fritzi drew her legs up on the cushion, wrapping her arms around her shins. The smile remained and could even be called winsome, what with the tears. The way you're standing over me, Selina. I used to do it to my sons.

Sons?

Yes, offspring of the male sex, as opposed to solar bodies. I had two of them.

Had? Selina backed away. Intimidating people is not only wrong, sometimes it is dangerous.

You're right. I still have them. There's no way to undo that or take it back.

What?

I mean nobody can erase my signature in their genomes. I fucking made them, fucking fucking John. They're still mine, aren't they? Even if they're with him.

Fritzi's crude and angry words indicated that she was out of control. When people are out of control they speak in a way that they would not normally speak, saying things they would not normally say or formerly have kept hidden. Fritzi was saying things she had previously kept hidden from Selina—that she had had children, with someone named John (or a John?), and now the children lived with their father. Clearly, that meant Fritzi had lost custody. Interesting.

Fritzi had just shared some of her past, and might share more. But her words had been crude and angry and the folded knife was right behind her, on the bookshelf. When you have a choice between information and personal safety, you will always pick personal safety, unless the former somehow contributes to the latter. That is instinct or self-preservation, and so what if Fritzi had lost her children. People lose their children all the time, usually because they are irresponsible or out-of-control. Like Fritzi was, right now. The doors were just a few steps away, and then, to the right, was the hallway leading to the entrance. But the front door could be locked, the bolt complicated, especially in the dark. You could just walk swiftly out the back through the patio doors and around to the front of the house and the Beemer. Though the Beemer would not start, so then you would have to run.

Suddenly Fritzi started to laugh, really laugh. Pure hoots of laughter, not a strangled mix of hilarity and rage. What was going on? Maybe it was all a big joke, that fake-out game she used to play with her little friend. Only the rule there was that you had to let the other know when a game had begun.

Pardon?

Fritzi stopped laughing, panting a little. Selina, sit down. Please. You should have seen your face. It was like watching someone watch a well-designed experiment go wrong. Or seeing a cat chasing a bird fall off of a roof. Crossing her legs, then cocking her head, she asked: Did anyone ever tell you how funny you are?

No longer out-of-control, but also not in it, Fritzi was contriving to regain control. She was trying to get on top of the situation by putting Selina down. Well, Selina not only remained standing, but also stepped closer again, to show that she was not intimidated. At the same time, Selina did not answer Fritzi's question, which anyways was not a question, but a putdown. When people are mocking you the best response is no response. If they can see that you feel stupid, then they can feel smart, in the mirror of their own mockery. You see, it is all about them.

From somewhere in the big open room beyond the French doors came a brittle, tumbling sound—probably ice falling into the dispenser in the refrigerator. Fritzi was still smiling, but only a little, her hands lying palms up in her lap as if she did not know what to do with them. On the shelf behind her, along with the knife, were the framed photos. In one you could see what appeared to be a very pregnant Fritzi, still dark-haired, standing beside a tall potted palm in what looked to be a glassed in lobby or atrium with a young man, also dark haired, who seemed vaguely familiar. They both wore white lab coats, their arms around each other's shoulders, and though the young man's face was partly shaded, they grinned matching white grins—like teammates on the winning team. In the other photo was what looked to be the same young man, though his face was now in profile and again shaded, this time by the brim of a Greek fisherman's cap, and his smooth, boyishly thin body clad only in black bathing trunks. He half lay, half sat on a beach towel, propped by his elbows as he gazed out at the sea. Timor came to mind for a moment, Timor the first time, though if the young man resembled someone, it was someone else.

I have a proposition for you, Fritzi finally said.

Once when Selina was a little girl home alone with nothing to do, a thunderclap rattled the windows. Within minutes, rain was pounding the roof. Standing with the front door open you could hear the rain, only the rain, no babies crying or mothers yelling or cars gunning in grass-cracked driveways, smell the rain, only the rain, no crockpot meals or dog crap baking in chain-linked runs, see the rain, though not only the rain, because rain is also see-through. Because rain is also see-through you could still make out the vinyl-sided ranches and split-levels, the stingy lawns, the wheelchair ramps, the petunia beds and plastic wishing wells—but nothing was the same as before. Sluiced by rain it had all changed, become swollen, both stretched and saturated, radiant and dark. You felt like you could burst. Or collapse. Burst or collapse or both unless you did something, anything, so Selina picked up an umbrella from the stand in the hall and ran barefoot out into the street, popping the canopy up into the wet.

The umbrella was red, an old one with a broken spoke that no one ever used. Still, it held up against the drum of the rain. Not only held up but cast a circle of red incandescence, bathing your arms, pooling around your feet, in a red letter moment that you wanted to go on and on, a new rubric for breathing, nevermind what that means. Nevermind.

Nevermind what that means although Selina once tried to explain to Timor. After it all became working and drinking, or drinking and work. With too much eating thrown in. After it all became about career advancement and consumption, but before it became hopeless. We can sell everything and go someplace, she had suggested. A village in Ireland. Or even the Black Forest. Eastern Europe was out of the question, because Timor once said he would never go back behind the Iron Curtain. Even though it had rusted all away.

I have to work, baby, to pay for all of this, he said, resting his hands on his swollen but never bursting or collapsing belly. Who's going to pay if I don't?

It was like he was no longer alive so Selina told him about that time in the rain, about how sometimes you just need to take a risk run out get wet fill your lungs, understand again what it is to breathe.

But you had an umbrella, he replied.

Well he was right. Selina had an umbrella. Or <u>had</u> had one. And she could get soaked. If Fritzi's scheme worked, Selina's share would last many a rainy day. No more debt, no more reiki, no more shaky commerce or back door maneuvers. All you needed was a little faith in Fritzi and dumb luck.

E12.03.11: There will be two of us and we will be graded. She will be an A. I will be a B+. I will be a B+ because on day three my eight blastomeres will be very slightly but visibly less spherical and uniform in size than hers. Also, there will be a small patch of blebbing along the inner curve of my zona pellucida. Inside, grades will not matter. I will occupy the best exit position, your cervix a firm cushion for my head, and I will receive the better part of all nutrients due to superior placental function. When I am born I will weigh almost a full kilo more than my sister. Dabbing the cheesy crud of vernix caseosa off my pink, well-oxygenated skin a young, newly-hired neonatal nurse will exclaim: "He's perfect."

But of course I will not be perfect. I will have a non life-threatening heart defect. The defect will cause a murmur. The intensity of the murmur will be low, the pitch high. The quality will be musical. I myself, however, will not be musical. The heart defect will be congenital. The lack of musical talent will be congenital as well, but I will try to compensate by learning to play the piano. I will play the piano like a bear wearing mittens. I will also look like a bear, although I will not wear mittens. From a young age I will refuse to wear mittens, as well as a coat. I will seem not to feel the cold, which anyhow will be less acute than before due to global warming. I will seem not to feel the cold, such as it will be, and you will think I have no feelings. You will think I have no feelings because I will often hibernate in my bedroom with earbuds in my ears listening to the music I cannot make rather than to you complaining about how you gave up your career to have us.

My sister, despite her embryonic excellence, will have defects as well: dyslexia and malocclusion. You will arrange for therapy for the dyslexia. She will overcome her learning disability completely, eventually achieving perfect scores on her CATs. You will write a longish piece about what a struggle it was for her, which will be published in the *New York Times' Sunday Magazine* and lead to an invitation to contribute regularly to "Motherlode." You will never become visible enough to compensate for the erasure of your academic identity, but between your freelance work and regular alimony/child support payments you will be able to pay upfront for my sister's orthodontia. Eventually, she will also have beautiful teeth and a perfect bite. You will not hear the words she hisses at me behind your back: doofus, bonehead, bozo, basket case, shrek face, disaster zone. With her sinuous body and long silky hair, she will not look anything like a bear. When she goes off to a university on the opposite coast, part of the same system but actually superior to the one in which you once taught, the two of you will skype several times a day.

I will enroll at the community college, and take a Great Codexes survey course so that you, your new younger even than the preceding boyfriend, and I will have something to talk about at dinner. You will have read only two of them. Your new YETPB, whom you will have met after a five minute facelift at the mall, as you were emerging from Sephora and he was standing handing out Heat Death Certificates for Green Peace, will have read none. While I stack the dishes in the dishwasher, you and YETPB will go out to the garden together, first to inspect the dripless watering system in the vegetable potager, and then to withdraw for sex inside the solar pagoda.

The next day, I will drop out of the community college, dutifully filling out all the necessary forms so that I can collect a refund from the Bursar's. I will now stay in my room nearly all the time, listening to Rachmaninoff and masturbating, emerging only to use the bathroom and to raid the kitchen when I know you will be out of the house. One day, just as I have begun to unbutton the fly of my parachute pants, you will walk in and yank the earbuds out of my ears. You will cut the two shrek green spheres in half. You will place the four shrek green hemispheres on the windowsill and then leave the room.

From below will come the mechanical clatter of the garage door. I will stumble over to the window with the shrek green hemispheres on the sill as your e-kart glides silently down the driveway. You will not look back at the house as you swivel the e-kart into the street and zip away. My dick will be still be hard, but I will not return to my cum scummed bed. Shoving the buds into the pocket of my parachute pants, I will leave my room, stomp bare footed down the stairs to the first floor, lift the keys from the hook by the kitchen door, and enter the dark garage.

Parked on the far side will be the old silver Audi station wagon you used to drive us to preschool, and later to therapy and lessons. There will still be orange goldfish crumbs in the crevices of the rear seats. The two tiny tv screens that face the rear seats will still be smeared with fingerprints. I will not sit in the back, however, but in the front, on the driver's side, where I will insert one of the keys I lifted from the hook in the kitchen. The heated seat will still work, warmth slowly seeping through the scuffed leather up through my thighs, my ass, the small of my back, pooling in my groin. As the heat rises up my dick will sink, my erection melting away into a mild, feckless arousal. My head will fall back into the headrest and I will close my eyes. I will sit there in the darkness, warmth lifting through me, around me, smelling the faint fruity odor of your skin firming lotion rising up from the leather. Eyes closed, my skull sinking back into the firm cushion of the headrest, hearing nothing but the hum of the motor, I will be in the best possible position.

I'd say I have too much time on my hands, if I had them. Which doesn't mean I've been jacking off. For one, I can't. For another, my new hobby is not just a hobby, but a scholarly enterprise as I boldly go where no academic has gone before, collecting cultural artifacts from the other side. Publication could be a problem, but at least I won't perish in the effort. Still, with all the hours I spend each day (even if I am not, strictly speaking, bound to diurnal existence), recording, archiving and editing, I have more than enough time to think of you. An eternity, *króshka.*

You're always on my mind, this free-floating epiphenomenon, this phantom hovercraft without a landing pad. You're always on my mind, for lack of a better term, even as you continue to pretend that I'm not on yours. So one thing I've been wondering is how a smart cookie like you could get mixed up with a sneaky *súka* like that. OK, you explain… the maze of rural byways, the ambush of postmodern architecture, the switchblade. You were addled, embattled, in fear of your life and behind on your rent. But surely your whore's sense told you the deal was Trojan, and I'm not talking about condoms.

If I could've warned you, I would've. But after the divorce proceedings, not to mention the death, I was out of it. Really out of it. What people don't know about dying is that it's not just an out of body experience but also out of mind. The mind simply *isn't* for a while. For while energy cannot be created or destroyed, it can be converted from one form to another. Imagine, Selinka, our phantom hovercraft disintegrating into fairy dust: then throw a sparkly fistful into space and watch it disperse. In other words, *one* is no longer one, as the glitter of self diffuses into *all.* And then gradually the entity, so to speak, drifts back to being, in the mental if not physical sense. I won't attempt a technical explanation of the process—I can't (I was a medical doctor, goddammit, not a particle physicist). But if it helps, consider the truism "old habits die hard." Finally, mind is just a rut (forget the hovercraft analogy) that memes stumble into. It should be noted that some of us return more completely than others. I won't pat myself on the back (I can't), but I will say you're lucky I'm not one of those half-baked *bolváns* perseverating about bloody hands, money beneath the bedroom floorboards, and tools missing from the shed. They're worse than Alzheimer's patients. You can't dump them in a nursing home—the dumb fucks will only come back to haunt to you.

Yeah, you're a lucky ducky, that I've got all my marbles (memes?). Sure, I can't keep you out of jail. I don't want to: the image of you in an orange jumpsuit, your sweet meat behind bars, is just too delicious. But maybe I can help you make sense of the whole mess—the savor of understanding is something we can both enjoy. So why did you get mixed up with Fritzi? Sure you smelled money. At the same time money doesn't smell the same on everyone, and your olfaction was more acute than most. What did money smell like on Fritzi? What did it smell like on *me*?

Let's start there, *détka*, with the hope of tracking the one scent to the other. What did money smell like on Timor Zinkovsky? Bury your nose in the engram of my armpit, in the pine-sol forest of American deodorant, and tell me you couldn't smell the piss-resined scaffolding of Brighton Beach boardwalk beneath. Not to mention the small reek of Odessa, like a rat scurrying into the dark. Be honest, you won't hurt my feelings, though there's no need to gag. You can't hurt my feelings. Like my baba said after the Fritzis (no wonder I don't like that woman) schnitzled her man and then krauted her kin (did I ever mention my mother was half German?), there's nothing left to hurt. Not that I'm trying to uncover old war crimes or put anybody on trial—what's done is done. I just want to help you so that you can help yourself, like one of those self-help books you're always reading. So fess up—admit that money never smells only like money, admit there's always something else. Even if you marry for it.

Especially if you marry for it, because nobody marries just for money, which not only isn't everything, but finally isn't anything—just a substitute for a being that it can never be. Sort of like a ghost, but let's not go there. Nobody marries just for money, because it just isn't worth it. There has to be some kind of collateral: the promissory note of limited life expectancy and/or career advancement (think of all the gals and guys, yours truly included, who've gotten a leg up on some gramps' shoulder), of a green card, of live-in medical care (who doesn't want a nurse attached to that purse?), or maybe just free maid-service.

So I know you didn't marry me *only* for my liquid assets, or even for my real estate, though I'm shit sure Bosky House cinched it. Yet if the house sealed the deal, it wasn't a deal breaker. No, there was something else you wanted. What was it? I've thought and thought, replayed the footage of our marriage again and again (stop here and take note: that was a figure of speech, not an admission to using a surveillance device), and come up with nothing. *Nishto*, my Selinka. My long pawed sphinx. In fact, if money always smells like something else, it was obvious you never liked the smell of mine. Hell, we hardly spoke about my Ukrainian roots, let alone my Brighton boardwalk rearing (pun intended)—it was as if I'd sprung, Cornell accredited and Board certified, from Irwin's forehead. An origin myth Irwin himself originated, introducing himself the first time you met as "Tim's dad," and one that you later passed on, telling your little nephews that I'd grown up in Cooperstown, New York. Yet no way were you fooled by Irwin's flimsy familial cosmogony, cutting him off as he started on some b.s. about "Zinkovsky" being a patronymic parting gift to his cherished white Russian wife who'd died in childbirth: "I have heard so many wonderful things about you, Mr. Bliss," you lisped and then swooped in to give him a kiss on the cheek. I can still see his startled leap back, as if a bat had flapped past his ear.

No way were you taken in by Irwin's wholesome fiction of my small town start as the adopted son of a literary scholar and folklorist of independent means: you knew the goods were fake even as you sold them to Andy and Wesley. And while every huckster knows that a good legend has its own worth (as the whole economy of Cooperstown rests upon the founding fib that it is the birthplace of baseball), you surely could have had the real thing. Tall blond banker Mark, for instance, born and bred in that wasp's nest called Westport Connecticut: it was obvious every time he dropped his two little larvae off for another weekend at Bosky House that he would've preferred to remain with you rather than return to convalescing Cara, laid-up by another spiral of the spirochete in the endless round of chronic Lyme. Totally obvious as the brats shot out of the luxury SUV yipping with excitement up the drive and into my house while he tried to hold you with chitchat not to mention a brotherly hug that always lasted several seconds too long. But you weren't interested in him in the least, breaking away with a backhanded wave as you power shuffled off in your Turkish slippers, a big footed concubine summoned away by the imperious cries of the two little princes who'd usurped my throne for the weekend.

Not that I ever got the royal treatment myself, at least not after the first few years. But for the princelets, no indulgence was too great. Take those overnight trips to Cooperstown, chauffeured and guided by "Uncle Tim," although no guidance was necessary: you all knew in advance exactly where you wanted to go, to what I considered Hell but you called the Hall of Fame, to Abner Doubleday Field, to the Batting Range, to Dreams Park with its mission "to Serve, Preserve, and Protect Baseball as it was meant to played" (or else. There's more than one way to swing a bat, thought the kid from Odessa), not to mention every rinky dink baseball souvenir shop full of crap at doubledah prices you could get it on-line. The monsters running ahead as you followed, bearing two big canvas totes each emblazoned with "Where Baseball Dreams Come True" and overflowing with signed balls, team endorsed gloves, hall of famer t-shirts, major league pennants and one-of-a-kind cards, round cookies frosted white with chocolate stitching and lemon sticks shaped like tiny bats—sagging a little under the weight of all those airy baseball hopes substantiated. And when the day was done there were two suites at the Otsega Hotel with views of Glimmerglass Lake (since Irwin's death, and even before, accommodations at Riverside were no longer available), booked and paid for in advance compliments of Uncle Moneybags, which might have been nice if they had stayed in their room and you in ours where a bottle of Moët grew tepid in a bucket of melting ice.

But instead, because at home the tyrants never went to bed before ten, you first had to escort them down to the golf course to tumble on the damp greens and catch bullfrogs in the cove and then, because they couldn't fall asleep without a "grown-up," to lie all three of you together in one of the two king sized beds where you'd inevitably drift off into a field of dreams that stretched out until morning. Then rise and shine at nine for the Otesaga breakfast buffet and fortified back in the car for the scenic ride back on route 20 and the mandatory stops first at the Tepee Roadside Treasure Shop for genuine Minnetonka moccasins manufactured in Belarus and then again as the hotel scrambled eggs and bagels had dissolved in youthfully efficient digestive juices at the diner in Duanesburg, for burgers and fries and quart-sized chocolate milkshakes that fast little metabolisms notwithstanding were still too much for pint-sized appetites (so that I always had to polish 'em off), but no dessert. No sirree. No dessert. It was the only thing you ever denied them, because there were always heaps of home-baked goodies back at home. Or "guzzert" as your nephews would say, even though they were no longer toddlers and perfectly capable of the correct pronunciation. Yet you'd insist your nephews weren't trying to be cute—they couldn't help it. No guzzert until we got home, but as soon as we were in the door you were off to the kitchen pulling cake or pie or whatever you'd baked before dawn the previous morning out of the refrigerator, serving up two big mounds of it. And when they'd gobbled those up, thrusting forth their empty plates for "more guzzert please," you'd give them each a pile of pastry even bigger then the last which they never finished, running after a bite or two to bounce off the oil glazed paneling of Bosky House. As for Uncle Tim, he never got so much as a thank you, let alone his own piece of the pie. Yet through it all I played the good humor man, genially smiling at your ricocheting little relatives as I enjoyed their leftovers, even joking like my *baba*, "Who put a *kopek* in you?"

The crap I put up with. The crap I put up with, which is not to say you didn't get treated like shit in court. Too bad you couldn't stick it out with me until after Cara did her dirty deed. Surely you would've had a better chance at getting custody of the boys with a fat doctor and his fat income. Further, if you had not left me, I probably would've left you, sooner or later. According to the post mortem doc, my fatal stroke, though stress-induced, was inevitable. Inevitable and until you dumped me and I had you removed as a beneficiary, your legal means (unlike murder or suicide) to my big, fat life insurance policy.

For not only could Mark's Colorado Christian sister provide a focus on the family, she could also pay for braces, ski trips and college. Silly *détka*, how could you think that without a husband or more importantly, a bank account, the court would consider *you* in *loco parentis*? Loco maybe, given your family tree, but certainly not parentis.

But to return to the subject of "guzzert," what was with the confectionary biz? You claimed that sugar didn't "agree" with you, but then even when those kids weren't around you'd be baking a kitchen full of sweet shit: plum tart and apple pan dowdy, strawberry rhubarb and blueberry crumbles, coconut and banana crème layer cakes, lemon meringue and key lime pie not to mention those lemon bars that set my heart racing the way you once did, macaroons and deep fried old fashioned donuts that turned the very air redolent with grease—I swear I could feel my fat cells swelling with each breath. And of course I did more than breathe—I ate it all. Sometimes when I came home from the hospital and found a warm fruit tart on the counter, I'd just start forking it up, stuffing myself with gobbets of filling and crust (store bought, Irwin insists. If so, you knew where to buy it.). Until finally you'd come down to greet me with the cold treat of your smile. Pie à la mode, anyone?

In spectral retrospect, I almost wonder if you married me for my body. Not to cherish it, for Lenin's sake (state mandated atheism runs deep, even after death), but to ruin it. Sure I was no longer the Best Ass on Brighton Beach when you met me, but I also wasn't a beached whale. I remember once I asked you to please lay off all the baking. All you said was "well you don't have to eat it, Ti-*More*." But I couldn't stop, anymore that I could stop wanting you, even though I knew you weren't good for me: a polysaccharide packing schemer who would give me heart trouble, for sure.

Thank Trotsky (another kid from Odessa, as well as a stand-up dude, to give credit where Gorbachev did not), that's all over. Like I've already said, without a body, you don't want no body. Which anyway is not the point: i.e., this is not about me wanting you, but about you wanting me (forget for the time being about that Fritzi).

I *know* it wasn't just for my money or my house. It had to be something else. Besides, you could have snagged both without snagging me. You would've figured out a scam: a secret photo shoot of me bare-assed on one of the office examination tables (unwittingly shaking down my own booty), or maybe some kind of Russian American roulette with you, me and Irwin (sexual preferences aside, he had a thing for you). You know, last one standing gets everything, including the house. Anyway, my point is that where there's a will there's a way: you had more than enough of the one kind to make sure you'd get the other, not to mention a property deed.

It had to be something else, but what else could there be? Dare I use the L-word? No.

I'm afraid this is just a dead-end, *détka*, like the cul-de-sac you grew up on. What did I expect, in my condition? They say that a near-death experience can lead to new insight; well after death, it's all just one big stab in the dark, with no one to stick it to. That's the worst of it, actually. Much as I'd like to see you in an eight by eight cell, orange melons pressing up against the bars like crated fruit, I'd rather you were here. Or better yet, that I was there. Funny how it worked out. A year ago, looking at that biopsy report, I would've predicted the opposite: you here, me there. Although not quite, since back then I didn't believe in an after life. By the way, *your* ashes would be on the mantel in a Chinese cloisonné vase, from the Qing Dynasty (the Ming, I'm afraid, would've been out of reach), like the trophy wife you weren't. Not in a couple of cardboard Nike shoeboxes, in the trunk of that piece of scheisse that I did *not* make you buy.

Yeah I'm still mad as hell, but since there isn't one, I'd rather be back with you. And if I was, you know what I'd like to do? Can you guess? I wouldn't want to fuck or to eat (that was bullshit, what you said about how the only rooms we ever used at Bosky House were the bedroom and the kitchen). Or even go car shopping, though even Marx knows you could use a new one; one of these days that old tank is gonna tank for good. Here goes: I'd like to find a kid, any kid except Viktor (who anyway must be at least twenty by now), too bad your little nephews didn't work out, and take him (or her) to a matinee in one of those old theaters with the marquee hanging over the sidewalk. I'm serious.

You and me and the kid—I can see us in the lobby, the two of you crouching in front of the concession case. You'd be wearing the glasses that magnified your mildly mydriatic pupils, making your eyes look bigger and blacker than ever, reading off candy names to the kid. Who would have bright curly hair like a storybook hero or a red headed stepchild though I'd never raise a hand to him or her—no sirree bob. Shit I'd even take hold of the kid's grubby paw as the two of you stood up again and stand there rocking back and forth a little on my heels like some proud papa, some flaming sire, as you ordered one Babe Ruth bar and two popcorns, one medium and one large, the first with butter and the second without. Some flaming sire who would conveniently turn squire toting an armful of detonated corn plus a supersized softdrink (indulge me) as you guided our candy bar chomping charge into the dark theater where images larger but lesser than life would already be flickering on the screen. Far lesser as we'd sit the three of us in those scratchy plush chairs, the kiddie in the middle already panting with excitement, a damp panting we wouldn't be able to hear above the blast of the previews, only sense like a couple of old cows grazing for spring clover at dusk. And if that sounds too pastoral for the kid from Odessa, well my dear old Scarsdale dad had a paneled library with heavy velvet drapes over the windows and a door that could be locked from the inside, where he used to ream me as I stood reading the leather bound spines of the complete works of Thomas Hardy. Anyway, this is my fucking fantasy—not yours.

To continue, we'd sit there, the three of us, kiddie in the middle, necks craned up at the screen, shoveling in unison from the cartons of corn, alternated with sips of carbonated syrup because this is my reverie and you'll drink whatever I say you're drinking, missy. What harmony, what bliss (though I can't quite bring myself to put Irwin in the scene, no matter how touching the image of three generations together). What joy, me and you together with that hypothetical boy, or girl, the sex doesn't matter because this isn't about that, even though you once said it was all I ever thought about. Even though our hands, when we reached behind the kid to clasp them, would both be slick with melted butter.

And that's it. Really. All I'd want, if I could get back—just some time sitting there in the dark with you. No fucking. No fighting. Just some time sitting there in the dark with you, *moya lubov.*

Oh, and the kid between us—I almost forgot the kid! Sure, why not. A full-time nanny, double for over-time—they both could've lived in the old chauffeur's apartment over the garage. And when the kid got a little older, I would've paid for a top-notch boarding school. Bendover, Buttkiss, you name it—nothing but the very best for our faraway darling who, come to think of it, might've gone to school overseas, not back in the Ukraine like Viktor, of course, though I sent yearly "tuition" checks to my aunt for ten years after he left, just to make sure they wouldn't send him back. But maybe some fine old institution in the UK or Germany where we could visit once a year, make a vacation of it, suite dreams for two in five star lodgings, champagne and chocolate strawberries as an amenity, complimentary Cuban cigars at the bar, an Audi A8 with Bluetooth and Cartesia alloy wheels (pineal gland included) at our disposal as advertised in the Hotel Adlon's Gentlemen's Agreement Package, kinder verboten.

Believe it or not, I'm a little ashamed of what I just wrote. Ashamed of leading you on like that, letting you believe I'd finally bought into this family business. Then canceling the check, so to speak. What is *wrong* with me—since when did I get so shady, my penumbral condition notwithstanding? What's with all this taunting, which I admit is just one letter away from haunting? Why do I keep trying to torture and tease you like some boy who claims he wouldn't touch a certain girl with a hundred-foot pole and yet keeps tugging on her hair? The truth is that if I had a hand, your pigtail would be in it. Then again, my sweet sow, what was *wrong* with you? Why did you marry me? Why did you marry me, if it wasn't just for money or even Bosky House? *Détka*, if you wanted kids, you should've gone with someone else.

Oh, and on the subject of kids, I am *not* responsible for "E12.03.11." I work purely in the folkloric tradition, as a collector of ghostly narratives, which very rarely derive from puerile sources (as noted by I.C. Bliss, only one ghost out of ten is the spirit of a child or youth), and when they do, are almost always devoid of psychological depth or interest. "I want my mama, whaaa whaaa whaaa..." Who gives a rat's ass? So how that embryo's whiny prophecy (which sounded more like a threat than truth to me, like "if you don't buy me that toy I'm gonna hold my breath until I turn blue") got mixed up in this is a mystery to me. Any ideas?

E08.07.11: On December 25, 2021, I will be given a palm-sized codex with a fur cover that will look like zebra skin. But not to worry, my mother will say, it is kanecaron fiber. The codex will have a little flap with a metal lock and little key to keep the lock closed. Inside, the pages will be blank and I will feel cheated—even though I will hate to read. Until my mother explains: it's a diary, a totally private place to write down your thoughts and feelings as you grow older. And then I will know that she knows. No more facespace. No more texting or tweeting. And when we have finished with the prezzis, she will hold out her hand for my foni.

Here is what I will write:

jan 1 2022
10:05am

deer zebe
gm. 2day is a nu day my rezo-lushins are

1. personaly to lose w8. shhh dont tell
2. to get better gradz
3. to have more thingz to do & not be BORD

11:51am

hey zebe
i mite go 2 the mall 2day w/nikki. but wut stinkz is that nikki all wayz wants to go to the butee sim centr at sefora & i dont care about wut i wuld look like with silvr hair, bft & no belli fat. i already kno what i wud look like skinni b/c i used to b & my boobies r big enuf. plus every thing all wayz goz on my kard

jan 2 2022
11:42 am

deer zebe
last nite nikki spent the nite this am she is b-in a BFB! she was up textn b/c she wuz BORD and tharz nuthn to do here now that i dont have a puter. then i herd her barfin in the nite & now my guess pillo smelz like cheez-its & vom-it! moms duznt care she all wayz takes out her own anger on me. uh oh, nikki cumin in b4n zebe

me and nikki maid up

jan 3 2022

deer zebe
i spent the nite at nikkis house we staid up til 3 playn V-girls. ther all lookn 4 LUV & so is nikki. im not so sure aftr what happnd with sean on fcspc. my gma has new kittns at her house but moms sez we cant get 1 b/c of the ferrets. i want a lil kittn so bad. it cld suck the end of my finger. i told nikki abt the kittns & all she cld tlk abt wuz how shed seen leo shulenberg at hole foods in albny with her mom. like it didnt matter what id sed. im glad im not on fcspc any mor but its hard u know. not all wayz but usully at leest 1 prsn will rite bck. i dont meen to hurt yer feelings zebe but its not the same
luv
mle

jan 4 2022

deer zebe
my moms is the BBITW she all wayz wants it her way. even my dad agreez. w/o a fon shes totally isol8td, he sed. it also seems a lil hippo-criticl gvn youv been ritin a blog abt her and yer life as a gr8t artst & a muther snc b4 she wuz born. its not the same moms sed. then dad sed u r never rong about anything Kyle r u? but he wont let me get a kittn ether
p.s. stayd home today. BORNG

jan 5 2022

deer zebe
2day i start back to skool. give you the info tonite

jan 10 2022

deer zebe

feb 18 2022

deer zebe
2day i got my prd i wuz so scared i wuz CMEO all the way home. i hope no 1 will find out!
luv
mle

feb 19 2022

hey zebe
i did not go to skool 2day i wuz 2 scard sum 1 will find out. i told moms and she sed sweetie its cool thers nuthing 2 be fritend abt its a little earli but totally nacheral sumtimes i cant b-leev yer my dawter. but if u don't want to go to skool 2day thats ok. just don't put yer bloody pads in the waist bin b/c the ferrets can still get them. then she went up to her la dee da stewdee-o. if she posts this on her blog i will kill her.

now heres wut really sucks Zebe. i just reel-ized after i rote that last bit that if she rites anything abt me i hav no way to find out. i cld look on the skool puters but if a tchr catchs me im fckd

feb 20 2022

deer zebe
2day it stopped and everything is ok. we have a field trip 2day to visit a working organ farm where they make cheez. Tchr Lindsay sez evry 1 will get to try it. yuk. if this is not fun dont blame me

march 9 2022

deer zebe

i am sooo srry!!! i have abundant u for a long time. i am home sik. moms thinks i am fakn but I am not. the grrls at skool are really BBs they treat me so bad. i had a fun w/end willo and sofee invited me to spend the nite i wish i had a twin 2. we played V-girls and everyone found LUV even me. then we went to sefora and the lady thought we were steeling stuff but we wernt. lots of laffs. then nikki spent the nite here. we had fun watchin 1 of dads old dvds on the fs in his stud-ee. shhh dont tell moms. the next day ther wuz sno! this is the 1st time sinc I wuz a lil grrl. dad let us take the bin tops to go sleddn in the woods and i didnt know it but nikki was tweetn in/s her hoodi the hole time abt how stupid and BORNG it wuz. she told me i should take off my vst and shrt and put sno on my boobis like princess pussy in that vid and i did it b/c i thot it wuz only me and her but then she pixd me with her foni and tweeted evry 1 WANNA LIK MY SNOCONES?

help me zebe

luv

mle

march 24 2022

deer zebe

srry i did not rite in a long time. im havn trubl keepn up with u. i joined baskt ball so i wud not be BORD & also lose w8. so ive been bz l8lee with that & also stuff from our last b-ball game. i saw the most gorgus guy thar hes luccas cuzin cooper. he lives in rensaleer his foni is 518-665-4973 hes not on fcspc and his

b-day is in may thats all i kno but i wish i culd kno him bettr. trak starts in 1 wk and im hopn my legs will get skinni
bye
mle

aprl 11 2022

deer zebe
ok heer is the deel i wuz goin out w/ this guy named a-den he is ok but then he sent evry 1 a text on the 1st day sayn he was goin out w/ sum 1 else is that stoopid or what. i startd trak but then i kwit. 2trd 2 rite any mor

jun 24 2022

deer zebe
2day is the 1st day of summr vacashun. its ben a long time i kno & i am so so srry. i wuz just reedn wut i rote 2 u b4. i cant b-leev how stoopid it sounds. how cud u stand me? pleez dont ever turn on me. proms? i proms to rite all the time & 2 rite bettr. Well a lot has changed since i last rote in u. dad is gone he moved back to hutsen to live in a loft with sum bodi who used to b his student. i dont kno if she is pretty or not. i herd him tell moms k-hook wuz nevr his seen and we nevr shud have movd. moms nevr comes dwnstrs any mor she is workn on a serees of sumthin in her la dee da stewdee-o. i askd her if i cud poz for her like i did when i was lil but she sed i no longer wrk w/ the humin figur. then the ferrets dyed they got in 2 sumthin we dont kno wut moms thinks it wuz bleech in the naybors fownten. nikki has gone to nu zeeland for the summer & any way we are not frends any mor after the SNOCONE thing. moms sez just go to the pool or sumthin mle u dont need a cell to tlk to peepl when

ther rite nxt 2 u in the water. but no way am i goin swimmin with this bod. maybe i will wach some of dads old dvds
luv
mle

jun 25 2022

deer zebe
wachd dads old dvds all day. that born guy is BORNG! tho i wunder wut it wud b like to frgt evry thing & start yr life over
luv
mle

jun 28 2022

deer zebe
went 2 dads loft in hutsen for 3 dayz. his gf is named tamsin & i still dont kno if she is pretty or not zebe. her eyez r super big frum injekshns. she warz 3 big nekrngs on her nek & she sez they dont hurt but they look like they do 2 me. dad teezes her abt them but i can tell he thinks thar sexc. he calls her nefer-teeti whtevr that meens & then he nibs on her ear. we went on a toor of olana wich was bilt 100s of yrs ago by a famuz panter. 2 of his kidz dyed wen they wer lil & now ther ghosts hawnt the plc. wen sum lady on the toor sed wut a terribl blo for him that must hav ben, tamsin laffed. but ghost chldren r the best kind she sed

jun 30 2022

zebe plse tell me wut 2 do i am so BORD i cant stand it

juli 1 2022

went 2 the playgroun 2day wher moms used to take me wen i wuz lil. at skool we lernt thats wher they used 2 berry the slaves. if i wuz a slave at leest id have sumthin 2 do. it wuz hot and i wachd the lil kidz w/ther moms. thar was 1 lil grrl w/curli brown hair like mine b4 i got it str8nd at sefora. she wuz ridn on the spaceship thingy yelling YAY im atomic betty & aWAY i go! if i wuz older may-b i cud babysit. moms used to babysit wen she wuz my age but that wuz a long time ago b4 9-11
luv
mle

juli 2 2022

deer zebe
went 2 the playgroun agen but 2day ther wuz no 1 ther at first. i sat in the shade on the spaceship for a lil while & then got up to go home. well i look ovr and theres this 2 totally qt oldr guy standin there starin at me!!! hi he sez & then we start talkin. his name is henri hawks and hes home from kollig 4 the summer. his b-day is in aug the same as mine wich meens were both leos and totally purrfect for each other. wen he askd 4 my foni & i sed i didnt have a foni he laffed thats even better u r like a girl in an old storee i just red in skool. wut storee i askd and he sed it duznt matter but can i call u loleeta? im meetin him agen 2morro zebe & i cant wait!!!
luv
loleeta

juli 3

he wuznt ther!!! w8d all day CMEO & then came home & 8 a hole lemon tart moms made 4 some party 2morro. she sed she wuz going to kill me and i sed goahed u alredy hav.

juli 4

deer zebe
just saw hh!!! he drove up to the playgroun yday but didnt stop b/c ther wer 2 many lil kidz & ther moms. i sed i wud not have cared but he sed r LUV is a prv8 thing. r LUV!!! we talked for a lil bit and then we saw sum kidz cumin. cum bck & meet me wen its dark he sed. will rite mor l8r
luv
loleeta

L8r

i LUV him so much. wen i got ther it was totally dark all the fireworks in town wer over & ther wuz no moon. jus the in-sex hummn & the air smelln like wet grass & then i felt his breth on my nek and his armz rapped arnd me like a prezzi 2 myself. he pulld me down 2 the grass & we wer just lyin ther doin lots of h & k but thats all b/c he sez im just a lil grrl and my 1st time shud be sum place nice. hes gonna take me thar soon

shhh dont tell any 1 but hes gonna cum in just 3 hours b4 moms gets up & im gonna meet him down the street so that she duznt heer his car. im so so happy & theres just 1 thing that makes me sad. i bet u alredy kno wut it is zebe. i cant bring u

& im srry. im srry but this is a fresh start & from now on every thing has to be nu

luv

loleeta

Not Okay: A True Crime Story,

by Selina Van Staal

Chapter Seven

"Rabbits Are Smarter Than People Think"

Three days after the silver haired but smooth faced embryologist made her proposition, the bank became the owner of Selina Van Staal's house. Actually, the bank had owned the house from the get go since it was the bank's money that bought it. In a sense, Selina explained to the young and spray tanned loan officer, she had never been more than a renter, a renter who sometimes had difficulty making the rent but always came up with it in the end. So why not continue as a renter, or even, during the months that rent proved scarce, as a squatter? Sure the bank owned the house but a bank, unlike a person, cannot live in a house. A bank cannot live in a house and in addition, does not need a house. But a person does. Unfortunately this argument made no impression. Jiving to her i-pod, the loan officer slid a copy of the notice of sale across her built-in desk.

When you have no place to live you turn to family. But Selina's mother and siblings were dead, her father as good as dead, last heard from in Tampa or thereabouts circa 2003, her former husband deader than dead having been released prior to his demise from all financial obligations by the misogynist state of New York. The next resource is friends if you have them. Earlier in life while attending school and working in the restaurant business there had been companions especially of the male sex who were good for a laugh and an occasional loan. If a boyfriend is a friend Selina had had more than her share. But after her marriage, contact with these companions slash boyfriends became infrequent. Of late, it had been restricted to business transactions with the few who appreciated good cannabis (one now a a graphic designer with a live-in masseuse, another a litigation attorney with an Ethiopian wife who liked to look down her long Ethiopian nose, the third an English professor who had been left with sole custody of three young children). All three lived downstate in close quarters without spare bedrooms let alone yard space for Florence to do her binkies.

So Selina had turned to the silver haired but smooth faced embryologist Fritzi Akdikmen. Well well, Fritzi had replied. Sure you can move in anytime.

Who would have thought, after the Mountain Dew business? It was for the best, now that they would be working so closely together, Fritzi said. Just don't reveal your new address to anyone at the clinic.

Selina Van Staal moved into Fritzi Akdikmen's big cobalt blue aluminum sided box on a Saturday, the seventh of August, 2010. Coincidentally, that was the anniversary of Selina's marriage to Timor, a marriage that almost happened on six occasions during the spring and summer of 1993, five times being called off or cancelled due to the illness or injury of one party or the other (Timor: hepatitis C resulting from an allergy to the sulfa drugs being used to treat a prostate infection and then broken ribs; Selina: two consecutive ectopic pregnancies, and one really terrible UTI), the sixth due to the hospitalization for a heart attack of Timor's folk historian friend Irwin Bliss, who recovered to live another year. The wedding finally took place the following summer. Irwin having recently died, along with Selina's mother, Dolores, and Selina's sister Cara being indisposed with Lyme Disease, the sole guest and witness at the Albany courthouse ceremony was Dean Van Staal. Que sera, sera, Dean said when it was time to kiss the bride. The day of August 7 was chosen spontaneously, Timor and Selina having agreed that a preset date would only tempt fate. Even still, the toilet in the master bath overflowed that night, for no apparent reason—a minor disaster that was jokingly blamed on the ghost of Irwin.

Que sera, sera. Selina's room at Fritzi Akdikmen's house was at the top of the stairs, at the opposite end of the second floor from the master bedroom. You could tell it had belonged to a child, or children. The walls were yellow, still warm with the glow of the setting sun filling the room through two big windows. Against the walls on either side were two twin beds with twin gingham checked duvets, one blue and one yellow, two twin stuffed black bears with open red mouths thick with red plush tongues propped on the pillows. On the floor there was a carpet patterned with what looked to be an aerial view of roads and houses, as if you were gazing down from a plane or a hot air balloon. On top of a bookcase filled with books, pushed up against the wall between the two beds, there was a row of toy robots. Oddly, there was a strong smell of cigarettes.

Selina asked if the room had belonged to Fritzi's sons. She did not ask if Fritzi's sons smoked. That is called making polite conversation. But of course Fritzi could not be bothered with polite conversation. Instead of answering, Fritzi pointed at Florence's cage, which Selina had set on the floor next to the end of the bed with the yellow checked duvet, under an open window, and countered with a question of her own. How did your rabbit lose its leg?

Selina did not like to think about it. At the pound they said that as long as the old superstition about the foot continued, good luck for people meant bad luck for rabbits.

There you go, Fritzi said. There's a bathroom two doors down that's all yours. I've got my own. See you in the morning. She turned around and walked out and then maybe down the stairs because it was only 8:00 at night. You could not hear creaking because Fritzi's house was new with shiny wood floors that were hard and slick. You could not hear footsteps and you would have to be careful not to slip and tumble if you descended the stairs yourself.

Selina fell back onto the bed with the yellow gingham checked duvet. The smell of smoke was in the quilt. Having finally revealed that she was the mother of two children, two children whom she never saw, Fritzi would say no more. Not even their names. How could she be so close-lipped? You would think she would be thinking about those boys all the time. It is very hard to always think about something and to never speak of it. You would think she would be thinking about those two boys all the time but then again, it could be that she was not. It could be that she had separated one part of her mind from the rest of her mind, to contain the thoughts she could not bear to think. They call this compartmentalization. You put what you cannot bear to think about in the present in a kind of mental storage unit, to revisit in a less disturbing future. Since only you have the key to your storage unit, you need to be careful not to lose it. You need to be careful not to lose your key, but this is easy to do—especially if you do not return to your unit for an extended period. Someday Fritzi might need help locating her key. If so, all she needed to do was to ask.

In the meantime maybe it was best to compartmentalize. After all, Fritzi had a lot to deal with—not just custody and real estate issues (her house had been on the market for a year!) but the logistics of the heist. A heist requires meticulous planning, to say the least. Fritzi could not afford to be distracted, even by her own children. No, Fritzi could not afford to be distracted. And neither, for that matter, could Selina. If you want a plan to succeed, you need to focus on the plan itself, not on any surrounding legal or ethical questions. It was like taking a test. If you think too much, you will fail.

If you think too much, you will fail. A great way to avoid thinking is to watch television but Fritzi did not have one. Reading will also do the trick as your mind becomes filled with the words on the page, rather than your own thoughts. Selina's mother had avoided thinking by reading, filling her mind with fantasies of other people's lives that even if they concluded with suicide as in her beloved Anna Karenina at least did not end on a dead end street on Staten Island. But Selina had not brought any books with her, and all the books in her new quarters were for children: Goodnight Moon, Ferdinand the Bull, Mike Mulligan and His Steam Shovel.

Plus reading is only a great way to avoid thinking if you do not stop to think about what you are reading. When Mike Mulligan and his steam shovel Mary Ann dig a cellar for the new town hall, they also dig their own grave. Ferdinand wants nothing but to be put out to pasture. And the end of Goodnight Moon—well what is that final "goodnight air" about if it is not about taking your last breath? If you think about what you are reading, you will often end up thinking about death, the ultimate failure. Or about lesser ones. Such as Andy and Wesley. Always Cara would say when she dropped the boys off at Bosky House for the weekend, you don't have to entertain them, they can just watch TV. Of course Selina had read to them for hours and hours. And not once was the word death mentioned.

Pulling her eyes away from the spines of the children's books, and the grim thoughts they raked up, Selina focused instead on the row of toy robots. Timor once mentioned that "robot" was the Russian word for "worker," but you could also think of them as mechanical dolls. Something of a tomboy or sporty type as a child Selina had nevertheless loved dolls, from baby dolls to barbies. One of the robots on top of the bookcase in fact looked a little like a barbie—more sleekly android less blocky in form than the others, it sat on its narrow bottom with its long molded metal legs stretched before it, pointy-toed feet jutting out over the edge. The skull was bare and the face a smiling silver mask reminiscent of the Tin Man but less expressive. Kind of like Fritzi actually. What had Fritzi been like as a mother? Why had her children been taken away from her? And how could she let that happen? It seems like you would fight to the death before you would allow it, if you had any feelings at all. If you were not a robot.

When Selina was a little girl, every night she used to tuck all her dolls in an old baby crib that had been in the garage but her mother said she could keep in her room. Because if the dolls were lying on the bare floor or even the cords of the braided rug, Selina would not be able to sleep. And although many a time she still could not sleep because her mind just would not stop thinking like a machine that will not shut down, putting the dolls to bed first helped. Putting the dolls to bed first made her mind hum like a smoothly running household appliance, rather than a brakeless vehicle racing down a mountainside, scary and out of control.

Selina stood and lifted the android doll from the bookcase. Straightening its legs, she slid it under the blue gingham duvet of the other twin bed so that all you could see, indenting the bottom edge of the white pillow, was the small smiling mask of its face no bigger than a silver dollar.

Was Fritzi downstairs? You could not tell because the hard slick floors here made no sound, not a creak unlike the floors at Selina's house that belonged to the bank or even worse, at Bosky House. The floorboards at Bosky House creaked so loud they could wake you up, even though Selina was already awake when Timor came in to take Viktor. Selina was awake that morning but her body was paralyzed, she could not move or even open her eyes. It seemed Timor had secretly administered some immobilizing drug, such as curare! Being a doctor and all, he had access to substances that ordinary people do not. It could be that was how Fritzi was when her ex took her children. Even if Fritzi, unlike Selina, was not actually paralyzed it could be she somehow felt like she was. That is what is called a psychosomatic condition, like Timor was always saying about Cara, before she lost it entirely. But that does not make the feeling any less real.

You had to feel sorry for Fritzi. At the same time it would be well to avoid her, the way she was acting. No one should have to deal with such rudeness. It would be well to avoid her but it would not be well to be trapped in a small room with nothing to do. It was way too early to turn off the light: not only would sleep elude you but negative thoughts would overtake your mind. That odd stink of cigarettes would lead to thoughts of lung cancer and inevitably, to thoughts of death.

Florence's crate wobbled. Looking down through the grill at the top you could see her pathetically flopping about on her haunches bashing against the molded plastic as she tried to scratch her right ear with her phantom limb. That decided it: poor Florence who had not been out of her crate since the morning deserved a romp in the cool sweet smelling grass. Poor Florence deserved a romp in the cool sweet smelling grass and as Selina lifted the crate by its handle, she immediately ceased to thrash about understanding that she would soon be released. Rabbits are smarter than people think.

At the bottom of the stairs (descended with care, one hand gripping the railing as the other gripped the handle to Florence's crate) it was dark, except for in the kitchen area to the right where the recessed lights in the ceiling cast a glow over the sink and countertops. A three quarters empty bottle of Bombay Sapphire along with a three quarters full bottle of cold diet gingerale stood next to the sink, the gingerale sweating down onto polished granite. On a cutting board there was one half of a fresh lime, plus several sprigs of mint. Those were the ingredients for a Ginger Rogers cocktail. Timor used to drink that cocktail with Irwin. Then they would say things they thought were over Selina's head.

On the shelf above the sink there were several tall frosted glasses etched with what looked to be old New Yorker cartoons. Selina took one down and poured two jiggers of Bombay Sapphire. Timor's favorite kind of gin. It makes me feel so Technicolor, like a Bollywood film he would say, as if he were a New Yorker cartoon. That magazine is not as smart or funny as people think it is, and gin can make you sick the next day. Still, better a little sick the next day than sleepless the night before. A big gin and diet gingerale sprigged with soothing mint could knock you out faster than a nineteen forties musical.

In the etching on the tall frosted glass a man sat slouched and smiling with a drink in his hand, as a second angry faced man pointed accusingly at the first's bulbous nose. YOU JUST THINK YOU'RE HAPPY, the caption read. Maybe so, but thinking you are happy is better than not thinking you are happy. If a jigger or two of distilled spirits can make you think your mood is good, even if you do not care for gin, then that is reason enough to drink it. And though it is best to avoid artificial sweeteners, aspartame is better than high fructose corn syrup, which in regular gingerale is 20 grams per serving.

If a jigger or two of distilled spirits can make you think your mood is good, then another jigger can make you think it is even better. Now the bottle of Bombay Sapphire was empty, but that was okay. Surely Fritzi had had her share of the bottle, which had been nearly finished, anyways. Surely she had had her share and was now out back, lolling on the grass beneath the woman turning into an amoeba, or wherever she was. Who knows it could be that she was up in bed already, lying there in a stupor. In that case you did not have to tiptoe around or worry about the sound of the ice machine because on a warm late summer night like this one where you could still feel the heat from the concrete patio wafting through the open louver window over the sink which was a waste of air conditioning, you needed plenty of ice.

When suddenly a volley of yips burst through the window screen, then Fritzi's voice overriding the noise: you boys leave that skunk alone! It sounded different than her usual voice—drunk yes but also raw in a way that seemed due not just to inebriation but to some other kind of excess. It sounded like a mother who has been screaming at her kids all day, which obviously was what those dogs had become for her, gin helping with the transformation. Whatever you might think about

Fritzi it seemed like she missed her children and if she had lots of money she could hire a topnotch attorney and get them back. She could get her children back plus no one would be hurt in a heist that would hardly even be a heist Fritzi said, but more of a storage solution. No one would be hurt and everyone's lot would be improved but in the meantime it was best to avoid each other. Picking up the Ginger Rogers cocktail with one hand and Florence's crate with other, Selina headed toward the front door.

Out on the overgrown lawn that you could also term a meadow to the right of the front door, beyond the circle of the security light that automatically turned on as you stepped through the threshold, Selina opened the door to Florence's crate. Florence hopped out then froze, her wriggling nose taking in the damp tumult of the grass the mint braced fumes of the gin and gingerale and possibly canine odors as well even though the dogs were way over on the other side of house and hopefully would stay on the other side of the house. You could tell as she crouched sniffing white fur rippling with fear that she was looking at you out of her right eye, even as her twitching nose pointed straight ahead toward the gravel walk leading up to the front door. When Viktor had been afraid he would do the same thing, look at you out of the corner of his eye only he never stopped moving. And he was just getting bigger and stronger all the time. It was not fair. That's how it is honey, Dean Van Staal used to say, meaning life. How it is. But that is not how it has to be. With the money from the heist you could go back to school for a degree if not an R.N. then some kind of alternative or holistic medicine and maybe even adopt a child a special needs or older child though not like Viktor. A child with not too special needs or even an adolescent because they are easier to get if you are single and over forty. It is never too late especially if you are willing to make compromises and keep an open mind.

It is never too late as Florence sprang forward into a twisting flip that landed her on her side. Immediately she was up again because you see the flop was just part of a leaping tumbling rolling routine with her white form going haywire in the tall dark grass like a carnival ride out of control or Wesley after he had eaten too many lemon bars or like who put a kopek in you? Who put a kopek in you whatever that meant it sounded like another language maybe from Timor like something he used to say to the kids even though he hardly ever spoke Russian or whatever they spoke where he came from in the Ukraine. Who put a kopek in you as you opened your throat and let the alcohol and melted ice slide down, as you fell back in the grass and gazed up at the clotted black of the night sky, feeling the soft scramble of Florence over your ribs, then a burrowing in the space under your armpit?

Lying in the grass on a warm summer night after a drink or two it is easy to think you are happy especially if you have something nice to think about which Selina now did because it is never too late if you are willing to make compromises and keep an open mind. And if you think you are happy who is to say that you are not? Who is to say that you are not happy if you think you are happy lying in the grass with a warm quivering bundle curled in your arm and something nice to think about because it is never too late, so happy and contented that you fall asleep? That is what must have happened because the next thing Selina knew her face and arms were wet from lightly falling rain and there was a sound like a car door slamming, then gravel beneath feet. Pulling herself up on her elbow, her bunny still nestled in the crook of her arm, she looked over toward the house. A smallish woman was walking on the path leading up to the front door.

As the woman reached the steps she hesitated for a moment, the motion activated porch light capturing her in a bright misted circle. It was Lyndon. She was wearing a thin caftan-like top, the cotton dampening and clinging to her torso. Her torso seemed to have gotten thicker. You might assume she was pregnant, if you still felt comfortable making such assumptions. Finally she stepped up to the door flanked by its two pots of wilting ornamental grass and raised the brass loop knocker. Then as if thinking better of it, she dropped the knocker and pressed the doorbell instead.

At the back of the house the dogs began to bark loudly. Then the sound faded, almost disappearing as they went inside, even as you could hear it funneling out toward the front of the house. The front door swung open and frozen in a backlit rectangle with the two barking white dogs fixed to her sides, stood Fritzi. There was a cigarette in her hand and the smoke drifted through the drizzle in the direction of Lyndon. Lyndon stepped back off the steps, waving the smoke away from her face. The dogs stepped forward.

Stay, Fritzi commanded.

I can't, but before I go I want to tell you something, Lyndon said.

Fritzi sighed: What do you want?

Lyndon raised her arms, then placed her hands on her stomach. The dogs dropped to their haunches, making a show of sniffing the pots of ornamental grass.

I'm pregnant.

Fritzi lifted her cigarette to her lips. The tip lasered for a moment and then she exhaled, turning her head so that you could see one black eyebrow of her narrow yet plastic perfect face was raised, like a derisive barbie doll. So I see. Goody for you.

Yes, Lyndon replied as she looked down at her belly her rain darkened hair sliding over her cheekbone. Then looking earnestly up at Fritzi: But goody for you, too.

Really? Fritzi's voice was too flat to call it unfriendly. But at the same time you could tell there was something there. One of the dogs crept forward, looking up at Fritzi and whining a little.

Fritzi, I don't want your children. I've never wanted your children. They don't like me and I'm afraid for my baby after what your Will did to Cindy Lou Who.

Sometimes your mind just freezes. Sometimes when your mind is suddenly filled with information you are not prepared to take in, it just freezes like a computer screen so that no further information can be processed or displayed. Such as the fact that suddenly Florence too had frozen in Selina's arms and both dogs were bounding through the grass two white bears with red mouths agape only these were not plush lined but full of sharp white teeth. Your mind just freezes but fortunately the survival instinct kicks in. Selina fell prone in the grass, protecting Florence as well as her own vital organs.

By the time Fritzi had collared the dogs and pushed them back inside the house, Lyndon was in her Volvo. Just before she slammed the car door closed, she yelled: You and I want the same thing: you want your kids back and I want you to get them back. If we work together I know we can make it happen.

I'm afraid it's too late, Fritzi murmured as she stared down at Florence. Florence was laying perfectly still, her body a damp flat parcel of fur like a toy minus its stuffing in a patch of smooshed grass. Probably Fritzi was referring to Lyndon's parting words rather than to Selina's rabbit (words that Selina herself was still processing even as she mourned Florence). But it was to Fritzi's credit that she was standing there next to Selina, rather than back in the house with her dogs. Or driving away like Lyndon. Fritzi was standing there next to Selina, and that showed solidarity, even if she was preoccupied with her personal problems. Poor Fritzi. It is hard to lose a pet but it must be even harder to lose your children. Especially to the sort of woman commonly known as a dumb bunny although bunnies are smarter than people think. And they are more resilient too, as Florence's leg suddenly twitched.

Amazing, Fritzi said. She pulled a flattened cigarette and a pack of matches from her back pocket. The rain had ceased and the match sizzled then flared as she struck it. As she exhaled, the tobacco smoke snaked around into Selina's nose. It smelled surprisingly good mingled with the damp air and the soggy leaves of mint at the bottom of Selina's glass, a mentholated counter to the gin sick in her stomach. Together they watched Florence slither sideways through the grass then drag herself back into her crate.

By the way, that was smart to throw yourself down on the ground. I'm sure that dim bitch didn't see a thing.

I'm on to you, my Sneekalinka. I know you've been reading my messages even as you do no more than glance at your laptop screen, as if at a night darkened pane. You can't pretend I don't exist (even if I don't). I know you've been reading my messages because "who put a kopek in you?" Admit that the currency of my words circulates in your mind, even after you've shut down your computer and gone to remove that obsolete Smith Corona SCM Electra 220 from its not so secret, secret hiding place (a.k.a. your sweater chest). Admit.

Or don't. Fuck if I care what rattles around in the spooky hollow of Selina Van Staal's head. Only one of these days you're gonna run out of ribbon, and then what will you do? Office Depot stopped selling those spools years ago. Maybe you can find another one on e-bay. Or you might try combing yard sale bins and flea market table displays. But eventually the last Smith Corona Electra SCM 220 ribbon spool will be gone and I'll be here waiting for you. Waiting for you to join me in my bit stream, for your murky and disjointed "memoir" to merge with a more clear-sighted perspective (lack of ocular apparatus notwithstanding), into one crystalline narrative flow.

But until then, patience. Like my *tjótka* Vera used to say to me each time Mama chased after a new *sponsora*, until finally she disappeared for good. Or more accurately, *past zakhlopni*, which in Russian means something like "shut your goddamn pie hole." As if we ever had pie—six meals out of seven were cabbage soup. But Vera fed me, and in a corner of her *krushcheby* flat I had a piss-scented mattress of my own piled with brown acrylic blankets thick and matted as mongol ponies. A mattress of my own in a corner of the kitchen while Vera and my cousins all slept together in the other room. The only person I ever shared that polyamide hide heaped mattress with was Mama, when she'd come back for a few days, her vinyl suitcase bulging with new clothes. The vinyl, cracked and split, was stamped with a red stewart plaid. The one time we visited your mother in Staten Island, just before she died, I saw one of her dogs wearing the same damn tartan but without the black duct tape patched holes. Still, the clothes inside Mama's suitcase would be mostly new—American jeans and black market lingerie that she would hand over to my aunt in return for my upkeep. Mama keeping just a few things for herself—bell bottom denims and a elastane underthing or two to package her goods for the next sugar daddy.

One morning I woke up after Mama had shared my mattress with me and found a pink lace underwire bra sprawled in the depression her body had left. In the cinderblock wall behind me there was a hole that Vera had stuffed with rags to keep the cold out. I rolled the bra up and hid it there, and when Mama returned to our mattress (the toilet was outside Vera's apartment, down the hall), her unsupported boobies wrapped in an essentially see-thru beige nylon kimono, I faked fast asleep. But my fluttering lashes gave me away. She grabbed me by the jaw, shook me and hissed methylated vodka fumes in my face: ya tebye sdyelayu yichnitsu!, which literally means "I'll make you scrambled eggs." Now maybe you're thinking she wasn't a bad mother after all, to promise her son such a nutritious breakfast. Well like the Spanish huevos, the Russian word for the ovum of the domestic fowl can mean more than one thing. But finally there was nothing she could do and later, after she hit the road (no doubt in the back of a van), and after Vera and my cousins had gone to bed, I took it out. When I was done jacking off, I examined it. On the back, sewn next to the hooks, there was a tag in Roman letters, and in the faint illumination of the kitchen window I studied them so that although I could only read Cyrillic at the time I memorized their shapes. Decades later when I picked up a similar item of yours from the floor I recognized the configuration of the letters before I comprehended them: *Maidenform*.

That is not to stuff your tits into my mother's cups, though they probably would've fit. Or to bitch about how kith and kinless you make me feel when your eyes glaze at the monitor, as if my words mean no more than the random nature scenes of your screen saver. As if what I have to say to you is less important than, say, a clothing tag in Chinese characters (which after all might provide important washing instructions). But no, the point is not to make comparisons or to complain. The mattress, the blankets, the bra (which Vera eventually found and confiscated and like some folktale fishwife, bartered for a fresh sturgeon providentially packed with roe)—what I'm trying to say is that I know abandonment from way back. From waaay back, baby—like you left me before you even met me. Meft me.

Yet I always stuck by you. Stuck by you through thick and thin because while you never gained or lost one luscious pound there were times when you really piled it on. I mean the shit I put up with. Like in Rhinebeck after your surgery—let me recount, for the record. For the record, and with the hope that a view from the other side will broaden if not correct your vision.

After your surgery: it should've been a good time for us, a healing process as they say in the low oxygen tent of American talk show teevee. A healing process that would begin with me picking you up at the Rhinebeck Women's Care Center (nothing but the best for my best girl; in the area of myomectomies and hysterectomies, they had Albany Med beat), solicitously wheeling you from your room to our car, valet parked at the entrance, and then after I'd driven you home, conclude at Bosky House: a sanatorium built for two. Tenderly I'd tend to you, fetching water and juice to wash down the pills, modestly monitoring dosages as well as your vitals, as if I was a nurse instead of a board certified physician, asking nothing but the med sour gratification of your breath as now and then, I brushed your lips. A healing process that would be a second honeymoon (two months early): out of your loss (of an organ no bigger than your fist), marital accord would be restored. Accord would be restored as the apple (though the shape more resembles a pear) of contention, or more accurately the paradise-despoiling tree that fruit could seed, had been preemptively removed. Then, still at the hospital, you got the call from Mark. Poor Cara was having another relapse and Mark had a Business Summit scheduled in London. What BS, what craptacular disregard for a valid invalid, as opposed to your lymingering sister, I raged (delivering an involuntary volley of puns and neologisms, since *you* were not the object of my wrath. Not yet.). For fuck's sake (and by the way, I wasn't expecting one for at least another five weeks, until everything was healed), you'd just gotten out of the hospital.

"Please do not use profanities," you lisped. "Andy and Wesley need me."

Like hell, I should've said. Neither you nor those organic milk and whole grain (not to mention guzzert) fed brats had any idea of privation. I could've told you about how at the age of five my ma had me waiting in line all day for the wonder of bread (drought having once again emptied the Soviet breadbasket), which in the end she traded for bootleg marlboros manufactured in Poland. Not that you would give a salad bar crouton.

Because your nephews "needed" you, I allowed Mark to dump his parental load (along with a hole foods bag of matchbox cars that must have weighed as much as a hyundai) on the front steps of Bosky House, from which I watched him drive off spitting gravel in his wake. And since you were still at the hospital, I spent the night locked in my room listening to the sounds in the hall outside—the whizzing of tiny wheels over floorboards, the thump thump of tiny metal chassis flipping over the Turkish runners on the landing before they ricocheted down the stairs.

By the time we picked you up at the Women's Care Center the next morning, after two stops for the bathroom over the course of the less than one-hour drive between Kinderhook and Rhinebeck, I was out of gas (though technically speaking, I'd filled the already half-full tank at the second convenience store). Out of gas because Andy and Wesley had totally taken it out of me. Still, I intended to wheel you from your private room out to the curb, to not only ease you into the passenger seat but to buckle you in, like the doting doctor husband I was (as the receptionist looked on from the lobby, dreaming that it was her breast that shoulder strap was skimming).

Instead you waved me away, swiveling your legs off the bed as the brats clambered together into the wheelchair. Gripping the bed rail, you stood or rather, stooped—bent like an old woman, like my *baba*, as if you were afraid that standing straight would rip the stitches, though you knew as well as I (leaving aside your "training" as a nurse, you were, after all, a doctor's wife) they wouldn't. Sure you must've been in pain, but surer still you were playing it, like an Italian footballer faking a collapse to draw a foul on an opponent. As if I didn't have your best interests in mind, as if I was not on your side (this was, after all, *before* I crossed over). Unable or unwilling to straighten up, you shuffled out of the room and slowly headed down the gray carpeted hall while your nephews raced back and forth orbiting you with the rejected chair in a series of rapidly shrinking ellipses that cinched to a circle as you reached the sliding glass exit: "Wait here Aunt Selina, I'll press the button for you." "No, let me do it for her, Wesley!"

After that, lunch: because the boys were "staawvin," a word they pronounced with an accent that could have been your mother's before secretarial school elocution lessons erased it—a linguistic vestige of Staten Island. Expecting lunch would mean some "kid friendly" corporate decorating scheme of old Coca Cola signs and Marilyn Monroe posters (cuz you know she wanted a pack of her own, but her mean husbands and producers wouldn't let her have any) and a menu of freshly nuked burgers with all the fixins, I was pleased when you suggested the pub at the Beekman Arms Hotel. A nod to our mutually mature tastes as well as my lust for their French onion soup (which even now makes me smack my spectral lips in reminiscence of melted swiss), I flattered myself. Turned out you just wanted to show the boys the antique rifles that hung over the fireplaces in each of the six first floor dining and reception rooms. As you left me in a corner of the dark beamed bar, I heard one of the brats ask if the guns had bullets in them. Why don't you check and see sonny, I felt like saying. Screwing around with firearms being a family pastime and all.

When the food arrived I was still sitting there alone, the room empty except for a single drinker at the bar and the bartender: a hatchet faced whiskey sipping oldster in a pink polo who looked a bit like Samuel Beckett (a wasted allusion, I'm sure. And in more than one sense, as the man was swaying in his chair) and the blowdried rural delivery diva attending him who was droning on about a recent midnight madness sale at Walmart: "never do it again...six deep at the register... total bedlam...I only needed four things... concealer, mascara, panty-liners, and kitty litter...so what do I do?"

Well I only needed one thing but you were off in one of the other rooms with someone else's family. And I sure wasn't going to go fetch anyone to the table like a butler or maidservant. Because even if you were there, it would be like I was not, as if it was my place at the table that was empty, the bowl of congealing onion soup an offering to some honored but long gone ancestor. Like I was ghost. My thoughts drifted back, as the bartender started talking about store security and consumer rights, to the last time we'd lunched at the Beekman Arms and heard the story of its resident spook from a woman at the next table (you were always, it seemed, making friends with someone at the next table). A cobb salad eating chatterbox who claimed she was psychic (even as she seemed completely unaware of the bits of spinach in her teeth).

Let me "refresh" your memory with her stale tale: "I heard the stomp stomp of heavy boots across the room…suddenly it was freezing cold…what looked like one of those Disney holograms sprang up…a man in eighteenth century clothing … buckled shoes breeches and a tri-corn hat… pacing back and forth to a desk where he'd pick up a letter, agitatedly read it, drop it, walk away then instantly return…" In other words, there were all the usual time-worn motifs of plodding feet and plummeting temperatures, the spiritless spirit locked in a cycle of repetitive behavior (although personal research has shown that perseveration is a pervasive if not defining trait of the revenant, so Cobb Salad gets one point here for accuracy). Remembering something Irwin once said about the ghost story being a reflection of the mortal informant's "folk attitudes" toward the spirit world, I concluded that they were also a reflection of said informants' imaginative limitations. But then what about me? Surely I could think of something better to do on an early summer Saturday afternoon than sit alone in the Beekman Arms pub like some relic of a revolution that wasn't even mine (though according to my *baba*, when the Bolsheviks rose up, the Zinkovskys laid low, stashing their potato crop in a secret cellar).

When suddenly there came a shout from the bar: "There was never anyone but you, talking to you about you!" Followed by a thunk.

His stool toppled behind him, the hatchet faced oldster emptied his wallet on the mahogany counter, raining a pile of rumpled bills. I couldn't see the denominations from where I was sitting but they must have satisfied the bartender, who after quickly stacking and counting them did not try to arrest the man's teetering progress toward the door.

"Jesus Christ," she said in my direction, "I was just trying to be friendly." Then she put two bills next to the cash register and stuffed the rest in her back pocket.

Well I wasn't going to be collared by that blowdried dollar snatcher, despite my resolve not to go searching for you. I found the three of you in the "library," a corner room lined with bookshelves filled with unreadable books (e.g. *Elbowing the Seducer* by T. Gertler. According to the dustjacket, he wants to stay young through womanizing, she wants to write a novel or be a man) and furnished with overstuffed chairs upon which no one ever sat (as evidenced by the lack of ass printz in the chintz). Nor was anyone sitting there now, as you and the boys were standing around a miniature glass-encased replica of the pub where I'd just been languishing.

"Oh I loved dollhouses when I was girl," you were saying. "I would make little furniture and then pretend I was inside, using it!"

And little Andy or Wesley, I could never tell 'em part though according to you one of them had red hair and was an inch shorter than the other, said, "Let's pretend that now!"

Why not just shoot me with that musket over the mantel, I thought. But then it gets worse. As I stepped up behind you, resting my hand on your shoulder in gentle summons, I happened to look down into the little vitrined arena. With the roof cut away, it was otherwise an exact reproduction of the room I'd just sat in, with its wood paneled walls, long L-shaped mahogany bar, fireplace complete with a rifle on the wall, dollhouse sized tables and chairs, the one in the corner to the left of the door seated with a bitsy but thick figure, his beetle-broad back to the wall, slumped over a teeny tiny bowl. What the fuck... That was exactly where I'd been sitting, the table and the place setting. I peered closer and saw the manikin crane up, eyes specks of humus in a mushroom cap visage. Then he dropped his face and I saw a pin-sized glint as his spoon dipped into the teeny tiny bowl. I closed my eyes and I must've swooned though I didn't fall, holding fast to your shoulder.

"Timor!" You turned around, irritated. "I am not a wall."

"Yeah," the boys chimed. "She's not a wall!"

Well neither was I, though there's a maxim in Russian, *kakza kamennoy stehoy*, which says I should have been: "as if behind a stone wall," is how a woman is supposed to feel with her man. On the other hand, I was busting my ass trying to be supportive.

So I let it go. "Lunch is on the table guys," I said, glancing back at the glass case as I turned toward the door. The soup bowl was gone, along with the manikin.

I chalked that vision up to a lack of sleep the night before, though in retrospect it may have been caused by a mild, localized cerebrovascular accident—a harbinger of the hemorrhagic Chernobyl on the horizon. About this I'm shit sure: there was no tiny Timor slurping soup in glassed off isolation. In the spectral state it's easy to cut through all the paranormal crap, to separate the pixies from the qbits, the impossible from the merely unperceivable. At the same time, I coulda paid more attention: just because hallucinations are internal psychic events does not mean they are irrelevant to interpersonal experience. Rasputin saw the bullets coming and I shoulda heeded that phantasmagoric tip-off to my fate. And I shoulda taken you with me—in one of those marital murder-suicides. There were six guns on the walls, for Chekov's sake, and if they weren't gonna be fired, why were they hanging there?

Coulda, shoulda. If I'd recognized my future sealed in that glass vitrine, would I have ended things there? Maybe in another place, another life. If the kid had remained on the streets of Odessa or even Brighton Beach. But here we were in pretty Rhinebeck with storefronts bedizened with wire baskets of peat moss nested pansies and pleasant portly Dr. Zinkovsky at the beck and call of his leggy wife. Self bound by convention (medical school followed by a thriving practice will do that to you) as well as alliteration, no way could I have shot your fucking head off and then my own.

So after lunch we went to A.L. Stickles Department Store. Again following your suggestion, and this time I had no illusions that the excursion was for me. The place hadn't changed since my Rhinebeck cockpit days twenty years back when I'd stopped in to pick up a pack of razor blades (which I hadn't found). The fecal green walls, the dropped ceiling with its discolored fiberboard tiles disguising whatever deficiencies existed in the plenum above, the peridontal disease red and presumably once white but now yellowed checkered linoleum floor, the long pine tables with two tiers of shelves displaying merchandise in an arrangement that appeared to be the handiwork of a brain with zero executive function—little glass vials of clear nail polish strewn with a candy selection of lemon heads, boston baked beans and cellophane wrapped twizzlers (should you decide to shellac rather than eat your candy), toothpaste with tinned cat food (no more stinky feline breath), packages of sewing needles with plastic bottles and wands for blowing soap bubbles (so you could burst your own, preempting sudsy despoilers), cheap plastic baby dolls with composition notebooks (because these days, everyone is writing her memoir)—and in the back a row of wooden dispensers to buy contact paper in various perky prints, I guessed to line shelves and kitchen drawers like my *baba* used to do, but do any women do that anymore, especially here in America, I think not: A.L. Stickles Department store, that stingy, dingy, senile perversion of Capitalist choice, depressed me then and it depressed me now. "Now" being the time of the incident I'm recounting. No longer possessing a body, I've become indifferent to consumer issues.

But you were just thrilled. Sucking in the stale fumes of unbrisk commerce (the expiration date on those lemonheads was long past), you said, "I love the smell of this place! It reminds me of the Woolworths I used to go to when I was young. Paper, glue, shoe polish…"

"What's shoe polish?" one of the boys asked. Given the little perforated orange plastic clogs on his feet, it was not a bad question. I don't know about you, but I haven't seen leather on a kid's feet in years.

The other, maybe it was the taller one without the red hair, was looking around with an expression like he was trying not to cry. On the way over, you'd told them they could pick out a toy. "Is this a real store?" he asked.

Well that was rich. Because it wasn't. Even your little nephews could recognize that the place was a poor substitute for a genuine emporium, like Target or Walmart, not to mention their beloved (More) Toys (fo)R Us (where Uncle Moneybags had been dragged on a torturous trip or two). A *real* store is pristine with printless sliding glass doors and gleaming white floors polished early every morning by people with brown skin. A *real* store has aisles with merchandise organized according to consumer size (so that the toddler toys are toddler height), gender (I'd noticed how the boys avoided the pink and lavender strip like the plague), and activity levels (including the board game burbs), along with signs at the end of the aisles so that even if you can't read you know that someone who can read has thought about you and your needs, not to mention your temporal convenience. A real store looks new and systematized—otherwise what's the difference between the shit on the shelves there and the crap in the toybox at home, minus a few grams of plastic packaging.

"Of course it is a real store!" you replied bending to give him a little hug. Then like a game show hostess you turned to the shelves, motioning expansively: "a real store filled with real bargains!" Plucking a moon colored Frisbee out of a pile of khaki sun visors you said: "Look at this. How much do you want to bet it glows in the dark?" Then turning it over to look at the tiny tag on the underside: "Only one dollar! That is *so* cheap!"

You began circling one of the tables, no more stooping I noticed, except when you bent to rifle through the merchandise. The boys followed suit, while I stood over by the door gazing out at the strolling, bag toting Rhinebeck shoppers whose dollars, going by the various designer logos on their bags, were being distributed everywhere but at A.L. Stickles. Not only were we the only customers in the place, but I'd yet to see a proprietor or sales clerk. Come to think of it, that had been the case that time twenty years ago. If I'd ever found those razor blades, it seemed I could've easily swiped them. Maybe that was how they deterred people from shoplifting: if you couldn't find what you were looking for, how could you possibly steal it? For at least forty five minutes that I'll never get back (even as eternity lies at my fingertips), the three of you rooted around in that jumbled sale, your nephews coming over and poking me every now and then with some new treasure ("Look at this, Uncle Tim. It's called a 'Grabber' and you can use it to grab things!").

But at the end of it all, the only purchase was the moon-colored Frisbee. At which point a sales clerk magically appeared. Had he noiselessly dropped through the dropped ceiling, although all tiles appeared intact? Pulling a dollar from your purse, you handed it to him, and then when he said "that's plus eight point one two five cents tax, Ma'm, four per cent for the state of New York and four point one two five per cent for Dutchess County, but you can just give me eight cents" you rooted around for change. You found it just as I was about to search my own pockets. Would things have turned out differently with a little preemptive digging?

As the three of you swept past me through the jingling door out onto the sidewalk, I felt a hand clamp my shoulder: "Please step back inside with me, Sir."

Three matchbox cars in each front pocket, plus two two-inch super hero figures (Spiderman and Captain America) in each back pocket, all bulked up with cardboard and plastic packaging: after I had emptied it all out at the request of the clerk, who looked to be about nineteen years old, we stood solemnly regarding my "theft." How could I not have felt all those toys in my trousers? Was it that you'd so unmanned me that I could no longer feel anything below the waist?

I explained that my nephews must have slipped the toys in my pockets when I wasn't looking.

The kid regarded me, stroking an invisible goatee. "I don't understand it, Sir. It's always the ones who look like they can afford to pay. I sure would hate to call the police."

One hundred dollars poorer (having shelled out fourteen dollars plus one dollar and fourteen cents tax for the toys, along with an eighty four dollar and eighty six cent "shoplifter's surcharge"), I found the three of you on the side street where I'd parked the Rover, sitting in front of somebody's house on somebody's patch of grass. Fanning yourself with the moon-colored frisbee (though it really wasn't hot at all), you looked up: "you forgot the toys."

Of course you know exactly what you said, as well as did. Forget what I said earlier about the "record" or broadening your vision. I only repeat it all here because I still can't believe it myself. The details—the wheelchair, the blow-dried bartender, the French onion soup, the T. Gertler novel, the drop ceilings, your outrageous remark—are for me, to provide what otherwise would seem like a total fiction with the cheesy texture of truth. Details, details—now that I've become so sketchy, I need them more than ever. You see, *détka*, without a body "I have only words to play with." Now there's a spirit I would really love to catch, but all I ever get are your dead relatives and suicidal zygotes.

And by the way, I did not "forget" the toys—I recycled them. In the alley behind A.L. Stickles there was a bin for glass and plastics.

File 2011/Electronic Copy of Revenant Composition, "The Ghost Writer," in Word DOCX (Former Sex: Female; Deceased: circa 2011)

The word "ghost" derives from the Anglo-Saxon *gast*, for breath or spirit. So to "give up the ghost" is to die. At the same time, in being relinquished by the body, the ghost escapes the confines of mortality: it lives on. The ghost "lives on" because, as Theodor Adorno writes, "it runs counter to consciousness to conceive of death as absolute nothingness; absolute nothingness cannot be thought."[1] Then again, the survival of the ghost

[1] "The Theory of Ghosts," *Dialectic of Enlightenment: Philosophical Fragments*. Trans. Edmund Jephcott (Stanford: Stanford University Press, 2002).

requires a certain commitment on the part of consciousness: the commitment to conceive of death. Truthfully, I do not have to think about death. I do not have to think about death, and in the face of more pressing matters, it seems I don't have the time. To genuinely die, first I need to insure that I am alive, a proposition that, these days, is not as easy as breathing. As the poet Kenneth Goldsmith has put it, "if you don't exist on the internet, you don't exist."[2]

To *not* have a presence on-line, to not be locatable by any search engine, is a kind of non-existence in the contemporary world. At the same time, the fact that your name can be pulled up on google does not necessarily rescue you from oblivion. Recently I did a search on an old friend—a person who as a child and young adult had seemed singularly alive. The sort of person everyone remembers years later and asks about: "What became of X?" "Do you ever hear from Y?" Restless yet acutely observant, both impressionable and vividly expressive—my friend was constantly taking it all in and constantly spewing it all back out, making wonderful "stuff"[3] when she wasn't making scenes.[4] In her early twenties she dropped out of FIT[5] to marry

---

[2] http://epc.buffalo.edu/authors/goldsmith/if_it_doesnt_exist.html

[3] On my twelfth birthday, after sitting in my room one day leafing through a copy of *Alice Through the Looking Glass* (with the original illustrations by John Tenniel. It was part of a two volume set that had been a present from my rich grandfather), she presented me with a shoebox decorated on the lid with a hand painted wooden carrot on the top. Inside, nestled in a lining of faux fur, was a cloth rabbit in a hounds tooth suit, cleverly cut from old scraps, if sloppily stitched. The expression on his face, drawn with ball point, resembled my own in my last school photo, an expression I'd considered sophisticated but which my mother called "cynical."

[4] In keeping with the nature of the artist or poet. As Wordsworth writes in

a French investment banker twelve years her senior. An act that one could say immediately weakened her professional prospects but strengthened her economic ones. And since money creates choice, an act that would in turn ultimately increase her opportunities for self-expression; i.e., instead of having to earn a living she would be able to focus on her art. However, she then spent the next two decades submerged in domestic service (as housekeeper, babymaker, nanny and driver all rolled into one) to the French Investment Banker, while simultaneously renovating and redecorating various upscale properties in New York City and environs, which were then sold, the FIB banking the profits. That is, she was not only a fulltime housewife, but a quasi-professional houseflipper (often of the very abode in which they were currently living), hustling on the side for the appreciation of the market (not to mention the FIB). In return for her labors, she was allowed unlimited shopping sprees at high-end Manhattan stores and provided with tuition for the

---

the Preface to *Lyrical Ballads*, the poet is one who "is endued with a more lively sensibility, more enthusiasm and tenderness...than are supposed to be common among mankind...who rejoices more than other[s]... in the spirit of life that is in him; delighting to contemplate similar volitions and passions as manifested in the goings-on of the Universe, and habitually impelled to create them where he does not find them."

[5] I.e. Fashion Institute of Technology, which my friend chose to attend rather than art school. This choice was no doubt a concession to the values of her upwardly mobile middle class family, whose members all went to graduate or professional school to become doctors, lawyers, academics or social workers, and collectively regarded my friend as "too intense" and "borderline" (as defined in the DSM). While my friend did not finish her degree at FIT, she acquired knowledge and skills valuable for her marriage to a successful businessman, including a refinement of her innate feeling for color and an understanding of the properties and potentials of fine fabrics

occasional studio art class.[6] In August of 2007, she freaked.[7] She cleaned out their joint checking account and kids in tow,

---

Effortlessly, she could achieve a couture look, not just for herself, but for her surroundings, which she dressed to impress her husband's clients and associates (new money and old), with silk damask window treatments and one of a kind pillows she sewed by hand from three hundred dollar a yard remnants purchased for "pennies" from old FIT contacts (because rich men do so admire thrift in their women, a quality that excites them nearly as much as an aptitude for slutty behavior in bed). Indeed, with her design training, she was able to superficially transform a house or apartment to the degree that the selling price far exceeded the buying price, providing profits that went beyond even the expected gains of the real estate market in the early years of the new millennium.

According to my friend, the profits from these deals went into an account that was supposed to provide for her husband's early retirement while she devoted herself (once the children were grown) to making "real art"—sculptures and paintings. Instead, the money funded their divorce and its aftermath, as the real estate bubble collapsed and her investment banker ex lost his job. You could say that my friend put her talents into what seemed to be a low risk investment—the solidity of real estate, marriage, family—but turned out to be a bundle of overleveraged securities.

[6] In the late 1980s/early 1990s, when I was still in graduate school, I would not have believed in a fictional character based on my friend (with whom I'd lost touch. We didn't reconnect until 2007, when she wrote to congratulate me on the birth of my sons). Did not believe, in fact. For instance, my chief criticism of the stories of a talented writing workshop peer was that her young and bored if not battered, bartering sex for baubles, housewife characters were Marilyn French relics, Doris Lessing dodos, female eunuchs of yesteryear. Back then it seemed implausible to me that any intelligent American woman, post 1980, would choose to be a housewife. We (my generation) had, after all, seen our mothers leave (or be left by) our fathers, then rely on loans from their parents to go back to school for a teaching degree or a masters in social work, or to start a sewing supply or yarn shop,

fled the 8,000-square-foot Greenwich tudorosity recently purchased by her husband after a transfer out of the Manhattan office. Back on the Upper East side, my friend and her two sons found refuge in a 800-square-foot condo just blocks from the park, a property she'd convinced the FIB to buy several years earlier as a potential flip. She then re-enrolled the children in their former schools and rented a tiny studio space nearby to sculpt in, banking on the banker (who subsequently lost his job),

---

while nobly resisting the urgings of their male attorneys to sue for alimony. We (here in the specific sense of my mother, three sisters and I) lived, after my mother left my father and returned to school, on "child support." The taste and texture of the casserole (only 25 cents a serving, according to *Family Circle*) my mother would assemble from six slices of stale Roman meal bread, six eggs and six slices of discounted American cheese for an early dinner, before she left for class, is still in my mouth: the tough brown bubbled skin of processed casein and whey like some kind of A & P proudflesh, the wheaty albumen laced mush beneath. Who would voluntarily relive her mother's married subjugation and subsequent abject "liberation" (my own mother, despite completing a master's degree and getting a good job with New York State benefits, only recovered the material security and comfort of her former life with my father, by remarrying)? I chalked up my writing workshop peer's dated tales to her Old World upbringing, to an antiquated notion of femininity inherited from her White Russian émigré mother (who was straight out of a novel by Irene Nemirovsky).

For a long time I believed that the American middle class (another fiction I used to believe in) woman could pursue a career *and* have a family, without marrying in bad faith or making shady sexual deals (although according to the latest scientific research, it's natural to be attracted to the bucks who can make bucks). Look at *Murphy Brown*. Never mind that personally I was only focused on the career, or more precisely, on the activity that would hopefully lead to a career (a "career" as an academic was never in and of itself a goal): writing. I didn't start thinking about having a baby until after I finished my first novel (in my early forties), having willfully

as well as the mariolatry of the eighty-year old, Italian-American Connecticut family court judge: i.e. she assumed she would receive a hefty settlement as well as full custody.[8] Instead, over the course of a two-year court battle, she lost the children, the condo, the studio, the social and professional contacts she had

---

ignored for years the statistics regarding reproductive fertility after age 35, like a creationist pooh poohing the evidence of carbon dating. I was sure I was fertile, going on the abortion I'd had at age 26 (a procedure which at the time I believed meant nothing, even as afterward I found myself inexplicably sobbing in the curtained recovery room).

Murphy Brown is long gone, and the networks are cluttered with Housewives, all of them desperate, whether explicitly so or not, with their masks of cosmetics and maxed out credit cards. And all sadly plausible, whether fictional or "real." Unlike a story I read recently in the newspaper by a woman in Brooklyn who raises her own chickens and grows vegetables in the amended chalk soil behind her house to feed her family, while at the same time serving as the "sole breadwinner" via freelance writing. By going "back to the land," she claimed she was able to provide her family with a "Waldenesque life" for less than a $100.00 a week, all year long. All it takes, she wrote, is "grit" and hard work. The writer didn't mention anything about canning, or a greenhouse, or a storage cellar for root vegetables, which made me wonder how she sustained Walden during the winter months. I also wondered how she afforded a place big enough for a family of four, along with a yard, in Brooklyn.

[7] My friend told me that the turning point was her discovery of a secret compartment in the FIB's briefcase stuffed with vials of oxycontin, dilaudid, percocet, librium, valium, xanax, klonopin, adderall, ritalin and fioricet along with a gram of marijuana in a small ziploc pouch labeled "trainwreck." A case perhaps of the pot calling the kettle black, as my friend also had her own pharmaceutical stash: the drugs prescribed over the years by various uptown doctors for myriad neurological and immunological symptoms that never coalesced into a definitive condition (e.g., first my friend was told she had lupus, then multiple sclerosis, then lingering damage from Lyme

made in the upper east side arts community, and for a while, her sanity.[9]

When I did an online search on my friend, I expected to find at least an old news item about her participation in an art show fundraising gala hosted by a famous shoe designer, an event she had mentioned a couple of years before. Zilch. What I did finally locate was a record for a real estate transaction on manhattan.blockshopper.com, with my friend (under her married name) and her ex-husband listed as the sellers. That condo has long since been sold and the life that was lived there with

---

disease most likely contracted the first time her husband sent her and the children off to live in Connecticut because he'd wanted to imagine them, as he worked late or drank at downtown hotel bars, "cozy as kittens" in their New Canaan beds).

[8] Rather than viewing my friend as a Madonna, the judge apparently viewed her as a species of "Trophy Wife," defined by www.Askmen.com as "The (rarely first) wife of an affluent (often older) man who is (often younger and) exceptionally (more) attractive (than he is). Prevailing synonyms include: gold digger, socialite, shopaholic, secret envy of countless women, and object of feminist scorn." Having determined, on the basis of the evaluation of the court appointed psychologist (i.e. not a psychiatrist), that my friend was mentally unfit to care for her children, he went on to observe that she was still "young and healthy" and to recommend that she "get a job."

[9] A loss perhaps precipitated by the ego depletion that results from decision fatigue. According to researchers, making choices takes a mental toll. And it does not matter whether you are a judge deciding whether or not a prisoner will receive parole (or a parent will receive custody of his/her children) or you are a bride-to-be selecting between china patterns: the resulting exhaustion is clinically the same. www.nytimes.com/2011/08/21/magazine/do-you-suffer-from-decision-fatigue.html?emc=eta1. One wonders why this would be so: why trivial decisions would be as psychically crushing as important ones. Maybe demoralization adds an extra weight. Imagine being in

two children, a slobbering havanese, and an art studio a few blocks away is no more. Just because you can be "searched" doesn't mean that anyone will find "you." Suddenly needing reassurance regarding my own digital substance, I googled myself. Near the bottom of the page, below the listings related to my professional life and accomplishments, I found one referring to an "Elisabeth Sheffield" from "upstate New York" (an autobiographical fact featured on the back of my first novel), a character in a novel by Tracy Ma, a Deerfield Academy student, about her prep school experience. Published in 2005, it came out two years after my book. Perhaps *Ma* had seen the name and info on a book jacket, perhaps not. At any rate, at that moment I "felt," as never before, the "death of the author" (and perhaps the birth of the scriptor, who as Roland Barthes writes, comes "simultaneously with the text, [who] is in no way equipped with a being preceding or exceeding the text," though the birth was not necessarily "mine").

If it is true that you don't exist unless you're on the internet, it is also true that if you're on the internet, you don't exist: the internet is the ether in which subjectivity exists as trace. The name is emptied out of life, and becomes the marker for a bundle of data, harvested and sold by the corporate collectors of consumer spending records and preferences. And "you" can't even properly "die," as demonstrated in a 2011 suit against Facebook filed by an Austrian law student, after he discovered the corporation had been keeping information he'd removed from his Facebook page. The student had put in a request at Facebook's corporate headquarters in Ireland for a list of the personal data the company had collected on him through his account, which he set up in 2008. He received a 1,224 page PDF file including not only data he had deleted, but also data he himself had never typed in but which Facebook had generated based on his entries. The file held revoked as well as never proffered information such as the student's physical location in Austria, and his time as an exchange student at a university in Southern California. And although his accusation could not be substantiated by the PDF, the student also claimed that the corporation was keeping a biometrical file of his face, in order to identify him with its photo tagging feature. Suits such as the one filed by the Austrian law student against Facebook have led to proposals to strengthen European privacy laws, including the "right to be forgotten."

But the "right to be forgotten" of *whom*? The right of a soon to be outdated collection of postings, pokes, tags, links, friend requests and rejections, invitations, deleted e-mails and discarded user names—the digital equivalent of charnel house scraps? And what does the right to be forgotten mean when even remembrance has become an empty gesture? After the Twin Towers fell, Anheuser Busch "honored" the victims with a 2001 commercial featuring the famous Budweiser Clydesdales, that was to be aired only once (though not only can *you* replay it on You Tube, ad[vertising] infinitum, but a "commemorative revision" was released on the tenth anniversary of 9/11). The commercial begins on a wintery dawn, at a farm somewhere upstate, and follows the solemn clopping of the Clydesdales along an empty highway (do they take the New York State Thruway or the Taconic Parkway?), over the bridge into Manhattan. Finally the horses come to a halt, facing the altered skyline, dark eyes glistening, nostrils steaming, great, white shrouded hoofs planted on a snow frosted lawn. And then, in unison, they bow. Viewers have described the animals as "beautiful and noble," their synchronized dip as a "tribute." Too bad the equine star of the 1950s sitcom, *Mr. Ed*, had kicked the bucket decades before: he could have given a speech.

According to Adorno, "the busy cult of the deceased [as evidenced perhaps by the ongoing buzz of controversy surrounding the memorial at Ground Zero, a project which still remains under construction ten years after the fact] or, inversely, the forgetting rationalized as tact, are the modern counterpart to the belief in ghosts."[10] The genuine remembrance of the dead, as opposed to active entombment or polite avoidance, requires an awareness of our own impending deaths. "Only when the horror of annihilation is raised fully into consciousness are we placed in the proper relationship to the dead: that of unity, since we, like them, are victims of the same conditions and of the same disappointed hope"(Adorno, 178). But how is such awareness to be achieved? People speak of the "life-altering" effect of a brush with death, felt as they hung suspended by their seatbelts in an overturned car or sat in the doctor's office and learned the suspected tumor in their lung was merely a fungal infection. But I wonder if such encounters only encourage our existential attachment to what we already know (what better time than now, to take out a reverse mortgage?). And what do we already *know*, anyway? Back in 1993, in an essay about the relationship between television and contemporary American culture and literature,[11] David Foster Wallace wrote that interactive television (a precursor of sorts to the interactive, multiplayer online games that millions of people world wide now spend significant portions of their lives playing, such as *World of Warcraft* and *Second Life*)[12] was no better than the old-fashioned, passive kind.

---

the position of the bride-to-be for years after the wedding, faced daily with paint chips, fabric samples and fixture choices, if not china patterns.

10 "The Theory of Ghosts," 178

11 "E Unibus Plurum: Television and U.S. Fiction, in *A Supposedly Fun*

Interactive viewers, in their manipulation of images, were still manipulating only "facsimiles of experience." In other words, they were still hooked "on image-technology," on a medium that let them escape "from the limits of genuine experience." That criticism feels somewhat hypocritical on Wallace's part, in the context of his own escape, sixteen years after he wrote the phrase "genuine experience," through suicide. Then again, given a world where people spend more time on Facebook than in face-to-face conversations with friends and family, a world that perhaps feels increasingly flat and thin (on *Second Life*, you can shop for "textures," should you feel dissatisfied with the slick look of your clothes and furnishings), death might have felt like the more authentic option.

Only it is not. I think we live in a time when we can't properly live and we can't properly die. Which is maybe why zombies and vampires are more popular in contemporary fiction and film than ghosts. Ghosts, though we speak of them as "living on," really must leave the body behind—that instrument that allows us to sensually experience and materially alter reality. Zombies and vampires, on the other hand, can still move about like you and I, partaking in human pleasures and vices, albeit in a

---

Thing I'll Never Do Again (New York: Little, Brown and Company, 1997).

[12] According to researchers, to a 2008 Nielsen report on PC and console game usage, in the US alone there were of 675,713 male players and 428,621 female players of *World of Warcraft*. Interestingly, the high number of female players (about 40 per cent) counters a historically male demographic. In the early days of video gaming, 14 per cent or fewer of players were female. Some feminist scholars see the fact that increasing numbers of women would rather spend their leisure time shooting orcs than shopping (even on-line) or getting pedicures as a positive development, as an escape from the bonds of the body and domestic subjugation—from what

restricted form (hard to get fat on a diet of blood, I bet). It's not incidental that the zombie movie classic, *Dawn of the Dead*, is set in the confines of a shopping mall.

After losing custody of her children, my childhood friend, the former shopaholic, quasi-professional house-flipper and amateur sculptur, left Manhattan and went to live in the family summerhouse in upstate New York (a property which after the crash has proved impossible to sell), on twenty rolling, wind-swept acres good only for growing onions or maybe raising draft horses. The first winter, she was numb with shock. She doesn't read a lot, the television reception was poor, and she'd given up her computer and cell phone, in the belief that her ex-husband was cyber stalking her. [13] But there were windows all around which together with the natural light shelf provided by the snow

---

Simone de Beauvoir termed "immanence" (as opposed to masculine "transcendence"). And to be sure, with the aid of an avatar, not only can women ditch their female bodies, they can even play as men.

[13] According to my friend, her husband hacked into her e-mail account and posing as her, sent various strange sounding e-mails to her attorney, the court appointed psychiatrist, and to her friends and family. He would also tamper with messages before her very eyes, making them shudder on the screen and disappear, then appear again moments later. Further, he impersonated her on their jointly held accounts, depositing a check from a former patron that was in her name and had been sent to the tudorosity, then withdrawing the money and pocketing it. Lastly, she claimed, he hijacked not only her iPhone, using it as a tracking device, to keep tabs on her activities and whereabouts, but the subsequent cheap cell phones she purchased to evade him, until finally she threw away all her mobiles (at one point she had at least five), keeping only a single landline with an unlisted number.

When my friend appealed to law enforcement officials, she initially received assurances that an investigation would follow. But it never did. Her

outside diffused the interior of her house with soft luminescence and each afternoon she'd go out in a pair of knee-high rubber boots and push through drifts until her legs ached and

---

siblings dismissed her as a lunatic, revising their DSM diagnosis from BPD to BPDPT (Borderline Personality Disorder with Paranoiac Tendencies).

I'm not so sure. On the one hand, I do think that my friend was, for a time, out of her mind. Those strange sounding e-mails to family, friends and legal professionals could very well have been hers. Or in the case of the shuddering, disappearing messages, there could have been a software glitch, which my friend in her relative technical naiveté attributed to her ex-husband's remote interference. As one computer expert has written, "a great many people are daunted by the power and complexity of computers and are deathly afraid of them...Paranoia is an integral part of the role computers play in society today"(www.rinkworks.com/stupid/cs_paranoia.shtml).

Or maybe my friend's conviction that her ex-husband was cyber stalking her was a subconscious act of self-preservation. Not from her ex, but from the soul-sucking distractions of her computer and smart phone. In those last desperate months before she lost the custody battle for the children, she was constantly receiving or tapping out e-mails and texts, from and to her attorney, the GAL, the children's psychiatrist, her own psychiatrist, the children's teachers, court appointed social workers, her skeptical and increasingly unsupportive family members: there was not a moment in the day that her attention wasn't fractured. Later she told me that during the last 18 months before she lost the children, she did not have, let alone execute, a single idea for a painting or sculpture. Only after she "unwired" herself did the creative thoughts come creeping back, like wild animals re-inhabiting an abandoned development.

Then again, it's not impossible that my friend's ex-husband hacked into her computer from afar. According to a news article at www.fbi.gov/losangeles/press-releases from September of 2011, a man in Santa Ana, California used malware to hack into a teenage girl's personal computer, which gave him control over the victim's webcam and allowed him to

beneath her parka, her t-shirt was wet with sweat. In February, she moved all the furniture out of the dining room down into the basement, spread the floor with canvas tarps, and started sculpting. In late March of 2009, I flew back east to visit her. When she opened the door, I smelled clay.

Denver, Colorado
December 23, 2011

"surreptitiously obtain naked photos of her." He was also able to listen to the victim's conversations, through the computer microphone. My friend's ex-husband (whom my friend said was always "very chummy with the tech support staff at the office") could have gotten into my friend's computer through similar means. So, my friend's claim could be feasible. In fact, sometimes when I'm sitting in front of my laptop, I feel like the screen is looking back at me. Right now, for instance.

Editor's Note: To begin, note how the subject begins the essay with an etymology, a common tactic of the academic type (not to be confused with the true intellectual or *intyelligyent*, which by the way is in Russia about the highest compliment one can give to a Russian over the age of 25. Very few Americans can be considered *intelligyentia*, including the subject.). These academic types, these bloodless bibliophages, must begin with a feed, you see—with a little transfusion from the dictionary to get the juices going. *Salut!* Without genuine thoughts of their own they need a prompt of some sort to start the associative process, the free flow of received ideas and borrowed experiences (observe how much of the substance of the subject's essay relies on the "story" of her friend). And the footnotes—well fuck me with your baba's cane. What a cliché, a dated affectation that exposes the subject for what she is: a hipster in need of a hip replacement. She should know better than to totter in the footsteps of her beloved DFW. Who by the way has been contacted repeatedly with the hope that he might make a little contribution to this infinite jest. *Nada*, as they say in the overrated story by Ernest Hemingway (there, no solicitation has been made).

Please consider as well the Siberia-sized conceptual blind spot in the subject's thinking about the limits of virtual experience: what the fuck is literature, if not that? Just the other day, for example, the subject consumed a novel by the lovely Irene Nemirovsky (with whom, by the way, a promising flirtation has developed, after overtures to Grace Paley were ignored), while supposedly caring for her children: "Yes you guys can watch another episode of *Conan* while Mommy finishes her book." And that's not even the half of it as she spends her days trying to put to paper lives she's never lived: a former trophy wife (re) turned to grifter; a sociopathic doctor who's lost her children; "they can even play as men" (see fn. 12 above), indeed. De facto, da subject has had her nose in a book most of her goddamn life, when it hasn't been up in the air.

Finally, that bit about feeling the "death of the author," well like the editor's baba used to mutter when he told her he didn't know who smoked her last ciggy, *ne goní purgú* (lit. "don't chase away the snowstorm," or "don't tell lies," "be honest."). Bad Betty checks her Amazon reader reviews more regularly than her blood pressure (which granted is way lower than the editor's ever was). Her dearest wish is to live on, as they say. More power to her. But as to who will be more "viable" fifty years from now, Elisabeth Sheffield or Timor Zinkovsky…it is just her words against mine.

Not Okay: A True Crime Story,

by Selina Van Staal

Chapter Eight

"Life is Not a Lab"

Only once as an adult had Selina Van Staal spent a prolonged period of time with a member of her own sex. Okay there was a female roommate or two. However the arrangement was always for convenience not company, a mutual place to crash or whatnot, without questions. The one exception being the fall after Selina's sophomore year of college, when her mother sent Selina and her sister Cara to Europe. For an entire month. Even though Dolores Van Staal could no longer afford Selina's tuition at SUNY on her secretary's salary, receiving zero assistance from Selina's dad Dean, who had driven off to Florida (the second to last time) one winter morning in a 1984 Airstream Limited, after cleaning out the family savings account. But going to Europe for a month or even six was what all the professors' kids did, coming back with nude beach tans, unwashed hair and backpacks infested with hostel bed bugs.

I want you both to have this beautiful, life-changing experience, Dolores said as she handed Selina and Cara round trip tickets from La Guardia to Charles De Gaulle and four week Eurail passes, all charged to Dolores' credit card, but no money for food or hotels. I know that you will take care of each other, she added. What did she mean by that? Maybe that shoplifting is easier with two people: one can steal a baguette while the other is talking to the person at the register. Cara could do the talking because she had taken two years of French.

For the first two and a half weeks Selina and Cara lived on money they had made over the summer back home, waiting tables and such. It was not a cushy time. Still, each night they could afford narrow bunks in a youth hostel or a hotel designated by one bed in Go Europe, one bed meaning the cheapest. And during the day they had enough lira, francs, deutschmarks or whatever, for a block of cheese or a stick of salami, bread and a bottle of wine, which when you are always a little hungry is enough to open your mind to a threesome with a young Australian trust funder whose looks are only so so. The threesome was two free nights in a four bed hotel on the Rhine, though there was only one bed, one large bed with smooth white sheets a white down comforter and French doors to a balcony that overlooked the water. Also several substantial dinners in das restaurant downstairs as well as a trattoria tucked beneath the ramparts of the Kastell.

Always a little hungry but open minded the sisters stretched their limited funds all the way to Copenhagen where they arrived stiff and dirty on a Saturday morning at the Hovedbanegård with only 70 kroner, or about ten dollars. That was just enough to pay for one bunk in a youth hostel near the train station and two yoghurts. Cara started to cry.

When a person with whom you have shared tough times starts to cry, it is easy to join in. Especially when that person is your older sister and in theory a person whose lead you should follow. Cara being older by four years. It is easy to join in the crying which after all can be a kind of comfort and even, with two attractive young women, an alluring scenario. That may be what Cara had in mind: fresh tear smeared faces pressed cheek to damp cheek soft shoulders heaving in tandem arms wrapped in mutual embrace. What man especially a fatherly type with hopefully a bit of fatherly dough could resist such dual distress? But you might also attract the attention of the police. One of whom Selina had already spotted—a stout woman in a navy skirt suit with gold buttons lurking by a kringle stand. Foreigners without funds tend to get sent home. It would be a shame to shorten the trip.

Yes it would be, Cara sniffed as she dried her face with one of the two Pakistani scarves (Cara's was green and white, Selina's red and white) they had purchased in Kiel, because the ferry ride could be cold and the exchange from deutschmarks to kroner made it hard to keep track of how much money you had. Together they spooned up their yoghurts in a shadowy urine-scented corner of the train station, as Selina told Cara her plan. The Danish yoghurt was richer in both texture and taste than the yoghurt in the United States. That in itself counted for something.

You can walk into a fancy hotel without raising suspicion, provided you are clean smelling and well dressed. Also, if you are a college student or college-aged, dressing well means no more than jeans that are not visibly soiled and an anorak or down jacket that is free of campfire soot and dumpster deposits. Add a new Pakistani scarf for a look of bohemian sophistication. Having bathed and spot cleaned their clothes, then checked their backpacks in the lockers at the youth hostel, Selina and Cara were now seated by a fire in the lobby of the Royal Hotel. We are waiting for our father, Doctor Dean Van Staal, Selina had explained at the concierge's desk. Please let us know when he arrives.

Comfy but increasingly hungry because even the richest tasting yoghurt is only curdled milk, Selina looked at Cara. Her sister's glassy green eyes were turned toward the glass doors of the entrance. Truth be told the plan contrived by Selina at the train station went no further than this—the swanky but temporary solace of sitting for a few hours in a five star (or five bed) hotel. It was Cara's turn to do something. With her surgically snubbed nose and her once dark but now pale honey colored hair, Cara could pass for a Dane or a Swede. Commonly, Nordic women are objects of male fantasy in film and elsewhere. Being objects of male fantasy gives them a certain power, if they care to wield it. All it takes is a bit of what is called blond ambition. Look at Ivana Trump, who was not even Nordic but East European. If only Cara would return the gaze of one of those well tailored brief case carrying men who kept strolling by on their way to the elevators.

Suddenly Cara's eyes widened. Touching Selina's arm, she pointed at the revolving glass doors.

Pouring through was a league of pale long jawed young men in polo shirts, maple leaf patterned pullover sweaters and tight designer jeans. Many of them carried what looked to be sports equipment of some sort that, along with their fit looking arms, legs and torsos, suggested they were professional athletes. It is well known that professional athletes have more money than they know how to spend. Having more money than they know how to spend, naturally they seek spending assistance.

As five or six older men later identified as head and assistant coaches and trainers of different varieties including something called a goaltending coach checked the group in at the desk, a delegation of three of the young men, one of whom had a piece of tape strapped over his nose, approached the sisters. Hello ladies. Do you speak English? Beautiful. We would like to party once we get checked in only me and my buddies here just had a brutal transatlantic flight. We are too beat to even look at a room service menu! Would you be able to help us out?

Much later, after several bowls of Doritos (Cara's favorite), pretzels, club sandwiches, crudité platters, fruit plates, plus innumerable Coca Colas and Carlsbergs, accompanied by a stream of cross cultural chatter about life in the States versus Canada interrupted only by occasional sideways glances at the topless "bitties" on the two color televisions, as all the while the head and assistant coaches and trainers of different varieties slipped in and out the door because sex scandals on foreign turf are bad sportsmanship, Selina and Cara found themselves in their own double room complete with a view of Tivoli Gardens. Thank you to

Tape Nose, who saddened by the plight of two girls who could have been his younger sisters if they were just Canadian instead of American, had taken up a collection. The entire team along with the coaches and trainers had pitched in, although the goal tending coach had muttered some rude comment about unfair exchange rates.

Cross-legged together on the bed nearest the window with the view of Tivoli Gardens the weary travelers tallied the heap of kroner notes and coins, along with a handful of crumpled Canadian dollars. In total it was enough for over a week of three bed hotels and pensionnes along with three square meals a day. There were still Dorito crumbs on Cara's lips as they curled in satisfaction. Foot five, she said, leaning back on her elbows and raising her right foot in the air. Selina raised her left foot, matching her sole to her sister's: Foot Five, Stay Alive!

Since the night that Florence had nearly died, the silver haired but smooth faced embryologist had been super friendly. Super friendly in the sense that you could tell it took a super human effort: Fritzi was not naturally gregarious and only interested in what other people had to say to the degree that their words confirmed her belief in human stupidity. That is actually not an intelligent way to think. As Dean Van Staal used to say, when you assume other people are idiots you make an ass out of you and me. That is not to say that most people are smarter than you think—most people are not. But just because most people are not, does not mean there are not some.

Fritzi was being super friendly and seemed to believe that Selina could not see through her phony overtures. At the same time it was fun watching dvds together at night in Fritzi's den—Bonnie and Clyde, Butch Cassidy and the Sundance Kid, The Sting, Thelma and Louise, and also fifties melodramas such as Written on the Wind and A Magnificent Obsession because Fritzi thought they were a hoot—sitting in Fritzi's leather club chairs eating bowls of wasabi peas, wearing Fritzi's Smart Wool socks. Plus when Fritzi would pause the dvd to refill the bowls of peas or take a bathroom break, she shared herself, offering information about her childhood or more divertingly, an until now hidden turn for whimsy. For you see, this previously concealed whimsical turn led to a kind of talk that is rare between adult women. Talk that is purely speculative and even silly like what would happen if suddenly your life was being directed by George Roy Hill? Or by Douglas Sirk? What would you look like how would you act what would be different and what would be the same? The sort of conversation that Selina used to have with Timor before everything became what restaurant should we go to tonight or did you look at the website for those speakers or check out the cruise brochure I left on the kitchen table? Before everything became about experiences that could be captured in a credit card statement.

Once or twice before, Selina had shared snippets of her spousal past with Fritzi. Fritzi had responded derisively. This time, the evening of October 15, was no exception.

Actually it's not all that different, Fritzi said as she popped a wasabi pea into her mouth. Either way it's the fantasy of being apprehended by somebody else's vision in order to make your own life memorable, whether the vision is the great auteur's or the staff of Grand Vacations'. The only difference is that the second is a fantasy you can actually realize: a carefully scripted week aboard an ocean liner with three all-you-can-eat dining productions a day and a professional entertainer every night is still within the reach of middle America.

With that snarky response Fritzi demonstrated that she was still a snot and that it was best not to share anything about Timor. Even as she went on to reveal a great deal concerning her own ex…

The fantasy of being apprehended by someone else's vision: that was how I ended up with John, Fritzi continued. She picked up another pea, but instead of putting it in her mouth began to roll it between her thumb and forefinger. In his eyes I was a princess. Not just any princess the kind who can be had with a little charming, but the true icy type, the snow queen who requires the most careful defrosting, an ice age of careful courting and glacial increments of warm attention. Too much too soon, his direct but always limited appraisals as he passed my carousel in the medical library suggested, and I would slip away into some impenetrable cold. He seemed the opposite of guys I'd gone out with in the past, the battery of flattery, the slobbering admiration and currish submission even as it always felt like I was the one who was getting humped. Guys who were always in some sense a variation of my father whose love bordered on invasion, whose boundless approval was a form of oppression.

Well that certainly did not seem like anything to complain about. The father who, as Selina recalled from one of Fritzi's childhood infommercials a few nights before, had also been a successful cardiologist, originally from Turkey, who had neglected his slavishly adoring German wife for his daughter. So along with boundless approval, Fritzi's pasha papa must have provided plenty of cash. But Selina did not comment, not wanting to stem Fritzi's unprecedented tide.

It didn't hurt that John was himself practically a prince back home, Fritzi went on, who'd grown up in a petroleum built palace but had decided to turn his back on all that and do his residency in the States after graduating from Weil Cornell Medical College in Qatar. A prince who although he didn't necessarily live like a pauper as his Lamborghini was the envy of all the male residents certainly applied himself. Here Fritzi finally dropped the last pea, which all the while she had continued to roll between her fingers, back into the bowl: You look skeptical, Selina.

Selina nodded, but at the same time demonstrated her willingness to hear more of Fritzi's tale by drawing her Smart Wool covered feet up onto the leather club chair and wrapping her arms around her shins.

Believe it or not, back then John worked harder than anybody. Worked harder and cared more. Patients weren't simply charts but precious psychobiological singularities, each to be teased forth with warm, bantering affection. The female patients adored him. When it was time for our medical elders to decide who would be chief resident, it was a no brainer. John didn't have to bust his ass to be the model young doc à la mode—but he did. Likewise I didn't have to act like I was unattainable, or attainable only with the greatest delicacy and tact, because probably I would've slept with him regardless, but he continued to pursue me as if I was some impossible prize. And I just ate it up, his vision of himself, his vision of me.

So when did it all go sour, you must be wondering. When did the model young doc à la mode turn out to be a pickled dick, when did the snow queen routine dissolve into a snow job? Well, it didn't happen in a day. We got married, left Weil Cornell to join the team at the posh new offices of Uptown Procreative Specialists, John as an endocrinologist me as an embryologist, had the twins without any fucking assistance though John's sisters back in the petroleum palace all said I was too old and suggested a little petri dish peri or some kind of scientific sorcery must've been involved.

Fritzi retrieved the silver ankh that she wore at all times from under the collar of her shirt and started to fiddle with it, her fingers covering the stem. About four years ago I noticed a shift, so slight at first that I just thought my judgment was off, that the lack of sleep that came with two young kids at home was screwing with my perception. It started with the way he'd talk about the couples who came to the clinic, in a tone I'd never before heard him use, a tone inflected with fatigue. But then gradually it wasn't just a tone but a discourse of unmistakable disgust with him referring to our patients as "zygote craving zombies" oblivious to their own "in vitro incrimination in technocapitalist dehumanization." And we, the "Doctor UnFrankensteins" who knew we were manufacturing monsters for these monsters, merrily pocketing the profits of our "embryo racketeering," were even worse. Far worse, implanting eight low quality embryos at a time in the uterus of a young Westchester housewife who thought a zit on the chin constituted a major deformity, or even just one A plus grade ivy league donor conceived morula in a fifty-year old law partner whose work load barely allowed for the two yoga classes a week needed to maintain a strength and flexibility that still fell short of the requirements for lifting a healthy eighteenth month old out of a crib.

Pausing, Fritzi lifted the looped end of the ankh to her lips, a gesture she had made on previous occasions. Repeated, characteristic gestures can clue you into people's feelings in a way that their words sometimes do not. So pay attention to body language, Dean Van Staal used to say. Pay attention to body language although if you do not know what a gesture means it might as well be written in Cyrillic.

John started drinking. Or more accurately, he started drinking more. He'd always drunk, but in the suave controlled fashion of the playboy who's chosen not to be a playboy on principle, of the son of privilege who decides to pursue a philanthropic career, like Rock Hudson in the second half of A Magnificent Obsession. In fact it was like A Magnificent Obsession in reverse, noble doctor reverting to a spoiled undergraduate brat. A spoiled undergraduate brat curdled further by one course too many in Marxist philosophy or poststructuralist theory. He started to miss appointments with patients, to show up late for embryo transfers. Yet he was still the prince perched on his moral charger, however unsteadily, while I'd been demoted to a commoner. Just because I kept doing my job,

Selina. On the increasingly rare occasions when we'd take the subway from Park Slope together to the clinic, I'd catch John looking at me like I was a stranger. A stranger on the F train but not the mysterious kind who compels fantasies of illicit rendezvous but rather the familiar grotesque—the scab covered hooker, the legless vet—who makes you reconsider populist means of transportation. Like he was wishing he was alone in a cab or car service limousine.

Just because I kept doing my job he began treating me like some unwelcome foreign matter or maculation, no longer at the center but the periphery of his vision. It was insulting not to mention grossly unfair as I was scrambling for him at UPS even covering his consultations though my comfort zone has always been the lab while working overtime at home being both mother and father to our sons praying that the new au pair wouldn't pack up and go back to Brazil like the last one.

Then one morning I reached my limit. It was 5:00am and I was due in an hour at the clinic to evaluate seven eight-celled embryos scheduled for a 9:00am implantation. John was asleep, his back turned to me, his thumb resting on his jaw his palm cupped over his mouth fingers fluttering on the pillow like an infant's. Let him deal with all the shit—his job at the clinic, our three story brownstone, the au pair, the twins. I'd find a hotel and then a studio apartment in the city. Hopefully the shock therapy of my departure would help John to get his head and his priorities straight.

Here's a life tip. Never fuck with an heir to an oil refinery because even though fossil fuel is not a renewable form of energy their resources are seemingly infinite. With the help of his family and an obscenely expensive Mob affiliated divorce attorney who managed to get the case reviewed by an eighty year old former Roman Catholic priest turned family court judge now retired but available on demand for cases of wifely insubordination, John sued me for desertion. He got everything—the brownstone in Park Slope, the Architectural Digest featured country house in Columbia county, and most painfully of all, the children. Full custody because after my quote unquote incomprehensible parental defection I could no longer be trusted with young children.

Well that sure made sense, what Fritzi had just said. Look at what had happened with Timor who though no petroleum prince had nevertheless left Selina royally screwed. One piece of the puzzle, or actually two, remained however. If Asani could no longer bear the IVF business, then what was he doing running his own clinic? And how had Fritzi ended up working for him?

Confronted with these two questions, Fritzi looked annoyed and even put out. Like she was not responsible for answering them. But then who was? Just as Selina was about to say something about loose ends and trusting your friends Fritzi drew a big breath and continued.

Okay, so John's had this big existential crisis and is suddenly too principled to assist in assisted reproduction. But if he's not gonna be in the baby business then he's going to have to rejoin the family oil syndicate. You see his father and uncles are fine with John's noble profession but they're not fine with no profession at all. It's a choice of continuing to play doctor in America or getting a real job back home bribing foreign business representatives and schmoozing with local sheikhs, a real job with a real purdah empowered wife or three all wearing the pants beneath their robes monitoring his every move through chador slits ensuring he adheres to the precepts of sharia or else. Door number one or door number two—otherwise the cash flow gets cut off. Neither door is a way out but maybe number one feels less like the entrance to a maximum security prison…

Fritzi trailed off, her fingers reaching for the fine silver chain around her neck. Having retrieved the ankh, she tapped her lips once or twice, then finally resumed: But the trouble is that he trashed the place before he left—there've been quote unquote incidents at the clinic and though no one at UPS ever explicitly says YOU FUCKED UP, he has. So John opens up his own clinic, once again drawing on seemingly limitless though not unconditional family funds as his father and uncles insist on being on the Board of Trustees. Fortunately for him, so far the trustees have been too tied up with domestic business affairs to pay much attention to the fiasco that is HVFC.

One of Fritzi's samoyed dogs, sprawled on the floor at the foot of her chair, began to whimper and scratch with its hind leg at its ear. Like there was a bug in it, which there probably was. Well Fritzi's account of John Asani's past explained a lot in terms of his alcoholism, lack of morale and loosely run reproductive enterprise. You can't sell a product you don't believe in, Dean Van Staal always said. You are your number one customer. But that still did not explain how Fritzi had gotten mixed up in the HVFC mess.

Fritzi was no fool.

Her jaw tightened, even as she allowed the ankh to drop beneath her neckline. She responded: Life is not a lab.

Exactly. So why choose to work in Asani's? Why not get a job at another lab? Or pursue a completely new career path? It is never too late.

Another long pause. At last, Fritzi replied: I'd lost my children. When I saw them, how long I got to see them for—John called the shots. You have no idea what that's like.

Well Selina could imagine, but made no comment.

And now he was taking them two hours away upstate—travel time that would effectively make each of my visits with them effectively four hours shorter. John needed an embryologist and he needed a mother for his sons, as Lucy Goosey Lyndon had yet to appear on the scene. If I moved to the Hudson Valley to work for him, I could have the boys every other weekend. Every other weekend, and if those went without incident, every weekend, which could eventually lead, following a court reevaluation, to shared custody. And oh, I could live in the Architectural Digest featured country house, which by the way, I designed and John had built by a contractor back when my wish was his command. Working for John, living in what was his house regardless of the fact that I designed it, allowed to see now and then the children the state of New York had deemed entirely his though I had conceived and carried them: it was a humiliating proposition. But what alternative did I have? Two tears seeped down over Fritzi's cheeks, one from each eye.

So that was how Fritzi had come by the big blue box. It was now for sale, though in the weeks since Selina had moved in no one had come by to look. Nor had her legally lost sons come to visit. Probably the latter situation had something to do with that knife and the death of Lyndon's dog. You could press for more details, but pressing would no doubt yield more of the same: additional bitter revelations that though they would be different bitter revelations in the way that no two snow flakes are alike would be indistinguishable in the end, one big frozen waste. In truth (and never anything but the truth), it all felt depressingly familiar. Depressingly familiar even though Fritzi was not family and barely even a friend. At a certain point in your life the mistakes have piled up so that there is no sorting it all out or even shoveling a path to the car. You are trapped, by the decisions you made, by the decisions you did not, by the decisions you let other people make for you. That is why Selina agreed when a few moments later Fritzi wiped her thin cheeks and suggested, let's just forget about all this for one night. I'll call the neighbor down the road to look after the animals. Then we'll drive into Albany, get a couple of motel rooms and hit the bars on Lark Street.

"Pay attention to body language although if you do not know what a gesture means it might as well be written in Cyrillic." Selinka, this is too much: you won't admit that you've been reading my messages, even as you flaunt your intimacy with their content. What is the preceding sentence if not an allusion to my Siberia bound mama and her contraband lingerie?: "I recognized the configuration of the letters before I comprehended them: *Maidenform*." An allusion that affects a neat reversal as the unintelligible language of the body (Fritzi's "maidenform"?) is figured in my cultural script instead of yours. Do you think I can't read what you're up to? Or do you know only too well, you cardiothoracically deficient bitch, that I can?

You know that I know what you are up to, yet with all your calculating insight you couldn't see through Fritzi Akdikmen. Once again, I would've warned you if I could've, or maybe to reciprocate for the above, to return your cryptic communications in kind, told you an old time American head-scratcher that Irwin once told me.

Riddle: A big Indian and a small Indian were paddling a canoe on a lake. Pausing between strokes, the big one said, "Child, you are my son but I am not your father." Then who was the big Indian?

Answer: The little one's mother.

Not Okay: A True Crime Story,

by Selina Van Staal

Chapter Nine

"Not Okay"

The morning after the night in Albany, Selina awoke, alone, in a room at the Ramada Plaza Inn. The date was the October 16, 2010, a turning point but unfortunately no turn was made. A note rested on the red-quilted bedspread, written in block print handwriting on a sheet of Ramada Plaza stationary:

YOUR KEY CARD IS IN YOUR BACK JEAN POCKET—ON THE CHAIR. HOPE YOU'RE OK. I LEFT YOU SOME OXYCONTIN (ALSO IN YOUR POCKET). FRITZI

No, Selina was not OK, or even okay. Okay being the correct spelling even though according to former English department secretary Dolores Van Staal, OK is an abbreviation for Oll Korrect. Also for Old Kinderhook, claimed Timor, who was always rooting around in etymologies like a pig looking for truffles. The choice bits that could be used to prove some lineage or another that all fed the same line of landed gentry or fat complacency with your own cultural command and socio-economic standing. Selina was not okay and had not been okay for quite some time.

When you realize that you are not okay and have not been okay for quite some time, that is a call for introspection. But it is hard to look inward when all you want is to get out—out of your own head that feels like it is in a vise, tightening then releasing, tightening then releasing. Standing brought a wave of nausea so strong Selina tipped on her heels, almost falling back into the bed. That would not have been an unwelcome reversal. Even better to have fallen back into the bed such relief to rewind rewind speeding through the hot suffocation of sleep the stuporous ascent assisted by Fritzi and those two boys in their fedoras to your motel room the crouching on the cement in a puddle of steaming vomit hands holding your racked gut the floating naked alone in the heated pool watching Fritzi with that kid Aiden his hat bobbing between her legs her head thrown back laughing laughing like there was no tomorrow or yesterday for that matter the smell of semen mixed with chlorine the other one Dillan on a plastic chaise lounge with his hat tilted over his eyes drinking from a bottle of Jim beam after the boilermakers at Suzis bar Suzis with no apostrophe as if there were multiple suzis though the only other people there had been Dillan and Aiden two hipster youngsters in fedoras neither a day over twenty three and the bartender Jordan another boy toy who didn't know that back in the early nineties suzis used to be called The Griffin a mythical animal with sharp claws that could seize you lift you up and carry you back to before Timor when you were still taking continuing education nursing classes at SUNY Albany getting by just fine on bartending when you still had a grip on things…

Such relief it would be to rewind to shuttle back to the place before it all started to turn the pages back to the beginning and start again. But life is not a movie or a book! Life cannot be refilmed or rewritten or even arrested in one of the early chapters before everything began to go bad. Life only goes in one direction, which is a cliché but also true. Like something Lyndon would say. Lyndon who was now pregnant, and would either have a baby or more likely given her medical history, miscarry, but still would miscarry on, you could tell. Lyndon was a trooper. Picking up her jeans from the red upholstered armchair, Selina fumbled through the pockets for the Oxycontin.

At the breakfast buffet in the ground floor restaurant called the Blue Cafe though there was nothing blue about it unless you counted the depressing atmosphere created by a sea of white cloth covered metal tables under an expanse of white ceiling tiles checkered with squares of fluorescent lights, Selina poured herself a glass of tepid pulpless orange juice.

Over on the other side of the room was silver haired but young faced Fritzi with her back to the buffet and what looked to be those boys, Aiden and Dillan, still wearing their fedoras. Aiden and Dillan with a capital A and a capital D because in the light of day they were not ken dolls or boy toys but actual people with proper names and probably surnames too displayed on the driver's licences they had pulled out at the liquor store on the way back to the Ramada Plaza Inn, as proof of age. Aiden and Dillan were young but legal adults that you had not had sexual intercourse with because although the opportunity had been available and the mind willing, the body had said no. The body had said no, absolutely not with your innermost being or at least the entire contents of the stomach: the two Luna Bars eaten in the car on the drive in to Albany, the beer and the whiskey, and then some—what had looked to be clots of blood but hopefully were just dried cranberries from the Luna Bars.

Selina sat down at an empty table in a corner opposite from Fritzi and Aiden and Dillan, counting on the camouflage provided by other hotel guests chowing down nearby.

On the white tablecloth was an empty white plate made of the heavy china available at restaurant supply stores. In restaurant kitchens they have stacks of them sitting on metal wire shelving, for the cooks to fill them and the servers to carry them out to the diners who empty them and then back into the kitchen to the dishwashers who clean them and then stack them, so that the whole cycle can start all over again. Jobs in the food and beverage service industry are easy to get but hard to leave, once you get caught up in the routine of late nights and drinking too much after work. In truth (and nothing but the truth), it would be very hard to go back, to before Timor. But forward was a challenge as well.

Odors of over grilled sausage and congealed cooked eggs wafted over from the steam table. Fortunately the Oxycontin seemed to settle Selina's stomach as well as to cure her headache. According to the NCLEX-RN study guide, Oxycontin, or oxycodone, is an opoid analgesic medication synthesized from opium. Probably the opium accounted for the drug's soothing effect, its ability not only to alleviate head pain but also gastric agitation. Too bad Oxycontin cannot be purchased over the counter. While temperance is the best policy, even people who are not alcoholics occasionally overindulge. When they do, a powerful prescription drug such as Oxycontin can work wonders, restoring a feeling of equilibrium.

Still, a feeling of equilibrium is not the same as a feeling of well-being. Or what is called sanguinity, a sense of not only health but also confidence. You see, confidence is the one thing Oxycontin cannot restore. Without confidence, the future looked like a white china plate—a plate Selina could not bring herself to carry over to the buffet table. So actually, there are two things Oxycontin cannot restore—confidence and appetite. But if you think of appetite in the more general sense of an appetite for life or vigor, and confidence as faith in your inherent strength or power, they are basically the same thing. What one-eyed Dean Van Staal used to call moxie. Although moxie was originally a soft drink called Moxie. So it did not come from within. You had to drink it.

What Selina needed comes from within. Introspection was necessary and now that the Oxycontin had taken effect, a throbbing headache was no longer an excuse. Plus she was just sitting there. Just sitting there she might have made that movement inward that can lead you out again in a more promising direction when someone tapped her on the shoulder: Hey Sexy Lady, may I sit down?

It was Dillan, the less cute of the two hipster youngsters, the sallow face beneath the brim of the fedora bony and flat with an off-center nose, a face like a mug shot from the nineteen twenties or thirties back when they still drank Moxie.

Selina nodded. In hindsight, that was a mistake. Not just a mistake, but a misdirection. With hindsight, Selina could have corrected her course, first by not letting the fedora hatted boy sit down, and second by leaving behind the Ramada Inn and the silver haired but young faced Fritzi. You cannot see behind you when YOU are in the way. Because life is not a book you can hold in your lap and read.

You should eat something, Dillan said. The food sucks but it comes with that room you paid for. And you'll feel better.

He reached over, touched the back of Selina's hand. Resting on an age spot, his finger was long and supple looking, the pink oval of nail like a cameo without the cameo. On his wrist there was what looked to be an old man's watch with a stainless band and a yellowed face. The time said 2:05 even though it was mid morning. Let me get you some eggs and toast, a cup of joe, he said.

It could have been the coffee, because Selina suddenly found herself talking. Telling the fedora hatted Dillan about the two years she had lived in Albany attending SUNY off and on after the years in the city off and on at CUNY, all the while bartending or working tables at various bars and restaurants. One of those had been the Lark Tavern, catty corner from Suzis that used to be the Griffin. Last night she and Fritzi had tried to go there first, but found the old brick façade sooty, random panes in the large lattice style windows broken, the peaked gable above the locked door charred, the little bronze plaque that said Lark Tavern est. 1933 darkly tarnished—found the once cozy tudor style pub not only closed but gone ghetto. Although according to Dillan the place had been crawling with preppies as recently as a year before until a kitchen fire had closed it down.

Back in the early nineties, Selina confirmed, it had been packed with preppies too, crew necked sweaters rubbing breast to shoulder boat shoe toes testing for boat shoe toes as they sidled past each other to the bar brushing their Daniel Day-Lewis waves behind their ears as they leaned in to order their Jaegermeister shots and Molson beers then sidling back trying not to spill one drop of the quote unquote correction fluids that would blot out GPAs, internships and clerkships, residencies and impending nuptials, just for one night. That sounded bitter but it was not. It would have been easy to go out with a docksider-shod Day-Lewis coiffed dork and even to marry one.

But preppy was not my type, Selina explained.

Dillan reached over and picking up Selina's fork helped himself to a bite of untouched eggs. He smelled like a thrift shop, probably the source of his what looked to be nylon white button down shirt and gray flannel slacks, as well as the hat. Chewing, he inquired so what is your type?

Sometimes people speak without thinking, using common terms like type without first considering their meaning. Sometimes people think without thinking, as well. Without thinking about Dillan's question, Selina thought Timor. If Timor were still around he would probably say something about how type derived from some ancient word or another that derived from some other even more ancient word that had nothing to do with anything. At the same time, when the question of type was posed by Dillan, the word Timor immediately came to mind. Timor, like that word was the epitome of Selina's type, even as the man that the word identified had toward the end seemed in no way related to any original ideal.

What is your type? Dillan repeated one elbow resting on the table, his chin cupped in his hand. The fedora shaded his eyes, but you could see the presumption in them. He thought he knew the answer and that he was it.

Looking at Dillan who with his crooked fedora shaded mug was in no way an ideal or even a preferred type though he possessed a lithe swimmer's body (last night, poolside, he had mentioned a high school state championship), Selina recalled the first time she had seen Timor, at the Lark Tavern. That was long before it had closed down from a kitchen fire, probably before Dillan had even learned to float. Although they say that babies are born knowing how to float, an ability that they already possess in utero. Plus last night at the hotel pool Dillan had guessed that Selina was no more than thirty-two.

Dillan did not need to know how old Selina really was. But he did need to know that he was not Selina's type, whatever that meant. Just because you have lost your confidence that does not mean you need to toss away your dignity as well, like the clothes you should have kept on or at least replaced with a bathing suit before you stepped into the water. This fedora hatted boy who was in no way an ideal, a skinny dip at best, needed to know about Timor.

So Selina started to tell Dillan about her ex-husband. She told the fedora hatted boy about Timor and then could not stop, going deeper than necessary into the details, as if pulled by some talk show undertow. She told him about working the lunch shift at the Lark one afternoon instead of the night shift because the daytime bartender had to do a DMV remedial class; about a stranger walking in just near the end of the lunch shift, wearing a pair of black Rayban sunglasses even though it was late afternoon and Albany, New York, and also a Walkman; about the stranger still wearing the glasses and the Walkman taking a seat at a dark corner table; about him lifting one headphone to order a ham and cheese sandwich on rye no mayo but extra mustard and a Heinekin forget the glass from the waitress then replacing the headphone; about the waitress who had then dropped the beer order off at the bar saying what an asshole; about watching the stranger pull a paperback from his back pocket, open it to a place marked with what looked to be some kind of leaflet or brochure, and proceed to stare down, either at the book or the brochure, you could not tell since he did not turn the page or unfold the glossy sheet; about the mushroom pale soft yet tough look of the stranger, about his high quartz-white forehead with the pillowy tuft of black hair above and the impenetrable glasses below that had hit hard, fast and unfair, taking advantage of some blind spot you did not even know you had.

Going deeper than necessary into the details, Selina continued to tell the fedora hatted boy about Timor who at the time was not Timor but a stranger. He was a stranger so alluring that Selina sank to following him out the door when he left, not above walking out on the job but luckily her shift was over. Then she tracked his wiry neither too short nor too tall body like a high school wrestler's or a welter weight fighter's with the square of the paperback bookmarked by the brochure disfiguring the back pocket of what looked to be expensive gray gabardine wool trousers ticked with fine vertical threads of red like rows of illegible type though not destroying the essential symmetry of his ass up Madison Avenue past Washington Park, left onto South Lake where in profile a small not unappealing potbelly was visible swaddled by a black what looked to be cashmere sweater all the way to Albany Medical Center and through the main lobby past the young attendant at the information station who said good afternoon to you too Doctor Zinkovsky to the stranger's retreating back and headphone covered ears, down the corridor and into the elevator slipping in behind a pregnant woman in a wheelchair just as the doors were about to slide closed, riding up covertly eyeing the stranger labeled but not explained by the title Doctor Zinkovsky, whose gaze in turn was trained upon the floor his hand pulling at his tuft as he listened to his Walkman or maybe just his own thoughts, out the elevator, down the corridor through the entrance that said Obstetrics and Gynecology, stopping only when it was possible to sink no further, at the reception desk where an appointment was scheduled for a complete exam, three months in the future, since until then Dr. Zinkovsky was completely booked.

So, Dillan said, removing his fedora and laying it to the side on the table, sounds like doctors are your type. Without the hat his sallow but unlined face looked about ten years younger, meaning about ten. Same with my mom, who's looking for a new husband on match.com: she says MD means more dough.

He pulled Selina's eggs in front of him. Stabbing a yellow clot he lifted it to his mouth: Not that I'm judging you sister. Late capitalism is a bitch.

Well no. Meaning yes, late capitalism is a quote unquote bitch, though it is mostly the men who are in charge—and in fact there had been something in the Albany Times Union the other day about how even restaurant jobs are not so easy to get anymore. But no about the MD or more dough being the source of Timor's charm, the magic, the moxie even that had pulled Selina through the streets of Albany New York like some will-twisting spell or an invisible string through the nose. Remember that starting out at the Lark he was simply a stranger, a stranger who could have been anyone and done anything, from washing dishes at a diner to directing films about devil worshippers. Timor's charm, his power even, had nothing to do with his degree or earning potentional and everything to do with that high pale forehead that had gleamed like a healing crystal in the dim light of the bar. What secrets did it harbor what craft did it contain? According to Dolores Van Staal's Everyman's Eggheads Edition of Freud, women are the dark continent. But that only means that you have to feel your way around without any lights. Which is the way it is with people in general. If you grope around for a bit you will find a way in, and usually sooner rather than later. Especially in the case of the ones like Lyndon, the ones that are wide open from the get go. But this stranger who could have been anyone—dishwasher, director, doctor, thief—seemed different. It was like you could feel your way in the dark, a task that would be no chore from the look of him, but you might never find any actual doors, only walls and corridors leading to more walls and corridors.

Leaving out the last part about Freud and groping for doors in the dark, Selina summed up: Money had absolutely nothing to do with it.

Well I like that healing crystal image, Dillan replied. So nineties new age. In the film version the soundtrack would be something from Enigma, maybe "Sadeness," the one where they juxtapose the Gregorian chants and panting over a dance beat. Before they got divorced, my mom and dad used to play it when they were about to go upstairs and get it on.

Obviously Dillan was dismissing Selina's story about seeing Timor for the first time. When someone dismisses what you say, it is a form of disrespect, or what is commonly called dissing. In dismissing Selina's story, Dillan was dissing her and yet at the same time he was leaning forward, smiling a little smile that seemed to be for Selina alone, as if there was no other woman in the room. It was the kind of smile that you see babies smiling at their mothers when they first learn to smile. It was a smile that, if you think about it, is the origin of all seductive smiles, the smile that paves the way to permission which is probably why when you have kids it is hard not to let them walk all over you. Even if they are not your own and more or less grown up. That is to say the dissing led to kissing, which led to panting if not chanting, which led to leaving the table, which you could do without paying because the breakfast buffet came with the room—which was still available for another hour because checkout was not until noon.

After, in bed, which is to skip the before, in bed, the part succeeding the breakfast buffet but preceding any post-coital conversation, the juicy but finally not terribly pertinent or interesting part, Selina felt once more what even the oxycontin had not been able to restore: a sense of not only health but confidence, or sanguinity. A demonstration of the power of the body to heal itself one-eyed Dean would say: the most powerful medicine comes from within. Although he would probably not approve of the means used to dispense that medicine. Messing around with a minor is a recipe for major disaster, honey. But Dillan, according to his ID, was a young adult and Dianetics has long been discredited.

Sanguinity thrives in silence. Or if you cannot have silence, then the near silence of two warm damp bodies breathing softly side by side. So when Dillan rolled away without saying a word, Selina was fine with it. She was fine with their two warm bodies lying side by side, not touching or talking, just breathing and staring at the blank flatscreen television on the opposite wall for the remaining forty minutes until check-out time. Fine even with the smell of musty second hand clothing combined with young sweat and sexual fluids, a mix that merged locker room, bedroom and nursing home all into one. But if Dillan were to suddenly get up, slide into his old man's slacks, clap on his fedora and beat it—well that would be okay too (if not OK). The sense of well-being would remain. You see, satisfying if uninteresting sex with someone barely out of their teens is like a long drink from the soda fountain of youth: pure moxie.

When suddenly Dillan started quizzing Selina about Timor, beginning with a smartypants question about whether healing crystals can lose their powers.

A tip: if you ever decide to sleep with a young person, young of course being relative to your own age, remember that different generations have different ideas about how to fill the down-time after climax. In the olden days, they used cigarettes. But not many people smoke anymore, Fritzi and college students seeking to appear cool or uncaring about their health being the exceptions. Dillan did not smoke, although he seemed like he was college age (and maybe even in college. At Suzis, he had mentioned something about studying philosophy). College age, he had grown up with the Internet and mobile phones, with instant messaging, texting and what not, which basically meant that he was used to chatting all the time. Why he did not go and pull his cellphone out of his pocket and call or text someone right then and there is a mystery. It could be that hook-up culture has its own code of conduct, just like any other. Could be that it is a rule that you have to have intercourse with the person after intercourse. Meaning intercourse in the sense of conversation, an exchange of thoughts or feelings rather than bodily fluids.

I'm serious, Dillan said, raising himself on one elbow. Small acne scars pitted his otherwise smooth skin, visible for the first time in the late morning light pouring through the large window at the far end of the room. MD aside, it sounds like you really dug this guy. If I felt like that about someone, I'd never let them go. So what happened?

Well clearly Dillan was not content to lay in silence or near silence for the forty minutes or so that remained before check-out. Nor was he going to leave of his own accord. Sure Selina could just get up, get dressed and leave him there. But the room had been reserved in her name, using her credit card and driver's licence. That is to say, any towels stolen or pay-for-view pornographic movies watched by Dillan in Selina's absence would be traced back to Selina.

It was like being held hostage, with your own history as the ransom, even though your abductor was still a child at the time you were being forced to revisit. You could try to turn the tables, maybe inquire about aspects of Dillan's past, like why his parents got divorced, but that would mean risking a dose of young adult angst—the opposite of drinking from the soda fountain of youth.

Not wanting to risk a dose of young adult angst, which will only make you feel old if you are past the age of thirty five (try rereading Catcher in the Rye, or rewatching Pump Up the Volume), Selina resumed talking about Timor to Dillan, who either out of genuine curiosity or post hook-up politeness was now interested. And like earlier at the breakfast buffet, talking about Timor once more took on a life its own, as if your words were some beat you had to follow whether you wanted to or not or shoes dancing you straight to hell like in the fairy tale by Hans Christian Anderson. If you think about it, that is really cruel, getting damned just because you liked flashy shoes. Especially if you did not actually care for flashy shoes or super high heels that you only wore that one time—goddess knows why. You could hardly even walk in them. Sometimes when people are interested in other people they say or do or wear things they would not normally say or do or wear.

Talking about Timor now was as irresistible as following him had been then though Selina managed to skip over the part about the shoes and the office exam. The fedora hatted boy did not need to know about the exam at Timor's office and the awkwardness of when you are first getting to know someone, when you are first finding out about their lives and who they are past and present and deciding how much you want them to know about your life and who you are past and present. You see, with every new intimate relationship people start afresh and some beginnings need to be fresher than others. Not that Selina had anything to hide or anything.

In truth (and nothing but the truth) the great thing about being with Timor was that you could be yourself, without affectations, Selina told Dillan. Without affectations even as, for instance, you shared an appreciation for quality and craftsmanship, for texture and depth as well as polish and patina, for threadcounts and fine grains. You see it was not about appearing rich or trying to impress anyone: it was about enjoying the world's wares, because there are interesting things to see, to touch and to smell everywhere, and you do not necessarily have to buy them. So you could be as happy browsing at a flea market as at Barneys, like the time they found a genuine bearskin at a stall in an old used car lot on Avenue of the Americas that Timor only purchased because the vendor said it was from Siberia and that was where Timor's mother was from or something—a genuine bearskin from Siberia that they had later made mothball scented love on in front of the fireplace without a fire because Naphthalene is a carcinogen and the fumes were strong enough as it was.

Let's try that sometime, Dillan interrupted. I love that old mothball smell.

Selina ignored the suggestion and went on, explaining that because there are interesting things to see, to touch and to smell everywhere that you do not necessarily have to buy they could have lived as well in a silverfish-infested three-room rental on Arbor Hill in Albany as at Bosky House, Timor's seventeenth century Dutch manor in the woods, although the silverfish, which prefer starches and glue as can be found in bookbindings but will occasionally eat fabrics, had destroyed a shimmering swathe of vintage duponi silk discovered at an Episcopalian church sale, even though there were plenty of old paperbacks as well as overdue library books to choose from. But then Selina had almost been raped on the way back to Arbor Hill from the Lark Tavern one night by an intoxicated man who had yanked her off the sidewalk into an alley and then just as suddenly shoved her back shouting I would not touch you with a ten foot pole bitch after Selina suggested that she would take his testicles as a souvenir of the experience. Violent sexual assaults can occur just as easily on country estates as in inner city neighborhoods, but emergency room statistics tend to link them with the latter, Timor had said after Selina had told him about the man but left out the part about the souvenir. Plus there was more room for two people at Bosky House.

A lot more room at Bosky House. That is not to say it was simply a matter of square footage or even premium living space. You see, Bosky House was not just a house, a high end property that had been advertised in the New York Times for the discerning buyer before Timor had purchased it, but a piece of living history. Or herstory, like they said in the Continuing Education Women's Studies course Selina had taken as a humanities elective one semester, then dropped. A piece of living herstory in the sense that Selina's family on her father's side had lived there before she was born. So Selina could claim it as her own in the sense of a heritage, if not an actual legal inheritance. You see, just because a house or piece of land no longer belongs to a person or her family does not mean that the bond between person and place has been dissolved. That is why indigenous peoples are called indigenous, even if they have been driven from their ancestral lands.

Well yes and no, Dillan said. Homo sapiens has been a nomadic species for most of its existence, the concept of land tenure being a very late development, and the concept of transferable titles and deeds conferring the right to occupy a particular property an even later one. What I'm saying is that it all comes down to concepts, or constructions of the human mind. So whether or not you have a natural bond with or right to a place is all in your head. But the same goes with a title or property deed: even if it has your name on it, it is just another story like Harry Potter or Star Wars. On the other hand, it is an entertainment for the masses that reaped blockbuster profits for the banks. Like it's all this big fiction created by our collective brains yet people still have houses worth less than they paid for them so forget about that equity we were building for for your college fund, Dillan, you'll have to take out a loan. Or as this famous philosopher dude Althusser said, ideology slides into all human activity… it is identical with the 'lived' experience of human existence itself. So yes you could say that house was as much yours as his but practically speaking the mortgage belonged to More Dough.

Dillan paused, reaching for his hat from the bedside table. He set the hat on his head. In old movies, when people put their hats on their heads, that means they are about to leave. He even made what seemed to be a parting remark: Not a bad deal for you, Sexy Lady—sort of like what I had with the rents before they split up and sold my childhood home.

But instead of getting up and picking his musty clothes up off the floor to put them on, Dillan settled back into the pillows, folded his arms over his chest, and asked so when and how did More Dough find out that you were having sleepovers in the old herstorical halls?

Well a judgment had been made: that what happened was adultery and that Selina was the adulteress. The judgement was laced with insinuation, you could tell from what Dillan had said about "not a bad deal for you" and "herstorical halls." The insinuation being that Selina was a two-timing schemer who had hooked for a house and then fished around on the side, the kind of person who gets tangled in her own nets. Or webs. Like a Black Widow spider or someone who would wear one of those strapless corsets with the garters attached. Selina would never wear anything like that or even thong underpants, which are so uncomfortable with that string in your crack. As for the shoes, she only wore those the one time.

Dillan's insinuation laced judgement was inappropriate, not to mention tasteless. It was time for Selina to walk out of that Ramada Inn room in her Church's wing tips that were still like new after ten years because that is quality for you. Nevermind the pay-for-view or the towels. She stood up, to look for her wing tips, as well as the rest of her clothes.

On the carpet next to Selina's shoes, a ladybug crawled. Maybe it had been brought in last night from by the pool although it was mid October and the season for manbug hunting was surely past. The lipstick red dot moved slowly and without apparent aim. Leaving meant figuring out where to go from here. Back to Fritzi's yes, because Selina had nowhere else to go, but then what? After last night, Fritzi seemed less trustworthy than ever. Certainly she did not act like a woman distraught over the loss of her children, unless having public sex with a boy young enough to be her son counted as a form of consolation. Yet getting her kids back was supposedly her motive for the heist. Like Selina's dad would say, it is never a good idea to launch a venture with a partner you cannot trust.

Leaving meant figuring out where to go from here. Then there was Dillan on the bed with his arms smugly folded, his uncircumsized penis nestled beneath a brown brush of pubic hair. Leaving could also be construed as a concession. Another thing Selina's one-eyed dad Dean once said was do not walk away when someone accuses you of cheating them, or in this case, of cheating someone else. Stand your ground and look them in the eye when you tell them that you would never do such a thing. Because if you look away they will think you are not telling the truth.

Never had Selina been unfaithful to Timor, not once. Not once, in any sense of the word, which if you think about it, has several. Betrayal does not have to be sexual, or even of another person. You see, it can be of an organization or even of an ideal.

Selina sat down on the satiny red spread. Timor was the one who cheated, she informed Dillan. You could tell the spread was polyester by the slight pilling of the fabric. Timor cheated not in the sense of sneaking around or romantic two timing but in the sense of hiding his true colors. It was like someone listing a car in the classifieds as Chinese lacquer red when it was really that old man's maroon, only it was himself not his car that he misrepresented.

Dillan snickered. So this guy wasn't really a More Dough? That's great.

If only it had been that simple. If only Timor had practiced the kind of fraud that once it is discovered can be documented and legally prosecuted. How could Dillan, who was basically a boy in a man's hat possibly understand how it felt to commit your life to one person and then have that person turn out to be another? How could you explain that kind of change that does not happen overnight or even over a year? How could you explain a change that is not really a change but more of an uncovering that happens so slowly you cannot be sure when the cover came off or even if it has been off all along? And in the meantime you are not getting any younger and uncovering the moment of uncovering does not mean recovering your losses. You cannot get back the years you have given nor can you be sure that it will not be the same with someone else—that he or she will not turn out to be someone other than someone else. Maybe even someone similar to that first person that was not the person you thought they were. How could you explain the unrecoverable investment of marriage to someone who was still in a highchair when you got your first bartending job? That was back when you were so young yourself you thought you might make an exciting career out of tending bar, forget the nursing degree. In the food and service industry you can work anywhere, even abroad—provided you do not mind working under the table.

To further confuse matters Timor was what he looked to be on the surface, which was like someone from abroad. When people asked him where he was from, he would tell them the Ukraine, in the former U.S.S.R. or Soviet Republic. But he would only tell people that if they asked him. He was not forthcoming about his foreign background. He hardly ever spoke a word of Russian or whatever they speak in the Ukraine, which he once divulged was very close to Russian. Talking like some snotty Talk of the Town columnist, he even went so far in the end to comment on Selina's English, saying it was stilted! Yet if Timor had looked to be someone from this country (a docksider wearing dork, for example), Selina would not have followed him out of the Lark Tavern.

It was far too complicated to explain all this to the boy wearing the man's hat, a boy who even though he looked and acted like a hardboiled detective or a seasoned criminal had no idea how subtly duplicitous people can be. They might not even know they are lying because they are lying to themselves as well. The subtle duplicity of people who do not know they are lying because they are lying to themselves is something it takes experience to see. Dillan would not possess experience for many years. In the meantime, all Selina could do was clarify why Timor was the cheater, not her:

It was never about the money or even Bosky House, Selina explained. Just because something is your heritage that does not mean you have to hang around it all the time like a bird guarding its nest. Anyways birds only do that when they have eggs or hatchlings in them. For goddess's sake, Timor did not even want children. He did not want children and he did not want to go anywhere, or only to the sunny vacation places everyone goes to—the Virgin Islands, Cabo, or even Key West—those tropical mortuaries where you embalm yourself with rum drinks even as you tell yourself you are living the life.

Yes, the real cheater was Timor. Absolutely. The real cheater was Timor because he acted like a person who came from places that were shady not sunny and who would return to such places. He acted like he would return to such shady not sunny places, and he acted like he would take you with him. Well it turned out he had no plans to go anywhere—his biggest accomplishment was to park himself right here. In his big pre-revolutionary war era house where he could pretend he was from America before it was America. Surrounded by old rare books that he never had time to read and antique furniture that collected dust for the cleaning woman. You see, he was always working, always at the clinic collecting, as Dillan had put it, more dough. Always he was collecting more and more dough until he could have been the Pillsbury Doughboy. But it was not the weight gain that ruined things. Just because a person puts on weight does not mean that they are not the same person inside even when it is fifty pounds in five years. They are still the same person inside unless they were never that person in the first place. It was the things and wanting to get more things that ruined things. Actually, you could say that over time Timor just started to look like what he really was: a fat American materialist, even though he was from the former Soviet Union.

Selina did not mention the hysterectomy, though that was part of it, too. That was part of it as well, the loss that could not be compensated for, the small empty cavity between whatever else was down there, kidneys and bladder and whatnot, like a pocket without a lining let alone contents. Selina did not mention the hysterectomy because it still felt like a defeat, like you had forfeited the only weapon you had, not against Timor, but against time. Yes, against time, even though Timor had said you would live longer without it, that the cancer would come back and then it would spread, those were the odds. Those were the odds but certainly Selina would not share them with Dillan who, from the sound of it, had never lost anything but college tuition. Besides, he could always get a guaranteed government loan.

Selina's eyes were wet. It was all so sad, Timor's materialism not to mention Selina's hysterectomy, which meant she would never be able to make something more important than money. But she would not cry in front of Dillan, who could always buy himself a future with a guaranteed government loan, training for a career that might even support a family, eventually. No she would not cry in front of this fedora hatted boy, who had remained sunk in the pillows, his arms still folded over his chest, hands tucked in his armpits, fat uncircumsized penis nesting between his thighs the whole time Selina was talking about Timor, but leaving out the part about her uterus because it was just too much, now that there was nothing there at all except a shriveled pair of ovaries, which do not count when you are forty three years old, no matter what Timor had said about the best endocrinologist money could buy. No, Selina would not cry in front of the fedora hatted boy, and she would not do any more clarifying like a crime suspect in an interrogation room: case closed!

Case closed, but then Dillan reopened it.

I'm not so sure this Timor guy was a materialist, Dillan said yawning and stretching his arms back so that his hard young chest pushed forward. Tossing back the sheets and red spread, he swung his legs over the side of the bed. As he reached down for his clothes, he spoke over his shoulder, from beneath the brim of that hat: In fact, I would say it was the opposite.

Dillan stepped into the gray flannel slacks, pulling them with his back turned up over pale swimmer's buttocks. The waist was high like in a nineteen fifties movie or television show, a Perry Mason affectation to go with the hat. He zipped them up and turned, panted and hatted but naked inbetween.

Au contraire, he continued. I would call him an idealist. What is matter, after all? Fact is, Sexy Lady, that what we take to be matter has very little to do with the way the physical world actually is. When you get down to brass tacks, there are no brass tacks—at the subatomic level matter loses its material character altogether. For an excellent account of this in layman's terms read Particle Physics for Dummies. Finally the only way we can grasp matter is through our minds even as our minds are only matter, whatever that is. Ideas have a material basis, and our only access to the material world is thorough ideas. That's Justin E.H. Smith recycling George Berkeley. I read them both online the virtual university being the only I can afford now that my college fund is gone, a fund that was never more than an abstraction like all money—though you can't pay tuition without it.

Dillan picked up his white nylon dress shirt from the floor, sliding his arms into the sleeves then shrugging the slippery fabric over his strong swimmer's shoulders. You say this Timor guy was too interested in things but what are things finally but ideas, both at the level of their supposed materiality and at the level of our desire for them? Why do we want them? Because our minds have invested them with ideas—that they will make us more this or that, more American for example.

Speaking of being more American, Dillan said as he finished buttoning his slippery white shirt and then pushed the tails into his pants, there are virtues attached to that. You know, hard work, self-reliance, honesty. You could have tried to make it on your own, without hitching your trailer to some guy.

Dillan looked at the broken watch on his wrist. Time to blow this joint: I've got an appointment at the army recruiting center in half an hour. It's probably not the deal it was back in your day, but hey, they still help put you through school if you're willing to commit to your country.

He walked to the door. As he pushed down on the handle to let himself out, he turned: Good luck, toots.

The Selina Van Staal who had sexual relations with a barely adult man twenty years her junior after a night of drinking and debauchery instigated by the infamous Fritzi Akdikmen is not the same Selina Van Staal who is writing this now. To be sure, no person is the same person they were one year ago. For instance, if you regularly get your hair cut and wear it at a length no longer than six inches, then you should have a completely new head of hair at the end of 365 days. Of course this is not just about who you are at the physical level but also at the mental level. Although if what fedora hatted Dillan said was right, the two levels are not all that different and maybe even the same. So nevermind about whether you are a new body or a new mind or both: what is important is that you are a new you. You are a new you because you have had new experiences and anyways, you cannot re-experience previous experiences because life is not a book or a document with pages you can flip or scroll back to and revise.

The Selina Van Staal who is writing this now would not have driven into Albany, New York for a night of drinking and debauchery with Fritzi Akdikmen or had sexual relations with a boy who was barely a man the next morning. These actions contributed to the nihilistic outlook that made it possible to take part in the heist. The truth is (and nothing but the truth) that the person who is writing this now would not have done many of the things that her former self, or selves, did. That is not to abdicate responsibility. Poor decisions led to poor choices, and even if you are not the same person now as you were then you have to own them, just as when you write a bad check or make a charge on your credit card for something you cannot afford, the responsibility is yours. You have to own it all.

Still, in a memoir or confession you are allowed to say what you would do differently if you could go back in time. You are allowed to say what you would do differently if you could go back because a memoir or a confession is not just about what you did, but about how you feel about what you did. When you say that you would not do that thing but something else, you are acknowledging that you feel badly about it. Likewise, you are allowed to say that you would do a certain thing again. So if it were possible to go back, Selina would still follow Timor out of the Lark. No matter whom he turned out to be. Selina would follow Timor out of the Lark again and again, no matter whom he turned out to be each time.

Where do I start, *détka*? How do I begin to pick apart the garbage that you write? And to what purpose? To uncover some measly morsel of love beneath the mountain of crapola? Some scrap of affection that we both know is only fiscal regret? Why should I waste my time sifting through the trash of your prose?

Then again, who am I kidding with the phrase "waste my time"? You can't squander eternity. The dismal, endlessly droning like a dial tone that never becomes a ring, truth of the matter is that I'll take any diversion. I'll take any diversion and you, you will simply take anything, with the emphasis on "take" (from the OE *tacan*, to take, which in turn derives from the

PGmc. *taekanan*, of uncertain origin. The OED calls it "one of the elemental words of the language." That is, taking has never been about anything other than taking, and neither have you, you greedy, grasping bitch.). Thus you persist with this pretense that you can't read my messages. To vex me, to provoke me, to spur me on! The bucks and Bosky House are gone, but who knows, the saga of Timor Zinkovsky (hooker to healer to hoodwinked hubby) might be worth something. Perhaps as a companion volume to your own *Not Okay*. You could title it *Not OK*. Or even *Knot OK*—a bit cryptic for the mass market you hope to hook, but at the same time provocatively expressive of the emotional bondage you practiced on me. Continue to practice. And when you've fleeced me of every last word (because unlike time, language is not inexhaustible), you'll finally let me go. No, I would not put it past you, Selina Van Staal—grifting a ghost.

So it's *Not OK*, or *Knot OK*—a companion and corrective (or korrective, as in Oll Korrect) to *Not Okay*. That doesn't mean that everything you've written is inkorrect. Admittedly, I was less than "forthcoming about [my] foreign background." But think about it. This was not exactly a heritage for a young gynecologist with a budding practice geared toward the wives of affluent capitalists to broadcast, i.e., a former life as a Soviet refugee and prostitute, the whoreson whore of a Siberian logging camp slut and blackmarketeer of western lingerie. The associations with venereal disease and cold war privations would not have helped my professional image, with my patients, my colleagues or the insurers who determined my malpractice coverage rates—already somewhat higher than American born MDs, despite my solid gold standard (Nixon shock or no) US of A medical education and training.

Yet if I was vague or even reticent about my "foreign background," certainly I was not ashamed of it as implied in your account of your Ramada Plaza Inn fling with that fedora hatted, philosophizing pimple face (if only you had seen me in my youthful prime: then you would know the difference between caviar and spam!). The kid from Odessa stood (and still stands) in good company, Isaak Babel, Nikolai Gogol, Mikhail Bulgakov, Sergei Prokoviev, Petro Illych Tchaikovsky—all hailed from the Ukraine. Not to mention the lovely Grace Paley (née Goodside, an anglicization of Gutseit, like the Bliss that was once Blizinsky), who though born in the Bronx hailed from freshly transplanted Ukranian stock. And oh, Lee Strasberg, him too, Lee Strasberg (née Israel Strassberg), the father of method acting in America. An art I sometimes wonder if you studied. "The human being who acts is the human being who lives…" Strasberg said. "He must somehow be able to convince himself of the rightness of what he is doing in order to do things fully on the stage." Or to quote the oft quoted Dean Van Staal, "the good salesman believes in what he sells. Even if he doesn't."

So it's not that I think you were lying when you told Silly Dilly about "the mushroom pale soft yet tough look of the stranger, of his high quartz-white forehead with the pillowy tuft of black hair above and the impenetrable glasses below that had hit hard, fast and unfair, taking advantage of some blind spot you did not even know you had" (by the way, I can see that my style has fertilized your own. Even as you continue to refuse to give credit where credit is due.) For one, back then I was still easy on the eyes, despite that supposedly unsportsmanlike maneuver with the blind spot. If you were conning me, you were conning yourself too: I never heard more genuine appreciation in the sack. Or didn't hear, as it was your silence, your silence but for your ragged jagged shuddering breath, that convinced me.

I'll even buy that you believe you would have followed Timor Zinkovsky out of that bar again and again, "no matter whom he turned out to be each time." I'll buy that is what you believe *now*, for whatever reason (out of fiscal regret, or the hope of writing a bestseller)—but not that you believed it *then*.

Then being that weekend at the Hotel Americana. The weekend of July 31 through August 2, 2009—exact dates provided at no additional cost since they are only numbers. Numbers will never hurt me, but words and images may break my heart. Words and images as I relive those two nights for you even though I am dead and have no blood pumping organ to bust may kill me a second time. Yet how else to make you see the cheap sentiment you have sold yourself? I mean that amour amour and then some more lifetime channel bath of tears salts and lavender-scented lotion included bullshit about how you would do it all over. How else to make you see that you wouldn't do it all over than to show that you didn't?

The Hotel Americana in Chary Springs, New York, formerly the Pavillion Hotel, an early nineteenth century upstate destination for downstate fancy folk, who came to wallow in the mineral waters and nudge croquet balls over lawns mowed by local farm boys. Passed over by the Gilded Age elite as Saratoga and its racetrack provided faster entertainment. Rediscovered in the early to mid twentieth century by rich Jews not rich enough to get by the yid sniffing Saratoga hoteliers and maître d's. Gradually abandoned in the sixties and seventies as local resorts were superseded by Disney family vacation packages and cut rate, Carnival Line escapes (for the record, those brochures I left on the kitchen table were for yacht rentals, not cruises). Purchased in 1997 for the price of a week in Orlando with all the mickey mouse trimmings by two city fellows who five years and several hundred thousand dollars later reopened it as the Hotel Americana. I only discovered the landmark lodge through Google, in a search for resort hotels and spas upstate, but if Irwin had been living still he would have found it first. Found it first and perhaps attempted to lure me there, to both numb and stimulate me with icy but not iced gin martinis on the long, bunting hung, white pillared verandah that with its austere décor of red, white and black stripe upholstered wicker, astringently scented by true blue glazed pots of rosemary, was American in quotation marks.

Oh say can you see it was exactly the sort of place that appealed to me, both historically pedigreed and up to speed, subtly reeking of but not rotting with a past that wasn't mine and all the more appealing for that. No matter what you think, I never wanted to exchange my own history for another. The aim, rather, was to affect a past, like an ascot or a navy blazer with gold buttons. Or even a fedora. It was just the sort of place that appealed to me, and I thought you would like it too.

You hated it.

Not at first, of course. You'd been primed to like it, by the foreplay of the drive west on route 20, through the rich rolling green of long ago mountains like eroded fortunes past abandoned storefronts, peeling clapboard houses, and collapsing barns, the sort of piquant decay that pasted you to the passenger window with parted lips and narrowed eyes because "Timor you never know what treasure can be found in an old tool shed." Thank god there were no yard or garage sale signs posted that day: like I said, you'd take anything. And as we pulled into the gravel lot filled with new Priuses, Volkswagen Jettas and Passats, Mini Coopers and even a Lexus hybrid or two, the low-emission transport of the high credit scorers, you must've continued to feel the thrill of potential commerce. Because even though the educated and gainfully employed New Yorkers the place attracted tend to be scheme resistant, every mark has his (or her) markings: if you can spot 'em, you got 'em. Sure you still had me, but I suspect already you were looking for new ventures, new saps to tap before the spigot turned off. New saps to tap, as you worked on your "healing touch"—a nontactile technique described in the books I'd recently discovered on our doorstep, pried from their cardboard Amazon mailers and then carefully re-glued: *Reiki Shamanism: A Touch Guide to Out-of-Body Healing* and *Reiki: Universal Gift of God's Healing Love I & II Training Manual.* I have a hunch you were also baking and dispensing "herbal remedies," as I'd return at night to a kitchen still warm with the smells of chocolate and marijuana. Really, my sneekalinka, the installation of spyware on your cellphone, to track your healing dealings, would not have been unjustified. That is not, however, to admit that said spyware was installed.

Every mark has his (or her) markings, and I fancied, as we stepped up onto the long bunting draped porch to the red door in its black frame, Hotel Americana in gold Copperplate style caps painted across the lintel, that you were scanning the guests loosely assembled on the porch for happy hour—the slim seventyish woman with the stem glass of white wine and the grimace of chronic pain beneath her scudding blue eyes or the thirty-something man with the blond samurai ponytail, madras shorts and converse sneakers, an open tin of tobacco and zigzag papers in his lap, deftly rolling a cigarette in mid air as his black cocktail dress sheathed college-aged companion chattered on about somebody's "over-the-top" wedding reception—for prospects. Fine with me. Like my long ago Scarsdale foster rents who tolerated my underage foster siblings' forays into the liquor cabinet so long as they did their drinking on the homefront, I'd decided to turn a blind eye to your transactions. And if you ended up in prison, well at least I would know where you were.

But then I saw that you weren't looking at the other guests, but gazing up at the bunting: "I am not a patriot, Timor."

We stepped inside. To the right was a small, empire style reception desk. Behind it was a small young woman scarcely out of her teens, in a white, empire style dress, cotton lawn gathered beneath a pair of small, pert breasts, standing stiffly like some central New York caryatid: "May I help you, Sir?"

"I have a reservation for two, for two nights, in room two. The name is Dr. Timor Zinkovsky."

The girl bent her smooth young neck to an open reservation book. Pursing her lips, she traced her finger down the first page, then the second, then back up the second, returning to the first where her buffed nail stopped midway: "The only 'Dr.' I see here is a Dr. Sink."

Recalling that the person who'd taken my reservation had had some trouble with my name, I asked "Is there a phone number?"

"518 758 8935."

"That's my number. Someone misspelled my name," I responded, though "misspelled" was an understatement.

"Well Sir, if Dr. Sink isn't here by 6pm, you can have his room. But his room is number one, not number two. Number one is here on the first floor, with an entrance right over there."

She pointed across the room. "It also has another door that opens onto the verandah."

"I'd prefer the second floor," I replied, already imagining verandah revelers, stomping and shouting, disturbing the post-coital peace, ruining not only our sleep but any chance of reconciliation. Call me crazy, but that is what I was hoping for, even after the Rhinebeck debacle and the seven weeks of silence that had ensued with you camped in your father's old quarters on the other side of the house. Seven weeks for you to stare up at that stamped tin ceiling tracing the stitches over your groin, exploring the dimensions of your loss. Seven weeks to calculate your price for an organ that unlike Dean's missing eye could not even provide perspective. Call me crazy but I was ready to pay, liable or not (the human papilloma virus doesn't care who had more sexual partners, Timor or Selina).

"I'm sorry, Sir, but all the rooms on the second floor are booked."

"Well then how about another room down here? Is there one at the back?"

"No, I'm afraid all the other rooms are upstairs."

"Then how about a room upstairs?"

"I already told you, Sir—the upstairs rooms are booked."

"May I speak to the owners of this establishment?"

The girl crossed her arms over her empire waist. "Mr. Douglas and Mr. Warren are out of town this weekend at the annual conference for the National Trust for Historic Preservation in Nashville, Tennessee. They will not be back until Monday."

"OK, then just put us downstairs in Room Number One."

"You will have to wait to check in. If Dr. Sink does not arrive by 6pm, I can give you his room. That is the best I can do, sir. In the meantime, you are welcome to join us for happy hour, either out on the verandah or at the bar." She pointed to the bar, a copper topped counter with a few bar stools, just beyond a partially open door through which I could see a dim space interspersed with white linen shrouded tables.

I was tired (sleep had not been my ally since your decampment to Dean's old room) and hungry: I either wanted to lie down or have dinner. I did not want to drink on an empty stomach. I pointed to the partially open door. "Could we at least get something to eat?"

"I apologize, but our award winning grill room does not open until 6:30 tonight. Our Ballymaloe, Ireland trained chef was delayed this afternoon by a family emergency."

You spoke: "We can just go somewhere else nearby, Timor."

Somewhere else nearby would be Cooperstown, which was still at least thirty minutes away and also sure to be thronged with baseball fans, hoardes of little Andys and Wesleys along with their huffing parents chasing after cheesedog dreams of family fun and togetherness. No thanks.

"I have a reservation here for two nights. If I have to wait an hour for myself not to arrive so that I can check into a room that is not the room I requested when I made my reservation, I will."

I turned back to the young woman in the empire dress, who in the meantime had sat down behind the empire desk and picked up a paperback novel: *The Marble Faun*. "I'd like a gin and tonic with Bombay Sapphire if you have it, and a glass of reisling sent out to the porch. Also a dish of pretzels, peanuts—whatever you've got."

Without lifting her eyes from the page, she replied: "I'm sorry sir—the person who normally covers happy hour on the verandah is ill. Please do feel free to get drinks at the bar with its antique copper counter from a nineteenth century tavern in Springfield, Massachusetts. Normally we only allow plastic glasses outside, but tonight we've run out."

Out on the long covered porch, we found an unoccupied wicker love seat. We sat down, sipping our drinks in loveless silence. Several swallows of gin later, sans pretzels, peanuts or any variety of alcohol absorbing carbohydrate," since according to the bartender "folks finished off the bar snacks half an hour ago," my brain was a leaking boat. Struggling to stay conscious (it was not simply a matter of sink or swim, but Sink *and* swim, at least until 6pm), I reached for your hand. You withdrew it. So I attempted to focus on the people standing a few feet in front of us. One of them was the woman I'd noted you not noting on the way in, the seventyish woman with the scudding blue eyes. With her was a man who appeared to be her husband or fraternal twin (they wore matching seersucker resort wear) and a boy with a head of glossy black curls. The woman's hands draped over the kid's shoulders. A thin blond man in his early thirties, all in black Hugo Boss from his polo shirt down to his suede driving shoes, a martini in his hand, had approached the three, his eyes upon the boy: "What gorgeous hair. You'll get plenty of attention with that when you're older."

"It looks like he is getting plenty of attention now," you commented, loudly.

The thin man ignored you but the woman turned toward our loveless loveseat: "What was that, young lady?"

"I said it appears that he is getting plenty of attention already. Maybe more than he requires."

The man in Boss black raised his eyebrows: "Well as Jenny Holzer says, any surplus is immoral." He took a sip of his martini.

"I do not care for the sound of that one bit," the old woman said, her hands cinching the boy's biceps.

"I hope you all enjoy your stay." The man turned his back, sipping his martini as he walked away.

You stood up and extended your hand. "Hello, I am Selina."

"How nice to meet you," the woman said, her expression of chronic pain momentarily turning acute as she suffered the grip of the dairyman's daughter. "I am Mrs. Eva Karetski, this is my husband Mr. Sidney Karetski, and our grandson, Sam."

"Hello, Mr. Karetski," and then squatting on your haunches, "Hello, Sam. Guess what? I have a rabbit in my car! Would you like to see her? What time are you leaving? Tomorrow at noon? How about first thing in the morning, when I take her out to exercise? Okay, we have a date!"

Soon the four of you were thick as thieves, or rather, the three Karetskis were thick with *a* thief. From the loveseat, drifting in and out of awareness, I caught snatches of your conversation. Reminiscences about childhood pets (Mr. Karetski's family, before his father became successful in "textiles," had raised both rabbits and chickens), which led to bromides about kinder, simpler times when you didn't have to watch children "like a hawk" to protect them from "predators" and how hard it is to raise a child these days in a world filled with "unregistered firearms" (as opposed to registered ones; I wonder which kind your father shot himself with) and "drug addicts," which turned to a discussion of prescription pain killers and modern medicine where the doctors never had time to talk to you because they were "too busy handing out the pills." Just before I fell asleep, I caught the word "reiki" and the phrase "a healing technique that relieves pain without physical contact," a phrase that seemed to reassure Mrs. Karetski (who must've still been feeling the squeeze of the dairyman's daughter): "why that sounds just wonderful."

When I opened my eyes again, the porch was deserted and voices were sifting through the dining room window screens to the right. I went inside. In the lobby, the girl in the empire dress was still reading behind the empire desk, but the paperback copy of the *Marble Faun* had been exchanged for a Kindle. She looked up: "Oh hello, Dr. Zinkovsky. I have some good news! Dr. Sink never arrived, so Room Number One is all yours. Your wife has already checked in."

She handed me a brass key with a brass tag engraved "no. 1": "Mrs. Zinkovsky said you might need an extra key. She's in our award winning grillroom having dinner with the Karetski party." Returning to her Kindle screen, the girl added "Please do let us know if there is anything we can do to make your stay at the Hotel Americana more enjoyable."

Savory smells and appreciative murmurs drifted through the entrance to the dining room. But while my hunger remained, my appetite was gone. The thought of attempting to join you, those two old seersucker suited suckers and their curlicued cutie turned my rumbling stomach. Anyway, I knew it wasn't worth it. Dinner, slow-grilled, would be followed by dessert, preferably something flambé, if that was in the culinary repertoire of the Ballymaloe, Ireland trained chef, because "you know the alcohol just burns off," and then tea and coffee in the sitting area of the lobby, dragging on and on until every last ember of conversation had died and Sam was sacked out on the settee, his curly head pillowed by his grandmother's lap. Or maybe even by yours. Getting anything going after that, back in Room Number One, would be hopeless.

But tomorrow the Karetskis would be gone. Further, I planned to be fortified by a full night's sleep (klonopin addiction be damned, I'd take two of the little yellow fuckers if I had too. And I would have to, after my verandah nap.). Turning my back on the empire-waisted receptionist and her "award winning grillroom," I walked across the lobby and inserted the "extra" brass key into its hole. Tomorrow I would regain my wife.

When I woke the next morning, you were gone, but the imprint on the mattress to my left, your suitcase on the luggage rack (mine had been displaced to the floor, even though if you'd bothered to look, you would have found another rack in the adjoining dressing room), and the open animal crate on the floor attested to your proximate presence, along with that of your three-footed familiar (do you ever wonder about the luck lost with that missing leg? Maybe things would have turned out better for you if the animal had kept all four.).

You were gone, but I could guess where you were—out behind the hotel on the big shade tree ringed lawn we'd seen yesterday afternoon as we walked from the gravel lot around to the front. "What a perfect place for Florence to do her binkies!" Or for a bald eagle to swoop down and seize her in mid caper (too much, probably, to ask of the Hotel Americana guest services, though I'd just read in the *New York Times* that the birds had been removed from the endangered species list). So I had a choice: to go view the grotesque antics of your pet from a red umbrella shaded table on the back patio where, according to the guest services binder on the bedside stand, "fresh baked scones and Freedom roast coffee" were served until 9:30am, or to relax a while longer in bed. Coney freak show complete with clapping Karetskis or a little quiet wanking time under the

600 thread count white sheets? You decide. And actually you did. Imagining your face souring at the sight of me, I decided the scones and Freedom roast coffee could wait.

As I took my soft self in hand, I surveyed the room from the four poster bed: the tomato bisque painted walls, the creamy white wainscotting, the porcelain pineapple shaped lamps, the tapestry print armchairs, the gilt framed mirror and two paintings, one of a clipper ship and the other of a horse and its owner or trainer. It was the kind of room that makes a man feel well fed even as the sheer muslin curtains fluttering a little in the breeze from the open (though shade drawn) windows hinted at less substantial pleasures. See-thru nighties, peekaboo panties: in my mind's eye I dressed you in them, not just for my own titillation but for your imaginary humiliation. "I am not a sex doll or a servant, Timor" you said when I ordered the Parisian parlourmaid outfit, still het up by your get-up that first time in my office. I didn't know then the occasion was a one-time deal. Not a sex doll or a servant and as it turned out, not a patriot either, but what the hell, you were my wife.

You were my wife like my dick was dick (and yours too, to have and to hold, until death did us part). My dick was my dick and yet it resisted all my efforts, both physical and mental, to excite it, like a protestor passively resisting arrest. I flopped back on the mattress, yanked up the waistband of my black silk boxers, size XXL.

I lifted my eyes from the silken morass of my groin back to the tomato bisque walls. If I couldn't enjoy myself, at least I could enjoy the atmosphere. The painting on the wall to my left was the one of the horse and a man who, as I crawled over the mattress for a better view, was clearly the owner. His full, brushed beard like a white ruff over a tailored chestnut colored frock coat, black derby hat and polished black boots bespoke his buying power. Not to mention the horse itself, which likewise sported a chestnut coat, a muscle-binding hide that shone a uniform glossy brown except for two white stockinged hind hocks. The horse, like the derby hat and the boots was a commodity—just like you, my Selinka. Only you sold yourself. You sold yourself the day you tottered into my exam room on your own two hoofs.

How angry you will be when you read those last lines! No more blank impassivity, as if there is nothing to see but your screen saver: your nostrils will flare and you may even mutter, "You did not own me, Timor." My response? Of course not. You sold yourself to me but I never "owned" you, just like I never "owned" that sad sack between my legs (my dick was my dick but there was no deed of sale). Sure I refer above to "regain[ing] my wife" but only in the sense that people speak of regaining the use of an injured limb or mental faculties lost due to brain trauma. You were part of me and I was part of you (til death did us divvy). And even still something of me remains with you, like the vapor over a recently flushed crapper—a feculent perfume I can smell on your otherwise flat prose, whether you will admit it or not. So if I remind you that you sold yourself to me, if I remind you that you acted like a whore, it is only to set the record straight. You were the one who tangled love with commerce and that is *Knot OK.*

Heaving my bulk off the bed, I stood to read the text at the bottom of the painting. "Risdik's Humbertorian" was the name of that fine animal. Risdik's Humbertorian, "sired by Abracadabra, he by Mumbo Jumbo, and he imported by Messenger. His dam was Penelope, mare by imported Beckett's Bellfounder; grand dam Goldsmith Maid, by Old One Eye…"

I returned to the image of the horse descended from "Old One Eye" and the plutocrat in the derby hat. The man stood beside the horse, gripping the halter just a few inches beneath the animal's nose—no slack allowed. No slack allowed as the rich man assessed the viewer, collaterally assured of his own net worth, while the horse appeared from a side view, its gaze downcast. I touched the glass over the horse's powerful rump, the slope where its croup merged into a black cascade of tail. It occurred to me that I should have kept a tighter rein on the daughter of Old One Eye. I might be enjoying her still. Then again, the horse's head was in profile: what would another angle reveal? The creature's other eye (assuming the progenitor's ocular singularity had not been passed on) could be turned in the direction it was preparing to bolt, after giving frock coat a good kick in the balls.

Hell maybe you planned it all along: a horse trade where you were both horse and trader. I wouldn't put it past you. Fill up the saddlebags and make a run for it—giddyap and go. Giddyap and go because there's no law against women who don't have a dime marrying men who do. Indeed, as I learned in Survey of the British Novel 1800-1900 at SUNY Purchase, circa 1976, it is a truth universally acknowledged that a man possessed of a fortune must be in want of a wife.

No I wouldn't put it past a horse-trading whore like you, swapping sex for your trough of golden oats and a two million dollar woodland stable. Taking your dutiful groom for a ride that was good for a year or two, but then got rougher and rougher. Rougher and rougher until it was all I could do to hang on, hoping that you'd let up, slow down, back off from your quest for kids or "quality of life"—whatever mirage it was that you dumped me for. I write "mirage" because for all your whore's sense, I'm not sure you knew what you were after.

A heads up: next time you turn on your computer, I'll be watching, spectrally recording the minutest movements of your facial muscles, along with every ocular shift, including the dilations and contractions of your pupils. Even if you do not utter a word, I will know that you are reading this. And with the help of some recently installed malware (a gift from a government spook who used to work for Homeland Security), I will be able to accurately gauge your emotions. But I will not be able to penetrate your thoughts even as mind and matter are essentially the same "stuff" (to recall pimple face's tutorial). Something to do with interface issues, my spook friend says. All the FEDS (Facial Emotion Detection Software) can tell me when you read this is whether I am getting hot or cold. Hot or cold, even as the cache I want—your thoughts that weekend you walked out on me—is, more likely than not, inaccessible. A lockbox buried under layer upon layer of self-deception, that even if we could reach and then manage to pry it open, would reveal a mess of self-immolating contradictions, cremating before our eyes like a surgically excised organ in a hospital incinerator.

But onward ho (in full acknowledgment of my own venal history), with *Knot OK*. Ceasing my investigation of Risdik's Humbertorian who with his long pedigree and short leash only served as a painful reminder of past oversights (always meet the mama before you wed the *dotchka*) and indulgences, I walked around the four poster to a window with the intention of opening it further. As it was, the three-inch space between sash and sill permitted barely enough air to flutter the curtains and suddenly I felt the need to fill my lungs like bellows, to take the bracing breath I needed to slap the bitch face of day. And then I'd deal with you.

Only the window wouldn't move, up or down—it was stuck three inches open or three inches short of closed, gummed in place with thick white paint. A good, hard downward shove might free it, but also shatter the thin paint freckled panes. And then I'd have to pay for damages, on top of everything else. I tried another window, also a few inches short of open or shut, but like the first it wouldn't budge. What did they do with them in winter? The remaining two windows, which I didn't bother to inspect, were closed.

In accordance with the room description provided by the reception desk caryatid, there was also a door that opened out onto the verandah. You'd set the rabbit's crate on the floor before it. I gave the empty crate a kick to the side, rattling the metal hatch but also stubbing my bare toes on the hard plastic shell.

The interior door opened easily, but the screen door beyond was, like the windows, glued into its frame with paint. I pressed my nose against the mesh, sucking the morning air, already warm and thick with a vegetally laced humidity, into my nostrils. Foot phalanges throbbing, I thought of one of the "fun leporid factoids" you'd shared with me following your adoption of that three legged freak: that rabbits eat their own excrement. The purpose was to extract "maximum nutrients" from their food, and wasn't that admirable—not only were they vegetarians (at that point you'd given up meat entirely and it'd been years since we'd shared a plate of steak tartare) but "recyclers." Then you went on to pontificate: "It is like she does not waste a minute of her life, Timor—even the past." Would you be happier with me if I started eating my own crap, I wondered (actually, you could say that's what I'm doing now:

if only you could see my shit-eating grin). I smacked the frame that held the screen hard with my palm, and to my surprise, the door swung open. After fishing a robe from my floored suitcase and securing my girth, I stepped out.

Half empty (or half full, depending on your perspective and drinking habits) glasses from last night's happy hour sat on the railings and I caught a whiff of stale alcohol that mixed with the steamed vegetable air brought back the borscht and vodka dregs of my baba's country kitchen. The verandah was empty except for a lone figure at the other end, a plume of hair falling forward over his face as he twirled something between his fingers: it was the man with the blond samurai ponytail, rolling another cigarette or possibly, in the absence of fellow guests and staff, a joint. I was about to sit back in a white chaise lounge on my end, to give him as wide a berth as I could for his activity, which if he went on to light up on hotel grounds was probably illegal either way—wacky tobacky or simple sedating nicotine leaf—when he turned his head in my direction.

"Good morning. Care to join me for a toke?" he called, in a voice that mixed Brahmin with beach boy.

I imagine his plan was to counter any objection I might make to fumes drifting my way by making me his accomplice. And as you know, I never smoked pot or tobacco—couldn't stand the feel of that acridity in my throat or the herbal stench, an aversion that dated back to my hooking days in lower Manhattan—to yellow stained fingers pressing down on my shoulders, clouds of secondhand smoke settling on my head like phantom laurels even as I fought for breath, struggling for the finish. But then I imagined you returning to our room, noting the open inner door, and stepping out on the porch, noting chubby hubby at one end and samurai swinger at the other. I decided to make a preemptive alliance with my own sex, before you got the chance to choose sides.

He licked and sealed the flap of the joint as I sat down, on the other side of a wicker and glass coffee table with a black potted red begonia in the center.

"All yours, man," he said, stretching his long arm across the table. "Need a light?"

I waved it away: "Don't smoke, dude—makes me paranoid. But you go ahead and have fun."

I watched him pull a pink plastic lighter from his shorts, his eyes crinkling with satisfaction as he lit his spliff and drew. He looked older at close range, forty five or more. But over all, he was what both sexes would term a "hunk": at least six foot three, with a lean, rangy body and long blue eyes riding the crests of strong cheek bones. His loins girded in leather instead of madras, he would've fit right in with a Viking crew, pillaging and impregnating his way down the pre-modern European coastline, gifting whole populations with his haploid group. Easily I could see one of your ancestresses over his shoulder, black hair spilling down, fists beating his back. The thing I hated most about his type was that even when they put on weight they looked good—their big frames could carry it. Less reach vertically gives you less leeway horizontally, although I remember you once calling my height, only one half inch greater than your own, "perfect," because we would "always see eye to eye." But what about that other eye, the wandering one?

He picked a fleck of pot off his lip, then licked it from his finger. "Delectable. You don't know what you're missing man." Raising the joint to his lips, he took another deep toke. The miasma of his pleasure drifted across the table. My nostrils twitched.

"So is that your girlfriend or your wife?" he asked, reaching forward to tap a bit of ash into the begonia plant.

"My wife."

"Not bad, not bad. Even better if she was wasn't though, don't you think?"

"Excuse me?"

"I'm referring to the notion of 'friends with benefits.' Froggy doesn't have to go a courting anymore. Or worry about some princess sinking her golden claws into his estate. We've got feminism to thank for that. Is your wife a feminist?"

An interesting question. For all of our kitchen talk those first years, I could not recall you defining yourself by *any* ideology. Feminist, pro-choicer, pro-lifer, leftist, centrist, democrat, republican, libertarian, capitalist, socialist, communist, anarchist: never had you identified a political position. Sure there was the time you quoted Rosa Luxemburg to me: "Those who do not move, do not notice their chains," but that was only to get me to consider buying real estate in Eastern Europe, after you read an article in the *New York Times* "Home & Garden" section about renovated pre-Soviet era flats in Prague. Did you ever once even register to vote? I don't think so. "Then they will call me up for jury duty, Timor. I once lost a very good job that way." What it was you never said. All I knew was that in the sixteen years you'd lived with me, you'd never had a job to lose. And that you were *not* a patriot.

"I didn't think so, bro," he said, even though I had not spoken my thoughts.

"You've got to get yourself a feminist," he went on. "Or better yet, a post-feminist. Twenty-something, college educated, or preferably still in college because they're more malleable, on the pill. One of those chicks (and that's right, I said 'chicks' because if you haven't noticed our politically correct nineties lexicon is extinct. Too bad, so sad.), one of those babes, who says 'I totally believe in feminism.' But of course she's wearing a wonder bra under her button popper and a pair of juicy pants that scream 'objectify me as a whole but focus on the T&A, boys.'"

He reached again into the pocket of his madras shorts, pulling out a flat silver case. Inside were what appeared to be business cards and a tiny pair of manicure scissors. Removing the scissors, he snipped off the head of the joint over the begonias and I heard a faint sizzle as the cinder burned through tender leafage. "You have to know your limits," he said. Before stashing the roach in the case, he removed one of the cards. Stretching across the table, he placed it before me on the pebbled glass.

"Of course she's beautiful if ten years past her expiration date, and sexy, even with those big feet and the wingtips. And old habits die hard. Believe me, I know. I once dated the same woman for three years. Just don't forget you have options."

He stood up, sliding the silver case back into his pocket. "Enjoy the rest of your day, bro," he said as he bent to retrieve a cordovan valise that had been stashed behind his chair. Possibly I glimpsed the sheen of scalp through the swept up hair of his samurai do, but that might have been wishful thinking.

I watched him step off the porch, then head swinging his bag and whistling what sounded like an old blues song toward the gravel parking lot. I didn't look to see which expensive car was his, but I did pick up his business card:

Kirk Rinehardt, Esq.
Divorce and Matrimonial Law, Trials and Appeals in All Courts

435 Madison Ave, New York, NY 10022
Phone: 212 832 1877
Fax: 212 832 0912
e-mail Kirk@KirkRinehardt.com

The room was still empty when I returned inside. I decided I would get dressed and join you, Karetskis or no: I would do whatever was needed to save our marriage from that blond tufted shark and his ilk.

Showered, shaved and fully attired, I studied myself for a moment in the full-length mirror on the door of the white coin tile and gold fixtured bathroom. If well over fighting weight, I was still a contender. Still a contender with my plush brush of silver threaded black hair (grown out, there would've been more than enough for a pony tail; enough for a fucking draft horse), my hard-planed Slavic visage polished with Clinique aftershave lotion (a part of my anatomy that along with my legs seemed lard-resistant), my invincible taste in menswear, as evidenced by my Oswald Boateng linen silk sportjacket. What happened to that Savile Row treasure, by the way—whose bespoke booty did it become, yours or Sandy Giersten's? (Sometimes I wonder if I would have been any worse off with Kirk Reinhardt, Esq.; Giersten was not just a money grubber but a soul sucker. As Irwin warned, when he advised a preemptive pre-nup, getting the best divorce lawyer in the business is like getting the best devil in Hell. Oh well.).

No one was attending the reception desk, nor was anyone at the bar. The lounge area to the left (where I'd envisioned the slow libido draining drip of after dinner conversation with the Karetskis taking place) was empty as well. I stepped through the white painted French doors leading to the back, onto the abandoned patio with its several red umbrella shaded tables and koi pool the length and width of an open grave in the center, thick with water hyacinths. A cloth napkin lay on the flagstones at the foot of a wrought iron chair, scant testimony to the meal that, according to the guest services binder at my bedside, still should've been taking place (it was 9:20, according to my Rolex). Not a crumb of scone or splash of freedom roast remained on the pebbled glass tabletops. The only movement came from the fingerling carp in their pool, lacerating the stem-snarled dark with orange and gold.

I retreated back through the French doors into the lounge area. An antique grandfather clock ticked in the corner, pendulum sweep sweeping the seconds. Where were all the people who had crowded the verandah last night? Where were you? A sudden wave of heat passed over me, a metabolic fluke that left my skin clammy and my legs shaky. Maybe the Boateng jacket was a layer too much that muggy morning, or maybe the old mortal coil was already starting to malfunction (my medically documented death was less than three months off). I lowered myself into a club chair. On the other side of the room, in a room or recess behind the bar, dishes clattered. Eventually, someone would emerge and in the meantime I would sit and wait, cushioned by cool smooth leather, the arms of the chair curving round like a loose embrace. In front of me there was a Franklin stove on a dais of brick, mercifully cold. But how cozy to snuggle before it some December afternoon, your honey in your lap. Maybe after a day of hitting the slopes at a local ski resort, like the one advertised in a framed vintage poster on the wall behind the stove. Exhorting the viewer to "Ski Mount Otsego: Slopes, Trails, Tow," it featured a white toothed young man in a nineteen forties era red parka brandishing a ski pole like a sickle. In fact, the poster brought back propaganda images from my Soviet youth. It also summoned up all your past attempts to get me to go hiking, camping, berry picking, canoeing, snowshoeing, and yes, skiing—all your mostly failed efforts to get me to accompany you out into "nature." Even as you knew that "nature" for me was always a phenomenon best enjoyed from a bay window, balcony, verandah, portico or patio, preferably with a stiff drink in hand. Now I wonder if the nature crap might've been the price of the honey in the lap.

As anticipated, someone did finally appear behind the bar. It was the reception desk caryatid from the night before, only the empire waist dress had been replaced by a zippered navy nylon cyclist's jersey which as the girl turned to place clean glasses on a shelf behind the bar displayed "BETSY" in white block letters. I walked over and took a seat at the copper topped counter. The jersey was part of a sporty ensemble—red spandex shorts spangled with white stars and a pair of blue and white striped cycling shoes that clicked over the floor as she walked back and forth, lifting glasses from a plastic stacking crate and putting them away.

"Betsy?"

"Oh good morning, Doctor Zinkovsky. How is your room?"

"OK. Have you seen my wife?"

"No sir, I only arrived ten minutes ago," she replied, pushing a damp strand of hair out of her face. I caught a whiff of young female sweat flowered with antiperspirant.

"Well, is there anyone around who might have seen her this morning?"

"I would be happy to inquire in back. I think one or two of the breakfast wait staff are still here."

"What do you mean 'still here'? That book in the room says breakfast is supposed to be served until 9:30. It's only 9:25."

"People don't come to the Hotel Americana to loll around all day, sir. Most of our guests want to get out as early as possible to hike, to swim, to fish or to go kayaking on Lake Otsego, or as James Fennimore Cooper dubbed it in his fabled *Leatherstocking Tales*, the Glimmerglass. Even the less physically active may find plenty to do, as the region is home to numerous museums and family fun centers, including the famed Baseball Hall of Fame in Cooperstown, all wheel chair accessible."

"Fine. Go see if you can find one of 'the breakfast wait staff.' Please. And if you could get him, or her, to come out here, I'd appreciate it."

A few minutes later, Betsy returned with a gangly teenage boy in black pants and a white polo shirt spattered around the breast pocket with what looked like egg yolk and Tabasco sauce. He wiped the grease from his mouth with the tail of his shirt, revealing a long, tanned and fat-free torso: "What can I do for you, Doctor Sink?"

I considered asking the kid if he'd had anything to do with the reservation mix-up, but decided to let it go. "I'm wondering if you might have seen my wife this morning, a tallish woman with long dark hair. I believe she had a rabbit with her."

"Yowza. I mean, yes. That rabbit was tearing all around on the lawn. Our pet policy is no free pets. Not free like they don't cost nothing, but free like off leash or not in a crate. So we had to ask her to take it away. Well she got all amped, I mean, annoyed, and stomped off. The older folks and the kid went with her."

"Do you have any idea where they might've gone?"

"Well Dave, that's our dishwasher and kitchen deejay, Dave heard them in the parking lot when he was taking out the trash. They were talking about the state park at the top of the lake. Now if you'll excuse me, Doctor Sink, I need to get back to a Guest Services Staff meeting."

The state park at the top of the lake. We'd stopped there one wintry spring, early on, after an unpleasant visit with Irwin in Cooperstown. As I recall, he called you an "opportunist" to your face. When I apologized in the car on the way home, you lisped "thsticks and thstones may break my bones, but words will never hurt me." Knowing, however, that that occasional lisp, along with the remnant of the Staten Island accent that accompanied it, was a symptom of distress, I instantly obeyed when you pointed out the "Skate and Snow Tube Rentals" sign at the entrance to Glimmerglass State Park. "Oh look Timor, Thstop!" I ended up that day with two fractured ribs, after flying so fast through the rock strewn brush that I couldn't tell the "thsticks" from the "thstones." My ribcage still ached in remembrance. While it was many years later and a different season entirely, I decided to wait for you at the hotel. Who knew, in your aggrieved state, what natural resources you'd find in that park to express your displeasure.

With recent issues of the *London Review of Books*, *The New Yorker, The Atlantic*, and *Town & Country*, all originally gift subscriptions from Irwin, I'd pass the rest of the morning on the verandah, maybe even, as lunchtime approached, indulging in a bloody mary with good gin (always gin, never vodka. "Ah Jennifer, Juniper…" as Irwin used to sing). Or two. And if you weren't back yet, I'd lunch alone in the "award winning grill room," and doze afterwards in Number One, which lacked nothing but ventilation.

Good thing I had a plan, since it was late afternoon when you returned. I opened my eyes to see you nudging the rabbit into its crate. I had every fucking right to be pissed off. But my first feeling was simple pleasure. Simple pleasure, I swear, at the sight of your slick dark hair falling forward over your sun pinked cheekbones as you latched the crate's metal door. You stood, your back to the bed. You were wearing white clamdigger shorts that set off your tanned calves. There were grass stains on the seat. Curled blue in the back of your knee was a varicose vein: I wanted to kiss it.

You turned around. Your face was a rose suffused brown. Beautiful.

"I missed you," I said.

You crossed your arms: "Timor, you said that pets were welcome here. Clearly that is not true. I could not leave Florence locked up all day."

And that was it: shazam. With a wave of your wand, my longing turned into resentment: "You might've told me where you were going, or left a note; it's called courtesy."

"Okay. Right now I am going to take a bath. Here. In the bathroom. I hope you do not mind if I lock the door. It is called privacy."

I remained in bed. Unable to follow the columns of tiny print in the *London Review of Books* (and having read *The New Yorker*, *The Atlantic* and *Town & Country* cover to cover), I found a home improvement show on the television that until your return had remained untouched—in a faux antique cabinet appliqued with pineapples. What would it take to improve our home; what would it take to make it habitable for us both? On the show, they started with radon mitigation and asbestos abatement. "These are proven carcinogens that we dealt with first thing," the show's expert intoned. "A pure, nontoxic atmosphere was crucial for the health and happiness of our homeowner and his family."

An hour later the bathroom door opened, a cloud of steam pushing through the small dressing room area into the stuffy bedroom. I smelt your shampoo, the therapeutic coal tar formula that you used to keep a slight case of psoriasis at bay, an astringent woodland pitch. You hung back, hiding yourself like some forest sprite or fright, but in a moment or two you would have to emerge. You'd want to exchange your chlorophyll smeared clamdigger outfit for something else, and your suitcase was on the luggage stand by the window. I wondered if you'd walk out naked or wrapped in towels. Before you'd never been shy about displaying your body, but that was before. I hadn't seen your bare torso since the surgery.

I kept my gaze on the television screen but out of the corner of my eye I saw skin. You rustled around in your suitcase, then retreated.

Skin was a good sign. Skin was surely a display, not just of epidermal imperfections and scars, including the eight centimeter long red pelvic cicatrix that in another year or two would become a thin white line overgrown with pubic hair, but also of good faith. Good faith and trust in my expert opinion that the surgery had been necessary. No drug or radiation treatment could eradicate the possibility of another endometrial uprising: the only solution was the final solution: getting it out. "It" not even being all of it, a subtotal of the total, as sister cervix and her reproductive crew, fallopian tubes and ovaries, remained. You still had everything you needed to breed, thanks to me, because as you damn well know, the pathologist's report initially indicated an even more radical procedure. Thanks to me, to my insistence on not just two biopsies but three, since slides must be placed under a microscope by technicians who are sometimes poorly trained and often overworked. You still had everything you needed to breed, but to whelp you required help.

You required help and after seven solo weeks of soul searching, I was ready to provide it. My thirteenth year anniversary gift(s) to you: the gestational surrogate of your choice. And if your aging ovaries failed to respond to the ministrations of the best endocrinologist money could buy (an attractive brunette I'd met at an AMA conference in Denver, Colorado) and/or both a vasovastomy and a vasoepididymostomy failed to undo my seminal deceit, an egg donor and a sperm donor as well. Together we'd make a baby, no matter how many of us it took. Sliding my hand deep into the pocket of my loose linen pants (like I already said, I was ready to pay, liable or not) I imagined making my candle-lit procreative pledge over dinner in the award winning grill room, imagined the six hundred thread count reconciliation that would surely follow in Room Number One. With good faith on both sides we would regain all that we had lost, and more.

In the bathroom, the hairdryer blasted. A sound that did not normally accompany your grooming routine: "Heat damages the protein shaft. Healthy hair is unprocessed hair." Although you'd recently begun to dye your glossy tresses, after discovering the first pigment deficient strands: "I am not yet ready to look like an old woman and now that I cannot conceive, toxins do not matter." Well with a surrogate's uterus (and egg too, if necessary), you could keep your color and have your kid, too.

When you finally emerged, my dick lifted even as my heart sank (Dr. Sink, redux). What were you thinking with that electrocuted hair, your eyes glittering through mascara-rimmed lashes? Where did you get that get-up, the silver fish scale mini, the plunging nylon net top, the lucite platforms with what appeared to be small winged insects embalmed in the heels? Was the look come hither or run away screaming? My heart sank some more even as my cock crowed. Finally, I let past precedent, the historical fact (long consigned to erotic fantasy but no less true for that) of those shiny black, granny tie ankle boots with the six-inch heels decide. You wanted to get it on, but after all the weeks, weeks become months, without discourse (let alone intercourse), you couldn't get it *out.* The hair, the make-up, the clothes, the see-thru shoes—all were nomenclature for a condition that would not, could not speak its name. Horny.

"You look great," I said, and meant it.

"I am ready for dinner, Timor. I assume you have made a reservation."

I had—although it was for eight o'clock, not six fifteen. "Wouldn't you like to go have a drink at the bar, first?"

"I would like some wine with my meal."

Early to dinner, early to bed, makes a woman willing, filthy and fine. That was how I spun it to myself, a long self-deceiving skein about extended foreplay and after, protracted replay. And if they couldn't accommodate us an hour or two earlier in the dining room, we'd just have to order room service. I would make my reproductive proposal just as we'd finished our chops (if not before) and then, greasy fingers, crumbs, resveratrol-charged kisses—what a romp it would be.

As we stepped out of our room into the lobby, I took your arm. You did not resist or pull away, maybe because you realized that with those polished floors, tattered Turkish carpets and tottering shoes, you could ill afford to refuse. Arms linked we walked across the room, past the empty reception desk and through the door into the dining room. I imagine we were a risible sight to the half dozen or so occupied tables, the squat squire and his leggy underdressed and overshod lady, but I didn't care: it felt good to be in public together, a couple again. And the way you towered over me (as I never "towered" over you, not once, despite your claim earlier in *Not Okay*), filled me with a pride that was almost paternal, as if I'd raised you, somehow.

The maître d' appeared, a pretty thirty year old with a mother's mussed mien, her blunt cut blond hair a little dirty, her red, white and blue Provençal print dress rumpled, with those mary jane sport shoes that make adult women look like dowdy dolls (thankfully, you never bought a pair). During my solo lunch, she had served me herself, as well as taken my dinner reservation. Not unsexy even with the mary janes, and as I'd learned over the course of that earlier meal, single too (depending on how you did the math. Do children have a numerical value of their own?). I don't remember her name, but let's call her Martha. Or Marta, because American girls are rarely named Martha anymore. Marta the maître d'. She looked you up, she looked you down, she looked you right out of town. You stared over her head. She shifted her gaze to me: "You're early, Dr. Zinkovsky."

I apologized, said it had been a long day and we were both feeling "peckish": would she be so good as to find us a table now? I did not let my eyes drift to the more than half empty dining room beyond her as I spoke.

"Of course, Dr. Zinkovsky. Follow me."

Marta started toward a table adjacent to the swinging doors leading to the kitchen, then abruptly veered in the other direction. Leading us past several empty window tables with views of the verandah and the Chary Springs thoroughfare beyond, one of which I'd sat at during lunch, she halted before a corner round top six feet across, set for six. A pair of oil paintings in eighteenth century American "folk' style hung on the walls behind: one a portrait of a man with a face as smooth as an unhatched egg perched atop a high collared shirt with a floppy black bow tie; the other of an equally bland faced woman, her flat dark hair covered with a white mob cap. Irwin would've crowed with delight over that twinned example of new world artistry (or the lack thereof).

"I'd prefer a window table, if you don't mind. This is a little large for us."

"So sorry, doctor, but all the window tables are reserved for parties who will be arriving later."

"Is it possible that one of those was reserved for us? We could just take it now."

"Unfortunately, the reservation list and seating arrangements are all on the computer, which froze just a few minutes before you arrived."

"How convenient," I said.

"Would you like to wait at the bar? I can call you in when I get the program up again, but I can't guarantee that the table I reserved for you earlier is any better than this one."

"Timor, this is fine," you said, sitting down on the side of the unhatched man.

Marta the maître d' scooped up the extra napkins and silverware, leaving one place setting untouched, on the side of the table opposite yours. "I'll send someone over to take your drink orders in a moment," she called over her shoulder.

I snatched up the wine list. "A bottle of your Côte d'Or 'Aux Beaux Bruns' and a basket of bread, *now*," I yelled at her retreating back.

I thought about moving around to your side of the table. I thought about it and then looked over at you, bent over the menu card, studying the evening's selections. The way you were sitting, leaning forward with your arms spread out and hands splayed over the expanse of arctic white cloth on either side of you, as if staking a claim, made me think it was best to wait. Maybe after a glass or two of "Aux Beaux Bruns" had broken the ice

Eyes scanning the evening's selections, you commented, "I think the service would be better if you were alone." Then, "Oh super—they have grilled fresh frog legs. I will have those."

"I thought you didn't eat meat anymore."

"I still eat fish. Frogs are cold blooded animals, like fish."

Like you, I felt like responding. Only it wasn't true. You had once been warm, so warm it made me hot to think about it, and you could be warm again. You would be warm again, once I shared my plan with you, and then I would finally be content. I see a happy future hatching for you someday, *Timorchik*, my baba used to tell me. But then she also would warn, do not count your chicks in the fall. Do not count (Timor's) chicks in the fall (and especially in the summer). In the meantime, be gentle with the hen, I told myself.

The boy waiter from the morning stepped up to our table, bearing a basket of seeded whole wheat rolls, wafting annealing glutens, and the bottle of côte d'or. The food-stained polo shirt of the morning had been replaced with a button down made out of the same red, white and blue Provençal print fabric as Marta's dress.

"Hello, my name is George and I will be your server tonight."

Adeptly uncorking the wine, boy waiter George splashed a little in my glass. "This wine is from the burgundy region of France. Burgundies are divided into two categories, masculine and feminine," he recited. "This is a girl, I mean feminine one, and it tastes of dried flowers and chanterelle mushrooms." He rhymed "chanterelle" with "cinderella."

It did taste a little like fungus, if not flowers. Mostly it tasted like grapes. "Fine," I said.

"Notice the translucent red color, miss" he went on, filling your glass. "People think that a lighter color means the wine is less complex but that is not necessarily the case. This is among the most complex. However the complexity is based on delicacy, not power. May I take your order, miss?"

"Frog legs."

"And what would you like for your entrée?"

"Frog legs."

"Ma'am, the frog legs are an appetizer. There's not a whole lot of meat on them. May I suggest the lamb for your entrée? It's awesome tonight."

"I will have two orders of frog legs. Thank you."

I ordered the grilled duck breast and sent George off.

You slathered a roll with butter, then gobbled it down. Then you did the same with another, chasing it with gulps of wine. And you called me the glutton…

"How was the state park?"

"Pretty."

"How was the lake?"

"Nice."

"How were the Karetskis?"

"Kind."

"How are you?"

"Fine."

I looked up at the portraits on the wall: "What do you think of those paintings?" Hoping to get some derisive comment, knowing that you hated everything folk, an antipathy dating back to Irwin, if not before. Yet kitsch was another category altogether. (How you cut that cheese, I wonder still.)

"Nothing. If you will please excuse me, I need to use the restroom."

You were gone for at least twenty minutes, our dinner arriving a few moments before your return. Maybe you timed it—watching through the glass, from the verandah, to make sure it was on the table before coming back. Although when, tired of sitting and resisting the rolls, not to mention the wine (I did not want to compromise my post-prandial performance), I'd stepped over to the window and looked out, the porch was empty, last night's cocktail crowd consigned to an engram that didn't necessarily mean any of those people—the man in the Hugo Boss black, the Karetskis, Kirk Rinehardt, Esq.—existed. Neural tissue can't tell the difference between memory and hallucination.

The grilled duck breast was wonderful, a huntsman's dream of wild flesh filling the mouth with a private marsh of herbaceous grease. Even still I can taste it, sans tongue and tastebuds, sans neural tissue to record a gustatory experience too good to be true. Like I said, a huntsman's dream, a free floating hallucination without even a brain to anchor or debate it. All I know is that that duck was a lot more enjoyable than cocktails on the verandah of the Hotel Americana had been. Five minutes went by, at least, before I looked across the floe of linen to ask how you liked your frog legs.

A bony limb jutted from your mouth, foot first like a breech birth. You mumbled something that sounded like "great" as you pulled it from your mouth, both femur and tibiofibula sucked clean. You added it to the small heap of bones on your salad plate. A chorus line of grilled legs on a bed of lettuce remained on the platter before you. You picked one up, and first dipping it in a bowl of butter, slipped it into your mouth.

Another saying of my baba's came to mind: "not fish, not meat." I dropped my eyes back to my own plate. Duck was a dish I'd first encountered under Irwin's tutelage—one that still held a certain mystique for my Odessa born eyes, but the flavor was always recognizable, its gaminess recalling the stringy piece of goose or two I'd eaten as a child in the village. Recognizable, and here in America, so incredibly delicious. I could eat and eat. Maybe you felt the same way about frog legs. I decided I would wait until we were both finished before I made my proposal.

But thirty minutes later my plate had been cleared from the table, and you were still gnawing and sucking. Gnawing and sucking on what might have only been bones at that point; I'd left my glasses in the room and could not tell if there was anything remaining under the romaine leaves, tossed and rumpled like a nightmare bed.

George had left a finger bowl and a wedge of lemon. I cleaned my hands. I opened my mouth, I closed my mouth. I opened my mouth again: "I've been doing a lot of thinking these past seven weeks, about you, about me. About us." I made my proposal.

You dropped your twig of bone. Picking your napkin up from your lap, you wiped the grease from your lips. And then you said what you said. You know what you said, I don't need to recount it all here, all that poison, that noxious torrent about me controlling you, controlling your mind, controlling your body, controlling your world a world that was always the perfect temperature for me filled with the things I liked but what about you, controlling until the controls were broken and the eggs turned rotten the milk to sour curds the fruit to mold and now it was too late. You know what you said, and you know my response, you barren, self-negating bitch, you *baba yaga.*

You know what you said and I only recount everything that came before because I want it known what I put up with that weekend (like I said, a companion and corrective to your *Not Okay*). What I put up with and yet still I did not walk away.

That was you.

After you left the table, I sat for another half an hour, nursing a gin rickey. Would things have gone differently, without George (who was clearly to blame for the room mix-up), without Marta, without that ice floe of a table, without the frog legs (did you really need two orders)? Not to mention the catalytic Karetskis—without them the links between events would not be links, the disastrous coupling of circumstances that had led to dinner's toxic spill.

I swilled the gin in my mouth, bitter juniper soured with lime. On the other hand, I had only myself to blame for the Karetskis: without the Hotel Americana, there would have been no Karetiskis. Oh sure, the Karetskis and their ilk were everywhere, or at least at the pricier hotels and resorts in the New York environs, but if I had consulted with you before I had made reservations, maybe you would've been less inclined to shy from my company. Maybe you were right: maybe I was too controlling.

Marta herself delivered the check. "Will there be anything else this evening, Dr. Zinkovsky?" she asked. Hope hovered in her voice.

I waved her off. "No, thank you. Not tonight."

I knew what I had to do. It would stick in my throat like a bone, like a tiny webbed foot (whether frog or duck, it didn't matter), but I would get it out: an apology. The lights were off when I opened the door to Room Number One. In the dim, I saw your form on the fourposter, back turned toward me. Leaving the table, you'd announced you were going to bed, if that was "allowed," but I knew you could not be asleep. It was not even eight thirty, and you do not fall into sleep easily. You do not fall into sleep easily, and you'd refused my most recent offer to write you a scrip, after a recent two in the morning meeting on the stairs ("I am no longer in pain and do not wish to be drugged anymore, Timor.")

The windows were still open three inches but the room felt airless. I opened the inner door to the verandah, to let in the fresh of outside. One of the lucite platforms was lying on the floor by the rabbit crate. I picked it up, examined it in the porchlight spilling through the screendoor. The insects trapped within the plastic heel were moths. I set the shoe on top of the crate, which was empty. Then I moved around to my side of the bed, bending down over the mattress. Your eyes were closed and in your arms was that rabbit, ears folded back, muzzle tucked beneath your chin. Its fine fur rippled slightly with your breath, which even as it was did not quite pass muster as the respiration of slumber. I know you were awake, and I will repeat what I whispered to you here, because even though I am sure you can recall every word that I said, I want you to hear them again. Hear them again and weep, if only for assets liquidated down the drain.

"I know I've been a shit. I'm sorry for tonight, I'm sorry for everything. I'm sorry for everything and I will do anything, whatever it takes to make it right between us. I sign the check, you write in the amount, and I'm not just talking about money. I mean it, Selinka."

I kissed your cheek, and then I went into the bathroom and took another pair of klonopin from the vial beside the sink—the cap was still off from the night before.

A cooling breeze was blowing through the screen door when my consciousness returned. Out on the verandah, I heard voices, none of them yours. None of them yours, though my ears strained with hope even as I saw your suitcase was gone, along with the crate. I sat up, bracing my hands to either side of me on the mattress to take a deep breath, and felt a small substance under my left palm, a pebble-like form that was both hard and gelatinous. Turds. Turds in a little trail that crossed over your pillow, leading to the edge of the bed and no doubt to the floor below. Poor little rabbit: she'd had no time to eat her shit.

And oh, that brochure you mentioned earlier, that mysterious brochure? I've thought about that a lot. I've thought about that brochure a lot, and I'm sure I now know what it was: a real estate brochure for Bosky House. That famous lunch at the Lark Tavern must've happened the day I was trying to decide whether or not to make an offer. Did you come over to my table? Did you ask me if I wanted another beer? I really can't say. I'm not sure I would've noticed you—without your big whore's shoes.

File 2008/Revenant Provided PDF
(Former Sex: Male; Deceased: circa 2008?)

AUTO SKIDS, KILLS GIRL.

Young Daughter of Sheffield Farms
Head Dies From Injuries.

POUGHKEEPSIE, N. Y., May 20—
Miss Elizabeth Sheffield, 14, daughter of Edward Sheffield, head of the Sheffield Farms Dairy Company, died from a fractured skull suffered in an automobile accident near Highland, Ulster County, last night. Mr. Sheffield

> and a son suffered slight injuries. The party was on its way from Bogota, N.J., where Miss Sheffield attended school, to their summer home at Hobart. The car skidded on the slippery road and crashed into one tree and then into another. Miss Sheffield was thrown out, and struck on her head.
>
> **The New York Times**
> Published: May 21, 1922
> Copyright © The New York Times

Editor's Note: The above was provided by a particularly uncooperative revenant subject, deceased, to the best of our knowledge, in the spring of 2008, somewhere in the vicinity of Tallahasse, Florida. While contact has been established, communication is unsatisfactory. The above was accompanied by a quote from Scientology founder L. Ron Hubbard: "The only way to handle a journalist is to give him a story."

Our research indicates that the Edward Sheffield referred to in this *New York Times* pdf is one and the same as the twenties tycoon who used a significant portion of his fortune to add a wing to Bosky House, the seventeenth century Dutch manor on the outskirts of Kinderhook, New York. Bosky House is included in the New York State Historical Association's registry of important historic structures. According to local lore, the ghost of the tycoon's daughter would periodically fiddle with Bosky House's ancient intercom system, in a futile attempt to reach her mother. (An aside: no such calls were ever received while the Editor resided there.). It is also possible that there is a connection between Edward Sheffield and Elisabeth (with an "s," not a "z") Sheffield, the writer, if anyone gives a rabbit's shit.

Not Okay: A True Crime Story,

by Selina Van Staal

Chapter Ten

"The Intelligence of Absence"

Most crimes have motives. But not always. Sometimes people commit crimes just to be mean. Sometimes people commit crimes just to be mean even though the experts would not agree. They say that the seeds for mean, seemingly unmotivated behavior are sown by earlier mistreatment. In one book, they referred to a study showing how young men who have been physically abused in childhood are more likely than others to acknowledge having threatened to hurt someone, having hit someone in a fight, and having engaged in illegal acts. But the experts are not always right. Plus there were only men in that study, not women. Selina was abused as a child, emotionally if not physically, but that did not make her mean. And Fritzi, from the sound of it, had wonderful parents.

A seed is a seed, before it is sown, and sometimes seeds are simply not good, like in The Bad Seed, which Dolores Van Staal read and then put in a box in the basement of their Staten Island splitlevel because the shelves upstairs were reserved for Literature. When Selina retrieved The Bad Seed from the basement box (which also held Rosemary's Baby), it smelled like mildew. For many people, that is an allergan.

Mildew was not an allergan for Selina, who went on to read many a mildewed book, but it was for Fritzi. Of course, if a book is mildewed, you do not have to read it. You can always throw it away and find another copy somewhere. Particularly these days, when so many books are available on Kindle.

With a house, it is another story. With a house it is another story, since sometimes you cannot simply abandon a house (even an already abandoned one): maybe you need to stay there because of the plot.

What was the plot? In a nutshell, it involved a heist at HVFC followed by a hostage type situation at another, secret location. A hostage type rather than a true hostage situation because embryos are not legal persons, Fritzi emphasized. Grand theft, at worst. The embryos would be held at the secret location until what the silver haired embryologist called KEY CONDITIONS were met.

Fritzi had spent months devising the plot, and had finally revealed it in full, except for said KEY CONDITIONS, the afternoon following the Ramada Plaza Inn sexcapade. Now we are truly partners in crime, she smirked, after they dropped Aiden off in front of his parent's cape cod bungalow in Slingerlands, New York.

The empty old limestone estate house with the boarded-up windows, on the grounds of HVFC, was a crucial element of the plot—the abovementioned secret location. After the heist, it was where the Embryo Incubator containing the embryos would be hidden. No one had entered the estate house in years, and no one would think to look there, Fritzi said. In her months of scheming, it seemed as if she had thought of everything, including the perfect place to hide the embryos. But no one can think of everything, no matter how smart they are, because people's brains are stuck in their bodies. Or as Dean Van Staal used to say, everybody has to use the john sometime. Well the silver haired embryologist need to use the john like everyone else. She also had allergies. Fritzi scoped out the empty estate house in early September. Ragweed season. With her allergic response suppressed by Claritin, little did Fritzi know that the house was infested with mildew! Now that allergy season was over, she had stopped with the Claritin.

That was a mistake, but again, little did she know.

[An explanatory aside to the reader, just in case anyone is mystified by the progression from unmotivated meanness to mildew in this chronicle of true crime. First of all, both cruelty without cause and the capacity for a fungus commonly found in uninhabited structures to trigger an anaphylactic attack in a susceptible person bear upon how things turned out. Without one factor or the other, things would not have turned out as they did. Plus, when you are trying to remember a painful experience, you cannot separate the emotion from the event. The experts say strong emotion colors and even muddles thought, sometimes making it hard to get from **a** to **b** to **c**. As mentioned in the beginning, people who have gone through painful experiences may tell their stories in a disconnected fashion. They may even sound like liars. If you have had painful experiences of your own, you will understand. If you have not, why are you still reading?]

Fritzi failed to discover in advance that the empty limestone estate house with the boarded-up windows, situated off to the side of the entrance to the Hudson Valley Fertility Clinic's grounds, was infested with mildew. But otherwise, she planned with care and foresight for the heist and the hostage type situation that followed, scheduling both for two days after the Ramada Plaza Inn sexcapade, for the evening of October 18, 2010, when the HVFC doctors, nurses, laboratory technicians and staff would be attending a baby shower at the Asani residence. Coincidentally, the eighteenth of October was also Timor's birthday (which made him a Libra, or on the positive side, romantic and empathetic, on the negative, materialistic, self-indulgent and cruel). Maybe no one cares about Timor's birthday, but certain dates are hard to forget. Certain dates are hard to forget even if the person they pertain to is no longer part of your life, and has not been for some time.

Anyways.

Anyways, readers may be curious about the set-up for the heist. Hopefully, information about the set-up will not be used to commit copycat crimes (which are the worst. If you are going to commit a crime, you should at least make up your own.). Anyone who is thinking about copycatting this particular crime, be forewarned: you need to be an ART insider. You need to be an ART insider such as Fritzi. Obviously Fritzi knew all about reproductive technology, and so forth. She also knew the code to HVFC's security system. You see, while John Asani did not trust Fritzi with the children, he did trust her with the embryos. Going on Fritzi's true past at Uptown Procreative Specialists (as opposed to the fake one recorded in chapter eight of this book; more on Fritzi's true past at UPS below), he should not have trusted her with either. However, it seems that he assumed that Fritzi would not do again what she had done before. He assumed that she still had something to lose, or to re-gain. Trusting Fritzi, his top as well as only embryologist, he had given her the code to HVFC's security system—so that she could monitor the growth and development of the embryos after hours, count cell divisions and what not.

In addition to knowing the code to HVFC's security system, as an ART insider Fritzi also knew about the workings of ART equipment. Sure the operation of the Embryo Incubator itself was normally overseen by one of the technicians, but in monitoring the development of the embryos during off hours, Fritzi had to be able to troubleshoot for mechanical problems, malfunctions and such. Knowing something about the mechanical side of things, Fritzi foresaw the need for a portable generator. Yes, Fritzi foresaw the need for a portable not to mention silent generator, since you would not want to attract the attention of any passers by on Route 9J (such as a late night jogger), who might notify law enforcement officials! The arrival of law enforcement officials would make it difficult to negotiate with John Asani and ensure that KEY CONDITIONS were met, Fritzi said. To this end (that being the need for a quiet power source that would not disclose the fact that the empty house was, temporarily, occupied), Fritzi had purchased a portable GEN-Z 1500 Watt Battery Based Emergency 120 VAC Power System.

Or actually, she had had Selina purchase the generator for her, the Monday before the heist, from the Home Depot, with five thousand dollars in cash, without telling Selina what it was for (as mentioned above, full disclosure concerning plot details, with the exclusion of KEY CONDITIONS, did not occur until the day before the heist.). You see, with three egg retrievals scheduled for that week, Fritzi had her hands full at the Lab. Plus without those eggs, there would be no fresh embryos. And without eggs, you can't make an omelette, Fritzi laughed. Sure, there were some frozen ones around the Lab, but with the potential for chromosomal fragmentation during defrosting and so forth, they were not worth a whole lot.

A collaborator can be useful in an ART heist and hostage type situation. A collaborator can help with the preparations (including equipment purchases) for the heist, as well as the actual execution of it. They can also help guard the hostages if, say, one person has to go use the john. Though embryos are not exactly going to run away. A collaborator can be useful in an ART related crime, but it also seemed like the silver haired embryologist could have worked alone.

In fact, she sort of was working alone, by not telling Selina the set-up for the heist and hostage type situation until the day before. So that was odd.

In the meantime, Fritzi made the heist and hostage type situation sound like fun. She said it was not a kidnapping but a kind of robinhood stratagem where all the little robins would get their eggs back in the end. Put in those terms, the heist and hostage type situation were a thrilling game that you would be gutless not to play—everyone would get their eggs back, and at the end of it all, you would have something for your own nest, too. This is not to make excuses but only to explain how you can get caught up in an activity or situation and not think about or reflect upon what you are doing and how it might hurt others, like the people who go to Atlantic City and play Black Jack for twenty four hours at a time, until all their family savings are gone (like Dean Van Staal once did, according to Dolores.).

This is not make excuses but only to explain how at 7:30 on the evening of October 18, 2010, sitting in Fritzi's Nissan Quest in the parking lot in front of HVFC, waiting for Fritzi to ring her cell and say that it was time to pull around to the rear of the building, Selina was not thinking at all about whose embryos would end up in the back of Fritzi's minivan, or how they would feel, if they knew. Selina's head was empty of thoughts, even as the images streamed in. Her head was empty and yet smoothly receptive, like an expensive new video camera, taking in the night scene: the horizontal roof-line of the clinic, black against a matte-gray sky, the glowing ground floor square of the lobby, Steph behind plate glass at the reception desk, working late, before she drove off to the baby shower at the Asanis, like everyone else. Or more specifically, knitting late. Her little helmet of bronze curls bent over her needles, her shadow looming on the wall behind her like a giant knitting mantis. You could not make out the clicking of the needles, of course, but through the rolled-down window (it was unseasonably warm, as well as overcast) you could hear the last of the cicadas, humming the insectile score to Steph's handiwork, which looked to be a baby sweater, or maybe a bunting (presumably the second of two pieces of knitwear; the scuttlebutt was twins). The air smelled like decaying leafage, moist dirt and faintly, of skunk, which if you open up your mind is a kind of perfume, or at least the beginning of one, as the glandular secretions of animals are the basis of some of the world's most exquisite bottled scents. Once Selina had tried to tell Timor this but he would not hear it: that is nothing but a foul stench, sweetheart, a pure and simple stink.

But as already mentioned, on the evening of October 18, 2010, Selina's head was empty of thoughts, including thoughts of Timor, whose birthday it was, even though he was dead—thoughts that since the night at the Ramada Plaza Inn had become a thick and tangled mess. This shows the attraction of a life of crime, in that criminal activity is completely absorbing—it sweeps your brain clean, then stuffs it with NOW. Stuffs it with NOW, leaving no room for the past and its aftercrop of regrets, no room for the future and its anxieties to come. When you are commiting a crime it is like having good sex: you do not think, you just do. Selina had not had good sex since Timor, but she was not thinking about that, either. She was not thinking at all. Really.

When a horrible sound rent the dark. A horrible horrible sound that for a second sounded like a woman a second like a newborn infant and a second like a cat. And then all three roped together in a writhing sack that kept ripping open again and again somewhere in the field to the left of HVFC, behind the empty estate house. It was a sound that sent shock waves through NOW, so that now NOW was no longer that pure packing between your ears but something else, a dividing shifting ground without bounds where first you were running one way, then the other, like an animal that cannot decide whether it is predator or prey. That is what it must have been, by the way—an animal.

Either a pheasant or a fox, Fritzi said, after Steph had finally driven off in her Camry and Selina could pull around to the rear of the Clinic. It was now 8:00pm. With Fritzi's minivan backed up to the service doors, they loaded the vehicle with the Embryo Incubator (tied to a dolley), along with the GEN-Z 1500 Watt Battery Based Emergency 120 VAC Power System. Both animals, Fritzi added, can sound like a screaming woman.

In Literature, when nature is like a person, that is food for thought, a pheasant for a fox. But a chronicle of true crime is not Literature, so no comment. No comment, but for the record, the night was not the same after that. The nevermind yesterday or tomorrow attitude Selina had put on since moving in with Fritzi like a pair of those 3D glasses they have at the movies, except for an hour or two here and there when the glasses had slipped off like the morning after the night at the Ramada Plaza Inn, was gone.

The night was not the same after that and in the meantime, it was getting harder and harder to follow the dark of Fritzi's thinking. As she slammed the backdoor of the minivan closed, she asked have you ever done it in the back of one of these? When this is all over I'm going to fuck my brains out.

If Fritzi's purpose with the embryo business was to get her children back, then why did she care about having sex in her car? Could be she wanted even more children, but still, her post heist and hostage type situation plans were not reassuring.

Selina should have said something, instead of nothing.

In silence, Fritzi drove the minivan the quarter mile to the empty estate house. She pulled around behind it, backing up a few feet away from the rear entrance. The letters VH were etched in the stone over the lintel, initials for the name of the family that had built the house, Van Hoesen. And though it was only a back entrance, not the front, the door was large and thick enough to keep a castle, with three stone steps leading up to a small open porch, and a stone ledge fanning out from each side. Beneath the big brass knob, there was a big keyhole, the kind that you see in storybook illustrations. The kind that needs a key that was lost once upon a time.

Fritzi, per yesterday's disclosure concerning the details of the heist and the hostage type situation, had scoped out the house in early September, so she had to have a means of entry. Yet she had not mentioned what that means of entry was, and Selina had not thought to ask. At any rate, the back door did not appear to be it. The back door did not appear to be it, and then, presto, it was. The key to the door being the one that Fritzi wore on the chain around her neck, that big silver thing that Selina had taken first for a crucifix and then for an ankh, but had never seen close up or in full (it was always at least partly hidden by her clothing, or when she picked it up and touched it to her lips, by her fingers).

After Fritzi had unlocked the back door with the key on the chain around her neck, they pushed the generator up the steps, using the dolley as a ramp, and over the threshold. Next they carried in the incubator (keeping it level as possible so that the embyros would not slosh too much in their petri dishes), setting the appliance next to its temporary power source.

The dim sweep of Selina's flashlight revealed a kitchen, with an old tile floor drifted with dried mouse droppings, long wooden counters also covered with mouse droppings and bigger things although nothing bigger than what looked to be a bread box, metal with the letters WON still visible on one side—the rest of the letters, if there had been any, were eaten away by rust. Above the counters there were a few cabinets and stretches of wall painted white or some other pale color at one time, but now mottled with patches of dark. There were also a refrigerator and stove, circa 1950 going on their rounded contours, and a metal and vinyl dinette set with the seats torn and clumps of filthy foam sticking out. There was no faint hum of appliances, there being no electricity, but you could feel things stirring, rustling, in the corners and in the stuffing of the dinette chairs. It did not seem like a good place to store in vitro embryos, even temporarily, because in vitro embryos are even more vulnerable to pathogens than the other kind. That was why you had to wear sterile scrubs and a gauze mask in the Lab. Yet, Fritzi did not seem worried!

They'll be fine—safe as houses, she said, plugging the incubator into the generator, just in time (the incubator, according to Fritzi, was designed to maintain set temperature for twenty minutes without power. Fifteen minutes had passed since they had loaded it into the van behind HVFC). The GEN-Z generator, as stated on the laminated specs card at the Home Depot, featured "Silent Operation," but a little manmade sound would not have been unwelcome right then. Sometimes nature does not sound so great.

Fritzi stood and wiped her hands on her jeans: Just don't open the door. Opening the door will break the vacuum seal that is keeping everything sterile inside. Then she sneezed hard, twice. Selina did not bother to bless her. Fritzi did not want anyone's blessings, you could tell.

Sniffling a little, Fritzi resumed: I'll be back in ten minutes. I think it's fine to sit outside, by the way. No one can see you from the road. You could even have a smoke, she added. I'll leave my pack and lighter on the back steps. As she walked off into the dark, she sneezed some more. Achoo, achoo, achoo until the cicadas swallowed all.

Per the plot, Fritzi was going to return the minivan to the parking lot behind the clinic. As she had explained during her plot disclosure, John would never think to search the empty house for Fritzi and the embryos (unless he saw Fritzi's car parked outside). It was just like he would never think to pick up an empty vodka bottle, even to throw it in the trash.

The ground on each side of the limestone porch was overgrown with mint, still going strong even though it was the middle of October. The smell was damp and pungent. People think of it as soothing, that smell, but the night of the heist it was not. You see, mint always makes you think of other mint, of when you had mint before. Selina did not want to think of when she had mint before because that would lead to this mint, that is, the road from past mint to present, from that night at Fritzi's house drinking the Ginger Rogers cocktails, when Lyndon showed up and Florence almost died, to now. Okay, those were not Lyndon's embryos in the incubator; Lyndon's embryos had made it through the incubation process and were now planted safely inside her uterus, as Lyndon presided over a baby shower in their honor. And even if they had been Lyndon's embryos, well Lyndon was a ditz. But so were the others. Ditzes every one, the women who had passed through the halls of HVFC, even Portia with her la di da doctorate—clueless, platinum card carrying patsies who had trusted their baby bearing dreams to Asani's bungling. But who is to say ditzes with credit lines do not have just as much of a right to become mothers as anyone else? Too bad the skunk smell was gone or just too far away to detect over here, closer to the road. Skunk would be better than mint. Best of all would be fresh skunk. Whether you hate it or not, the smell of fresh skunk is too strong to think of anything else. It fills your nose and your head, chasing anything else away, the doubts, the misgivings, the skittering thoughts that run first in one direction and then the other.

Fritzi had left her cigarettes on the steps for Selina. Even though Selina did not smoke, Fritzi assumed that she did. Fritzi assumed that Selina shared her taste for tobacco, just as she had assumed that Selina shared her taste for young men barely out of their teens.

Selina picked up the pack. Fritzi's brand was Marlboro Lights. One of Selina's boyfriends, way before Timor, had smoked Marlboro Lights. Barely out of his teens, he was a fellow server at the Ponderosa Steak House. But in those days, Selina too had been barely out of her teens. Once in a while, Selina would smoke one of the Marlboro Lights, but she never got addicted. In those days, Selina had a different boyfriend every six months. Every six months for years until she was well out of her teens she would get a different boyfriend because face it, strong sexual attraction only lasts about that long. So then it would be over, no hard feelings and we can still be friends. Until Timor.

Timor claimed he had never smoked, and Selina believed him. You could tell by the way he acted around cigarettes, the opposite of how he acted around sweets and alcohol. Timor had never smoked, and Selina had only smoked now and then, before Timor. Why would you want a burning desert in your throat, he would ask, when you could have a refreshing dessert or a drink, a creamy spoonful of gelato, a cold swallow of good gin?

Still, Timor did not expect Selina to share his desserts or his drinks. If you did not want a bite or a swallow, he did not press you. It was more the other way around, like he wanted you to press him, press him to eat and drink less. Well adult men should not expect their wives to act like their mothers. But he never did try to make you get fat with him, or drunk. When you wound up with a hangover, you had only yourself to blame. With Fritzi, you had to do whatever she was doing, even as you were not entirely sure what it was.

Even though yesterday Fritzi had gone over the plot in detail, she had left out parts. One of these was the method of entry into the empty estate house. Why not say beforehand, I have the key around my neck? Just because someone forgets to ask does not mean that the other person should not tell. Okay, sometimes one person fails to tell something because the other person fails to ask. Or they fail to tell something because they think it does not matter. But then what about the KEY CONDITIONS? Those were different than the key around Fritzi's neck. The key on Fritzi's neck was an instrument for turning the bolt of a lock. A key can also be something that gives an explanation to a riddle or a puzzle. A door may need to be opened or a puzzle to be solved, but not necessarily. That is called leaving well enough alone. But if you look in Webster's Dictionary, you will see that key has another meaning as well: important or fundamental. If Fritzi's plot was to succeed, KEY CONDITIONS had to be met. Plus Selina had actually asked about them, during the plot disclosure. And what was Fritzi's answer? I'll tell you later.

The last of the cicadas trilled on, though usually they were finished by this time of year, Timor's birthday. That was probably due to global warming, another good reason not to have kids Timor used to say. When suddenly the pheasant or fox screamed again. The scream had come from the line of trees behind the house. It was that close. That close, it sounded bigger than a bird. More like a fox. Although a fox is nothing to be afraid of if you are a person. A fox is nothing to be afraid of unless you are a bird, a pheasant sitting on its nest, instead of a woman guarding an

Embryo Incubator. You have nothing to fear if you are a woman who has harmed nothing or no one in a robinhood caper where every robin will get her eggs back in the end. At the same time, a woman who has nothing to worry about can feel anxious. Many women with nothing to worry about feel anxious and find various ways to sedate themselves. Selina did not normally smoke cigarettes, but many women do, for the sedative effect. And just one, under duress, would not hurt. Before Timor, Selina would smoke a cigarette now and then, even though she never got addicted.

The smoke rose up in the dark and then just hovered there, like a genie from a bottle or a spirit. Maybe the smoke hovered like that because there was no breeze. But still it did not feel right. It felt wrong, unnatural, the way the smoke just stayed like that, as if someone or something was keeping it there. It felt wrong, unnatural, but of course the smoke was only smoke from a cigarette that due to a lack of air current or whatnot was just hanging in the air in the shape of what looked to be a person. Timor would say it was just apophenia, a fifty cent word that means the tendency to see patterns everywhere, even in random data. You are always seeing patterns, Selina, even when there are none. It was apophenia, which made you see the shape of a person in what were only cigarette fumes floating in the air due to a lack of air current or whatnot. And now

Timor was dead, never coming back because there was no such thing as ghosts only the desire to see patterns, the shapes that used to be there and are now forever dissolved. It felt wrong, unnatural that you would never ever see him again but that is the way things are, the way the laws of physics work something having to do with heat and entropy that you could never understand even though you always scored pretty high on standardized tests.

When your eyes are wet, it is natural to wipe them. If you do not have a tissue you can use the back of your hands. Then you can wipe your hands on your jeans, but all this takes a while. When Selina finally looked up again, the smoke was gone. The smoke was gone and there was Fritzi. Silently (sneezing fit over, it seemed) she had stepped out of the shadows, on sneakered feet, black Pumas, to be exact, that looked to be new, maybe purchased just for the heist and the hostage type situation, though you might wonder how she had found the time, with all those egg retreivals.

In her hands, Fritzi held two small silver and cobalt blue cans. She extended one: Have a Red Bull; it'll keep your eyes open. Selina took the cold can of sports drink, but did not peel the tab. She set the unopened can down beside her on the steps and then stubbed out the cigarette. Sedative or no, the feeling it had given was sad.

Fritzi perched on one of the ledges and pulled out her iPhone, sipping as she gazed down at the small glowing screen: I sent a message to John from the parking lot. The reception's not great over here, but there is a signal.

What if cell reception failed? What if Asani's reply could not get through? Or what if he turned off his cell for the night, being that there was a party going on at the Asani residence? On the laminated specs card at the Home Depot it said that the run-time for the GEN-Z 1500 Watt Battery Based Emergency 120 VAC Power System was six hours. Come to think of it, six hours would be over in the middle of the night—about 2:15am. Asani could be asleep by then, unaware that KEY CONDITIONS needed to be met, or else!

Then you'll have to use your powers of extra sensory perception, Selina. Phone in through the chi channel, calling all gestalts, breaker breaker, can you hear me doc, breaker breaker, spiritual entities could be lost, depending on where you locate the moment of ensoulment, at or after conception, depending on whether you even consider the fusion of gametes in a petri dish conception. Breaker breaker, get your ears on, breaker breaker you better deal or its rock a bye baby broken petri dish and all.

Fritzi finished her riff with a laugh, then lit a cigarette. She took a drag, then added: don't worry. I'm sure he got my message. If we don't hear from him soon, I'll start walking back through the trees until I get better reception.

Joking about killing the embryos (rock a bye baby!), then lighting herself a cigarette, Fritzi looked like a witch. Her whole face seemed drawn to a point by the burning ember—like everything that had once been human was incinerating there. But that was just a perception, right? Just because someone looks mean and crazy, that does not necessarily mean they are. So Selina just let the witch go. She should not have done that.

Something hooted somewhere. Something hooted somewhere and the smell of burning tobacco mingled with the mint. Mentholated secondhand smoke that you had no choice but to breathe. Unless you were just going to walk away. But it was too late for that.

It was too late for that, and Fritzi had said everyone would get their babies back in the end—including Fritzi. Fritzi, whose babies had been taken away by Asani and the attorneys he had been able to hire with all that money from his family in Iran or Pakistan or wherever. With her babies back, Fritzi would no longer resemble a witch. Fritzi would no longer resemble a witch because the face of a mother is the opposite of the face of a witch, the opposite of a face that is drawn to a point. Just look at those paintings of Madonnas, and you will see. You will see what Selina used to look like when she was young, working the salad bar at the Ponderosa Steakhouse. You had to wear a hairnet that covered your hair like a veil and the older waitresses would tease, you have such a sweet, giving face, like a Virgin Mary. No wonder they keep coming back for more croutons.

Fritzi would look like a mother again instead of a witch because she would be a mother again, the opposite of a witch. Being a mother again, Fritzi would not only look like one but have to act like one—there would be no more nights at the Ramada Plaza Inn. There would be no more nights at the Ramada Plaza Inn, at business travel centers or corporate crashpads for anonymous, illicit sexual rendezvous—from now on it would be family style hotels for family style fun.

Looking off into the dark trees beyond, away from Fritzi's face that in the meantime had drawn to a point, to the zero sum expression of a witch or a hag, Selina suggested that when everything was over Fritzi and her boys could go to Disneyworld, or even Legoland, in Denmark.

Are you kidding? When this is all over, I'm headed for the beach. Bora Bora or Santorini: I can't decide whether I want balmy languor or sizzling torpor, Polynesian lover boys or Greek godlets with fire in their board shorts.

Why was Fritzi talking about boys at beach resorts when she would have her own boys with her, at last? Why was she talking about boys at famous beach resorts known as adults only playgrounds dedicated to adult pleasures and vices—the kind of places responsible parents keep their children away from, unless the parents, due to employment as chambermaids, waiters and bartenders at said resorts, have no other choice?

Neither Bora Bora nor Santorini sounded like a great place to take the kids, was all Selina said.

But you'd have a good time, wouldn't you?

Before Fritzi could press further, her cell, resting beside her on the ledge, lit up and started chirping—a swarm of electronic crickets drowning out the background trill of the last of the cicadas. She picked it up, pursed her lips, tapped the screen once, before sliding her finger across the top. Then with her nail she turned off the sound switch on the side.

Who had just called? Why had Fritzi turned off the sound on her iPhone?

Fritzi said nothing. The owl or whatever it was hooted some more. Who had called? Who, who?

He can wait, Fritzi said at last. He can wait like he's made me wait. I told him very clearly what I wanted, but he refused to hear. He said it was a breakdown, a derailment, a midlife smash-up even though I wasn't even forty yet, he said I would get over it with some time to think, to be alone.

Get over what?

You once asked me how I got on this quote unquote career path. I was good at math and science, my father was a doctor. Yadah yadah yadah. I have a mind like a steel trap so medical school was a snap. A snap of the trap. I didn't want patients, of course: the human comedy only interests me from afar, filtered through a script, projected onto a screen. That explains how I ended up in lab and research work. But helping self-serving fools to bring more self-serving fools into the world? Go figure. She paused, touching the key that Selina had once mistook for an ankh, a symbol of life, to her lips.

If you're wondering why I went for the biological sciences rather than, say, particle physics, Fritzi continued, well, I wasn't <u>that</u> smart. Plus I was interested in the complexity of biological systems, especially in the human body. The immune response, for example. The intricacy of it, the finely calibrated sequence of biochemical events initiated by an invasive agent or an instance of physical trauma. The incredibly precise machinery of it, engineered by no one. By no one. I liked that, the sense of well-thought out design, without thought. Well thought out, without thought. Not the absence of intelligence, but the intelligence of absence.

That sounded like intelligent design.

No. Fritzi lifted the Red Bull to her lips, swallowed. I'm talking about something else, a kind of invention without an inventor, human or otherwise. Creatio ex nihilo without a creator, so just forget about ex deo. Forgetaboutit, she repeated in a mobster accent. I'm talking about the intelligence of absence, pure absence, not the absence of intelligence.

The fruity, chemical smell of the sports drink wafted over, momentarily displacing the smells of mint and tobacco.

The intelligence of absence is what interested, even thrilled me: we're all brilliant, at the cellular level. Cytoplasmic savants… Fritzi trailed off, took another long drag of her cigarette and exhaled. The smoke did not look like anything.

Dropping the burning butt, Fritzi snuffed it with her Puma, then took another swig of Red Bull. A shiny trail of the sports beverage dribbled down her chin, like leaking plasma.

People are so fucking stupid, she continued. Morons. Even people with years of scientific training and advanced degrees. They look at seven eight-celled embryos and see that six of them suck, that the blastomeres look like squashed grapes, centers flecked with blebbing. Six of them suck and probably won't implant so hey, let's use them all, team, just to increase the odds, because sometimes low grade embryos do implant and as far as we know, the children born from low grade embryos are just as adorable, healthy and intelligent as those born from high grade embryos. Except for when they all implant and end up, at 21 weeks, in the NICU. Because human beings are not equipped to have litters. And maybe most of them will make it, with only one or two cases of cerebral palsy, and learning and behavioral disorders in the rest. But no worries, treatment can be found for the precious survivors, at therapeutic services providers near you, all costs at least partially defrayed by the health insurance industry.

The smell of mint, mixed with tobacco, was overpowering. Selina stood up, walked a few feet away from both the mint plants and the smoke, into the rank overgrown lawn behind the empty estate house. The line of trees loomed beyond, darker than the sky. Fritzi continued to talk, as if Selina was still sitting there, on the steps beneath her ledge perch.

Fritzi continued to talk, like a recording, like a machine that will not turn off, her words and phrases spinning into the night air, gyrating, reeling beyond comprehension even as they made a kind of sense that made you think you should have been listening more carefully from the beginning—but it was too late now. Words and phrases like zygote craving zombies, embryo racketeering, and Doctor UnFrankensteins that previously Fritzi had attributed to Asani, but that were actually her own! Along with additional ones like I never really wanted children; John was the perfect fuck; maximal pleasure, minimal sperm count; the pill seemed unnecessary at the time; a single seminal mishap followed by a twin catastrophe; fullterm and still fucked up; both ADHD; I'd try to read to them and they'd hit me and pinch my tits; already little beasts, even before they killed Lyndon's dog, stoning birds' nests, spraying squirrels with the au pair's mace; boys will be boys, and girls too, that is, stupid and bestial; though for deliberate cruelty of nature, human might be the greater insult, Isaac Asimov once said; either way I couldn't stand it anymore; and, it was John who covered up for me.

It was John who was covering up for me, the machine said, the machine that had once been a woman, a woman you thought you knew, thought you had a grip on, however loose.

Selina stood, frozen, with her back to Fritzi. The weeds felt thick and tricky, like if you tried to move they would tangle around your ankles and trip you.

Not the other way around, the machine continued. It was John who did my egg retrievals, cultures, sperm evals, fertilizations, including ICSIs, fertilization checks, embryo biopsies, and assisted hatchings though he'd been trained as an endocrinologist, not an embryologist, when I was gone for days at a time. He even performed three embryo transfers for me.

Selina wanted to keep walking, to slip through the dark bars of the trees, but could not, because of the weeds or something else, because of the tricky tangle that was not just around her ankles but in her head.

You're probably wondering where I went: I don't know. I don't know. But I always came home, usually early in the morning, my heart feeling too big for my chest, both swollen and hollow, like I'd swum for miles in the Hudson or run the length of Manhattan, although I doubt, going on the smoke in my hair, the taste of booze and tar in my mouth, and the slime between my legs, that I'd been engaging in athletic pursuits. I'd feel like shit, but shit with a shine, a golden glow that I couldn't hide even after a shower and twelve hours in bed with the shades down and the door shut to keep out the sounds of colicky babies and despairing au pairs, a shimmering shit cloud that stayed with me even when I finally made it back to the Lab, raining over the counters, the tables, the gurneys, the appliances and equipment, settling every surface with its radiant dirt.

I don't know where I went but I know how I felt after with my heart too big for my chest and swathed in golden filth like some primal force that had climbed up out of the muck and ascended into the atmosphere, like all the power was mine, raining down over everything. All the power was mine, only there was no me—just that crappy shimmer, that crepuscular shittiness descending over every available surface in the Lab. All the power was mine, only there was no me, only the power spreading over every available surface.

Sinking to the ground, Selina listened as the machine droned on.

No me, only the power spreading, over every available surface until there was not a centimeter left uncovered. Not a centimeter, and then, silly me, I realized that there were surfaces inside of surfaces, drawers to be pulled, doors to open, lids to lift. When John walked in, I'd removed four petri dishes, thirteen embryos total, from the incubator. And though John immediately put them all back, by the next morning they'd stopped dividing. A baker's dozen of buns that would never make it to the oven.

Well, someone did the math and there was an investigation. But there were no security cameras inside the lab, only out, so no one knew exactly what had happened to the embryos or who'd been responsible. John took the blame for the contamination, with some byzantine explanation about protracted postnatal depression, misplaced masculine protectiveness, domestic stressors and sleep deprivation, uncertain protocols, and plain poor judgement. He even claimed he'd been drinking and reading the work of a "dispiriting philosopher" that night—though in fact, that was me. John didn't hit the sauce or the Schopenhauer until after I left. Regardless, we were both asked to leave the practice.

Sitting in the damp weeds with her back to the empty estate house, Selina waited for the machine to continue. Even though it really did not matter. As with a puzzle that is three quarters completed, you could quickly put the rest together yourself. Who would hire Fritzi to help people make babies after that? It would be like letting a fox into the henhouse, a screaming, half-crazed fox that chewed its own tail. Needing a job, Fritzi would have no other choice but to follow Asani upstate to HVFC. There was only one piece missing: why would he want her around? Asani had a new wife, Lyndon, who might be an airhead but better an airhead than a shimmering shitcloud, or whatever it was that Fritzi said had made her kill those embryos. No worries: the machine formerly known as Fritzi went on to supply the lacking puzzle part.

I'm not crazy, it finally said. I'm not crazy, at least not anymore. Three fully licensed, practicing psychiatrists certified my sanity, after John paid for six months at a private mental hospital, one of those places you see the discrete little ads for at the back of the New Yorker magazine. They attributed the disappearances and the petri dish incident to episodes of fugue, which can be caused by bipolar disorder and depression. Depression. Everyone gets depressed, and ten percent of the population is on anti-depressants. Join the crowd, they told me, and so I did.

I'm not crazy, I told John when he picked me up. I just don't want to do this anymore, I said. Give me give me five thousand a month and

I'll disappear, into the crowd. I'll be out of your life forever.

He said no, you need to be what is called gainfully employed and the children need a mother. But I understand that you aren't yet ready to return to us, so you may reside in the house I built for you, until you realize your priorities.

Like he was some goddamn tribal elder, permitting me to keep my tent.

And in the meantime, he'd found that dim bitch. My replacement. Only the replacement apparently doesn't suit him. Or maybe she was never meant to be my replacement, but more like a supplement, a supplicating simple-minded little dick sucker to fill in until I came to my senses, and finally lifted up the flap.

Headlights rounded a curve down the road, approached the empty estate house and then passed on.

Well, I've spent a lot of time thinking these last few years. A lot of it sitting in that room you've been sleeping in. John and I painted that room together: fucking sunflower yellow. If you sit on the floor with your back against the closet door, all you can see is the sky—no fields, no trees, just sky. I'd imagine myself just floating away, away from everything…

It paused, maybe to fill its lungs with more nicotine. Maybe to float away. But then it resumed: Once this is over, I'm going to the beach.

There was a light thud, the swish of feet stirring wet leaves. The smell of mint.

I want to feel the hot sand burning my soles.

The voice came closer.

I want to feel the hot sand burning my soles, then the cooling wash of brine.

Closer.

Swim out as far as I can. Back again.

Closer.

I want to feel the salt dry on my skin. I want to feel the rum rake my throat.

Closer.

I want to drink until I can't see. I want to roast in the sun like a pig on a spit.

Closer.

I want to be eaten all night by native boys.

The voice lowered in both position and pitch, dropping down behind Selina's ear: I'm going to the beach and I want you to come with me.

I want you to come with me, the machine repeated, its breath in Selina's ear warm yet somehow lifeless. Like air vented from underground, like an escaped puff of sewer gas. I want you to be the girlfriend I never had in highschool because my father said young American females were too stupid always shopping at the mall for skimpy transparent clothes, wrapping their overweight bodies like beef in cellophane to attract young American males, phony baloneys who nevertheless wanted real sex. I want you to be the girlfriend I never had in highschool to talk to about the boys who were not allowed to even drive past the house where I sat reading and studying night after night. The boys who used to make fun of my father as I'd stand hiding the next day in the cove of my locker: you no touch my Fritzi. You no touch my Fritzi or I cut something off! Even though my father's English was English public school perfect. I want you to be that highschool girlfriend I never had so that when I wake up in the morning after a night in the dunes and it's all a shimmering shit fog, you can tell me what I missed.

Not everyone wants to go to the beach. Some people even hate it.

Oh but not you, Selina. Not you. You were made for the beach. Your permanently tanned skin tells me so, the tale of melanin levels elevated by long term sun exposure, baby oil bastings baywatched for the perfect shade of brown. You were made for the beach with your beachballs bursting out of your bikini top—you must have been hot. A real sizzler. And now that you're not, what else are you going to do with yourself? You can't stay here.

Well Fritzi was right about that. When you commit a crime (even a crime where no one gets hurt and there was still hope that no one would because probably all Fritzi wanted from Asani was money, that five thousand a month to disappear into the dunes or wherever), you must leave. That is called fleeing the scene of the crime, which is another crime but there is no stopping once you start. There is no stopping once you start which means you have to go. Still, there are choices. Canada, for instance. And if you are not so hot anymore, just look for someone who was never hot in the first place, like a retired ice hockey player. There is no stopping once you start but at least you can head in a new direction. You can head in a new direction, just keep it to yourself so that no one can prevent you from turning around. Planning to head in a new direction once the heist and hostage type situation were over, Selina said nothing.

Selina said nothing, which the machine formerly known as Fritzi seemed to register as an agreement to go to the beach. Sinking into the damp weeds beside Selina it babbled on about mindless fun in the sun, mindless endless fun in the sun like cells dividing on and on without variation but maybe mutation and wouldn't that be something melanoma arriving like the masque of the red death only it would be brown and black and assymetrical a spreading amorphous blob the party crasher that would mean partyting all the harder partying under the dizzying strobe of sun until you drop and the light goes black and the sound goes out but the party is not over it goes on without you…

The party goes on without you in your absence without your intelligence or your lack thereof and the machine would not shut up even as Selina had stopped listening. Selina had stopped listening when suddenly the machine was up on its black Puma covered feet, walking away. Walking away and still talking, but no longer to, or at, Selina.

Selina turned to see the machine heading toward the abandoned estate house, its iPhone pressed to its ear. It sounded crafty:

Don't worry, they're fine. Perfect little morulas, each merrily dividing in its cozy dish of culture: they'll be blastocysts before you know it, the cunning machine said into the smart phone.

A bird or a bat swooped out of the trees, skimmed over the machine's head, ascended again before vanishing beneath the eaves of the empty estate house.

As the cunning machine ascended the steps to the back door, its voice both faded and lowered. There was something more about when the banks open and transfer the money to my account and tell you then and plane takes off at noon and loved me? and just the two of us, we could have been happy… Then it disappeared inside.

The back door of the empty estate house, recessed in the shadow of its frame, looked bigger and thicker than ever. If the machine had wanted Selina to accompany it inside, it would have said something. It would have said something instead of going in alone for some unknown reason maybe just to use the john although from the looks of that kitchen a bathroom with a working toilet seemed unlikely. A working toilet seemed unlikely in such filth where the embyros were best left undisturbed vacuum sealed within the incubator powered by the portable GEN-Z generator everything at the perfect temperature, probably human body temperature 98.6 or whatever that was in Celcius, until the GEN-Z's battery failed. At about 2:15am… What would the machine formerly known as Fritzi tell Asani after the banks opened in the morning?

Or did Selina already know? Did she already know what the cunning machine would tell Asani, and that it would be at least seven hours too late? John would have to meet KEY CONDITIONS, Fritzi had said back when she was still Fritzi. Fritzi had never revealed the terms of those KEY CONDITIONS, but going on what had been said about when the banks open, transfer the money to my account, and plane takes off at noon, as well as what had not been said (bring the kids to the airport) you could not claim you did not have a clue. You could not claim that you did not have a clue, either before a judge in a court of law or in your own mind.

If the machine had wanted Selina to follow it inside, it would have said something. At the same time, the key that Selina had once mistaken for an ankh still glinted in the lock, where the machine had left it. Whether the machine wanted you to follow it or not, you could not claim before a court or in your own mind that you had no clue what it was up to.

Twisting the key then shouldering open the door, Selina flicked on her flashlight.

Next to the counter with the old breadbox resting on top stood Fritzi. She held a clear fluid-filled disc in her hand, which glowed faintly in the flashlight's beam. Her face too was lit and no longer drawn to the zero sum point of a witch or a hag, but smooth and smiling down at her palm. The breadbox was open, the interior blacker than it should have been, even in that unlit kitchen.

Fritzi (because the machine looked like Fritzi again) lifted her gaze into the flashlight's beam. It's a wonder, she said in a soft voice. Fertilization, cleavage, morphogenesis. I think I loved them best at this stage, the point before the germ layers have begun to form, when they're just transluscent clusters of cells, so precise yet unassigned, tiny ornaments without trees to hang on. It's impossible to tell what they'll be, what they'll become, without genetic testing—boys, girls, pheasants, foxes—they could be anything. But even later, I remained smitten. I still remember the ultrasounds from 22 weeks, the arms and hands and fingers waving around, the legs, femurs within the legs. Kidneys, bladders, hearts (both atrias and ventricles), skin stretched smooth and taut over spines, mandibles, smudgy views of faces like strangers speeding by on a train. Just amazingly cool. Until I heard them crying in the delivery room, first one and then the other, the platitude of new lungs filling with oxygen… If only they could've stayed there, inside me. If only they'd never been born.

A wonder, Fritzi murmured, as her gaze shifted back to the petri dish resting on her palm. Her face was soft and smiling. So that for a second or two it truly did seem a wonder—the miraculous moment where fate turns around and inside out, the monster's maw into the mother's kissing mouth. A wonder, as Fritzi's own lips touched the lid of the petri dish. Then she removed the lid, sliding it into the back pocket of her jeans, and placed the lidless dish inside the too dark interior of the breadbox. Along with the letters WON painted on the box's rusted metal side, there were faded images of what looked to be balloons or bubbles.

And you know it grows strong bodies twelve ways, she added. Twelve ways, when suddenly she sneezed. And sneezed again. Which did not prevent her from heading back across the room toward the generator.

At this point events become hard to recall in terms of exactly what happened and in what sequence, so that what follows might be more of a jumble than a chronicle. Apologies to anyone who has been reading carefully, though if you have ever been through a traumatic experience yourself, you will understand.

Most likely, Selina lunged at Fritzi. Because you could not claim that you did not have a clue what Fritzi was going to do next, either before a judge in a court of law or in your own mind. But it is also possible that Fritzi, whose sneezes had become serial and increasingly violent, stumbled over one of the dinette chairs, and into Selina. Either way, the two women ended up on the floor, in a tussle.

Earlier in this narrative, Fritzi was referred to as a machine because she was acting like one. Well she also felt like one: she had arms of steel, it seemed! Selina tried to hold down the crazed embryo killer, to prevent her from rising and stumbling over to the incubator for another of the two remaining petri dishes, but Fritzi's force was unrestrainable. Her force was unrestrainable, both in terms of the strength of her limbs and in terms of the spasms that wracked her body each time she sneezed, spraying Selina's face with mucous. You had no choice, however, but to ignore Fritzi's fluid if you wanted to prevent future losses of future lives, no choice even though it already seemed like you had no choice because Fritzi was so strong there was surely no stopping her. No stopping her, when the sneezing turned to wheezing.

The sneezing turned to wheezing and suddenly Fritzi was headed for the door or maybe Selina was pushing her, either way, the door swung open, with Fritzi first who looked to be leaping from the small porch and next pitching to the side like on a rocking boat, smashing into the left ledge then flipping forward onto the ground and rolling off into the mint where she gasped and thrashed for a moment and then was still. Still as the unopened can of Red Bull that glinted in the flashlight's beam, a few feet beyond the bottom step.

A wetness darker even than the too dark interior of the breadbox had tarnished Fritzi's silver hair and seeped into the mint beneath, but you did not want to lift her head to look closer. It was enough to check her pulse, which was already gone. To check her pulse and to look at her face that no longer looked like a machine or a witch or a mother, that no longer looked like anything one living person would call another.

According to the postmortem, the "trauma" to Fritzi's head neither fractured her skull nor injured her brain. So, Fritzi's death was not caused by trauma to the head. Instead, Fritzi's death was the result of "acute anaphylaxis." Human Biology, one of the books Selina purchased long ago when nursing seemed like a possible career path instead of just another conning opportunity, says that when the cells of the immune system mistake an allergan for a pathogen, "they release histamine and other substances that cause secretion of mucus and constriction of the airways." On occasion, they can also send these chemicals "into the bloodstream. The increased capillary permeability that results from this can lead to fluid loss and shock." That means Fritzi's own cells, her "cytoplasmic savants," stopped her life. In other words, she was killed by the intelligence of absence.

But Dean Van Staal, who also suffered a trauma to the head and did not die from it, would say that is all water under the bridge, honey. Life goes on and Selina, who could have just walked away, called Asani from Fritzi's iPhone and told him where he could find his dead ex-wife and the embryos. Even though Fritzi had broken the "vacuum seal" taking out the one dish of embryos, there were still two others. If just one single embryo survived after all that had happened, it would be worth it. Right?

Selina sat down on a limestone step to wait. Fritzi was dead along with a petri dish of embryos, but from the sound of the trilling cicadas, you would never know it. Just like that last night at the Hotel Americana, after dinner and back alone in the room—you would never know it was the end from the sounds of late summer floating through the screens, the cicadas, ice clinking in glasses on the verandah, somebody laughing about somebody's sock tan. Listening to those floating sounds, waiting for Timor's little yellow pill to take effect, your bunny soft in your arms, it seemed like you might as well continue on like

before. It was not unbearable. It was not unbearable, and who was to say, things might get better instead of worse. Life is full of surprises, until it is not. But then the pill took over and the next thing you knew, the morning sun was streaming in. The morning sun was streaming in, yet Timor was still snoring, gray faced and open mouthed on the pillow.
At the time, he had looked dead. Hopelessly dead. If only you could have seen Fritzi first, sprawled with her silver head blackening the mint, that thought never would have come to mind.

So this is what it comes too. *Menjá nadúli.* Literally, you conned me, you filled me with air. But you know that. Literally. It is in the ten pages of "Russian slang and colloquialisms," that you cribbed from http://everything2.com. Ten pages of virile *mat* thrashed into Roman serfage, because Cyrillic is Greek to you, *súka.* You filled me with air, inflated me with linguistic esprit, only to kill me, once again. A whack job, a hack job, a bumbling though evidently not humbling execution of this misbegotten faux-bilingual sequence of phonemes, this so-called Timor Zinkovsky. Oh sure *I* may live on, if our pile of *otstóy* finds a publisher—live on, as much, or as little, as you,

"Elisabeth Sheffield." You, who have snatched away all I had to live on *for*. A dangling preposition, as my darling, dimwitted amateur grammarian would point out, referring to *Practical English and the Command of Words*, if she could read *these* words.

If she could, but she can't. She never could, I understand that now. Not a word, from the very beginning, or should I say end, from the moment of the fictive death of Timor Zinkovsky in the fictive life of Selina Van Staal. For shame. Or to quote sweet Graccy P., your literary superior: "Everyone real or invented deserves the open destiny of life." Even after death.

I am not going to let you off. You have committed a murder, ended a life, if only on the page. Not to mention plagiarized the plot of a Hollywood movie. Two crimes against literature in one book. But all the more reason for me to dog you: what use is a paper trail, without a tracker to follow the pulpy reek? And already Bad Betty, in my investigation of your capital offense, I've found in these pages answers to nearly all the classic capital questions: the Who (you), the What (me), the Where (here), the When (now), the How (no need to reiterate). Only one capital question remains: Why?

Why?

That answer is not *here*, in these writings, in this file you have titled WIP for "Work in Progress," in imitation of the inimitable James Joyce. Maybe it is somewhere in your head, entangled in some neuronal sixth sense mess inaccessible even to you. If that is the case, no help there. I believe, however, that it is in the looseleaf notebook that lies next to your laptop. Snorting around, I found these scribblings—stopped short by their stale intellectual stench:

Epitaphs. They once spoke to us. "As thou art so was I. As I am so shalt thou be." As I am so shalt thou be…

Now we speak to them, even though "over six million accounts on Facebook belong to dead people…"(http://www.creative applications. net/webapp/above-the-cloud-archaeology-of-social-networks). But it's just us doing the talking, tagging their photos, posting mylar balloon sentiments on their pages. Crap like wish you were still here, bro. Miss you, sis. Hi Mom, I'm a mom now, too. Hey pops, just bought a new Infiniti. You'd love the ride. No attempt even at projection or to summon a voice from beyond the grave. No conception of anything beyond the banal pay-for-view here and now…

We can't stop yakking on, to listen, even if they could speak.

So I suspect that you killed me for irony's sake. But irony is dead, *détka*—everyone's known that for years.

E01.06.11: I will be born at the end of twenty-eight weeks of gestation, my twin having died in utero. Quick as a cat can wink an eye, I will be whisked off to the NICU. She will call me Kitten and cradle me for hours everyday, while I am fed through intravenous tubes with the milk she pumps from her breasts. She will call me Kitten, sing Kitten don't fret I've found your mittens and hey diddle diddle the cat played the fiddle. And I will be able to hear her until the middle of week thirty, when an intraventricular hemorrhage in my brain will wreak havoc with my premature nervous and motor systems, depriving me of sound and normal motion, though not of sight or feeling. Not of sight or feeling, as I remain in the NICU for weeks and weeks afterwards, my breathing assisted by a ventilator that will overstretch the air sacs in my lungs, damaging the delicate tissues. The lung injury will heal, eventually, leaving only a susceptibility to viral pneumonia during the winter months and a certain tenderness I cannot communicate. But she will still call me Kitten, as the weeks go by, as the months go by, as the years go by and my spastic limbs lengthen, kicking and batting at nothing.

I wIll still be her Kitten, as first she mouths the word, then her soft light hair pup tents my face, so that all I can see are her eyes, shining. Shining, her breath smelling always a little like the baked tofu she hand feeds me in cubes. Still her Kitten when three years after bearing me and additional fertility treatments she will give birth to my sister, who will be full term and perfectly healthy. Still, when eight years after bearing my sister she will be diagnosed with stage three ovarian cancer. And still, even when she has become too weak to hold or even touch me, when all she can do, as they roll me in in my chair, is look at me. Shining.

And after? After there will be a day:

My sister wheels the chair around from the back of the ecovan and my father lifts me out and into it. His arms feel strange. He pushes me over a gravel path as my head lolls back and the clouds skim over the sky. The sun warms my face and I can smell earth and rock, baking. He pushes and pushes and then he stops. My neck snaps forward, jerking my eyes away from white skimming over blue to motionless mottled gray. A hard slab that my sister kneels before and embraces and my father absently pats. Unmoving mottled stone then back to skimming clouds and gravel crunching wheels although I can't hear anything, only feel through my spine—feel crunching give way to soft thumping and bumping.

Grass. Bright grass flecked with white clover and as the chair ceases to bump along, a large pine with a long horizontal limb stretching out over the lawn like a suspended bench or a log floating in water. I sit with my head lolling back, but my eyes are just fine. They clamber up, my sister going first, straddle the branch and then hitch their bodies along until they reach the center where my father shifts around so that they sit each facing the other. He points overhead, she looks and he tweaks her nose. They laugh, then she says something, her smile gone, gesturing down at me. He looks back over his shoulder, at the ground. His face flickers something. He returns to her, takes her hands in his, their heads tilting together as their mouths move. Two birds on a branch, floating away.

The skimming clouds clot, covering the sun. I have no coat and I grow cold. I can smell the resin from the pine tree, the sap. If I could feel the bark beneath my hands. Rough and sticky. If I could climb. Past the long horizontal limb where they perch, their heads tilting together. If I could climb hiking my body up branch by branch, each one skinnier than the last. My head breaking through the boughs bristles scratching my cheeks like whiskers. Sap in my nose. Climb up and up. Up.

I sit in my chair, kicking and batting at nothing.

And then the clouds break. Shining. On my forehead and cheekbones, on my shoulders, on my arms. Heating through the fabric of my pink stretch pants. Sinking into taut muscles and tendons, softening and loosening, seducing. My limbs stretch, my spine lengthens, my fingers and toes unfurl. The smell of grass, baking. I gasp, I suck. I suck in all the air I can. It hurts.

Acknowledgments

I would like to thank the following persons, both the extant and the deceased, for their lore: Patricia Ackerman, Emmanuel David, Theresa Coleman Delp, Samuel Dean Delp, Gordon Delp, Sue and Warren Delp, Rochanya Generous, Patrick Greaney, Dragan Ilic, Louis C. Jones (whose "The Ghosts of New York: An Analytical Study," *JAF*, V.57, 1944, inspired Revenant "File 1994"), Melanie Sheffield, Joan Sheffield, William Sheffield II and William Sheffield III. Last but not least, I would like to thank Jeffrey DeShell, whose wit and ways helped to conceive this book.

I would also like to thank the National Endowment for the Arts and the University of Colorado. Grants from each helped to support the research and writing of *Helen Keller Really Lived.*

Revenant "File 2010" appeared in *Gargoyle* (V.57, 2011) as "i live in a hole"; Revenant "File 1994" appeared in *Denver Quarterly* (V.47, no.3, 2013).